Sam looked across the d[...] of his sails and to the moun[...] green with the lush foliage of a fog-bound coastal forest. Enjoying the sight and the feel of the wilderness, he was surprised when a woman came running out of the trees onto a barely perceptible cliff ledge. Sam watched her try to sprint on weary legs over the crumbling granite, each footstep breaking loose weathered stones. A hundred years from the trees, the path disintegrated with a puff of dust as dirt, rocks, and the woman plummeted into the water.

Glancing at his chart, he knew that the swiftly-changing tide would pull her away from the island and into the overfall—the deadly collision of currents that formed a rolling wave and a saltwater whirlpool larger than most. Her only real chance was climbing onto a dry dock or making it to a pocket of beach. Surely enough, Sam caught the white of her shirt against the dark granite of a partially submerged rock. She was hanging on, struggling in the frigid water.

Now he had a decision to make.

Cursing through clenched teeth, he pulled the hatch on the yacht shut. Even if he managed to keep the boat off the rocks long enough to snatch her out of the water, the engine didn't have enough power to fight the current. If he attempted the rescue, they were both going into the overfall. Few yachtsmen had survived Devil's Gate on a heavy tide.

He threw the engine into gear and watched the woman thrashing with her legs, trying to get a better purchase against the flowing water. As he drove the boat forward into the building chop, the hull pitched and rolled and the wind rose under a black sky.

"I see you," he muttered. "Just hang on."

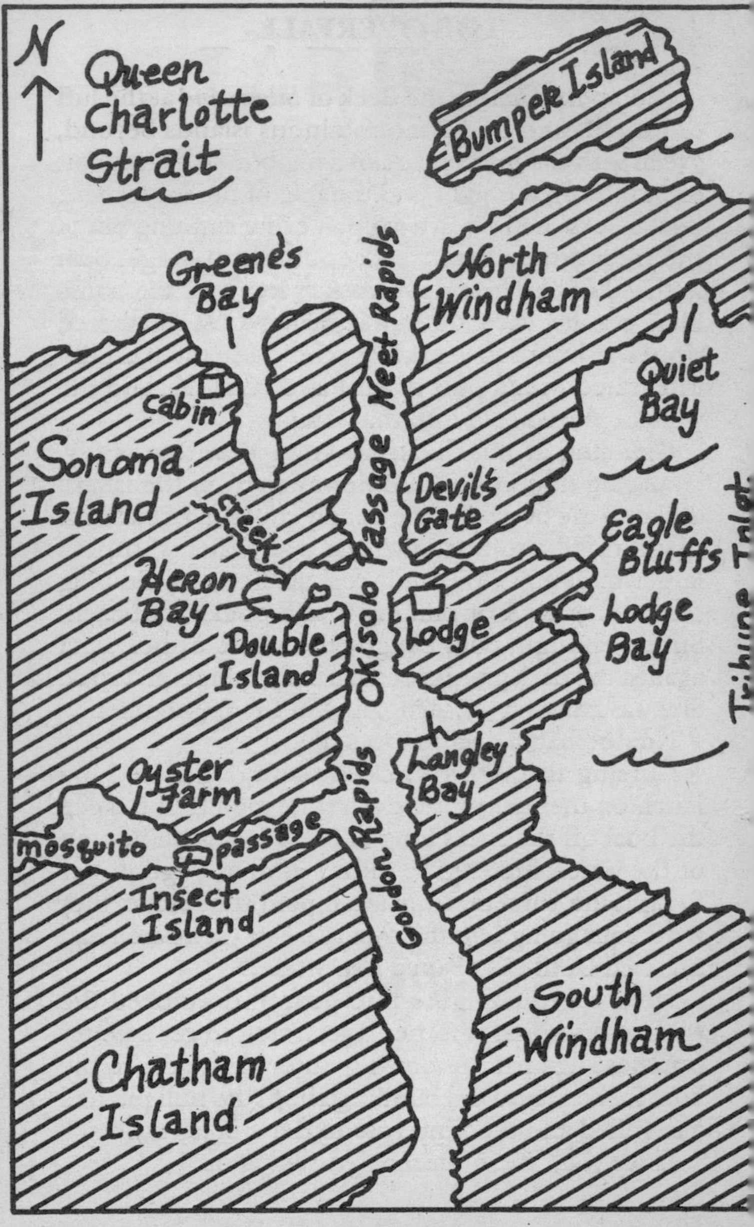
N
Queen Charlotte Strait
Bumper Island
Greene's Bay
North Windham
Meet Rapids
Quiet Bay
cabin
Sonoma Island
creek
Devil's Gate
Eagle Bluffs
Okisolo Passage
Heron Bay
Lodge
Lodge Bay
Tribune Inlet
Double Island
Langley Bay
Oyster Farm
mosquito passage
Gordon Rapids
Insect Island
South Windham
Chatham Island

OVERFALL

David Dun

PINNACLE BOOKS
Kensington Publishing Corp.
http://www.kensingtonbooks.com

ACKNOWLEDGMENTS

Professional Acknowledgments: To Ed Stackler, my friend, editor, and inspiration meister; to Anthony Gardner, my agent, for being a great advocate and a terrific advisor; to all the creative people at Kensington Books, Laurie Parkin for making it all happen, and Ann Lafarge for her editing and thoughtful editorial assistance throughout the process; to Ruth Johnson for her extensive research efforts; to Dr. Michael Kinsella, of the University of Washington (a heck of a fun guy), for his assistance with the science; to Amy Stewart of Eureka, California, for her poem "Day Care"; to Anacortes Yacht Charters of Anacortes, Washington, for many years of fantastic bare boat yacht charters into British Columbia; to Justin Kirsch for great moral support and computer wizardry; to P. Scott Brown for the website; to my high school English teacher Bert Ring, for general inspiration; to Daniel Bridi for assistance with language and culture; and to Perry Yuen of Sacramento for technical assistance in the art of investigation.

Personal Acknowledgments: To all of my friends, family, and co-workers from whom I have received a large measure of encouragement and inspiration, some who helped with a few words, some who devoted themselves to many hours, even days, of thought and helpful editorial commentary; not all of them are listed here. I thank you all for your generosity, support, and hard work. I will undertake the risk of naming a few of these fine folks (in alphabetical order) who had extensive remarks concerning various plot points and character comments and who were a source of great personal encouragement: Mark Emmerson of Redding, California; Charles Gillihan of Columbus, Indiana; Russ Hanly of Seattle, Washington; David Martinek of Eureka, California; Bill Warne of Sacramento, California, and Donna Zenor of Los Angeles, California. And to my wife Laura who keeps the home fires burning, always roots for the good guys, and manages to love me (which ain't always easy).

One

The small jib was taut and straining in the northerly wind, the weather turning, the sky azure in the evening sun but for the near purple of the approaching dark clouds. To the east lay Tribune Inlet, a long fjord bounded by steep mountains and creating a great funnel that ended in a narrow, rock-walled passage called Devil's Gate, where wind and water rushed, making dangerous work for sailors.

Before him, the sea was already starting to mound, as if little hands were forming humps in flattened dough. The whitecaps made logs and other debris harder to see, causing Sam to squint and stare over the bow of *Silverwind*, his custom-made, forty-eight-foot cruising sailboat.

There was the sound of parting water, and of spray falling back to the sea, the quiet thunder of wind in sail, the rise and fall of a gentle swell that underlay the chop, and a slight harmonic vibration as he drove the boat north and east to windward across the mouth of Tribune Inlet. The wind was unsettled, the barometer falling, but that was expected to change as a new high-pressure system built.

Sam wore yellow rubber sailing boots and athletic gloves for handling lines. The Farmer John rain gear featured pants so watertight he could sit in a puddle;

a jacket with Gortex over goose down that blunted even the late October wind.

On the seat next to Sam stood Heraldo, known as Harry, Sam's mostly Scottish terrier. It had been his son's dog. Harry eyed Sam, and with a lip-licking expression, distilled his hunger into long swipes of his tongue.

"You've been saying that for an hour now."

Harry repeated the long lick with innocent eyes. Sam then emulated him, running his own tongue around his lips, watching Harry's canine eyes stare fixedly at the show. Harry lay down, his chin on his front paws, expressing pouting disquiet at Sam's mockery.

The white-hulled boat—36,000 pounds of fiberglass, lead, and teak—floated featherlight over the sea. From his cushioned seat, Sam handled the wheel deftly with his feet, steering a straight course toward Quiet Bay, some fifty minutes distant.

Silverwind looked salty when compared to the vacation boats that jammed the big-city marinas and yacht clubs. It was loaded with the trappings of wilderness cruising: sheepskin on all the stays at the spars to protect the sails; dinghy and gas can lashed to the deck; netting on all the lifelines; canvas wind and spray breaks around the cockpit; solar panels; wind vane; a heavy-duty canvas and plastic windshield known as a dodger; a fold-away bimini top; and two diesel generators. The list of extras was formidable. After buying the *Silverwind,* Sam had spent another $250,000 preparing her to cruise.

There was nothing to this sailing on the so-called Inside Passage from Alaska to Victoria in summer except rocks and currents, intimidating to the uninitiated. The rocks made holes in boats and the currents from time to time made swirling holes in the water, aptly named whirlpools, and even more frightening, rolling waves called overfalls, created by the force of water meeting water at great speed in a narrow passage. A severe overfall could swallow a yacht in seconds sometimes swamping and sinking it, other times pounding it into slivers on the rocks.

The tides sluice the salt water in from the Pacific Ocean through the Queen Charlotte Straits behind Vancouver Island and between the smaller islands and up into the inlets, bays, and estuaries. Wherever the land constricts the flow of tidal water, the current races. In a few places the water moves like a white-water river, and boats dare not cross it during the tidal surge.

The spring tide was ebbing and the sea was tugging *Silverwind* toward Devil's Gate, where the current on occasion reached a solid seventeen knots, one knot faster even than the infamous Nakwakto Rapids at the mouth of Seymour Inlet to the north and at least two knots faster than the Skookumchuck to the south. Last Sam heard, the Skookumchuck had killed sixteen people, and Devil's Gate was way ahead of that, having eaten ten in one summer when a large yacht wandered down her throat and slit its belly on the rocks.

On one occasion Sam had seen a Devil's Gate whirlpool pull down a telephone-pole-sized log, then free it, to burst to the surface three hundred yards down current with such force that it shot for the sky like a breaching whale. Devil's Gate wasn't a place to make a mistake, but it intrigued Sam and he had his binoculars ready to take a look at the overfall that would be created by this ebb tide. On a few rare days when the wind swung from the northeast in a roaring williwaw, it stiffened the overfall at Devil's Gate to heights normally not found on sheltered waters. Some said it reached fifteen vertical feet and stood nearly straight like a concrete wall. Today was becoming one of those days, with the dark of the clouds and the blustery winds coming ever closer. Williwaw was a winter phenomenon not uncommon in late October. It referred to times when weather conditions in these water-filled canyons drove the winds to near-magical speeds. The natives said the word with a hint of reverence.

Down through the companionway door stood two screens—one radar and one GPS. The GPS was an electronic map showing islands and channels enhanced by a satellite signal that could depict the precise location of the yacht, while the radar painted an outline of the surrounding shores. Sam had noticed the drift in his course and continuously corrected.

His current course would take him abeam the opening where he would turn toward Devil's Gate for a quick look before he did a 180-degree turn to escape the cold-eyed rock walls that sucked the sea through and into the small passage between North and South Windham Islands.

As the wind tousled his hair he slipped into a familiar reverie, in which the rushing of water and wind and the vibrations through hull and sail functioned like a sniff of good food or the sound of enticing music. It drew him. In sailing, as in most areas of his life, Sam was a purist. If the wind blew, he traveled; if not, he sat, except in dire circumstances such as when he was running out of Cuban tobacco leaves for a good cigar and he needed to get to the appointed mail stop.

He was looking forward to dinner and an anchorage that was almost Zen-like in its serenity where he could sit out what felt like a building williwaw. When beating to windward, as he was now, there was no competing with the lift offered by the big diesel, but he wouldn't use it. What he took from the wind was too important to him. It caressed his face, fed his spirit, shivered the boat through the mast, dampened the roll—a thing in harmony with the earth and not a thing in opposition.

Besides her seaworthiness, *Silverwind* offered something just as important to Sam. He could pull her into a harbor and not be noticed, not a single eye turning his way. If he had chosen a hundred-foot international yacht the same could not be said. Although beautiful in her lines and certainly in her abilities, *Silverwind* was close enough to ordinary to suit Sam's purposes.

Sam was a long-muscled swarthy-skinned man who stood all of six feet two inches in his stocking feet, part Tilok Indian, handsome with curly dark hair that fell down over his ears. His face was more angular than round, with fine features, smooth and unblemished except for two scars, one over his right eye maybe a half inch, and a small nick at his chin. His eyes were amber.

Since his retirement he had taken to wearing a gold earring in his left ear. Around his neck, usually out of sight, he wore a braided rawhide necklace with turquoise stones and a golden sun locket the size of a half-dollar. When it had belonged to his grandfather, the picture in the locket had been of Sam as an infant. Now the picture was of his grandfather, Stalking Bear, in ceremonial regalia at the annual gathering of the new beginning. His grandfather had said about Sam that he had a look of eagles in his eye. Whether it was there or not, Sam had a strong personal presence that he had learned for professional reasons to disguise. Usually he sailed in a raffia hat and sunglasses but

wore his work clothes, a loose pullover shirt and simple pants—again by design, nothing to call attention
and nothing memorable.

Sam's ultimate destination of the moment was Sydney, BC, just across from Vancouver. He'd have dry
dock repairs made while he wintered in the mountains of California, where he would feed his soul.
After that perhaps he would come back to this watery
evergreen wilderness or maybe head to the South
Seas. Sam no longer made plans more than a few
months ahead.

Looking along the rock faces that bordered the entrance to Devil's Gate, he focused on the sharp tide
line where the salt water had killed the small ever-
greens, as if some giant made a regular trimming.
Farther along toward the pass itself the rocks were
gray black, steep, and treeless, although every little
ledge seemed to harbor a scruffy green bush or two.
Maybe he would get a good look at the overfalls. A
camera with a 300mm lens sat on the seat next to him
but the light had faded too much for a photo. Using
binoculars, he studied the wave. It was awesome. By itself it would never sink a blue-water boat, but by
deflecting them into the whirlpools and finally the
rocks, it broke and sank even oceangoing yachts with
ease. He came about, knowing it was time to escape
the current, bringing the nose into the wind, then settled into another broad reach back in the direction
he had come.

As he reveled in the wildness of this place, his eye
caught movement. It appeared to be a woman, running on a narrow trail that traversed the face of the
treeless portion of so-called Eagle Bluffs of South
Windham Island near the island's sharp point.

"Go figure," he said to the terrier.

There weren't many tourists in this part of BC in October. South Windham Island, as far as he knew, had no residents, no government parks, and no resorts. At least none showed on the chart.

Harry barked in response to Sam's concern.

Two

Hurrying but purposeful, Anna Wade slipped on her tennis shoes, took nothing but the computer CD-ROM entrusted to her by her brother, her considerable wallet, and her satellite phone, all of which she stuffed in a waterproof bag that went into her fanny pack. The seaplane would meet her on the backside of the island in an hour and a quarter, but there might be a long wade to reach the plane as there was no dock.

When she walked up the trail away from the lodge she felt as if someone was watching. She knew she was rattled and perhaps imagining things. Normally she felt freed, calmed, by this wild place, even the shivers of isolation and the creatures casting wary stares. Today instead of wonder she felt fear.

She tried to tell herself that a major company would not be committing murder, but at this point, alone on this island, she couldn't come to any conclusions. As she jogged past their pen the rotweillers' ugly snarls caused her to pick up her pace.

Soon she found herself running on the forest trail just above the steep shoreline headed toward the large cliffs—the long route to Langley Bay on the opposite side of the island. It would be less obvious if she didn't take the direct route. The dry leaves of October made the forest noisy and her passage through it anything but a secret. After several minutes, she stopped. She thought she heard a snap above the wind sound a little distance back, perhaps a footfall breaking a stick. More sounds came—maybe something moving behind her along the brushy trail.

It stopped and she could feel it listening. Or was it just the wind? She bolted and ran. If they discovered that she was sneaking off to a seaplane, the fear now crouching in her mind might become reality—an outright confrontation with Roberto or worse. They might let the dogs loose.

She was in good shape and thought she had a good chance of outrunning them. Unless they brought the dogs.

As if summoned by the thought, she heard the snuffling and yelping of hounds eager for blood. Anna's stomach knotted and her throat tightened. Ahead ran a nearly invisible path that eventually cut across the middle of the cliff. Although she had never taken it, she had seen where it emerged from the tree line. The cliffs were one place where she might face an attack dog and win.

Quickly she jumped off the main trail and scrambled down the hill toward the water. It was much steeper than she imagined but the dense brush made her feel safer. The forest, shades of green above her and choked with huckleberry, salal, and salmon berry, grew like a wall. Adrenaline made her gut hollow and her body light. Suddenly it occurred to her that it would be easy for someone to force an accident on these cliffs.

Uncertain, she stopped. Maybe she should fool with the satellite phone. But what could anyone do? First she would get distance between herself and any pursuer.

Her heart was pounding and her breaths were deep and hard. She tried to listen, but heard only herself and the wind. She supposed that a person on the cliff trail would make an easy target.

Again she ran. She could not go back, and going upslope would be impossible without slowing greatly and releasing a cascade of stones and creating the crackles and snaps of walking in a dry forest.

After what seemed a few desperate strides around a corner the trees gave way to the vertical drop. It was a couple hundred yards to more forest. She paused and wiped the sweat from her eyes.

Then Anna saw the sailboat throwing spray in the whitecaps, its sails looming and its sleek body, and the man at the helm. She glanced down at the whirling of the bending water green like moss on marble headstones, strong enough to move a train, sufficient to drown an army. The boat shined at her like mock salvation, a world away below her.

As Sam watched her try to sprint on weary legs, the trail collapsed. Dirt, rocks, and the woman plummeted into the water. Glancing at his chart, then at the GPS, he knew that she might have fallen into the current.

Sam took a deep slow breath, and flipped off his hat, angry that this was happening to him. Harry barked in earnest now. Meaning to take a better look, Sam once again came about, heading back down into Devil's Gate. On a broad reach the boat shot ahead, requiring that he completely luff the main. He had seconds to decide. The wind was still increasing and driving the black clouds overhead.

Always things went wrong in multiples.

With the mainsail flapping he knew he was about to attempt a nearly hopeless rescue. It would be a regression into his old life—a life he had forsaken.

He punched a button to furl the main inside the mast. Incredibly, the sail bound and it stuck. Never in a whole year had the mainsail furling jammed and now when he needed it to work—it didn't. He cursed gadgets and reversed the process. Fortunately the bind came free and it unfurled. Not wanting to waste precious seconds, he released the halyard, ran forward, and yanked with all his weight to pull the big sail down. It piled on the boom in a sloppy mess.

Out of habit his mind calculated the odds of survival—his own and hers. This area was a wilderness with an occasional passing yacht or commercial boat. The instant she hit the fifty-five-degree water she would be swept away, probably dragged under by a whirlpool, and if by some miracle she did not drown in that fashion, she would be dead in three or four minutes when she was pulled into the overfall and then buried by the huge whirlpool underlying it, down thirty or forty feet under the sea with little hope of making it to the surface in time to breathe. And if somehow she did struggle to the surface, she'd probably die from cold shock before she could swim to shore. Her only real chance was climbing onto a dry rock or making it to a tiny pocket of beach.

While he started the motor and ran down the channel he looked for some sign of her. Normally he'd have left himself a spot of mainsail to steady the boat. With the main down the boat set up a roll.

He waited for the next piece of bad luck.

His eye caught the white of her shirt against a rock. Glancing at the GPS, he realized he was being drawn toward the pass, but there was still time to escape the current. Quickly he looked with binoculars. Even with the boat's motion he could tell that she clung to seaweed-covered granite. She was well away from the cliffs and the point from which she had fallen. From her location it was too far to swim to shore in this current.

For just a second his eyes left the figure in the water to look for another boat—any boat. Nothing.

The wind was increasing fast, blowing right at the overfall. He knew the result: It would push the wave up, perhaps making it half again as high.

He pondered whether he could save her. He loved his yacht as much as a man could love a material thing and still possess a soul. He loved Harry. If he went much closer he would risk losing Harry and the boat, maybe dying, and for a stranger who would probably drown anyway.

Then he saw the solitary figure on the trail from which the woman had fallen. He breathed a sigh of hope. There were two dogs running, noses down, barking their frustration at the cliff and the vanished track.

Through the binoculars he managed to get a shaky view of a man standing, looking down into the water, and then turning to walk away.

She was waving frantically, but at Sam, not the man on the cliff. The man didn't run or even look agitated. Assuming that he saw her, he plainly didn't care if she died. Perhaps he even wanted her to die. A moment later he had disappeared.

"Unbelievable," Sam said aloud.

With the wind the sea was building fast and the waves were washing over her. She would be swept away in minutes. Glancing at the wind indicator he saw the wind at thirty-five knots and building. It was going to be a williwaw.

He brought the boat around into the wind and furled the jib, then ran to the wheel and concentrated on positioning the boat. Because he was upstream from the woman, the current, the wind, and the breaking sea were sweeping him toward her. With the sails down the boat rolled even worse in the building chop. He added power.

According to the GPS, the current was pushing him at seven knots over the bottom. Sam was accustomed to risking his life, but there was still an adrenaline surge.

In the distance the roar of the overfall filled his ears. Even from his location he couldn't escape the white wave that sat just ahead of the largest saltwater whirlpool and undertow in the world. The boat would be drawn into it and the treacherous rocks all around as surely as the moon pulls the oceans. He wondered if his boat could survive the water that might fill it or bash it against the green-tinged jaws of rock that guarded the Paradise Channels.

The wind was rising fast under a black sky. Forty-one knots, the incandescent numbers blinked.

"Harry, go to your bed."

The little dog jumped up on the bulkhead, then dived down the hole of the companionway hatch into the pilothouse. Sam pulled the hatch shut. There would be water everywhere once they hit the overfall. He could see the woman, still clinging to the rock, thrashing with her legs, obviously trying to get a better purchase. She couldn't climb out of the water, and with everything but her shoulders and head immersed she would develop hypothermia in minutes. She was still looking in his direction, waving one arm.

"I see you," he muttered. "Just hang on."

With less than two hundred feet to go he swung the boat into the wind and current, letting the rushing water push him backward against the full power of the diesel. It was like the middle of a river, and the force of swirling water jarred the boat, making it hard to hold the bow on a heading. Even with full power into the current he was going backward at about five knots over the bottom. He threw a strobe-lighted life ring with a safety line out the stern for her to grab if she missed the boat. The current was increasing—the fierce wind was doing the rest. Finding the lee of some islets that broke a little wind, twisted the water, and reduced the current, he was able to slow the boat's backward movement. *Silverwind*'s stern was headed very near the rock to which she clung.

Soon the current would roar to seventeen knots and life on his boat might well come to an end.

"Let go after I pass," he called out, over an electronic megaphone, hoping she wouldn't hit a nasty whirlpool and disappear. It was a billion-ton washer with the water beaten frothy, the current swirling and eddying. The clouds looked worse, and at the heart of the gorge he suspected the wind would rise to more than forty-five knots. Ninety knots had been reported in winter gales. The land was shaped to multiply as much as twofold any normal wind.

Everything was rapidly becoming more difficult. The first whirlpool caught the hull and shoved the boat over on its side until the weight of the keel pulled it upright. The boat jerked, shuddered, and careened before straightening out. Less than fifty feet to go. She looked grimly determined. Worried about running aground and ripping a hole in the bottom, he swung the stern slightly outward and eased the throttle for just a second, letting the current push him a little farther off.

"Do I swim?" she screamed.

"Wait," he blasted over the loudspeaker.

Twenty feet.

"Get ready."

Going backward past the woman he shoved the nose behind her rock as if he were trying to drive the boat aground. The current created a massive eddy and a giant whirlpool just to the stern of the woman's perch and of *Silverwind* that allowed the boat to move forward. With a swipe of his hand on the throttle he reduced power. There was an ugly crunching and he was slammed over the wheel as the lead keel hit the granite.

"Now?"

"Swim!" he screamed at the woman, not bothering with electronics. She began a powerful crawl stroke.

He heard her hit the hull and saw a hand trying to grab. He thrust a huge salmon net over the side, almost falling overboard himself. Her legs went into the net first as she slid down the side of the boat. Holding on to the net with all the strength he could muster, he watched helplessly as the bow swung from the rock and the boat turned broadside to the current, gaining speed. Her hand grabbed the gunwale.

"Hang on." Desperately he hauled in the net. She got a foot hooked over the edge of the boat's rail.

"Climb!" he said. Still grasping the handle of the net with one hand, he used the other to throw the transmission into forward and move the boat away from the rocks toward the center of the channel.

"Grab me," she screamed.

"Just hold on," he said as he continued his efforts to get clear of the downstream rocks. The overfall was around a slight bend and about two hundred yards distant. He decided to take it bow first and that meant turning the boat ninety degrees. Just as he hit another whirlpool he spun the wheel. Tipping far over, the starboard rail went under and the woman with it. Quickly he stepped above her, grabbed under her arms, and hauled her body half over the lifelines. Around them the water roared and the boat careened, but he kept pulling.

When he had her torso in the cockpit with her feet still over the lifelines, he pulled, deliberately falling to the side and using his weight to take her with him. Landing on a seat corner, he slammed his ribs into the fiberglass. Water was everywhere as the boat righted itself. Had it been anything other than an oceangoing sailboat it would have filled quickly.

He took the woman by the shoulders and moved her around the wheel to the bottom of the open cockpit, tossed a life jacket at her, and tightened down his own. Then in little more than the time it takes to sneeze, he recognized her as Anna Wade, actress, Oscar winner, two Golden Globes, $20 million a picture, and still a nice person. At least by reputation.

"Stay there." He calculated the boat's entry into the wave. It wasn't the size of the wave that mattered but its steepness, and the down suction from the whirlpool. He could see that there'd be no climbing it. They would be buried.

Here the canyon created the venturi and the wind howled. The digital readout of the wind indicator was showing fifty-plus knots and still climbing. If Sam hadn't seen it and heard the stories he wouldn't have believed it. Lines were tangled in the cockpit. Some were wrapped around his leg.

"Haul this in," he said, handing her the safety line. In a whirlpool it could catch in the propeller. She pulled like a seasoned deckhand. "It will be okay," he said. Then a whirlpool spun them and he fought to keep the bow pointed at the wave. Unless he kept it straight the rocks would punch holes like an angry fist through tissue paper.

"A hundred feet," he said, as the boat careened around the whirlpools. "Grab," he said to Anna Wade while planting her hands on two chromed bars to either side of the steering column. Her grip was vice-tight.

The wave loomed, rising up thick and green with a dimpled belly and its head rolling white like a great ocean breaker. There was a slick on the surface and a steep dip just ahead of the wave. They shot through the slick like a toboggan on ice, the wave coming and going with a hiss, then a roar. The sounds shook in his head. Green water poured over the yacht's nose as the current sucked it down so hard Sam could feel it in his gut. Rolling over the decks the water submerged the cockpit, and everything but the mast disappeared.

Green water, bitterly cold, hit him hard. His hands dug into the wheel as the water yanked him off his feet, his body nearly prone. When his feet were back under him he stood in water to his thighs.

Suddenly the yacht rolled almost completely over to the port side. There was a hard jolt as the keel bounced off a rock and then the frothing water was gone, leaving only a series of whirlpools more than two hundred feet in diameter.

With water pouring from the scuppers and the boat weighted down at the stern, it began to spin. As if on ice the boat glided stern first to the center of the whirlpool. In seconds he realized that the transmission was in neutral, the lever knocked back by the force of the water.

Feeling the yacht slowly sink below the horizon, he knew they'd been caught in a whirlpool's vortex. They were falling backward down a watery shaft. With his boat in a bewildering spin, Sam shoved the transmission into forward, grateful that the motor was still running. With full power the boat clawed over the funnel's lip, careening out of the first whirlpool only to be knocked in a circle by the next. Using the power again and again, he managed to escape each whirling eddy until their strength diminished.

They were inside the Okisolo Channel, one of several watery fingers penetrating fern-covered granite walls whose patches of moss, lichen, and grasses made natural corridors of pristine beauty. They passed through to Heron Bay a couple hundred yards distant as the current slowed to a mere two knots. The wind had been cut by half by the bluffs around the bay but still moaned in the rigging and thrashed the sails. Lines ran everywhere, even streaming down the boat's sides, and the mainsail still lay across the deck, draped over the rail.

Sam put a hand on her shoulder and studied her face. She was shaking badly. "I'm okay, let me help," she said in response to his silent concern. Then she struggled to pull in sails and every line that could reach his prop as if she were regular crew. He let it go on maybe three minutes, then ushered her down below.

His inflatable raft was gone, ripped from its tie-downs on the front deck. The diesel was still running and sounded good. In the relative calm came the discovery that the *Silverwind* had a broken rudder. And a broken weather vane—an automatic steering device that held the boat to a preset angle to the wind. The aft solar panel was a shambles.

"What a mess, I'm sorry," she said as they went through the pilothouse and down into the cabin.

Although the diminishing wind was still pushing

them, he kept the engine in forward with the auto pilot on so they would be certain not to drift past the bay down to the Gordon Rapids. Using the remnant of the rudder, the boat held a heading after a fashion. Quickly he showed her how to work the sumps in the head and got her in the shower with her clothes on.

"Don't undress yet," he said as he left her for topside. Soon they were motoring into Heron Bay and turning in eddies as they went.

The islands' steep terrain appeared only as imposing textured blackness against the night sky. The clouds were mostly gone, the wind reduced to gusts of twenty miles per hour.

Down below, Anna could only take in the mood of the bay through the porthole, but was more probably lost in thoughts of death and the sweetness of life. He thought about her with her wet hair hung in her face, the borrowed life jacket draped with seaweed. Before he got her under the shower she had to have been on the verge of serious hypothermia.

Once safe in the bay, Sam put the boat in neutral and went below. "You all right?" he asked outside the door.

"I'm okay. Thank you so much."

"You still decent?"

"Yeah." He opened the door and found her seated on a bench in the small shower looking much warmer in the steamy little compartment.

Harry barked and wagged his tail ferociously.

"This is Harry," he said.

"Oh," she said, reaching down, even in her drenched condition, to pat him. Sam ran into the galley for a plastic bag and some gauze to wrap a cut on her hand. Now he was starting to chill pretty badly despite all his high-tech underwear and outer garments. For the first time he noticed blood on his own hand and a modest cut that had been dripping red about the teak floor. He made a makeshift bandage with gauze wrap and tied it off.

"And, Harry, this is Anna Wade," he said when he returned.

"That's pretty good," she said. "I must look like a drowned rat. You're turning blue around the lips."

He grabbed towels, blue jeans, and a shirt. Sam had a thirty-two-inch waist, so the pants could be cinched up with a belt even for a woman who probably measured only twenty-six.

"When you're warmed up you can dry off and put on these," he said. "Are you okay?"

She was looking better already. "I'm fine. Especially with the warm water."

"One-handed shower," he said, wrapping her hand and pulling the bag over it.

Getting out of her clothes might be awkward, but he thought better of offering assistance.

After satisfying himself that she knew how the toilet worked—always problematic on a yacht—he closed the door and went topside. Normally it would have taken him ten minutes to drop and set the anchor, but with the cold wind making it nearly unbearable, he just loosened the windlass and let it go. Making its usual whine, the anchor chain payed out some forty feet until the anchor hit bottom.

Belowdecks, he stood outside her shower door. Harry was perched on the settee, watching.

"You okay in there?"

"Great," she said.

"I'm going to take a shower myself."

"Okay," she said. "Not in here, I hope."

Sense of humor's intact.

When he finished warming himself, which took a good ten minutes, he dried off, pulled on his pants, and opened the door to his stateroom. He saw her with the door of the forward stateroom ajar, wearing jeans but nothing else. Her beautifully tapered back was covered by her long curly dark hair. Seeming to have eyes in the back of her head, she closed the door with her foot. A couple of minutes later she emerged in his shirt.

"Is the boat going to float?"

"Oh, yeah. But the rudder is mostly gone—God knows what else. I'm ready to call it a night."

"Look," she put her hand on his arm. "You risked your life to save me. No one has ever done that for me. So, I hate to bring this up but I really need to get off this boat. So do you."

He pulled a large first-aid kit from under the seat at the navigation station. After washing her cut, he went right to work using the cotton, gauze, and cream.

He didn't respond to her comment. There was no practical way to leave the yacht.

"I will never be able to thank you enough for what you did. I'll pay to fix your boat." She shivered just a bit, the chill obviously still inside her.

"The clothes don't quite fit but they work. There's a down coat over there on the couch." He stopped for a moment while he grabbed the parka and she slipped into it.

She pulled back her hair from her face and smiled. "When did you recognize me?"

"When I pulled you in."

"You weren't the least bit uncertain?"

"Why would I be uncertain? I see you on the magazine racks several times a year in every grocery store. What's to be uncertain about?"

She raised a brow. "Do you watch many movies?"

"I've seen a few of yours."

She had her eyes on his hands. "I think you hit a punching bag with your knuckles. I couldn't help but notice a scrapbook in the stateroom. Articles about celebrities, a lot of them in film."

"Yeah." He shrugged.

"What picture won Peter Malkey an Oscar?"

"*Sandals.*"

"He won it for?"

"Best Director."

"Who produced the movie?"

"Hey, I'm neither Siskel nor Ebert."

"You know, don't you?"

"Only because my mother loved the movie. Raved about it."

"Who's my agent?"

He smiled. "You're a woman with a lot of questions."

"Either you know the name or you don't."

"I know her name. I'm making spaghetti tonight."

"One of the articles was about how they found Peter's thieving CPA—the one that took him for two million—and a lot of other people as well—handcuffed to the steel railing in front of the police station with a sign around his neck."

"Pretty amazing."

"And your name is?"

"Sam."

"Sam . . . ?"

"Sam of the *Silverwind.*"

"Well, obviously I'm pleased to meet you. You're brave, Sam of the *Silverwind,* and I'm alive because of it."

He cleared his throat. "I neglected to mention that in the drawer of the forward stateroom—the same place you found the scrapbook—you'll find a brush, makeup, that sort of thing."

"Sounds good. " She rose and disappeared while he pulled out the spaghetti pot and began cleaning up. There was going to be an issue here.

"How can I get out of this bay? Back to civilization?" She had returned with the brush, trying to draw the tangles out of her hair.

"How did you get here?"

"In a seaplane."

"Well, then, tomorrow we find a seaplane."

"I really have to go, and I'm going to need your help. It might not be safe here in the open."

"Why is that?"

"I don't know. Call it intuition."

"You could swim to that beach, on Sonoma Island, get hypothermia, and warm yourself inside a bear's gut." He grinned. "Just intuition of course."

"Come on," she said. "Be nice. You know that New York traffic is more dangerous than the bears."

"Absolutely. You're much more likely to be eaten by the cold, and then the crabs, but eaten just the same. The dinghy and emergency life raft are both gone. There is no good way ashore and then no place to go should you happen to make it to the beach. Unless you know something I don't."

"Or we could stay here, is that it?"

"The beach is not practical. So a delightful evening with me and my spaghetti is really the only option."

"Now you're trying to make the bears sound good," she joked as she walked toward him. "Look. I can't talk about my situation. You apparently have lots you can't talk about either. But we could trust each other."

"Who was the guy who walked off and left you?"

For a split second she looked troubled. "What guy?"

There was a story here. For her sake he hoped

nobody in the media found out. *Stars* magazine would pay a fortune for this piece. BACHELOR ON SAILBOAT SAVES BIG STAR AFTER MYSTERY MAN LEAVES HER TO DIE.

He wanted a smoke.

"What is your last name, Sam?"

"I'm just Sam. Here's my card." He handed her a neatly embossed, gold-lettered card. It read "Sam of the *Silverwind*," with nothing but an e-mail address.

"People usually have a last name."

"Yes, indeed. But then when someone is fleeing for their life they usually talk about it."

"You're making a lot of assumptions."

"Okay. Tell me what happened so I can understand the desperation to get out of here."

"Do those toiletries you told me about belong to anyone in particular?"

"Yes. My mother."

"She travels with you?"

"Occasionally."

"She's the one who put together the scrapbook. Probably forgot it."

Sam shrugged.

"I need to get off."

"You know a lot more about what's going on here than I do. So why don't you enlighten me?"

"Look, I know this is strange. And you did save my life. And I'm very grateful. But please trust me. We both need to get off this boat."

"We'll trust each other, and we can begin by you telling me what we should run from."

She shook her head no. Sam could see that she was anxious, but he needed to know why she wanted to leave. Running was often more dangerous than waiting. There was a dry suit on board that he hadn't mentioned, and he could start the motor and proceed more or less aimlessly to the beach, where he could ground the boat on one of many rocks perhaps fifty yards from shore. A less expensive alternative would be to use the dry suit and tow Anna to shore. There was a kid's blow-up boat that would hold two adults maybe, half submerged and totally soaked with this chop and the wind. With one adult it would be just as wet but not as deeply submerged. But keeping her on the boat, or seeming to, was the only leverage he had to get her to talk. Unless he knew the why of it all, he couldn't make a good plan.

Outthinking ill-intentioned people had been Sam's calling in life—all kinds of criminals, but sometimes the worst of the worst, those who by natural gift were uncommonly intelligent and by some means, natural or unnatural, had become twisted and/or nearly conscienceless.

Those with no conscience were less a problem for businesspeople or celebrity types because they were psychopaths devoted to killing people they encountered in their daily life. They remained the province of homicide detectives who worked long hours under the influence of black coffee and nervous politicians.

Sam's company worked both in the private sector and under government contract. Powerful people, celebrities, and governments paid small fortunes for his skill and the cold logic of a silicon beast called CORE (an acronym for Common Object Repository for the Enterprise), affectionately christened "Big Brain" by Grogg, the man who helped conceive her according to Sam's vision.

Sam's greatest asset was a strong mind, housed in a near-perfect tabernacle tainted only by the occasional doses of cigarette smoke that he perpetually swore would end. Scholarships at Yale and MIT—specialty:

computer science—had enabled him to create a so-called "expert system" that revolutionized data analysis using a programming method known as forward- and backward-chaining heuristics.

His skills had forged for him a unique occupation, a job that kept him in high demand, a job that he had found profoundly satisfying until recently, when he'd left it altogether. It was a line of work that required he keep an extremely low profile, something that, even in premature retirement, Sam did not intend to abandon.

Anna Wade was no exception: Unless she became a client, she could know nothing of him or the exotic trade he had once plied.

"I'll make the spaghetti sauce. Relax. You have been talking about both of us leaving the boat. Somewhere along the line you decided I must leave too. Why?"

"I was going to get you accepting my exit and then drag you along."

She walked back to the forward stateroom and closed the door, obviously disappointed. He was acutely aware that she hadn't answered the question.

Sam went to his stateroom, took out night-vision equipment, and went topside. It was uncomfortably cold in the wind. He looked to the near shore, then out across the channel behind him to Windham Island. A small island called Double Island that lay off the shore of Sonoma Island formed the shelter for their secluded anchorage. There was no one and nothing that looked like trouble. It didn't appear that anyone else was anchored in the bay, not surprising since this place made sailors nervous even when the tide was slack. The rocky channel was a little tricky to negotiate—high tide at slack water was definitely the preferred time. No bilge alarm was sounding so it was unlikely that he was taking on water. The next high tide was many hours away, and it would be dark. Without a rudder they would run aground if they attempted to weigh anchor and leave.

He considered whether he should just leave with Anna and trust her judgment. Anchoring overnight or longer with no one aboard would require putting more scope on the anchor, so he went topside and released more chain. It was wise to be prepared for any eventuality. After the boat drifted off he would drop a stern anchor with very little scope.

The boat wouldn't go anywhere. He wanted a smoke and a drink, but first he should take care of an emergency escape method. Rummaging around in a locker he found the kid's raft and pumped it up in the wheelhouse, wondering how long it would take for Anna Wade to stop pouting or whatever she was doing. He lashed the small rubber boat to the lifelines midships where it could easily be cut loose. As he was turning to go back inside he noticed that the rubber boat had lost its turgidity. Leak. Typical with kids' rafts. Then he remembered the relatives' kids in the early part of the summer and the barnacles. After dinner he would try to find the little pinhole and fix it. In the meantime, if he and Anna had to leave they would use the dry suit and an air mattress.

When he returned to the cabin, he opened a cupboard and took a look at a bottle of Caymus Cabernet, 1996 vintage. He considered it. He had quit the hard stuff completely, and would have a glass of wine only when he knew he could stop at three. Or even more likely, a German beer with similar limitations. So far he had never been wrong. Taking a careful measure of himself, he closed the cabinet. The arrival of Anna Wade and the near destruction of his sailboat could put a man on the bottle.

He filled his wineglass instead with sparkling water

and fed Harry. Judging from the homey little galloping noise, his guest was running water in the sink. It made him smile that in the midst of begging to jump overboard and swim, this woman was still going to be well groomed.

He closed the companionway hatch and turned up the diesel heat. The sound of the sink pump stopped. Like a lot of landlubbers she ran the water whether she needed it or not. He proceeded to clean the galley and main salon of the few items that had fallen from cupboards. Most of his things had stayed put behind heavy-weather barricades.

His thoughts were interrupted by the sound of a blow-dryer. Quickly he started a generator so she wouldn't drain the batteries through the inverter. At the rate she was going she'd find his mother's curling iron. Better whip up some vegetables and rush the spaghetti sauce; it seemed she was settling in for the evening. If it was that easy to persuade her, perhaps she wasn't desperate after all.

He went to the cupboard, and beside the wine was an unopened pack of Marlboro smokes. He studied them. "Come on, Harry," he said. After he was up topside, he tapped the carton until a cigarette slid partway out. "I know," he told the dog. "But I've got Miss Manhattan on board. One smoke is understandable." He lit up and took a drag, inhaling deeply. The wind was still whipping and he could feel the chill even in goose down. Once more he pulled the smoke into his lungs, the ember a tiny glowing furnace.

After the third drag he ground out the smoke with a pinch of two wet fingers. Then he took one more look around with night vision and was reassured by the isolation. Never before had he left his sat phone behind, but it had broken last week and it hadn't seemed a priority until now. At this moment he would give a lot to call Grogg and get Big Brain started on some probing questions about Anna Wade. He figured he'd better get down to his guest. As his last act topside, he opened a lazzarette and put the butt in a plastic garbage bag.

"Filthy damn habit," he told Harry, promising himself it would be his last.

It would take two hours to cook the spaghetti if he did it half right, twenty minutes if he sacrificed quality and cheated. She could drink wine while he decided exactly how nosy he was going to be.

He had the pot full of Italian-spiced tofu balls, beer, more Italian spices, tomato paste, and stewed tomatoes.

The curlicue pasta was on and he was marinating the avocado for the salad when she walked out of her stateroom. It was a mere fortuity that he had fresh lettuce. He had bartered it from the captain of a packer boat coming down from Alaska.

"What you been doing up there?"

"After my makeup, shivering under a blanket, looking through your books, and snooping."

"Least you're honest."

Her hair was soft now, her lipstick even, smooth, and warm; the touch of eyeliner and mascara made pools of her eyes. He saw it coming—at any moment the next assault would arrive.

Harry trotted over to her for a second pat.

After fussing over Harry for a moment, she came to Sam and put a hand on his arm. "Can't you think of some way to get us out of here?" These words and the warm hand were accompanied by her truly charming smile. It would make most men want to please her. It made Sam want a drink with another smoke. This was the old life and it had come roaring back with the adrenaline rush.

He shrugged. "I'm sorry you don't want to stay for dinner. It's a good recipe. Ever had beer in the red sauce?"

"Beer?"

"Don't knock it until you've tried it."

"Could you use your radio to call someone—a seaplane maybe?"

"We went over this. It's a line-of-sight VHF radio, we're in a natural bowl, the shortwave radio is in the shop. I don't have a sat phone that works. There is no cell signal here."

"Get me off this boat. Yes or no?" This time she was direct.

"No."

She looked at him with a level stare and he looked right back.

"Don't you have a beacon?"

"An emergency locator beacon won't get anyone here tonight."

She folded her arms and exhaled as though it were her last breath on this earth. It moved him but not enough to overcome his own determination. He made it a point not to be impressed by celebrities.

"The Mounties could get me off the beach," she said.

"With some luck we'll find a way out of here tomorrow. Of course if I knew what was going on, I might try to figure some way off this boat . . . some way that didn't entail freezing my ass in the salt water and then facing death from exposure on shore. Maybe."

He returned to the stove and stirred the spaghetti sauce. Without a word she walked back into the stateroom and closed the door.

So it's going to be like that, he said to himself. *Maybe she really can't even pretend to be like the rest of us.*

Three

Anna Wade had been aboard a few yachts, some lavish, some ordinary. Sam's seemed compact but cozy and tasteful. In the forward stateroom there was a walk-around queen-size pedestal bed and a small vanity next to a door to the forward head. Additionally there was a desk. The woodwork was lustrous and warm, a little reddish in tone, and looked very custom—similar to handmade furniture that she had specially ordered for her Manhattan apartment. Obviously expensive. The fixtures were also unusual. From what little she had seen of yachts in this size range, they usually had flimsy doors and elf-sized handles that rattled in their holes. Everything on this boat was substantial and solid, nearly as large as the fixtures in an expensive house. Sam cared about his things.

She couldn't tell if she was making headway with him or not. For a second she had thought he might be about to give in. As a last resort she would try a few minutes of the silent treatment—just sitting with the door closed while he wondered.

The way the boat was stocked—the books, the stuff in the drawers—it was owned, not chartered. There were scented candles, and she couldn't put that together with the man who had yanked her from the sea. So Sam was a man of some means. Definitely not a reporter, and no garden-variety businessman either. Despite his firm insistence on secrecy, she felt for the moment that he was trustworthy even if stubborn. Something told her he'd had a hand in nabbing Peter Malkey's thieving accountant. Perhaps he was some sort of high-powered investigator.

The shelves held books about Native American mythology; one compared New Age mysticism with Native American spiritual beliefs. An interesting woven-cloth bookmark protruded from a volume entitled *Tilok Life*, and another from *On the Trail of the Tiloks* by Jessie Mayfield Wintripp. There were some spy novels along with some traditionally male biographies. Even more interesting, he had a copy of *The Mind*. In trying to learn about her brother, she had read the book and others like it. Although not per se about paranoia, it was a stunning discussion of human consciousness and self-determination, a look at how mind might be derived from matter.

The desk was sizable, even out of proportion, and obviously served as his workplace when he didn't have guests. On the desktop she found a map with many notations apparently having to do with Native American tribes—the Salish, Kwaikutl, and Nuuchahnulth. Historic villages were marked in black, whereas currently existing villages seemed to be marked in blue. Sliding open the drawers, she found more maps of larger scale with notations about various sites. Perhaps the man was an archeologist. No, that didn't seem right.

In one drawer she found a collection of cosmetic items including shampoos, hand lotion, skin cream, lipsticks. Some of the liquid materials were in a large Ziploc plastic bag. Although the plastic case had remained nearly dry, she had been careful to rinse

Jason's plastic computer CD in fresh water to remove all traces of salt, but if she went in the ocean again she wanted better protection. Feeling only slightly larcenous, she emptied the contents of the Ziploc bag, inserted Jason's CD, and carefully sealed the bag. If she did nothing else, she had to preserve that CD. The Ziploc then went into the waterproof bag in her fanny pack.

In the corner of the large drawer was an album full of pictures of Sam with a young man. The way they stood she could tell they were close. It was probably his younger brother—Sam seemed too young for such a son. In one of the plastic sleeves, on the back side of a photo of the young man dressed in cap and gown, presumably at graduation, was a folded-up piece of personal stationery. Feeling a little guilty, she pulled it out. It was a letter. It was only four lines.

My only son. You came from me. You will go on with me, then without me. Carry me with you in your heart as I will always carry you in mine. Do not neglect a good beer and a sunset.
Dad

So Sam was the young man's father. Odd to have a letter that you'd sent to someone else.

Several pictures toward the back there was one of Sam with an older gentleman, obviously a Native American, wearing a heavy wool shirt, blue jeans and what looked like lace-up hide boots, and a green medicine bag around his neck. Behind that picture was a letter, very brief but written in a foreign language and bearing a signature that was obviously a foreign name.

For some reason she was sure the book belonged to Sam's mother. Perhaps the mother had found Sam's letter in her grandson's possessions and kept it. But why would she have left it on the boat? Anna felt a great curiosity and a little sadness. Seeing the letter had put confusion in her mind. There was a softness in the simple words that she had not seen in Sam.

Anna stopped snooping and sighed. She had tried reasoning with Sam. For just another moment she would sit and soak up the warmth and wait to see if he came knocking. If he remained steadfast she would act.

According to her watch it had been five minutes, and ignoring him was working no better than talking with him. She stood up and stretched, utterly determined.

Mr. Macho would follow, she was sure.

And what choice did she have? It had to have been Roberto that Sam had seen above her on the cliff. If it was Roberto who walked away (and not her brother, caught up in some absentminded daze, enthralled with the elegance of the universe), Anna was in great danger. All her life she'd depended on her instincts, and right now her instincts were screaming.

She popped open the front hatch over the front berth and crawled out on deck. It was black dark and the wind screamed in the rigging. The cold pierced her clothing, as the sound of it pierced her soul. Suddenly she decided that swimming in this hellish scene was too much. What had seemed doable in the comfort of the cabin now seemed impossible. Her eyes cast about. Three feet away in the dim light emanating from the wheelhouse she saw something against the lifelines. She ran her hand over it. A tiny rubber boat. The lying sneak.

* * *

DuShane Chellis was in fair condition for a fifty-two-year-old man, handsome with a decent physique, and he planned to stay that way. He kept his salt-and-pepper gray hair impeccably groomed, swept back with natural waves but close-cropped without sideburns. He was dark-complected and rough-skinned, and as with most fit middle-aged men, his face was unrounded by fat, more distinguished than pleasant. With his serious dark eyes and the flat line of his mouth he appeared to be a man who counted his conquests, a predator, which in fact was in keeping with his character.

DuShane Chellis had become a fabulously successful corporate takeover artist. He made most of his money on the third company that he raided, a small company enjoying newfound but unheralded success in the medical applications of certain mapping software. Chellis got control of the board of directors, ousted the founder, and went on to assemble a medical supply conglomerate that adopted the name of his first company, Grace Technologies. A small but not insignificant and growing portion of Chellis's great success came from his conversion of the takeover target's medical software into a variety of military applications. For that endeavor he had joined forces with Samir Aziz. It was Samir who handled the dirty part of the business.

Chellis walked down the immaculate halls of the Grace Technologies Kuching Laboratory with great anticipation. Around him, the building, which sat at the base of a densely forested mountain in central Borneo, bustled with activity. Most of the corporation's clinical tests involving animals took place here—a political expediency, since Malaysia had few animal rights activists and even fewer animal rights laws. In addition, Kuching was no mecca for probing journalists or government investigators.

Chellis stood inside the doorway of the office he had appointed lavishly as a gift for Jacques Boudreaux, his lead researcher. The imported antique furniture displayed the fantasies of glory dear to its occupant. More significantly, it was a measure of the scientist's importance within Grace Technologies.

"I am anxious to see the practical application of all this theory," Chellis said by way of greeting.

"You have Samir Aziz coming in. The largest arms dealer in the world. A dangerous man."

"Maybe not so dangerous; a little tamer when you are through."

"Yes. But if I knew . . ."

Chellis held up his big left hand bearing an oversized gold ring. "Jacques, I do the business, you invent the goodies. It's a division of labor."

"But . . ."

"I know you are going to tell me that if you know the application you can better tailor the product. Well, I don't care and I own the company. I had to bring Samir. I'll tell you that much. The Mossad paid a visit to his private residence in Lebanon and they wanted to know what I was up to in medical technology. With a very big gun under his nose they told him that they're interested in the brain research. They went into his safe, ransacked the place, and believed him when he said he knew nothing. Samir should have been happy that he had nothing in his safe. Instead he was very unhappy that they knew something about Grace Technologies that he did not. Samir is a powerful man and he is not used to being pushed around by the Mossad or anyone else, and it has put him in a very grumpy mood. He and I have a very tidy arrangement and I want to keep him manageable. Like Jason is manageable. That's where you come in and that's the only place you come in."

"I called security. Talked to Claude Balford himself. I asked about the man who came to visit without authorization. Devan Gaudet I believe he was. Our security man, Mr. Balford, was so silent I thought the phone had gone dead."

"You forget about Devan Gaudet. You assured me you told him nothing. Is that right?"

"Nothing."

"I am shocked you know that name. You wipe it from your mind, my friend. I cannot afford to lose you."

"Lose me?"

"In the purest sense, Jacques."

Jacques looked troubled, and Chellis knew that he should be.

"So am I going to see the real thing used on a monkey before I see it used on my good friend Samir Aziz?"

"Let's go." Jacques stood and led the way, apparently ready to accept the fact that there would be no more information. He was short and blond and had a strut that might have suited Napoleon himself.

Chellis followed him to double doors over which hung a sign indicating MOLECULAR BIOLOGY. Inside, a second set of doors was marked PRIMATE WING NEUROLOGY.

They stopped in a large room with multiple cages housing pigtail macaques. In all there were six. Four appeared completely normal.

Behind a plate-glass stood a large cage outfitted with gray tree trunks, rope swings, and a multilevel climbing frame. An obvious effort had been made to introduce natural elements to the enclosure.

"Aren't these critters mostly terrestrial?"

"More than most but they are still monkeys."

To one side of the plate-glass was a door that admitted them to an area immediately outside the cage that contained four chairs, small writing desks, and a console. Housed in the cage were a male macaque, Centaur, and a female, Venus. Centaur busily groomed Venus, his eyes concentrating on his fingers as they picked through her coat. Each monkey wore a harness with a small pack in the center of its back. Standing by was a young man dressed in a khaki uniform.

Jacques walked to the console. "Where we can control everything and have instant injection of the various juvenile hormones, we are making rapid progress in our behavioral studies," Jacques began. "Of course to get the range of behavior that I will now display, we need to have altered neurons from several regions and a direct-access IV drip of the various juvenile hormones. Note Centaur's calm demeanor." Jacques reached to the console and typed in a code.

Centaur sat back on his haunches, yawned, and looked out at them, Buddha-like, as if he were gazing into eternity.

"He looks like the Dalai Lama," Chellis joked. "I understand macaques are cannibals."

"No. That's chimps you're thinking of. But then people are cannibals if they are hungry enough." Jacques punched in another command.

Centaur began vocalizing and pacing up and down the cage, stretching his arms and making breathy screeching sounds. Again Jacques punched in a code, and the monkey began racing at the bars and screaming with a blood-lust trill. Suddenly he charged Venus, who at first cowered, then ran to a perch in the tree. Centaur followed. When he arrived at the perch, he stood over her, shrieking. Again Jacques typed a code, and the male grabbed the female, attempting to push her from the perch; a fight erupted, and quickly Jacques typed in another code.

Immediately Centaur sat on his haunches as if nothing had happened. After a moment he climbed down and approached the female, who was still trembling and baring her teeth in a grimace.

"That's actually a submission display."

"It looks like she's pissed."

"No, that means she'll play ball by his rules."

Methodically he began once again grooming her, and gradually she calmed.

"And what if you had not canceled the last command?"

"He would have become progressively more agitated and aggressive until he killed her."

"Very impressive. When will it be ready for the real world?"

"Don't know. We're working on it. What you observed is much more advanced in the mood control than we can get without IV access. And of course we placed the receptors over a long period and with much trial and error. We went through five animals." Jacques stepped away from the console. "Jason Wade is a phase one. These animals are phase three. We use both activating cells and suppressor cells in many cell types."

"Let's go get some lunch," Chellis said.

Jacques did not care for cafeterias, so they adjourned to a conference room adjoining his office that each day was turned into a private dining room, where he entertained various researchers and high-level staff. Chellis was perfectly happy to eat in the cafeteria, and even enjoyed the curious glances of all the employees, but he deferred to Jacques when in Kuching.

Chellis only visited every couple of months, and he appreciated that with Jacques running the facility more frequent visits weren't necessary. Benoit Moreau, his assistant and his mistress, came a little more frequently. Marie, Chellis's wife, didn't care for Malaysia, and although, for appearances, he did not like traveling alone with Benoit, he would not be without a woman. That was the main reason he'd assigned Benoit to monitor Kuching. She had been his assistant for eight years and his mistress for seven of them, and therefore only occasionally resided in Kuching. Chellis's life was further complicated by that fact that Benoit was Marie's sister.

This trip he had Benoit meeting with the heads of each department to obtain research summaries and to keep her away from the macaques demonstration.

"You don't think the aerosol is ready yet, even if we just limit ourselves to a phase-one paranoia continuum."

"Not quite."

"If we want only to achieve phase one on Samir with a simple paranoid continuum, do we need to put him to sleep?"

"Yes."

"But you know the effect?"

"We'll get the receptors, but the magnitude of the effect isn't completely clear. It's a question of how well the gene expression comes through, which depends primarily on the volume of vector particles. And frankly, the human will has incredible powers of adaptation. The mind with all its abilities is created by an odd composite of neuronal activity. The neurons, billions of them working together, trillions of interconnections create consciousness, but they are not consciousness. People can literally sometimes think their way or learn their way out of a change in physiology. Maybe we could say that training or thinking creates physiology. In the end physiology wins."

"So if I go ahead with my little plan, we don't know exactly how good the result will be on Samir?"

"That's right."

"But he will be nervous."

"Yes. It would be shocking if he weren't at least somewhat paranoid. Especially for the first few months."

"But not completely crazy. And we alone can provide him relief."

"It should make him a lot more manageable. We will see. You know I can guarantee nothing. We are reasonably sure but we don't have the controls, and the volume for a human-sized mammal remains a question."

"I know. I know. But let's do something."

"Imagine what you could do to a head of state, or an entire parliament . . ."

Chellis didn't mind Jacques's probing; he wasn't going to get anywhere with it.

"Is the gas chamber foolproof?"

"You must get him placed between the nozzles. If you don't we'll have to try again on the way back, maybe use force and rely on memory blockers."

"Samir should be here any moment; I need to get to my office."

"You could use mine," Jacques said.

"No. No. I don't need to impress this man."

When Samir entered Chellis's office, Chellis stood and greeted him in quiet tones. Samir was a big man, thick like a wrestler with glasses like Coke bottles, and an aura of confidence that was palpable. They had met for the first time fifteen years earlier, and since then had actually met face-to-face on perhaps a dozen occasions. They had become not so much friends or acquaintances as uneasy joint venturers, each keenly aware at any given moment of what the other might hold for him.

"Well," Chellis said, interrupting the mutual pleasantries. "I know you're a busy man and would no doubt like to get on with business."

"I'm not like the Orientals who require an hour's socializing before getting down to work," Samir said, "but I do need to see what you're developing so I can begin thinking about how we might employ it."

"I'd like to ask that only you view the demonstration. It's top secret."

Samir hesitated but was unreadable. "My men can wait outside the door?"

"Of the molecular biology wing."

Samir nodded, clearly not pleased but amenable. Weapons carried by Samir's men were hidden only in a crude fashion. There were obvious lumps in their clothes.

They went down long halls, and finally emerged into the main molecular biology lab, but this time Chellis led him to a different door. It was metal and heavy.

"What is this?" Samir asked.

"We go through an air lock. An anticontamination measure."

They walked to a second heavy metal door that said: AIR LOCK. CLEAN ROOM.

Chellis removed a plastic card and inserted it into a shiny stainless box. As if to ease Samir's mind, he explained:

"We have to keep out foreign bacteria. Ordinarily we wouldn't traipse through with street shoes on, but today it's okay."

With a sucking sound the heavy door opened to reveal a three-meter-by-five-meter chamberlike area with all-metal walls and to the left, hanging on the wall, heavy white suits looking rather like astronaut garb. They approached an even more massive door. Chellis determined that Samir was perfectly placed between the two gas nozzles.

Chellis took a deep breath and held it. A whirring could be heard as the sliding door began closing behind them. There was a loud pop and rushing gas. Samir, startled, took a breath, then began to look wildly about, gasping. Within ten seconds he began to stagger and to lose motor control. Chellis grabbed his own throat and swayed as if drunk, turning to look in Samir's alarm-filled eyes as he fell to the floor. Chellis stepped back to the door through which they had come. A crack remained to allow his exit; then the door closed. By the time Samir's eyes had rolled back in his head, Chellis was outside the chamber with the door closed.

Two hours later Chellis, as was his custom when under stress, went on a ten-minute screaming tirade. Jacques, appearing pale, began to stare down at his shoes, and Chellis realized that he was repeating himself badly. "You never said he would get uncontrollably angry." Jacques blinked his irritation but said nothing. "Answer me! I had Samir Aziz in the lab. We gassed him. How could you screw this up?"

"There is no indication that we screwed anything up. He is angry. He probably always gets mad when he feels powerless. Mad is different from aggressive. Aggressive means killing people; it comes from phase two, and he received no phase-two-vector particles. No receptors for those areas of the brain. You watch, the fear will increase, but he won't become more hostile or aggressive. When you have had a chance to introduce him to a masseuse, the massage oil will work perfectly. He will calm himself temporarily with each introduction of the hormone. More than that, he will crave it once he tries it."

At that moment Benoit arrived with Jacques's right-hand man, a bearded fellow with a round face and stomach. He stood back and nodded toward Chellis, who looked at Benoit as she put a hand on Chellis's arm.

"I am sorry. I wondered if I might interrupt."

"I want it working," Chellis said, no longer yelling but ignoring Benoit. "I'm going to see him in a few hours and he's mad as hell."

Chellis escorted Benoit down the hall, knowing he should not have alluded to the Samir situation in her presence. He kept her out of such things.

It was a short walk to her comfortable six-bedroom home, a small mansion set carefully at the jungle's edge with lush gardens and a ten-foot brick wall to ensure privacy. Benoit held his arm as they came up the walk and he nodded at the servants whose names he could never remember. Benoit seemed to know them all. It bothered him that she held his arm, as it gave the appearance of impropriety.

In the study he found a bottle of Glenlivet. After the first sip he turned his attention to Benoit. She was dark-haired and with the same stark-white unblemished skin as her sister Marie, his wife, but with large, doelike, brown eyes. She was slightly more squared in the shoulders than Marie, which he liked, and unlike Marie she was petite in the torso with a small bust.

Two years younger than Marie, Benoit looked more like five years her junior; at forty-one she looked to be in her early thirties. While Marie was a witty observer, an arranger of things, passively inviting sexually, and generally warm to everybody, Benoit was calculating and aggressively sexual, a small tigress with a killer instinct. In his most private thoughts it seemed to Chellis that they were two halves of a marvelous whole: sweet and succulent but tart and nourishing; luxurious and classy but practical and gritty. Where Marie was sexual crème brûlée, Benoit held the hot tang of his favorite chutney. Together they had it all, and which of them he wanted in his bed depended on whether he wanted to rhapsodize or sweat.

He made sure the shades were drawn and the door locked. Although he was still not quite in the mood, he gave Benoit a long, slow kiss, very carefully, with enough of his tongue to warm the heart but not so much as to move over the line to disrespect. If he hadn't made it right, she would be a bitch for a while. It was one of the few concessions he made to another person playing with his carefully spun reality. Never would he tolerate diffidence from a man, but the two women in his life were different.

Benoit gave him a good smile. She was pampering him. And he knew it was because she had a strong opinion about Jacques and his value and she felt the need to manipulate his mood any way she could.

"It will be fine. Give it time and it will work just like it did with Jason. You know I would never tell you your business, but it strikes me that Jacques is very capable. Perhaps we should not unfairly blame him."

"I don't know what you're talking about."

"DuShane, darling. I know what you tried with Samir."

"How do you know these things?"

"I snooped in your briefcase on the jet when you went to sleep."

"There was nothing in my briefcase."

"There was a planned experiment for this afternoon on a macaque with a body weight of 240 pounds."

"Maybe a young gorilla."

"Okay."

"You knew it was Samir Aziz?"

"Of course."

"Just how did you know?"

"Jacques's secretary booked a hotel reservation for him. He weighs about 240 pounds. We don't have any young gorillas. They don't stay in hotels."

The phone rang.

Even in Kuching there was a screening computer on his phone system that would not allow a call unless the computer recognized the phone number of the caller or unless the caller knew a code. He picked up the phone.

"Yes."

It was Roberto, insisting that Chellis hear the story of Anna Wade's tumble into the saltwater rapids. Chellis could feel himself being dragged into something and he didn't like it.

"Are you certain the scrambler is on?"

"Yes, we checked."

Roberto told the story twice, repeating each and every detail and taxing Chellis's patience.

"Get the CD back or make sure it's gone for good." Chellis interrupted when Roberto tried to respond. "If she had an accident, that would be . . ."

"Yes, an accident," Roberto said.

"And don't forget who you are dealing with here.

Even in Canada this won't go away quickly if something else happens to her."

"The currents here are fierce."

Immediately after he hung up Chellis knew he had made a mistake. This was happening too fast. He shouldn't be involved directly with this.

Four

While fidgeting for the want of another smoke and on the verge of surrendering to Anna temporarily, Sam heard the splash—a body hitting the water? He ran to the stateroom and tried the door. Locked.

Damn it. She had climbed out of the hatch.

Harry barked and ran to the companionway. Sam jumped over Harry and hit the third stair and one other before making the top. He dashed through the wheelhouse and made the aft deck in three strides.

No rubber boat.

"It leaks!" he shouted. "Come back. It's dangerous."

"Help me." In the wind he heard nothing more. With only a piece of his rudder it would be difficult to drive the boat after her and there was no time to pull anchor or don a dry suit. He had seconds to decide. He could feel himself drawn into the old life as surely as his boat had been drawn into that wave. His mind sat on a high wire, contemplating the possible opposing forces, the risk of falling and losing what little peace he had left. His son was dead. His hero days were over. On the other hand, dying might just be easier than living.

"Damn her."

Reaching under a hinged seat, he grabbed a life jacket. For a second he rummaged around until he found a large waterproof light that he snapped to a ring on the jacket. Then he thought about the drag and figured he could make shore without the jacket, so he snapped the light to a belt loop instead. He had to move fast and catch her before she got headed in the wrong direction. If she missed the point, about two hundred yards off, she would no doubt drown. Dumb woman.

Harry whined.

He needed waterproof matches. She was getting too far away. Taking off his topsiders, he tied the rawhide laces into his belt loops so he could swim with bare feet. "Stay, Harry." Then he dived neatly over the lifelines and as his head emerged, gasped from the frigid water. He forced himself to focus, creating a perfect rhythm to his stroke that melded with his breathing, losing himself in motion. He imagined himself in a pool and thought of his mind as a warm light that retreated deep within. Soon the cold was far away. Clouds drifted, but he was sure he found the North Star and kept it a bit to his right.

Every third stroke he saw the trees of the ridge against the stars and kept himself straight. After a time he slowed to hear the splashes of her paddle, and with the thought of it came the cold, driven away only by reclaiming the rhythm. The current was running enough that he knew they would be swept up Heron Bay. It appeared she would miss the point. He had to catch her. Once more the barely audible splash of her stroke drew him on and once more the cold invaded his mind. He was a powerful swimmer in superb shape. Steadily he gained until he saw her—nearly sunk.

"Get out. It leaks. You're barely moving. Wrong direction."

"Okay," she said. "Thanks for coming."

"Tie your shoelaces to your belt."

She also swam well. It took him minutes to guide them to the point and the shore. It was too far even to think about getting her to swim back. His foot touched bottom and he grabbed her around the waist. She was very weak from two major dunkings in the frigid water. The last fifty feet he carried her. On dry land he put her down and they put on their shoes.

"Come on," she said, wobbly but obviously determined to go someplace. He caught her and grabbed her shoulder.

She turned.

"What are you—" he began.

"Took you a while," she said through ragged breaths. Turning back toward the trees, she kept going.

He followed. "You could have killed yourself."

"Thanks to you once again, I didn't, though, did I?"

"What the hell does that mean? You are one frustrating—"

"Frustrating what?"

"Just how were you gonna keep from freezing to death?"

"That was your department."

"What made you think I'd be stupid enough to follow you?"

Astounded at her grit, he trudged with her down the beach next to the trees. He had no dry matches, no smokes, and he would have to make a fire.

"There's a cabin inland over on Greene's Bay," she said. "It's almost two miles. We can break in."

"How do you know?"

"I saw it a couple days ago. Jason and I crossed over to Sonoma with Nutka and went for a walk. She's a native."

He filed away the names for future consideration. "Are we looking for a trail?" He snapped on the waterproof light.

"Turn it off!" she said. "Wait until we're out of sight of the Windham Island shore."

"Who's on the Windham shore?"

"If we walk along this beach there is a tiny creek. I'll recognize it. If we go up the channel about three-quarters of a mile, we'll come to this concrete box with a pump at a spring with a plastic pipe going into it. We follow the pipe."

"They have a generator?"

"I guess they must. They have a pump."

Just then an eerie rushing sound echoed across the channel. He turned toward the boat as it erupted in a ball of fire.

"You can thank me later," she said.

"You should have said something."

Neither spoke for a moment as they stood with the heat of adrenaline moving through their bodies.

"Give me a break," she said. "You weren't listening."

"You weren't talking."

"Why are we arguing? You would have been dead."

"I liked the damned boat," he said. "And I loved the dog."

"I'm sorry," she said.

"Not as sorry as the guy with the rocket launcher."

Within two minutes the boat was gone to the bottom.

"Who did it?"

"We'll discuss it. I'll make everything right. Better boat, everything."

"You can't give me what I lost!"

"I'm so sorry. I didn't know they'd do this."

"Do they have a boat?"

"Yes."

The words weren't out of her mouth before they heard the sound of whirling rotors, the thump of metal beating air, and saw a brilliant light skimming the water.

"Do they have a chopper?"

"They have one. I didn't know it was here now."

"So you don't know if the chopper is friend or foe."

"I don't know who is friend or foe."

"Move," he said in a harsh whisper as they ran up the beach and into the trees.

For a moment they watched as the brilliant beam of an incandescent light skated over the wind-crinkled black surface to the spot where the boat had been lying at anchor. Like a mad mosquito the copter searched the area.

He noticed that in addition to the shaking, Anna was starting to lose her balance.

"So now do you want to tell me what's going on?"

She stood silent, with her teeth chattering while she rubbed her arms.

"Let's go," he said, frustrated that she still wasn't talking.

Until they heard the copter leave they walked just inside the trees with no light. By the time they found the creek, they were turning blue around the lips and she was shaking to the point that speech was difficult. He had been similarly cold before and had a few layers of muscle to help. Anna had very little womanly fat. If she was right about the distance, they had a long way to go.

They clawed their way through low-hanging branches and walked hard for what seemed like nearly half an hour until they found the spring. As she had said, the water pipe led right to the cabin some fifteen hundred yards overland on a small saltwater bay. In the circle of the flashlight the board siding was weathered gray but appeared intact. The tarpaper roof looked in good repair. On the door there was a sizable padlock and there were shutters over the windows.

"How do we get in?" She slurred her words as if drunk. Any minute he was afraid she would fall over and go permanently to sleep. He had to get her warm fast.

"How were you going to get in?" he asked.

"I was going to let you figure it out."

Surveying the door, he realized that ramming it with his shoulder would likely break his collarbone if they had a hearty bolt on the inside. Everything about the place seemed pretty beefy; he supposed they'd have a door latch to match. Maybe even a crossbar.

"And how the hell did you know I would be here?" he said, fumbling with a window sash.

"You didn't let me drown the first time."

"Don't tempt me again."

She was almost smiling when she patted him on the shoulder and kissed his cheek.

On the second window, he found enough purchase to yank it open. After that it was simply a matter of breaking the window and unlocking it. They both crawled through the open window and found a spartan cabin interior.

"Aim the light at the wall. And if you plan to leave before I get back, let me know."

"I love you for saving me. But otherwise go to hell."

"It'd be a lot warmer."

Sam unbolted the door and went out front. With the shutters and door closed, only the tiniest crack of light shone through at one window. It was easily fixed by propping a discarded board. Satisfied, he went back into the cabin and took a more careful look around. It was lined with some type of pressed board that retained a golden brown mottled surface. There were two hanging lights with frosted glass shades. The floor was painted concrete. When the place was occupied there would be a generator to run the meager electrical service, the few lights, and the water pump. On the lone table sat a gas lantern. They verified that the place had no food or matches.

"Search for lighters, blankets, matches, and clothes," Sam muttered. There was an old woodstove and a little kindling beside some hardwood logs. They rifled through more cupboards and drawers, desperate to find matches. She started to sit down.

"No." Sam stopped her and made her lean against the wall. "You can't go to sleep. You'll die on me. And then there would be a police report and they'd want my last name." He started rummaging through cabinets. Although she was barely able to move, he watched her emulating him, trying to help. In a closet they found two threadbare sleeping bags, a folded-up rusty three-burner Coleman stove that looked about twenty years old, and a blanket worn thin and barely green, with a few holes and sun-faded with age.

"I thought, given the antenna outside, that there would be a radio in here," she said.

"Well, there isn't."

"We need to get you a new boat and we need to get back to civilization."

"I've got to find the men who sunk my home."

"On the other end of this island . . . someone is building. An oyster farm, I think."

"It's not on the chart. Even if you're right, it must be at least four miles down this island through a brush-filled forest."

"We can go in the morning. First thing."

It was about forty-two degrees, near as he could guess.

"Dry off and crawl into the bag," he said.

"What are you going to do?"

"Take care of things."

"Turn off the light," she said.

"In just a minute." He unfolded the Coleman stove. "Yes!" he said, finding a box of wooden matches. She turned her back. He grabbed the paper towels, put them beside her, and doused the light. Quickly he stripped and dried off. He felt for his sleeping bag.

"I'm in," she said.

Sam crawled into his and could detect only a slight barrier to the cold. It had been a lightweight bag maybe five years ago. Now it wasn't worthy of the name.

"This won't work." Sam turned on the light. He went to the woodstove, took the small amount of remaining kindling, and placed it on a loose wad of paper towels. It burned nicely; he added more kindling. When it flamed he added a thick piece of branch. He was breathing hard and shaking slightly, but at least there was warmth on the palms of his hands. The sleeping bag over his shoulders wasn't doing him much good. Soon the branch had ignited and he added a larger piece of wood, leaving the stove door ajar for maximum draft. Anna hopped over in her bag and sat down against the stove. After the flame was established, Sam went out in front of the cabin and studied the stovepipe. There was no visible light, nor were there sparks. Uneasy, but satisfied that the fire was not a dead giveaway, he went back inside.

He lay on his back next to the stove with the bag over him, put his hands on the floor, and raised his abdomen so that his body was arched with only his feet and hands touching the Doug-fir planks. He began taking deep breaths.

"That's a very good *Ūrdhva Dhanura.*"

"So you do yoga too. It's hard to be original anymore."

"Control the breathing, slow the heart, the body will warm from the quiet exertion. Defeats the cold. I know what you're trying, but if you're that good I'll be jealous, and you probably aren't that good, so either way let's huddle close to the stove."

"Yoga is a way to stretch. I think it's nothing more."

After a full minute of stretching he crawled into his bag and they sat close.

"I'm still freezing," she said.

"We could put one bag inside the other, then wrap you in a blanket and both get in."

"Only in the movies."

Five

Jason lay on his desk, facing the ceiling, the fear still there. Always there. Every morning he woke and knew that there was something wrong and that it would not go away.

When he smelled breakfast cooking and opened his eyes to look from the window by the bed, he might try to find something bright, perhaps the sunlight as described by a bard who knew the look of a tree with its tufts of moss-life and the speckling of bark, the sap in the white wood, the bursting of crinkled green shoots, the tireless withering of old leaves before the new. But each time Jason found the bright it was bounded by shadows, dark spots in the crooks of the branches. The darkness ate at him, turned his stomach sour even before he rose. Maybe a bird would flit by, but he knew it would die in winter with little things crawling over its skin, rotting it, smelling like yesterday's fish. Wind harbored soulless ghosts, the mountain was cruel, and everything on it died, and nothing lived that hadn't risen from the ashes of another's death.

Fear lived in his chest as if a barbed hook were stuck fast in the wall of his gullet. He couldn't swallow his spit, let alone sing, without knowing the fear.

They said that without hope you die, and he realized

his hope was so dim it barely lit the back rooms of his conscious thought. It helped being naked, especially when he got his massage. Before he picked up a three-ring notebook and walked over to the *Principia Mathematica,* he sat on the floor and stripped himself of every stitch of clothing. It felt better, but only a little.

Roberto walked in through the kitchen and startled him.

"Relax, Jason. Everything is fine."

"I understood it was a plaything."

"Oh, no, Jason, you wondered." He punched Jason gently in the shoulder. "You always wonder and you never know for sure, do you? But it's at the bottom of Heron Bay now. Right now I need you to tell me where the CD is. You had two CD-ROMs, the regular and the backup. Did you give the backup to Anna?"

"No. It's around. If the Nannites didn't take it we'll find it."

"There are no Nannites. You know that. Now where is the CD?"

Jason did not reply.

"We're counting on you," Roberto said before he turned around and left the room.

Jason detested those words. He turned back to his office. Down both sides of the room ran bookshelves lined with math treatises. Set apart from its companion volumes, in the center, was Bertrand Russell's five-volume work, *Principia Mathematica.* It was a signed edition. Also set apart in their own special slot were Einstein's initial publications, papers really, on the general theory of relativity.

Most of his library comprised texts on quantum mechanics and quantum math.

There were two photographs in his office, one of Anna, another of his daughter, Grady. Memories of his life before moving to this island were disturbing. Memories of his life before France were even more disturbing, and hence seemed to have washed away, like sand castles on an incoming tide. He had had several girlfriends, but only one of note, and she had borne him a daughter when he was a nineteen-year-old prodigy at Georgia Tech and about to transfer to MIT.

There had been a court order before he went to France to work for Grace Technologies, and he was not able to keep his daughter. Grady's mother had wanted no part of him. Although she had given the girl her own last name, Lasky, Grady so despised her mother that upon turning eighteen she had changed it to Wade. Jason knew that his daughter cared little for him either, but he wasn't sure how he had come to that realization.

The picture of Grady had come from Anna; without it he wouldn't know his daughter if he met her on the street. But he thought about her, and he used to dream that one day he might shake the Nannites and go find her. Now such a thing seemed impossible—it would be dangerous for Grady—and he wanted more than anything to believe that she was safe. Anna, for whatever reason, wouldn't talk about Grady, so he let his daughter rest as a picture on his side table.

There was a phrase that he had heard somewhere about a millstone around the neck. Life was becoming like that, a steady weight of worry and fear. Any little thing could seize his mind. Only one small focus for his hope had not yet been extinguished. He had hacked his way into the Kuching sections of the Grace computers. It had taken him months of playing to breach the firewalls.

Within the Kuching laboratory files he had discovered encrypted file folders. He did not have the software to break the code, although slowly but surely he was developing software that might do the job. But it could take years. Although he couldn't open the files, he had developed a program that would download them. Those files were on the CD he had given Anna, and they might hold secrets of the Nannites. Curious minds would not rest until they opened them. Of that he was certain.

In forty minutes Nutka would give him his massage and there would be some respite to his misery.

Inevitably, his temper had risen like a cobra from its basket. Chellis erupted.

"Roberto is a disaster. Now we've got to bring Gaudet in. I don't give a damn what it costs. Roberto's foul-ups will cost us more. He's gotten Jason to sink a sailboat with a rocket launcher. A rocket launcher, for God's sake! What'll be next? If this keeps up, Jason will end up in a sanitarium. And if that happens, it's the end of some big programs for us."

"You are right to use Gaudet for this one," Benoit said. "Would you like me to get him?"

"I don't like it that the bastard is becoming a habit. But you better do it now."

"Thank you again," Anna said. "I'm not sure I could have made my way to this sleeping bag."

"You might have, had you paddled in the right direction. You are resolute and strong."

"Thank you. That's a better compliment than most I get."

"They tell you you're beautiful?"

"Incessantly."

She was fading fast, and he waited to see if another sentence would come. It didn't. His hand was on her shoulder. She reached up and patted it before the final deep breath that sent her into sleep.

Once the cabin started to warm, things seemed less desperate. Sam's old world was rapidly coming back and with it the old habits. He would have paid a couple grand for a smoke.

The problem was that Anna had a jump on his imagination. She was beside him, nearly in his bed. Being close to her and feeling her body sleep made for a sexy coziness.

If Sam was anything, the old Sam or the newly emerging version, he was in control. Cool. Objective. This unilateral interest on his part that he thought might be forming would not be cool, and that was the first problem. The second was that she was a celebrity, and he could never be with a celebrity again. It was one of the few absolutes in his life.

In the darkness he could see the barest outline of Anna's head. Finally she had uncoiled her body, stretching out on the floor, but he was still spooning her back in an attempt to stop her shivering. It seemed that the swim in the cold water had taken hold.

He could still smell the shampoo odor in her hair, like oranges, and a slight salt smell mixed with her natural scent—all of it focused his mind like a rifle sight before his eye. Her butt was tight but nicely curved and her shoulders were squared. Made extraordinary by the novelty, the tactile sensation of his thighs touching hers even through the bags, his chest against her back, was good. It put a craving in him.

It was odd about women and what made them attractive. It was never a single thing. But Anna had some freckles on her back that made her seem less a woman on the marquee and more a woman in his bed. He had noticed them in the sailboat before she did the move with her foot and shut the cabin door. Right now he wanted to run his fingers over the skin, contemplate the attraction, and forget that she irritated the hell out of him.

With his nose in Anna's hair, he put his mind to drifting—some would call it meditation—and his body followed suit. Cutting off the odor of her was the last effort. After several minutes he concluded that the scent of her was more difficult to quell than the pain of cold. Smell was one of the earliest and most primal senses of the mammalian brain with a very direct neural pathway to the cerebral cortex. There was no ignoring her and there was no leaving her because she needed the warmth. Unless he could sleep, he would live with the gentle torture of his own desire.

"You're not sleeping," she said.

Scrambling out of bed in the dark, he moved near the stove, which was draped with their clothes and now thankfully warm. He went back to a cupboard where he'd seen a small jar of moldy salmon eggs. The stink disintegrated any remembrance of the Anna smell. With an old rag he cleaned out the slimy contents, put two candles in the jar, and placed them on the stove to melt.

"If you plan to sneak off," she said, rolling onto her back, "perhaps you could let me know."

Sam allowed himself a smile. "I've got to coat these wooden matches in wax. We'll need them."

"You need to sleep if we're going to run."

"This cabin isn't that far from the inlet and there is smoke. The scent could carry."

"I don't know anybody over on Windham except Nutka that knows about this place."

"We can stay awhile."

"Promise me you'll let me buy you a new boat and that you'll keep quiet about this."

"Nobody kills Harry and walks; they don't blow up my boat without hearing from me."

"Please help me."

"Tell me what we're running from."

She didn't answer, and he hoped she would sleep. Although he was used to celebrities in general, this one at this time was a pain in the ass. The last thing he needed was somebody to take care of, a mission—especially when the mission involved a strong-willed actress who did what she damn well pleased. He wanted a drink in the way he used to want a drink. The way it was after his son died.

The mind was a peculiar thing, capable of rebuilding and renewing itself without necessarily growing a lot of new cells, just new pathways through the old cells. With some patience and a fair degree of effort, he had been reorganizing his approach to living. Life had become well ordered with his return to his roots.

One part of his beginnings involved his father, a man who had made nature a challenge and man a conqueror. It was a one-dimensional worldview that Sam could never fully understand, much less put a name to.

All that had changed when Sam found his mother and his grandfather, Stalking Bear. Until his death, his grandfather had been his pipeline to his heritage; these days it was his mother and Kier, his cousin. Sam saw himself as the strangest of paradoxes: fascinated and nourished by the old of the Tilok past, but made rich, and by some calculations successful, in the technology-driven world of supersleuthing. Although he retained only remnants of his professional life, it was that life that had bought him his freedom in more ways than one. Of course it had also bought him his son's death. Now, apart from his involvement with the Tilok, his days were mostly workouts and the usual sailing routine of reading, hikes, maybe a little flirtation with the tourist ladies, and exploration of ancient native sites and landmarks throughout the British Columbia coast and Vancouver Island.

It had been months since the last time he had seriously wanted a drink. The good in his old personality, the keen instinct, the incredible memory, his ability to organize had all remained. But the cravings and the restlessness, the need for alternate kicks of booze and adrenaline had finally left him. Before the moment he decided to go pull Anna from a rock, skydiving or rock climbing and other artificially created risk was all he needed. An annual near-death experience wasn't a requisite for life.

But from the moment this woman had fallen into his world, he felt like a guy with something big to do.

He tried to tell himself that his feelings for Suzanne, the only major love of his life, were like the populist love for Kennedy that may have grown considerably once the president was dead and gone forever. Nevertheless Sam persisted in his nearly sacred feelings toward the memory of Suzanne. Further complexity came when he tried to unravel Suzanne's and his son's deaths. Maybe to his poor mind, honoring his son somehow went hand-in-hand with preserving his feelings for Suzanne, for whom his son had died.

He looked at Anna as she slept.

Occasionally, Sam became possessed of an urge to uninhibited, screaming copulation, distinguishable from the urge to make love, but during the year since

Suzanne's death there had been only an occasional warm body from women who wanted a bump in the night before Sam sailed on. As to serious romance, there hadn't been a whiff.

Of course when he sat under a clear night sky with chocolate-covered coffee beans to clear his mind, and the grandeur of the firmament to bring out the truth, he realized that he hadn't a clue how he could have managed with Suzanne's celebrity status—even assuming he could have found something in the humdrum of glitz that might have saved them from the usual unhappy end.

Sam had always stayed cool when the fires of romance would have taken lesser men to the altar. His father had been the ultimate Mr. Cool, never getting excited—not even about his own death, because he ended his life so unobtrusively. It could also be said that he didn't give a damn about Sam's life or he would have stuck around to watch. Sam recognized the bitterness in himself, but he considered his feelings about his father to be realistic, even inevitable. Of the three souls that he might have loved, only his mother still lived, and he loved her very much.

Anna stirred and blinked.

"You look like you're thinking. You're no doubt pissed. I can understand that," Anna said.

"So for the sake of my dead Harry, why don't you tell me what's happening?"

She hesitated. He could feel her indecision.

"How do I know you'll keep my secret?"

"You'll have to figure out what kind of a fellow I am. Tough assignment on short notice. Or you could take a leap of faith and trust me."

"Why is trust so good for me and so bad for you?" She didn't wait for his answer. "The truth is I don't have any better choices. So swear to me you won't betray my confidence."

"You and I both know that no amount of swearing buys you anything. I'm either honest or I'm not."

"Humor me."

"I promise I won't reveal your secrets unless compelled to do so by a court, or unless it will save the life of innocents, including your own. How's that?"

"Spoken like a lawyer."

Astute, he thought.

She inched her bag closer to the stove and began the story of her morning.

Six

Anna sat on the back step of the lodgelike facility on South Windham Island and watched Nutka paint. Jason's house had a name—Cedar Spirits, a reference to a common Kwaikutl phrase, according to Nutka. Anna had befriended her and found her to be unmarried, thoughtful, and unburdened by cultural expectations, a confident woman who seemed to be able to make her own freedom. Surprisingly, Nutka managed the household staff and groundskeepers, most of whom were men and many years her senior. Although Frank Stefano, a Grace Technologies employee from France, officially ran the place, he always spoke with Nutka in order to get the work done.

Nutka had good-humored eyes and was small of stature, maybe 110 pounds and five feet four inches. She kept her hair braided and wore a clean and pressed slightly faded house dress under an earth-toned, elaborately designed, hand-made blanket that she draped over her shoulders.

Nutka was painting from memory a stream that poured into Knight Inlet, an immense fjord to the south that penetrated well into the British Columbia mainland wilderness.

"Many artists have to look at what they are painting," Anna said.

"I prefer to see it through the mind of the child I was when I first saw it," Nutka said. "I used to go there every summer with my grandparents. We said it was a place for owls because the spirits were strong there; my grandfather said they were wise spirits and you could feel them in the breeze."

"Was it a spiritual place for you?"

"Oh, yes. It is where old men go to build a sweat house and see visions. They find meaning in being Salish."

"I thought you were Kwaikutl."

"I am half and half. This is the Kwaikutl land and my mother's family is Kwaikutl. My father's family is Salish. The Salish are in the south. But I am painting a place near a village of people called Kwak-waka'wakw. Confusing, isn't it?"

"It certainly is hard to say."

"I don't go there anymore, at least to the place I'm painting. As my people say, the government's giant giving hand tends to take more than it gives."

"You know, I'm worried that it's that way with my brother and Grace Technologies."

"Yes," Nutka said, her eyes shining and gaze direct.

"Tell me something about my brother."

"Yes?"

"I know that your massage must be good, but why does he crave it so?"

"When I miss more than two days he is very nervous until he gets the massage, unless one of the other girls does it, which he doesn't like."

"And why doesn't he like the other girls?"

Nutka looked away and giggled. "He is, uhm. I don't want to say it."

"But if I could understand . . ."

"Maybe he has a crush on me. It embarrasses him."

"You mean he . . . can't help being drawn to you?"

"Yes. Most definitely."

"Well, maybe he just likes you."

"Then I wish he would say it. But the oil will give him relief no matter who puts it on him. I think the oil is some kind of medicine."

"Medicine? Where do you get it?"

"Grace provides it. It comes on the helicopter. I'm careful to save a little bit from each container. I think about what would happen if they stopped sending it."

"And you massage him every day."

"Not every day, but usually at least every other day."

"Can you get me some of the oil?"

"I think so. I would need to sneak it."

Just then one of the Grace security people walked by with two rotweillers straining at their leashes.

"I do not like those dogs," Nutka said.

"Me either."

"You never explain exactly what you do," Nutka said. "I know you are famous in the movies."

"You know what? Next visit I'll show you what I do."

"Good. I would like that."

"I'd better go find my brother," Anna said.

She walked through the large kitchen into the great room where her brother did his work. In the middle of the room stood a dark walnut table, crafted without frills and graced with a single roller-wheeled desk chair. On the table sat two computer screens with cables that disappeared into a brass fitting in the middle of the hardwood floor.

Anna sat alone in the room in the overstuffed chair that Jason had designated as her seat.

Footsteps and the whoosh of a swinging door announced Jason. He looked healthy enough. Curly-haired and dark-skinned, five feet ten inches, solid but not fat, he had a spot of jet-black whiskers on his chin and a sly smile that looked a little whimsical. Because his eyes smiled with his lips, you tended to like him. When he did not have the soul-starved look of worry, just by looking at him, you assumed him to be a man of compassion and good humor. As he stared down at her, his eyes found hers and for a moment he looked more serious than she had ever seen him. It almost seemed as if he'd read her mind.

He glanced around, wary, then led her through the back door into the garden. He touched Nutka's shoulder and smiled at her in a way that made Anna feel good and sad at the same time. If he were near normal he might be capable of loving Nutka, and there were few women as worth loving as she was.

They walked to a stand of Douglas fir trees, where Jason removed a Celine Dion CD case from his pocket and handed it to her.

"You best keep this where it's safe. If you show it to anybody make sure it's someone you can trust. There are people at Harvard and MIT and places like that who might understand this at least a little bit."

She wondered what could be on the CD he'd hidden in the album jewel-case. "Do you have a name?"

"I don't know who to trust. I can't think about trust. Maybe Carl Fielding." Then he looked at her and touched her cheek. "This could get you killed."

"Can you tell me what's on the CD?"

"Consciousness, time, space, energy, and uncertainty. See, everything at its core is uncertain until a conscious mind apprehends it. I have assisted in removing some of the uncertainty in the universe. Or rather, I am developing the equations for understanding it. We will probably need a quantum computer for me to finish. It's a race with the Nannites, you understand. We're toe to toe. Head to head. We're lip-smacking, French-kissing close." His eyes showed that he at least understood that he was losing her. "To answer your question, all of my new work is summarized on this CD. There is also something on here that may help fix brains that have been ravaged by the Nannites. You understand me?"

"Has your brain been ravaged by the Nannites?"

"I stand strong, but they have made their inroads."

"I'm afraid what you do is . . . a little beyond me. And I . . . I . . . think maybe the Nannites aren't real?" Her voice intoned the courtesy of a question.

"It's easier for you to believe my photon paradox than Nannites? Good gracious, sis. I tell you about electron spin and the hope of quantum computing and you look as though I've just explained where babies come from. But when I say Nannites, you struggle not to roll your eyes. I don't get it."

"I'm trying, Jason. Please remember what your doctors—"

"The quarky quacks? They still think like Euclid, and you believe them?"

"I promise I will try to understand the Nannites. Now how can I help you with this CD?"

"You keep it. It will help you understand me. I'm serious about not making a mistake with this. They'll kill you." Then he put his hand on her shoulder and gently shook her. "Remember, just because I'm paranoid doesn't mean they aren't out to get me." Then there was that wry smile and she ached—wondering.

"Tell me what you think of Nutka," Anna said.

"I love her."

"Jason I'm so sorry about what happened . . . I mean way back when you called me from France. It was my fault. You see, I believed . . ."

At that moment Roberto joined them under the

firs, his eyes on Anna, then Jason, studying. Anna had already put the CD in her coat pocket. She kneaded nervous fingers.

"What's going on?" he asked.

"We were talking," she said. "But I'm going for a walk."

"The rest you know," Anna told Sam. "I grabbed a few things, called for a plane to come to the far side of the island, and ran. That's when you saw me, before I fell." In the telling of her story she still had omitted any reference to Jason's CD and she hadn't told Sam what she had been trying to tell Jason. "My brother is owned by Grace. They control everything about his life except what little I can interject. He is a captive of his own paranoia so they can construct a prison that fits his paranoid fantasies. What keeps others out, especially the Nannites—his fantasy enemy—keeps Jason in."

"And you don't know who was following?"

"Roberto or one of his men. Does it matter?"

"It does if Jason blew up my boat. You'd assume it was part of some fantasy, I'm guessing?"

"I just don't know."

"They give a paranoid crazy guy a rocket launcher?"

"They just let him shoot it at the hillside. I think it's a game for him. Look, it's unbelievable. I know it. But I'll fix the boat. I'll do something about the rocket launcher.

"There's one other thing. Last night I heard Roberto yelling at my brother."

"And?"

"I have been wanting Jason to go to another therapist, Dr. Geoff, for a second opinion. Not just this guy hired by the company. While Roberto tells me he's trying to get Jason to go, I hear him trying to scare the hell out of Jason—trying to keep Jason away from Geoff."

"What does the company doctor say?"

"Incurable but very rare form of schizophrenia. Paranoia, but not a lot else wrong with his brain. I guess that's obvious. I wanted him to write up my brother's case in a medical journal, but it's never happened. I thought somebody might read it and know something."

"So this fear of Roberto is why you jumped into the rubber boat and why you were uncertain about the helicopter."

"It's more like a fear of Grace Technologies. They're huge, and definitely not on the up-and-up."

Suddenly she smiled. "I'm sorry. You remind me a little bit of someone else. Except he was not a pushy tough guy."

"And he would be?"

"Jimmy—a man I met who helped me when I was really down."

Sam nodded and screwed the lid on the jar of wax-covered matches. "This Nutka you told me about. How does she figure in all this?"

"Someone I trust. Jason trusts her. And she cares about my brother more than she cares about the company and certainly more than the company cares about my brother."

"I'm gonna take a nap," Sam said. He put the bottle of matches on the rockwork next to the stove and crawled into his bag. She wriggled up in front of him and got close.

Talking, telling the story had wakened her and set her mind in motion.

She had done some things right in her life and some things wrong. Nothing about her life before age twenty-four, when she started getting paid for her first big movie, had been particularly easy. Up to age twelve her life was a blur of day care and baby-sitters. Her mom taught drama at the high school. Her father sold cars. It was more than full-time employment because Dad sold as many cars at night as he did during the day, and Mom's plays were put on after school and practice often ran into the early evening.

She never really questioned in her head whether she was loved, and she told herself and everybody who would listen that her father was probably one of the better people that had ever walked the earth. Pretty much, she ignored the defining moment in their relationship.

It was May 14, 1979, two days after her twelfth birthday, and it hadn't been hard to fool the baby-sitter—one good lie did the trick.

It was 4:10 when she walked into the hospital. The walls were light yellow. There were tubes coming out from under the sheet. The tubes were full of fluid and it made her sick.

He was mold-gray and breathing oxygen.

Everything that she was going to say whirled in her mind. About loving him. That he was the best dad ever. That she would keep a special place for him in her soul.

Her father's hand waved. The arm was rail thin, the skin under it loose, the muscle gone.

She went to him and took the hand. It trembled badly. It seemed like he couldn't catch his breath.

"Dad . . . Dad . . ." He put a finger to her lips and beckoned her. She drew close.

"You didn't get your butt tattooed, did you?"

A joke. Dad did that a lot. He joked. When he read the newspaper and she waited patiently for him to look up, he always smiled. He usually patted her on the head and then he joked. Like now.

"Dad, I wanted to talk about that day under the tree."

"We didn't tattoo your butt under the tree?"

He laughed and then he choked. He couldn't quit. There was a cord and he pushed the button. The nurse came running.

"We'll just be a minute, honey." There was a hole in his throat that had a plastic lining and that was normally blocked off, airtight, allowing him to breathe through his nose and mouth. Now they unplugged it and put a green tube down inside. The sucking sound, the green fluid, brought a gut-wrenching sadness. She could tell they didn't want her to watch, they didn't want to feel her pain.

Figuring to start over in her talk with her father, she went into the hall and took a seat. She thought about the tree. Big hot tears rolled down her face. A second and third nurse came down the hall.

"No code. No code," she heard the big one say. Then they closed the door. It was taking a long time. She went to the door and just then they opened it. They were fixing his hands. His head was thrown back and his mouth was open. There was a stench. Her knees shook, and the big nurse came over and pulled her to her bosom.

"Honey, I'm sorry. He's gone." Her knees shook and she wanted free. The woman's flesh and perfume were suffocating. Her head was spinning.

"I'll be okay," she sobbed, and ran down the hall.

When she got outside, it had stopped raining. Life was cheating her. *Please let it rain.* She said it all the way home. To this day she remembered nothing of the walk. The tree in front of their house was no longer dripping. Just the same, she went and stood under it. She tried to remember. But there was no rain.

Lying on the ground next to the house was the garden hose, right where her father had left it not two weeks ago. She went to the faucet, turned it on, and took the hose to the base of the tree. Using her thumb she created pressure and squirted water on the leaves of the big maple, letting it drip down over her body. Three years ago there had been a swing from the large branch, but it was no more. He had pushed her on the swing in the rain with the water pouring down. It was a simple moment. There had been no joke. He had said: "I love you and I'm so proud to be your father." That was all.

Sam realized that maybe she was crying. There was no sound, it was just a feeling. Maybe a vibration in her body.

"You okay?" he asked.

"Sleep," she said. Then she wriggled even closer. Of course the heat of her and the smell of her filled his mind.

He breathed deeply and thought about his grandfather and a place of old trees—fir, hemlock, cedar, and pine. A lake, opal smooth, cooled the eye while the leather brown of its sand shore rippled the air in the afternoon sun. There was the emerald green of spring-fed meadow dotted white, yellow, and fireball red. Around the cabin, mountain bilberry grew, heavy-branched with sweet fruit. He was walking through the pasture to the trees and there was a tunnel shaped by the foliage as if elephants had passed through. When he looked down the dark of the tunnel, there were people running and hearts pounding. Anna was there, out of nowhere, and she was panting bent over and the crowds were rushing past. Then the fire came, a ball of yellow and red rising, tearing through the trees and opening a hole to the sky. Fear was in her eyes and she was shaking him, talking, trying to tell him. But he couldn't understand.

Sam awoke with a start, still glued to her back—sweating. "We've got to go now."

"What? Why?"

"Out." He jumped out of his bag, pulling at her.

"You were dreaming."

"Yeah."

He turned his back as he pulled on his clothes. "We've got to get off this island and get to a place we can really build a fire."

"How do you intend to get off this island, or do I want to know?"

"We can make it. Misery doesn't usually kill, it just hurts. Staying here we could be instantly crispy. Like one rocket into this place and pufffff. A fireball."

She fingered her still-damp clothes. "What if we stay here and dry off a little more by the stove?"

"You stay. I'll go check around and see if anybody is coming."

They were both nearly dressed when he turned and looked at her.

At that moment the roof exploded over their heads and it began raining fire.

Seven

On this clear night in the wilds of British Columbia the sky was splashed across with stars in myriad swipes and trails set against the black. So luminescent was the three-quarter moon that one imagined warmth but for the bitter cold edge to the air. It lit the meadows nearly green and left the forest in deep shadow. The wind had blown away the clouds.

Under the trees it was still darker, and Anna understood they dare not use the light. So when they left the creek, they crashed through the brush in cold wet misery, feeling their way like blind people, stepping into holes, trying to find trails and to stay on them. Finally they found what seemed like a real pathway.

"I'm vibrating like those wind-up teeth," she said. The cold was terrible and wet. It ached the bones and palsied muscles until she thought she couldn't stand it; then she would take another step, only to be clung to by a wet branch or torn by a prickly vine; and there were more steps, and it seemed a mockery of her self-awareness that she considered each step to be her last, when there was always another.

"You Manhattanites are tough."

"I'll take that as a compliment."

"It was a compliment. But don't get any ideas."

Despite her abject misery she laughed.

They stooped through a mucky thicket of something Sam called salmonberry with water running down the leaves all over her and gnashing prickles irritating her arms and legs. They exited into some sort of overgrown pathway.

"It's an old logger's skid trail cleared by a dozer," Sam said. "But someone has been hiking it, probably the people from the oyster farm you've been telling me about."

After a time they came to a small patch of moonlit, knee-high grass forming what appeared to be a natural meadow. They stopped and listened. In the distance there was a crashing sound in the forest that signaled pursuit. Then they heard the muffled sound of a helicopter rotor. As it drew closer it grew into a distinct thump-thump, thump-thump. Sam took Anna's hand and stepped back into the forest, picking up the pace. Soon, above the sound of slapping branches, there was the rush of moving water. For ten minutes it grew louder until they could smell the stench of low tide. When they arrived at the beach, green-slimed rocks slipped beneath their feet with every step, and they looked out over moonlight blazing on the roiling sea.

Down the way construction at the oyster farm was obvious. A large gable loomed against the sky.

Now they could see the copter's spotlight working along the beach a half mile distant. It was coming at them.

"You're not going to the oyster farm, are you?" she said.

"They'd find us in minutes."

"Then where do we hide?"

"We don't. We're going to swim Mosquito Pass and get to Chatham Island and then make a nice warm place to sleep. In the morning we'll find people."

"Swim? Again? Oh, God."

"Come on."

Ahead, the beach became a cliff, and the water was edging ever closer as they approached the steep ground.

It was a hundred feet across Mosquito Passage to Insect Island, and then only half that far to Chatham Island, where, after a long overland hike, they could find a wilderness resort that would have a radio and air service. But the water through Mosquito Pass flowed like a river when the tide was running. From the sound of the faint roar, they were walking up-current and away from the overfalls.

"You do hear that roar in the distance?"

"There is always a roar in the distance. You're just listening to this one. We're going to swim fast."

"No way. I'm not going," Anna said, the terror of the sailboat ride fresh in her memory.

"This isn't nearly as big or bad as the overfall at Devil's Gate," he said. "And the tide isn't running as hard."

"Will it kill us just as dead?"

"We aren't going through it. We're going to the kelp beds on the other side, hang on, and pull our way to shore."

"But if we don't make it?"

"We'll make it. This way they'll waste hours, maybe days, crawling over this island. They won't suspect we swam."

"You're damn right. They know at least one of us isn't crazy."

Now the helicopter was moving fast in their direction. Sam tugged her hand, starting to run. He was headed for the base of the cliffs.

The stench grew as potent as an old-style outhouse

with an added sulfur odor. At the base of the cliff were black holes. They ducked into a rock chamber exposed to the channel where flowing water had undercut the cliff. The eelgrass on the rocks made her feet slide crazily.

Then they heard it. Snarls and yelps from dogs in pursuit.

"They're killers," Anna said.

Sam grabbed something from the ground.

Out of nowhere there was a roaring bark, then another. It startled her.

"Sea lions!" Sam said. "We woke 'em."

Then two huge growling shadows came through the cave entrance. Sam put her squarely behind him up on a rock. There were splashes all around as the sea lions hit the water.

The rotweillers were ignoring the sea lions. Barely visible, Sam was moving. He held something large over his head. There was a hollow thud and growling. Sam had struck a dog. Then Sam screamed and charged. It was primal. He was more animal than the dog. Into the water they went, dog and man. Instantly she knew to follow. She ran down into the splashing, growling melee. Then came silence, but for the barking of the dog on the beach. Sam had pulled the dog under. The chopper flew low overhead, just outside the rocky hollow, then turned out over the water heading back down the beach.

Now she was in water to her chest and nearly out from under the lip of the rock. There was a slight current. Everything was black. There was a sound like a billion bursting tiny bubbles that was life in the rocks. The thought of crabs and bugs shivered her spine.

Sam burst from the water. The dog was growling but swimming for the beach.

"Bastard bit me," Sam said.

The first dog was now barking, but without enthusiasm.

It was plain the dogs would stay on the beach.

"I don't think I can do it. That damn wave."

He whirled and held her close. "You've gotta do it. Period."

"You could kill them."

"Right behind them will be guys with guns."

She was trying to concentrate. To summon her will against the fear.

He put his face close to hers. "You can do this. I won't leave you, but you gotta swim. Get your shoes off. Tie them."

She struggled, but got them on her belt.

He did a surface dive. She hesitated, then followed, and raised her head when she got beside him. The current wasn't strong.

Go, she told herself. When they were near the middle they were considerably downstream, and the current was rushing toward the jaws of the wave. Doing the crawl, she swam vigorously until her arms ached, breathing maybe every other stroke. Suddenly she once again heard the faint roar and it was growing closer, maybe a couple of city blocks away. And she was being pulled by a whirlpool. Her clothes felt as if they were lead-lined. Sam was strong and was leaving her behind. She swam harder. Then he was behind her—she felt his hand pulling on her fanny pack.

"Go!" he half shouted. "Go!"

Her arms and legs were losing strength. She seemed to be flailing. A gulp of water had her choking. The roar was now clearly audible.

"Swim!"

Then she felt slime everywhere, heavy and horrible,

miring her down. It was like swimming through wet towels.

"Grab the kelp, you're drifting."

Reaching out, she grabbed a handful of slime. Then she could feel the water pulling on her. It was fast! Looking over her shoulder in the distance, she saw the white of the foam. It was the wave. Once locked in the current, she would go there. The thought of the black water and its secrets put her on the verge of panic. Pulling with all the strength her near-dead arms could muster, she tried to make headway. She couldn't. In truth she was sliding slowly backward through the kelp, headed for open water and the wave.

Sam lowered himself backward through the matted vegetation, reached around her, grabbed her belt, and used one arm to pull her to him and the other to hang on to the kelp. He knew how her body would respond to the cold of immersion. Water lowered body temperature approximately twenty-five times faster than air. In water temperatures of fifty to fifty-five degrees, given her prior exposure to cold, it would take only five to ten minutes for her body to experience cold shock. Struggling would become a reflex as her brain, befuddled by cold-induced neurological impairment, told her body that she needed air and her respirations escalated into harmful hyperventilation.

All her instincts would be telling her to thrash. Movement would push the blood to her extremities cooling it, in the fashion of a radiator. Her motor control would go and her limbs would feel detached and spastic. As her blood cooled, it would lower her vital core temperature bringing on a loss of consciousness. She would begin to take in water and die.

He clung to the kelp for both of them. "Put your hands on my shoulders, your legs around my body," he screamed. She did it. "Lie back." She did that. Her arms were straight; her hands gripped his shoulders like talons, communicating her fear. Now he used both his hands to pull them through the kelp, pushing her body as if he were a tug moving a barge. As he methodically grabbed kelp, some of it gave way and some of it held. Even as they inched toward shore, they were pulled downstream. Over his shoulder the roar in the blackness created a palpable vibration in the air. The ocean wanted to feed its young.

Sam could feel himself start to gasp, and forced a rhythm to his breathing. Desperate, he reached down with a foot and felt for the bottom. Nothing. It cost him mentally, and he slipped a few feet downstream in the attempt. It was hard to concentrate. He had to get them out of the water. Pulling and kicking like a man possessed, he sensed the shore but couldn't see it. "More, more, more," he grunted as he pulled. His body had nothing left to give and he moved it by sheer strength of mind.

Then a toe hit a rock; he reached down and stood. Two more pulls and a stride and he was dragging her up the boulder-strewn beach toward some trees. As they neared the trees the helicopter neared them. Sam stumbled up the bank, carrying her, just as a brilliant wand of light encompassed them and they fell into the brush.

Through her chattering teeth she tried to talk. "Did they see us?"

"Don't know." The chopper was turning back. "They overshot us if they did."

Sam urged her farther under a dense tree. There was no way they could now be seen from the air.

When the chopper returned, it hovered, and its brilliant spotlight hit the uppermost portion of the tree and lit the area of the nearby beach.

She shivered uncontrollably. Sam knew this was going to be a bad night. "They may have seen us but there's no place to land."

Sam pulled her tight to his body for warmth, and she welcomed it. Her teeth chattered as if they might crack. In moments the helicopter moved off. They pulled on their shoes over bloody feet.

"They aren't sure or they wouldn't keep moving like that. Let's go," he said as they stumbled through the trees to another smaller expanse of fast-moving water.

"What's th-th-tha-that?"

"It's the last little stretch of water. We're on Insect Island. It sits in Mosquito Channel and goes most of the way across."

"No." She shook her head, backing away.

Sam grabbed her and put his face close to hers. "Do you want to live?"

She nodded.

"You have enough left. If you want it bad enough you can do it. You can live. But if you give up, you'll die. You've never given up."

Sam wondered if he really believed she could make it. Her breathing had become more regular, there was less gasping. Maybe she could get most of the way before he had to push her. They needed to make it to the kelp on the far side. Once again they went through the frustrating task of using shaking fingers to tie their shoes to their belts.

Taking her by the hand, he hobbled in the moonlight down the beach and into the second channel.

Sam felt the cold go straight to his innards—worse

than he thought. Once again they swam and to his relief, she did not lose her nerve or her will. On this side of the island the current was less and the overfalls smaller, but still lethal for Anna.

As they swam, he watched her constantly. They had covered about ninety feet, with only ten more to the kelp, when she began completely losing her strength. It was as if her coordination left her and her muscles spasmed crazily. Sam could begin to feel his own arms turning to butter. Grabbing her belt beneath her fanny pack, he sidestroked with the last of his energy and managed to get a hand in the kelp and to begin hauling her. The first giant strand pulled its anchor-rock from the bottom, but the second two plants held.

But he wasn't strong enough. They couldn't make headway. All he could do was hang on and prevent them from drifting with the current.

"You gotta kick," he said.

She thrashed, but it wasn't enough. The kelp snapped. Floundering, he grabbed again. The plant held, but he was getting weak fast. Before he realized it, he began gulping air.

"Damn it," he screamed at himself.

There was splashing from Anna. She was trying to swim.

If he let go of her he might swim, but if he continued to hold on, they were both going down. He tried in vain to sidestroke and hang on to her, but was too weak.

"Swim," she said.

So he let go and began moving ahead. Without the extra weight it was barely possible. He hit the rocks. Making his legs work, he moved through the water thigh-deep. She was drifting, struggling in the kelp's edge, but moving down toward the wave. The white froth from her struggles was all he could see. He couldn't let her go any farther.

"Hang on," was all he said as he leaped and grabbed her. Now they were drifting fast, but she had moved closer to shore and his feet were banging rocks. Suddenly the bottom came up and he found purchase. Scrambling, he heaved them into shallow water, where he hung on to a large rock with one hand and held her with the other.

Black water swirled around them. Normally he could have yanked her ashore in an instant, without a second thought, but now nothing worked. She splashed uselessly. The water was an inch from his gasping mouth. He fought with his body, but couldn't move up the beach.

His arms no longer felt attached. His legs seemed to move around on their own. In an instant he knew they were about to drown. Focusing all his concentration on his left arm, he tried to contract it. They moved a few inches. Somehow he managed to make it reach again and contract again. He got his upper shoulder out of the water. Still he clung to Anna.

"Roll," he told her. Like an infant she managed to flop over, moving up toward the beach.

"Grab."

She did. He let go and pulled himself up onto rocks in the shallows. Looking back, he saw that she was floundering but going nowhere. He tried to make the beach by crawling on his belly. Finally, his nose was on the dry pebbles that made the beach. He looked back. One of her arms was waving in the air. She was coughing and spluttering. She had swallowed water. It would take only a quart and a half to kill her.

"Hang on," he groaned. By getting his shoulders in the air, he slowed the cooling process, but the shaking was so bad he was nearly convulsing. He had to get control of his body. Forcing his palms under him, he managed to worm up the beach.

He looked around and found a long stick. Crawling back to the water, he flopped in and held out the stick. She was able to grasp it, but was too weak to pull or even hang on. Her choking grew deep and agonized. He slithered toward her and managed to put his arms around her. He got his feet on a rock. With all his strength, he rose up and fell with her toward the beach. He hit the rocky ground with a bone-cracking thud.

The chopper was coming back up the island, the edge of its beam just nipping the shore on which they sat.

"Come on," he said, trying to stand but unable. "You gotta crawl."

Even as he said it, he felt a tiny spark of strength returning. He managed to get up, put his arm around her belly, and lift her trembling body to stand next to his. They struggled up the beach and stumbled barefoot off into the trees as the copter whizzed past.

Once in the trees, Sam knew that their lowered body temperature was critical.

He was still breathing hard from the cold.

"We have ten miles," he gasped as if running. "Over rough ground. Got to get to the resort." He doubled over, and it occurred to him that maybe age was affecting him. But he shoved the thought from his mind. He was only forty-two, still young. The hopeful message pulsed through the structures of his brain. But his ever-present self, the thing that cowered at age, answered back: *Your dad killed himself at thirty-seven.* "We have to get away from the water."

They stumbled and meandered through the woods

for maybe an hour, the cold feeling slightly less extreme as they dried in the night air. The helicopter was an occasional buzz in the distance as it patrolled the other island. He knew the angry bird would soon have to leave for fuel.

He turned on his light. Trees and brush everywhere.

"I just need to sleep." She wobbled and he grabbed her.

"No way," he said. "You sleep, you die."

He pushed her ahead of him by the belt.

She started to fall, and he gently shook her. When that didn't work, he shook her harder.

"This is awful. I'm gonna die." She was shaking and her legs looked weak.

"You forget about the paperwork. I gotta keep you around."

It took him another thirty minutes to find what he needed. It was a house-sized rock with nearly sheer faces. They put the rock between themselves and the water from which they had come. There was a cleft in the rock and a niche maybe two feet deep.

"Help me," he said. "You can't be a lazy movie star out here. Pick up sticks, like this."

He began grabbing any wood he could find. Although she stumbled and fell repeatedly, she worked alongside him. Hollowing out a small area in the middle of the woodpile, he put in twigs and dry needles.

Then he took out one of the wax-dipped matches, cleaned off the wax, blew on it for two minutes, prayed, and struck it on the rock face. It lit.

"First time, every time." He looked down. When she sat down, she went immediately to sleep and appeared unconscious. Snapping on the light, he pried up a lid and saw her eye rolled back in her head.

"Damn." He began slapping her and shaking her to wake her. She groaned. The fire was burning. He nurtured it with more small sticks, then shook her some more.

"Wake up." He put her back to the meager flame and began rubbing her as if to warm her skin with the friction. As he fed the fire, the flame grew larger and began to put out genuine warmth. Now she began to groan in earnest. That was good. Her body was coming alive, starting to sense pain again. With all the bruising, she would soon feel as if she'd rolled down a hill in a box of rocks.

He began to clear an area of the forest duff. He found some stones the size of softballs and began stacking them next to the fire. He put some in the fire. He broke boughs on nearby trees and placed them in a pile. Next he took a stick and began digging in the dirt. It was rocky but not impossibly hard. As he pulled up more rocks, he also placed those in and around the fire, which by now had a three-foot flame.

The helicopter continued patrolling over the water, a mile or more distant.

Sam was pretty sure that they wouldn't see the smoke at night, and the flame was invisible from three directions. It was unlikely that their pursuers would fly out over a black forest searching for people on foot. And even if they did, the forest was so heavy they probably wouldn't see the fire. It took him ten minutes, but he found a long log that he dragged to the rock face. He put one end of the log in a notch in the rock next to the cleft that housed the fire. The log stood directly over the shallow trench and about three feet off the ground at the high end. Knowing he had what he needed, he set the log aside.

Now he dug pockets in the trench, put a hot rock

in each pocket, and covered each rock with an inch or two of dirt. Soon the entire bottom of the trench was filled with hot buried rocks. Next he stacked on about six inches of fir boughs and placed the log against the rock over the boughs. He leaned dry, stripped, arm-sized branches against it and then piled the boughs along the branches, making a tent of the boughs.

Anna was huddled by the fire with a bad case of the shakes. "Let me help. You're doing all the work."

"Stay right where you are. Keep warm."

He figured it had taken two hours to complete the tiny hut.

"It'll be warm enough." Sam doused the fire, hoping no one had spotted it.

Without hesitation he stripped off his clothes. She stared, obviously warn out and fumbling for some way to make the sleeping arrangements workable.

"Leave on your underwear and let's get in," he said. She retained her bra and panties, but Sam was happy naked. Apparently she had a thing about her fanny pack, or its contents, because she kept it by her side. He put their clothes under some spare hot rocks and watched with satisfaction as they steamed. He and Anna crawled into the tent, where he wrapped himself around her back as they sank into the warmth of the bough-lined trench. Heat from the rocks radiated through the boughs on which they lay, and as their bodies soaked up the warmth. It felt luxurious.

"You are quite a guy," she said. "Not a real diplomat, though."

"Maybe you know too many guys with their nose up your ass."

"You seem to be hanging on pretty tight."

"That's for warmth."

"Thank you for clarifying that. I'm going to sleep."
True to her word, she was gone in less than a minute.

They slept fitfully.

"My butt is too hot," she said after a time. By now
they had become partially unentwined and sprawled
on their backs.

"Actually, my backside is fried too. If it's not one
thing, it's another," Sam muttered, crawling out to
get more boughs to put over the rocks. Gray dawn
filtered through the trees. Birds were starting to flit
and chirp.

Weary beyond words, he muscled the boughs beneath them, spread them around, and once again
curled up tight against her back.

Just then there was barking in the distance.

"Damn. They dropped them on this island just in
case," Sam said. "They probably went for jet fuel and
left the dogs and a couple men to go after us. Come
on."

Sam pulled her out of the lean-to, snatched up her
clothes, and tossed them over her shoulder. She
scrambled to pull them on.

Sam listened carefully. The dogs were coming too
fast to be on a leash.

"Shoes now," he said, pulling on his own clothes in
seconds, then his sneakers. Nothing was buttoned.
She had done the same and put her fanny pack
around her waist. "Climb," he said.

She tried, but was obviously not a rock climber.

Sam sprang up on a small ledge on the rock. From
there he climbed around her, got above, and pulled.
Twice he repeated the process. Now ten feet up, she
spread-eagled on the rock using her fingers and feet.
Sam looked up to a ledge at least two feet deep. He
had to get her there. The hounds were running in a

meandering course, no doubt following Sam's and Anna's wandering of the night before.

"Lift your right foot."

"I can't."

"Yes, you can."

The dogs were close and barking, and then they were beneath them. One of them limped, but they both looked crazy with blood lust. They charged the wall, trying to climb.

"Don't look at them. Just move the foot." With momentum the dogs were climbing the wall, their jaws snapping within a few inches of her foot. She managed to raise it.

"Now your hand up here." He pointed. Painstakingly, she worked her way up the face until he could pull her to the ledge.

"I gotta kill them," Sam said. There were no rocks. No clubs. "Sit right here," he told her, and began to climb. The top of the rock was a good sixty feet, but he was there in five minutes. The opposite face was not steep. Even the dogs could have made it up. It was only about fifty feet down the backside to soil and trees. He hurried down the rock, still able to hear the growling dogs, knowing the handlers could be nearby.

One of these dogs had already tasted his blood, and he had nearly drowned the beast. There would be no confusion about Sam's status as enemy. He found a large branch, broke it to make a club, and instantly heard the dogs coming. They had heard the crack. He ran up the rock to make their attack more difficult.

Around the speckled gray base of the formation they came as if possessed. Without hesitation they charged, but they were single file because there was only one easy route. Sam kept the club behind him until they drew close. Then he raised and swung.

The lead dog scrambled back into the other, and they both tumbled down the steep slope. Instantly the lead dog whirled and came back, wary. Sam screamed and charged. This time the dog came at him and he swung the heavy stick, hitting the dog's head and knocking the animal off the rock. The second animal stopped and braced its feet.

At that moment Anna came around the outcropping with a club. And attacked.

For a second the animal turned. Sam swung again, catching him square in the shoulder. Feeling the force of the connection, Sam leaped, grabbing the dog by the head and lower jaw. Sam pushed off the rock, wrenching the animal's neck and breaking the jaw as he fell down the hill. He hit the slope's bottom with a thud, the paralyzed animal beside him.

He staggered up, blood running from his arms and hands where the animal had bitten and torn the flesh. The first dog was weaving, facing Anna, who was ready to swing.

"Hey," Sam screamed at the dog. It faced him with a low growl. Sam did a flying kick to the point of the animal's snout. Reeling, the beast hung its head low to the ground. Sam charged and pulled the animal's head tight against his gut. The dog fought and they rolled, teeth flashing, gashing his arm. Sam hung on, maintaining the headlock until he was able to rise. Lifting the dog off the ground, he fell backward using all his body weight to snap the animal's neck.

He looked up to find a shaking Anna with her club still ready.

"I couldn't see what was happening," she said. "I wasn't going to be stuck there if those dogs got you."

Sam walked over to her, dripping red as he went.

"I will never again call a man a girl as a term of denigration," he said. "Let's get out of here."

"Shouldn't we do something about those?" she said, pointing to his wounds.

"Without antibiotics we should just leave the gashes open. There's no artery involvement. We have to move. You know the men are coming."

An English wren was sitting on their shelter when they walked past.

"I'm gonna pee," Anna said, "and I'm not going far."

"Go ahead."

"Stare at your feet. And close your ears."

Sam laughed. She went behind a bush.

Eight

They walked inland from the shore, occasionally jogging seaward to make sure they hadn't veered off. The going was slow.

"Can they catch us?"

"No. They won't have a tracker, and even if they did, he would have to crawl in places. They're more likely to try to get in front of us or beat us to Echo Bay. It's the only settlement near here."

"Does it hurt?" she asked, looking at his bloody arms.

"Sure, a little."

"You're a tough one," she said.

"I love these islands," he said in response. "They have their own spirit. I don't know many places like this."

"I could tell by the care you took with your maps."

"These things were gouged out of the rock by glaciers in the last ice age. You notice that they are high and dry. Geologically they are young. Every hill is on its way to becoming a flat spot. We're standing on mountains."

"Do you know the natives here?" she asked.

"This is Kwaikutl territory. I've been looking at their old village sites."

"I could see that as well. Are you part Indian?"

"I am. I'm sure you saw the books and maps in the stateroom."

"Why won't you talk about yourself? Are you really that afraid of telling me who you are?"

"You can see there are bears on this island. See the claw marks on the tree and this spot here where the bear scratches his backside?"

She shook her head. "I'm already very impressed, so don't show off as a distraction. How much farther?"

"Sun's out—it's warm. Enjoy it. You know there isn't a thing we can do about Jason until we get back. You have to learn to enjoy the moment even in a crisis so long as you are doing what you can do."

"Yeah, well, I've never been chased by dogs and nearly drowned three times."

"Yeah, well, nobody has ever turned down my spaghetti before."

"Try me again in Manhattan. It seems like we're walking there."

"It's still about ten miles to Manhattan North."

"They don't seem to be following us," she said after a while.

"We'll have a greeting party at Echo Bay, but they won't try anything with people around."

"Fishermen?"

"Bird-watchers. It's the annual fall bird count— Echo Bay is their new hot spot. Great deal for the resort owners."

"How did you know about that?"

"I've stayed at Echo Bay."

"You're not a bird-watcher?"

"Not exactly."

"You are. You're a bird-watcher!" She giggled. "You are just a bundle of surprises.

"Tell me something," she said.

"Yeah?"

"Do you drink your coffee black?"

"All show-offs drink their coffee black. It's a rule."

"You drink your scotch straight?"

"Don't drink it anymore. Occasionally red wine."

"You smoke cigars, don't you?"

"Cuban."

"You don't smoke cigarettes?"

"I don't believe in it."

"Thought I smelled one on the boat."

"Strange."

"What are your vices, Sam?"

"Couple times a month, give or take, I have wild blackberry pie or a lemon sour-cream pie, but I usually only admit to the blackberry."

"Why?"

"Lemon sour cream is too afternoon-tea for me. So I eat it and pretend I didn't. I break the cigar rule more than the pie rule." He stopped for just a moment. "Are there right answers to these questions?"

"No. I'm just curious about you. Are you religious in any way?"

"I do yoga as physical discipline, not as a peek into something important. Hindus I don't understand. The Ganges is the most polluted river in the world, and religion or not, it can't be good throwing all that dead crap in the Ganges—a major water source." He was silent for a moment. "There is something out here with us—the universe isn't all cold and black and fiery infernos; somewhere there's love and beauty and whatever makes those values rock-solid in a person's gut."

Anna wondered if he had just revealed more of himself than he intended. To her it was far more important than his last name.

"My mom's a Catholic. But I'm not that."

"Christianity seems like a good idea if they could ever get anybody to practice it. I don't know if I could make 'turn the other cheek' work for me."

"Okay, back to vices. You don't gamble?"

"The sport of idiots."

"Jimmy would have said that."

"Again, Jimmy was?"

"He was a great guy. Like a father or an uncle. When I met him I was eighteen and waiting tables and crammed into a small apartment with three other girls eating macaroni without the cheese. I was being turned down for bit parts as fast as I could scurry from one audition to the next.

"I was going to acting classes when I could and determined that I was going to be an actress.

"I vividly recall the awkward blind date followed by continuous puking on the sidewalk. The restaurant did a great job with the food poisoning. That's what started it all with Jimmy. Anyway, I'm kneeling on the sidewalk in front of my place nearly unconscious with dehydration and I feel this hand on my forehead and another on the back of my neck. And I see this old guy with a big nose and wrinkles like canals and I'm thinking he's a pervert. I tell him I don't know him. And he says: 'Right now, do you really care?'

"Somehow he goes and gets this lady who has an apartment next door to his. He lives in the only really good building on the block. Next thing I know I'm in her place with a compress on my forehead and a compazine suppository shoved up my rear. It turned out that she was a nurse.

"They called him Jimmy Beam because he drank too much of the stuff when he was in the Navy. His real name was Erik. Crusty on the outside, a doll on the inside. He had friends everywhere he went. He always insisted, maybe demanded, that I would amount to something. I agreed with him. Everybody needs somebody who agrees with them contrary to all the evidence.

"Jimmy did come with a big dose of humanity: he picked his teeth incessantly and carried a metal box of cinnamon-flavored mints, constantly offering them to whomever as if he was conscious of his own bad breath. If he had a glass of apple juice, he'd fondle it like it was whiskey. After dinner his old bowels constantly farted. I complained about him, and I loved him."

"How often did you see him?"

"Like once or twice a week before I moved out of the neighborhood. You know, sometimes it was with my friends. They liked him too. Sometimes on the steps to his building. We talked on the phone. Every time something really big happened, I called my mom, my sister, and then Jimmy."

"What about your dad?"

"I was twelve when he died. Kind, humorous, always joking, upbeat. Never a down moment."

"You make him sound nearly perfect."

"A life as wrinkle free as a new starched shirt. I still idolize my father. But you know, there was one thing about him. I couldn't get him to be serious, I guess. I don't bring it up. My mom, my sister, and I, we just remember him as the perfect dad."

"But?"

"Well . . . it doesn't matter now . . . he died of cancer. Bowel cancer that spread everywhere. It was hard.

"I think I cried harder when they lowered Jimmy into the ground. Because my dad was so horribly sick, dying was deliverance from misery. Jimmy dropped through a trapdoor out of a happy life into the grave. I suppose the special thing about Jimmy was that he had no reason to love me and no nudge from mother nature. He didn't want fame or money. I guess he just wanted to enlarge his life with other people.

"Later, after my first big movie, Jimmy reminded me that I was just a girl from McLean, Virginia. Of course I would tell him that I was reminded of that every time I went to a party. I didn't sing or do the hoochy coochy or quote Shakespeare. So I'd say: 'Look, Jimmy, I go to a party and I'm a big deal that doesn't do anything.' Then he'd smile at my poor floundering ego. Jimmy died four years ago."

"Jimmy's talk must have taken. On those TV shows you always protest that you're an ordinary gal with an unusual job. Ah, shucks—no special insight, wisdom, or wit, you tell them. Of course nobody believes a word of it. Especially me. Then for the rest of the program you're expected to be very witty and wise in addition to being humble."

"I really do feel regular."

"Get over it. And don't tell us about it on TV. Maybe you once were normal, but you can't be normal or ordinary or whatever the hell you call it when you sneeze and the entire world offers you a hanky. If you act with kindness despite all that—now, that is golden."

"So, Mr. Publicist, what should I say when they stick a microphone in my face?"

"On national television, you can tell us that you were blessed with some good luck but that you still like being with your family and friends. You like doing the usual things. And for God's sake don't bat your eyes and act as if you suddenly woke up and noticed you were famous. That's crapola again."

"How long have you been waiting to say that?"

"Probably all my life. So then you had your mom and your sister?"

"Yeah."

"What was your mom like when you were growing up?"

"Catholic workaholic."

"Who always wanted to be a movie star but taught drama instead."

"You don't mince words, do you?"

"Peter told me."

"Peter? Oh, ho. So you do know each other. And you know each other well."

"Big clue there, huh, Sherlock?"

"So how did you meet Peter?"

"No more clues for now. I want to know about your mother . . . she was a wonderful inspiration in your acting career . . . you can skip that part."

"You are tough."

"I gather your mother was working a lot when you were little?"

"I had a baby-sitter or day care."

"Are you close with your mother?"

"Very."

"When you were growing up?"

"My mom was working her head off to make ends meet. Like any kid, I was probably disappointed a little."

"But you got over it."

"Yeah. I wrote a poem about it."

"Always embarrassing."

"Especially when you quote it in junior college English class."

"Can you still quote it?"

"No."

"Come on. Your memory for scripts is legendary."

"You would make fun of me."

"Because you're not a poet? No. Amateur poems can be very touching. I have a feeling about this one."

"I do not believe this. You are beer and football. Maybe hot cars or hot boats and maybe . . . maybe French restaurants where you order in French. You're a man of contradictions. But I won't stretch to poetry."

"How about I'm a collector of information?"

"I see. Poetry as fact-gathering. That's an emotionally challenged point of view."

"Touché. Touché. What about your brother?"

"Jason departed my life shortly after my twenty-second birthday. There was a major fight. His wife was asking for custody of Grady, their baby girl, and I got into it on her side. I thought he was an arrogant bastard at the time."

"You seem almost obsessed with saving your brother from his own decisions."

"I am."

"So when did you change your mind about him?"

"When Sydney, his ex-wife, told me that she had lied a little."

"Now you lost me completely."

"I'm too worn out to talk about such a heavy-duty subject. Your cuts look awful. I'm worried about you."

"I'll be fine."

"Yeah, that's exactly what Jimmy would have said. Okay, back to you, Sam. You were married and divorced and you don't want a repeat."

"Uh-huh."

"Kids?"

"My only son died."

"I'm sorry. Do you talk about it?"

"No."

"Do you have a girlfriend?"

"Friends who are girls but no girlfriend."

"I see."

"What about you? How are you and Lane Rollins getting along?"

"He's kind, thoughtful, caring, and a great companion."

"Doesn't sound good." He grinned.

"You see there? That grin. You're a know-it-all arrogant bastard."

"So I'm right."

"How do you get that out of what I said?"

"You say more than is in your words."

"I don't know your name and you're asking about my love life?"

They spoke of other things, and Sam revealed more than he intended, but he thought he managed to receive more information than he gave. Still, he did reveal that he was in the information business, and he knew that she was a perceptive woman and that she had an idea about him, and that for her and for this little game, that was something of a score.

"It's right through there." Sam pointed to a patch of sky through a fir stand.

"When we get out of here, I have to figure a way to get Jason."

"Have you considered just taking him?"

"I can't. We had a falling-out and it's public. So I don't look good trying to take over. See, Jason had this fascination with France, even became a citizen. He hooked up with DuShane Chellis's company, Grace, and when he started having problems—mental problems—they convinced him to make Roberto the guardian of his person and Grace Technologies the guardian of his estate. It's all legal. I visit only with their consent."

"Yeah, there are international treaties," Sam said.

"If the Canadians granted him resident status they'll honor the French law and courts. And as a matter of national pride the French won't want Americans taking over their brainchild."

"I know. I looked into it."

"You need some attorneys and a good investigator."

"My immediate concern is just walking into Echo Bay without knowing if they're there."

"They'll be there. And with a story, concerned about you, looking for you. They'll try to work the law. They aren't stupid. And they won't run off into the bushes somewhere and let you control the media and the government. No way."

"I hope what I've done hasn't put Jason in a bad spot."

"Nothing is going to happen overnight. Jason is in no immediate danger unless there is a whole lot we don't know. He has to be critical to their program. You and I just play it cool. Relax. Don't let them see any weakness or anxiety. You act normal. Pretend you're about to shake hands with your ex-husband's new fiancée."

"I'd be deliriously giddy."

"That's good. Giddy. We've just been out for a great hike. A survival lesson. We're on vacation. Or you're researching a part in a film. Got it?"

"I can do it. I think."

"They have to believe we aren't going to do anything precipitous. We want them to think that maybe we'll just blow it off if they buy me a new boat. Hell, maybe we think the yacht exploded."

"You think they'll believe that?"

"Maybe if we play it right they won't know what to think. Remember, you're Manhattan," he said, walking ahead. "Do it with class."

At first they were very careful not to show themselves while they scouted the small marina complex.

A blue-hulled aluminum catamaran Mountie boat with a lot of equipment was docked amid the pleasure craft.

"The cops are here," she said.

"My money says Roberto brought them. Hardly wait to hear the story."

"They've got brass balls."

"Let's go to Betty's and feed ourselves."

She grabbed his arm, careful not to touch the deep wounds.

"Wait, Sam. Listen, I need your help. I don't mean just now, I mean to solve this whole mess."

"I'm a sailor."

"I know people. You're no sailor. You're the one who cracked Peter's case. That's my guess. Peter said there was a sort of private investigator, but never said who or anything."

"That case was a long time ago."

"You aren't just going to leave me with this, are you?"

"Did I say that? I suggested a lawyer. I know investigators."

"You haven't said a damn thing. Not even your last name. But I feel we have some sort of connection here. And I don't know what you do in this world other than sail, but it's got to do with the spy or security business or something. And I know I need to . . . hire you."

"I'm a bastard, remember?"

"Try for one second not to let it show. And cut your bullshit. I'm an actor too."

"There are lots of people—"

She grabbed his shirt and looked up at him, hard determination in her eyes.

"I have never felt so incapable. I'm partly to blame for my brother's ruined life. Don't make me beg."

"I'll do what I can."

"Give me a commitment." Anna seemed on the verge of tears. "Once we walk back into the world, you're leaving. I can feel it. And you have not been leveling with me. All I know is that there's nobody quite like you to figure this out."

Sam hesitated. He knew he couldn't promise and then back out. Yes, he was his own man, but her words, the way she put it, made it difficult to say no.

"Please don't be a deserter when I really need somebody."

"I was going to help you; it's just a question of how."

"That's crap. There is only one way you help people. You take charge and fix it or you walk away. You're not a halfway guy, Sam. I know you nailed Peter's accountant. The story was about you."

"You would have to keep our relationship confidential and you can't talk to people about me. Got it?"

"Got it. You better not crap out on me."

"This will require some groundwork."

"I have your word that I can hire you?"

"You have my word."

"And you won't just disappear on me?"

"I won't."

With that they made their way to a white building with cheery blue trim. According to the sign, it doubled as the store and the post office. Merchandise was stacked neatly on the shelves, although it was a bit sparse. A slender woman with a feather duster stared at Sam.

"What happened to you? A bear?"

"Man's best friend."

"A dog did that? Gosh, Sam. Let's sit you down and

get you cleaned up. The Mounties are looking for you—if you're the captain of the ship that sank at Devil's Gate."

"That's me. And this is Anna."

"I'll call Rex." She picked up the microphone.

"This is Anna," Sam said again.

"Oh, my God."

"Yeah, it's that Anna. Listen, don't be too impressed—she passes wind even when she doesn't eat."

"I think you got your history ass-backwards," Anna said.

Betty rolled her eyes and Anna rolled hers back.

"A trivial stretching of history designed to make a valid point," Sam said as Anna knocked his hat down over his eyes.

"Northpoint, Northpoint, this is Echo Bay," Betty said into the radio.

"Switch and answer, Twenty-two Alpha."

"Rex, your captain showed up, a little the worse for wear, but fine. Apparently he had a passenger. They're gonna eat and clean up."

"I have my paperwork. And I've got to hear about Devil's Gate."

"How about after some lunch and cleanup?"

"Roger that."

"Echo Bay clear." Then she turned to Sam. "You heard. He wants to talk with you when you're done here."

"Are you and Rex still sweet on each other?"

"Now don't start on that."

Sam chuckled with the question still written on his face.

"Well, come on in. We'll start with the wounds and move to food. I don't know what you been doin', but these Mountie people and others are here looking for you. Said you might have disappeared off in the woods. They said a woman. They didn't say Anna Wade."

"Yeah, well, let's just relax about that," Sam said.

"Mum's the word." She sat Sam down at the table and in twenty minutes the wounds were covered with antibiotics and Sam had two dollar-sized bandages on his right arm and three on his left. After saying thank you and exchanging a few more pleasantries, Sam and Anna excused themselves to the washroom.

They tried acting as if they were strolling Fifth Avenue in jeans and Armani. They weren't completely successful, drawing wide-eyed stares from a pair of bird-watchers. The washroom was also the laundry room and was on a large float behind the docks. They made their way out the gangplank.

"I'm taking a shower. Despite the hunger pangs," she said. Then she leaned close. "When are they going to show up?"

"When they feel like it. You figure maybe they'll use a rocket launcher on the shower?"

"It's not funny. When are we going to make this plan?"

"It'll come. Relax. I need you to be on vacation."

"With a rocket up my you know what?"

"The Mounties are all over this place. It'll be fine. And if they use a rocket on you, you won't know what hit you."

"Well, that makes me feel better."

She went into the stall, stripped off her dirty clothes, and got under the hot water.

He came back with towels.

She interrupted the warm comfort of the shower, picked up her filthy shirt, and held it in front of her. Unlatching the door, she stuck out an arm. At that moment a shower of icy-cold water came over the door. She screamed. "How could you do that?" Then in came Sam's hand around the door with two fluffy dry towels, one of them with a big picture of a smiley face. The hand returned with a pair of wool trousers and a fresh shirt. Even a bra and underpants along with a blow-dryer.

"I borrowed them from Betty," he said.

"Sam?"

"Yeah?"

"Can't you pretend to like me just a little?"

He sighed. "Sorry, it's a tribal custom. We had a victory. You do this with people you like. Especially when you're on vacation."

The shower stall slammed shut.

Nine

Chellis waited impatiently for the phone to ring. Finally it did.

"They got to Echo Bay," Roberto said.

Chellis listened to the story for as long as he could, then cut Roberto off. "I want you out of this. You will do nothing more. Absolutely nothing. It's screwed up. If they're smart and we're lucky, they'll say nothing because the rocket launch would be pinned on Jason. I'm sending someone to handle this. You get a picture of the man with Anna, but do nothing else. Do you understand?"

"Tell me exactly what happened," Anna said, knowing that whatever Sam had said or done could make the press.

"While you were in the shower and on the phone, I went and talked to the Mounties. I'll tell you over lunch." When they went back inside, Betty gave them a bit of a funny look.

"Come on." Betty nodded toward the back. On a small table there were fried potatoes, a small steak, scrambled eggs, tofu, two apples, two oranges, two apricots, a large pile of lox, bagels, and cream cheese.

"My God," Anna said. "It looks good."

They sat down and Anna filled her plate with half the eggs and a pile of potatoes.

Betty came in, closed the door, and waited as if she had an announcement.

"There is a man named Roberto out here that wants to see Anna."

"Tell him we'll be right out," Sam said.

Betty nodded. "Take your time. I'm sure they can wait a minute while you eat."

"What did you tell the Mounties and what happened with Roberto?" Anna asked Sam.

"Roberto's buddy tried to take my picture. Seems the guy with the Minolta fell in the water and ruined his camera."

"You got in a fight?"

"I don't think I would call throwing a guy off a dock a fight. I told the Mounties our boat sank and we hiked."

"All this while I was drying my hair?"

They took a few more bites, concentrating on their food.

"Let's go see what the slug wants. For once you can be an asshole and I won't mind," Anna said.

"You bring your broom and I won't have to be."

"I need some shades," Sam said to Betty. She produced a pair still with tags, along with a new hat. "Now, that is service."

Before they could step outside, Roberto opened the door. "Anna, we were so worried about you. I need to talk to you about Jason."

Coolly, Anna said, "I'd like you to meet Sam. It was Sam's boat. And I think you're responsible."

Sam stared at Roberto. Nervously she put a hand on Sam's arm.

"We already met," Sam said. "And his buddy Ansel Adams."

"Let's go outside." Roberto was trying to look friendly.

Sam grabbed the hat and glasses; Anna took his arm as if he were escorting her for a walk, and they went out the door.

"Listen, Jason got carried away. I'm really sorry. Fortunately no one was hurt. That's a miracle. We came after you and couldn't find you. We thought after the boat thing that Jason was safe at the lodge, you know, calmed down. But he slipped out, got the rocket launcher again, and blew up the cabin as well. We had no idea until we caught up with him. We could tell the Mounties, but they don't even allow Mace in the country, for God's sake."

"Why then does my brother have a rocket launcher, for God's sake? It's insane. You're crazier than he is."

"It's gone. Destroyed. I agree it was crazy. But it's what Jason wanted. Now he wants another one."

"Can't you tell him no?"

"Of course. We have. But the question of the moment is whether we tell the Mounties that your brother blew up the boat and the cabin or we just buy the cabin and be done with it."

"The company will pay for the cabin?"

"Of course."

"The boat too? It's a million and a half dollars."

"Of course the boat too."

Anna looked at Sam.

"Anna, I need to speak with you alone about confidential company business," Roberto said.

Anna kept looking at Sam.

"Over there by the ramp to the docks," Sam suggested. It was visible from every direction including the Mounties' boat.

"Okay," Anna said, walking with Roberto.

"Jason lost a CD-ROM. It's his work, but it belongs to the company."

"I don't know anything about it," Anna told Roberto.

"You're sure." He scrutinized her, as intense as she'd ever seen him.

"I'm sure."

Perhaps it was her imagination, but she was certain that he was looking at the fanny pack, actually located on her stomach, and that he was suspicious.

"We're going to take Jason to see Dr. Galbraith in Seattle."

"Well, I guess I don't have a lot to say about it," Anna said, "but I appreciate your telling me." She walked back to Sam, feeling safer with every step she took away from Roberto.

"Let's talk." She led Sam back toward the forest.

"What did he want?"

"They want to take Jason to his doctor and they want to pin me down about whether we would press charges against Jason or anybody else for the boat. I told him no."

"You don't believe him about Jason and the rocket launcher, do you?" Sam said.

"It's possible," she said. "Jason could do anything. What I really wonder is, how can I possibly get control of my brother without years in court in France or Canada? The minute I start up, they'll hit me with a smear campaign—with the videos they have of my brother explaining our estrangement. Oh, and to top it all, his daughter is completely out of control and hates me even more."

"Grady, I think you said."

"Jason's daughter—now grown. She's half crazy herself. She's in LA. I've tried so hard to talk to her, but I'm getting nowhere. She's a stripper. She drinks. God only knows what else she does. She's twenty and hell on wheels."

"Tell me what you know about her."

Anna began with Grady's birth and recounted up through her life as a stripper.

"That's important," Sam said when she had finished.

"The seaplane is due in two hours. We're going to have to part ways in Vancouver. I need to know when I'll see you again and exactly how I hire you."

"I'll need time to research and plan. Let's meet in LA at the Capital Plaza in five days—next Friday evening. You'll hear from me in the meantime. You're going to your place in Manhattan?"

"Yes. I'll be there tonight."

"I'll send people. I'll be talking to you."

"Tell me," she said, "how exactly do I get in touch with a guy who has no last name?"

"E-mail."

"E-mail? That's it?"

Sam took Anna into Betty's apartment, sat her down where she could use the phone, and excused himself. When he found a public phone he paused for a moment, knowing that his life would take a major turn if he picked it up. As he considered this, he saw the would-be photographer come around the corner, a new cardboard camera in his hand.

Sam motioned with his head toward the dock,

careful to keep his face in the shadow of his hat brim. The man obviously understood that Sam meant to throw him back into the bay. He snapped a picture and ran, but Sam was on him before he had gone twenty feet.

"It isn't in my nature to fight," Sam said, shoving a hand under the man's rib cage and holding it like a handle. The photographer screamed and dropped the camera, grabbing at his chest, obviously in terrible pain. Sam smashed the camera under his heel while the man dangled.

"Next time take a picture of the natural wonders. It makes a much better souvenir. And don't bother Betty about any more disposable cameras. She's all sold out."

A man came around the corner in response to the screams and Sam let go of the ribs.

"Don't come back."

As the bird-watcher looked on in amazement, the wounded cameraman ran around the corner, holding his side.

Sam returned to the telephone. It was starting to feel like old times. The first call went to Shohei because he might be in Japan. Fortunately it turned out he was in San Francisco, and more significantly, he happened to be taking a little sabbatical and therefore had no contract at the moment.

Next Sam would need Jill, one of his assistants, and his mother, a Tilok woman everyone called Spring. But if he was going to call Jill about returning to work, protocol would dictate that he first call Paul. Paul's assistant answered the phone. He didn't know Sam's voice. Paul, who now ran a large hardware business, was with a commercial contractor, according to the anxious-to-please clerk.

"Tell him Robert Chase called."

Now he could call Jill. It was an easy call—they had been friends for years and lovers briefly. Jill's one weakness was that she liked reminding him in embarrassing little ways about what had happened between them—and about other women with whom it had happened. Jill was a bean counter by nature, and he supposed that just naturally carried over to counting more than beans.

Spring was an even quicker call than Jill. With Shohei, Jill, and Spring on board, Sam was gratified. He wanted a cigar.

He dreaded calling Typhony, but it would be gutless to have Paul talk in his place, and for what he had in mind he would need his whole crew. At the moment he had a dozen employees, mostly techies, working at feeding the Big Brain's database and keeping it operating for government contracting work. When Sam wasn't using his computer, it did work for the CIA, FBI, and other agencies, generating revenue. Grogg, a man whose glasses were epic in their size and magnification, was the craftsman who had implemented Sam's architecture and created the electronic marvel that was the heart and soul of Sam's business. Grogg remained on the job, but Sam would need to hire more investigators: the men and women who helped get the techies the kind of information Big Brain could use to solve real-world riddles.

Inside the store he found Betty.

"Hey," he said, giving her a casual look. "Anna is an occasional closet smoker. She needs a smoke."

"Well, I have them only by the pack."

"Okay." Sam bought a pack of Marlboros, removed one, and gave the remainder to Betty.

"Keep 'em behind the counter for customers."

"No way. They smell up the place. I can't believe she smokes."

"Toss 'em, then. She only wants one. Doesn't need the temptation of a whole pack."

Sam shrugged his shoulders as if it were a mystery, then went around the corner to the men's room. Inside he lit up, took two huge drags, snubbed it out, and tossed it.

Sam walked back to a wooden bench overlooking the bowl-shaped harbor where they would wait for the seaplane. Large conifer trees, lustrous and green, covered the upper slopes around the bay. The water was calm; the hillsides near the water were very rocky and produced gnarled trees in interesting shapes and arrangements; the ground was ornamented with salal, grasses, and fern, the rocks with lichen. Broken clouds let the sun stream through, bringing out the blue of the sky and sea. Something about the place was more than the sum of its parts, creating a mood unique in its intrigue.

"It's beautiful here." Anna had found him.

"Yes."

"Why do I smell cigarettes?"

"Maybe the shirt."

"Sam, could we talk seriously a minute?"

"I'm always serious. It's just that I occasionally feel compelled to be irreverent."

"Tell me about your mom and dad."

"Just like that?"

"Come on, Sam, you've given me nothing else, and you know you can trust me."

"Well, the only thing I knew about my mom when I was growing up was what my dad told me."

"Which was?"

"Drunken slut."

"That's it?"

"That's all of it."

"Did you ever see her or talk to anyone who knew her?"

"Not when I was growing up. I knew only my grandparents on my dad's side and never my mom's. My grandparents just refused to mention her or comment in any way. It wasn't until a few months after my dad died that I discovered my mother. I was eighteen and in college. At first I told myself I wanted to meet her or find her grave. Listening to my dad, I guess I had it in my head that she probably died of alcohol or drugs. I traced my dad's life back to when he was nineteen, found people who knew him then, people he'd lost all contact with. They told me about a beautiful girl, Native American, that he dated. I discovered the schools she might have gone to and started looking. Finally, I got a name, pictures, positive ID, and found her. I think I just didn't want to doubt my dad when he was alive so I hadn't pushed it."

"I want to be sensitive here. But there is this sort of looming question—"

"Why didn't my mother find me? Why did she let me go?"

"Well, yes."

"She was going to school, he was working. They actually met because my mother was renting a room in my grandparents' basement. They lived not far from the school campus. All of my mother's family at that time was pretty much centered in the reservation. Neither my mother nor my father wanted me on the reservation, so his parents took care of me during the day and my mom took care of me at night. My mom and dad were never married and my mom just kept on living with my grandparents and going to school.

My dad lived on a military base. Not long after I was born my parents quit talking. Then, when I was a year and a half old, my mom went on a travel class overseas for a month.

"When she returned, my father and grandparents told her I had died the day she left. Crib death, they said. Showed her an urn with my ashes. She totally believed it, and it really broke her down. She went back to the reservation, then on to the city and problems with drugs and alcohol, then back to the reservation and a dry-out facility. Then she spent time with her father and really changed. She went back to school, graduated. She is a psychologist and a spiritual leader in the tribe. When I found her and she saw me, she suspected who I was during my fumbling introduction. I mentioned my father and she started weeping."

"She must have felt horribly betrayed."

"It was hard for her to get over the hate."

"I can imagine. Your dad raised you?"

"I lived mostly with his parents until I was ten; then he took me full-time."

"And when you learned the truth you felt betrayed?"

"Horribly. But you deal with it."

"Did you and your dad get along?"

"My dad taught me three things—self-reliance, self-control, and survival. He was special forces military." Sam just smiled.

"Oh, I get it. It might give you away."

"My dad did that until age thirty-seven, when he faked an accident so he could die so he wouldn't have to retire and become an ambulance driver or something like that. He'd had knee troubles and his brand of special forces didn't go much past forty anyway."

"He killed himself?"

"Not what they called it, but that's what he did."

"I'm sorry."

"When I was growing up, he put me through a tougher version of what he went through. We went on trips into the Alaskan wilderness, British Columbia, practically naked, and lived like animals. We climbed around on Mount Denali, scaled ice cliffs. He loved to tell me about all the schools he went to. There were at least nine. Combat diving, paratrooper, underwater egress, survival, special ops medicine. He knew I was more suited to academic school, using my mind. I think he was trying to sweat it out of me."

"You never wanted to follow in his footsteps?"

"I never for a second considered the military."

"You just don't seem like a math nerd."

"Well, Dad made sure I was big and strong and athletic. I got out a lot and—"

The drone of the seaplane provided a convenient escape from what was quickly becoming an embarrassing topic.

"Sam?"

"Yeah."

"Did your father abuse you?"

"He didn't hit me except with boxing gloves on. But he did things with a young kid that shouldn't be done."

"Like?"

"Like it's time to go."

"Sam . . . "

"I loved him. I respected him. But at the same time I pretty much lost him even before he died."

"What do you mean?"

"In the winter I studied and played with my computer, primitive as it was in those days. I got totally enthralled with math and then computers and from about twelve on it was all I thought about. Any fun I had on the wilderness forays in the summer was blunted because it kept me from playing with computers. I was great with logic and math but not much else in school. I'm dyslexic and couldn't read a book to save me. The math skills got me pretty far, though. The high schools didn't pay a whole lot of attention to other subjects as far as I could tell. So I went off to the university young."

"What university?"

"A good one. Doesn't matter. Graduated at twenty and after that got some graduate degrees. Was out at twenty-four."

"What graduate degrees?"

Sam smiled. "You're narrowing it down."

"Don't be a jerk. You've told me this much. Now give."

"Computer science. Tech stuff. Ph.D."

"So you were at school a lot."

"Yeah, from about twelve on I was the boy wonder. The real key was this professor I had. He took me under his wing. He's the reason I did well in college. He figured out a way for me to read like a normal person, and after that I read fanatically."

"And your son?"

Sam hesitated. "My son was killed. We were on a job. It was my fault."

"What happened?"

"I'd rather not go into it now. Maybe another time."

She waited a few seconds, looking for the plane. "Okay."

Ten

In six hours Anna was out of Vancouver and on her way to New York.

After seeing her off in the studio's Gulfstream IV, Sam climbed into a Hawker 700 for the trip to LA. The Hawker was an old workhorse business jet, worth maybe one-fifth as much as the plane that came for Anna. It was owned by Sam's friend, who let him use it for a fee. Sam was a no-frills guy even when it came to his choice of jets.

At Sam's request the pilots had been good enough to obtain some tobacco leaves and a humidor that originally came from a Cuban national who for years had supplied Sam.

Inside the jet things were posh and comfortable. The plane's sidewalls were wood and, near the floor, carpet. On the ceiling and upper sidewalls it was two-tone, stitched leather. Sam settled into a seat with Atlas-sized armrests and watched the flight information display monitor for a couple of minutes before he cracked open his small tobacco box.

He could understand his friend's wife not wanting their plane to smell like a cigar, even a good cigar, but there was no law against rolling one. Sam took a large unblemished tobacco leaf and rolled the smaller leaves and pieces inside it to make a loose facsimile of a real cigar. When he had it all carefully rolled, he stuffed it in a cigar tube and screwed on the lid. Sometime this week he would smoke it.

He picked up the sat phone built into the plane and called Paul.

"Hi," Sam began.

"Well, well, well, you're coming back to work. I heard you've got Jill back in the saddle. And Shohei called me."

"It's a particular assignment."

"Hey, you know me. I'm in."

Sam spent a solid forty minutes telling Paul the whole story.

"This could only happen to Sam the History Man," Paul said when he was through asking questions. "Now let me get this straight. You're telling me that Anna Wade doesn't even know the rules?"

"No contract yet. I told her not to talk. She's not fooling me. I figure she'll go ask around about me. She's a control freak."

"From what you've told me she also has no sponsor."

"We'll fix that. Let's see what she does."

"From what you gleaned it sounds like she's most likely to spill the beans to her ex or her boyfriend. We gonna need somebody in New York?"

"Oh, yeah. For protection, mainly, but also to keep the lid on any snooper stuff. Let's impress her. We'll find out a lot in the first few hours."

They talked over the details of what they would need to do in the next twenty-four hours. It was a long list.

"Have Farris get the ESN number and the phone number on Anna's cell. They've got the contacts, probably cost a few grand."

"Use an oscillator?"

"Yeah. Record every word."

"You're gonna feel like a shit."

"I know. Do you think I should call Typhony?" Sam asked, now satisfied that Paul understood.

"She's one of the best researchers we ever had. She can make Big Brain sing songs and tell secrets. You already got one ex-lover back in the biz, why not two?"

"You think her boyfriend will be all right with it?" Sam said.

"Fiancé, you mean. Yeah, I do. He's a good guy."

"There's an undertone there."

"No undertone. I just never figured out why you and she didn't stay connected."

"One of those mysteries."

"Truth's truth, Sam. Commitment bores you. That was Jill and that was Typhony. So you gonna call Typhony or am I?"

"She's got another job, doesn't she?"

"Sam, she'll be crushed if you don't even call and ask. She's an executive assistant for some stuffed shirt. And you never know what she'll do till you ask."

"But for one assignment?"

"Hey, nobody believes that retirement crap. You want me to call?"

"I'll call." Sam now knew exactly how Paul's conversation with Typhony had gone. But it was necessary to play it out. It might be as long as twenty-four hours before she was back in the office.

Sam's finger was poised over the button. Once he dialed there was no turning back. The choice was still his until he dialed the number. It was about as awkward as a man finding his sister making love to his wife, but other than that the call was a breeze. After Typhony finished the verbal torture, Sam got down to the big question, and after appropriate hesitation and more than the usual verbal sparring she took the job.

"Talk to Paul, of course," Sam told her, "and get the full story from him. But do a complete search on Dr. Kenneth Galbraith, psychiatrist. Where he went to school, all the doctors in his class; any publications; every mention of him in the press; credit check; all the usual. And start having someone go through his garbage immediately. No doubt he'll have a cell. Figure it out, get the ESN, the whole nine yards, and get one of our contract guys listening to his calls. If we get anything at all we'll arrange more groundwork. If he lives remotely, use the drone, get blowups; otherwise drive-bys are okay. Then in the morning begin interviews immediately. Use Royce and associates. When you've got Royce going, help Paul on Grace Technologies: one Roberto Fresco, its vice president; DuShane Chellis, the president. I forgot to mention to Paul I think we should call our friends in Brussels and have them work on the France end. I'd like that outfit Discretion."

"I don't know how you end up with the most famous and the most troubled," she said. "But that's okay," she added before he could respond. "We knew you'd come back, and I guess Anna Wade is as good an excuse as any."

Devan Gaudet was looking forward to seeing the offices of Grace Technologies without its master ushering him around. Although he had been in the building a number of times as the need for his services increased, his movements were always controlled. Headquarters stood on the Rue de l'Arrivée, a block from the Luxembourg Gardens, where Chellis reportedly paced when in the throes of a deal.

For a Paris office, Grace's was expensive, which meant that by the standards of most of the world's cities it was exorbitant. Devan Gaudet looked up at the building from the small entry plaza just outside the main doors. Even he had to admit that Chellis had come a long way from Omaha, Nebraska. But the man still had the petty mind of an American.

The main doors led to a spacious atrium and waiting area that looked like a men's luncheon club. Large windows, painfully tasteful brown leather, and subdued plaids on the furnishings made one think of cigars and chess. According to Benoit, people congregated here to talk sometimes about business and usually when Chellis was out of the office. This was the policy center of the holding company, where business strategy at the highest levels took place.

Chellis's personal offices were through a second set of double doors off the atrium and down a long hall lined with other offices, making the path to his suite a little like an obstacle course for unwanted visitors. Chellis did not care for confrontation unless he had arranged for one of his rages, and then he sought it.

Gaudet used a pass provided by Benoit. He had arrived early deliberately; he wanted to get the feel of the place. Benoit had explained the sorts who hung out at the main office and she certainly had it pegged. Largely the working technical fellows would be found at the company's regional centers. Here scientists who no longer did science came to spend their last few years with the businessmen and MBAs and occasionally with the boss himself.

Gaudet made his way into the inner office without drawing a glance; he tried out Chellis's chair and used his phone for fifteen minutes before Chellis and

Benoit arrived, fresh from the flight in from Kuching. He heard Chellis well before he saw him.

"So they can screw themselves and go straight to hell and I want you to tell them that," he said. When he walked in the door he was pocketing a cell phone.

"Soon it will be time for your brunch," Benoit said as she put her purse down on Chellis's table. It irritated Gaudet that she occupied the man's space so casually.

"Why hasn't Roberto called back? What in the hell are they doing? Do I have to wipe his ass?"

At that moment they both saw Gaudet standing behind the desk.

Without smiling or offering a greeting, Gaudet walked to the sitting area toward the front of the office. He knew that when his clients needed him they had no alternative, so unlike in most personal service businesses the niceties could be ignored. When they were seated, each with a cup of coffee, Gaudet looked longer at Benoit than at Chellis.

"Your mistress is very beautiful. Like your wife."

"She is my assistant."

"Tell me the problem, then. But be more truthful about the problem than you are about your love life."

"You show respect or we have no deal."

"Relax. She is not ashamed of you. Why are you ashamed of her?"

"Get out."

Gaudet rose to leave.

"Wait. Just wait," Benoit said. "DuShane is not ashamed of me. He is protecting someone I love. Marie, his wife, is my sister. There is no disrespect. So why can't we all sit down and do our business?"

Gaudet hesitated.

"Sit down. I have always paid you. That should

mean something," Chellis said. "We know you are the best. There are others, but everyone tells me none as good as Gaudet."

Gaudet sat. "As I said before, I no longer work merely for cash."

"I'd heard. What do you want?"

"A piece of something. Part of a venture. I think you need me in the arms part of your business. Ten percent. I want ten percent. You've been holding out on me."

"That's ridiculous."

"Is it? Think of the future. In that line of business you may need a scapegoat who can disappear into thin air. Think of the advantages."

The men wrangled for fifteen minutes over their egos and their money.

"Five percent," Chellis finally said. "And that is asinine. You didn't build this business."

"I'm about to save your skin."

"And you have to take care of things without additional fees since you'd be a partner."

"Five percent will do, but I get full audit privileges. My people look at anything and everything any time they want. And of course I will still receive basic cash fees in addition."

"You're not being rational."

"To the contrary. The business of killing people is a precise science. You clearly need someone dead. Take it or leave it."

"My attorneys will make a draft of the assignment documents."

"My attorneys will make the first draft after conferring with your lawyers on the subject of the involved entities."

"It's only the weapons stuff."

"That's right. Samir's side," Gaudet said. "So let's start with the facts of the problem."

Chellis began telling the story, and when he was nearly through the phone rang.

"It's Roberto," Benoit said, looking at the name flashing.

"You'll want to hear this," Chellis said.

Gaudet nodded. They turned on the speakerphone. "What's the status?"

"They are afraid of Jason being arrested for the rocket launcher so they're saying nothing. They acted like a couple of rich tourists that lost another yacht. No big deal."

"Did you get the picture of the man?"

"No. He's smart and tough."

"For that you deserve a gravestone."

"We did the best we could. Oh, and we heard her call him 'Sam.'"

"So exactly what did happen?"

Roberto told them the whole story and Chellis vented his anger by hanging up abruptly.

"Can you tell me in a few words why this Jason is worth the dough?" Gaudet asked.

"All you need to know is that he's valuable."

"Why is he crazy?"

"I don't know. Paranoid schizophrenia. Rare form."

"What about this man that is with Anna?"

"He just picked her up in his boat. Had to be a co-incidence. How bad can that be?"

"Usually it is a coincidence that kills people like you and me. You don't know the name of the boat?"

"They never got it. Roberto couldn't see the stern when it picked her up."

"You need Jason all to yourself, the CD returned, and you need Anna Wade to forget about it."

"And her new friend or whatever he is. Someone took a rocket launcher to his boat. How would you respond? Plus we have one more problem."

"Another problem?"

"Jason has a daughter. Grady. She's a well-paid stripper. We have a handle on her, and we know she hates her father. Likewise her Aunt Anna. But if she turned and joined forces with Anna, a French court might give custody of Jason's person and estate to Anna or the daughter. It's not likely, but I can't risk it."

Chellis went on to give Gaudet everything they had on the girl.

"All right, the five percent interest will do. As for the fee, one million if it requires wet work. And if this man with the boat has to be killed, that's another million. Another half million if I have to kill Grady Wade."

"That's outrageous," Chellis said.

"Those are my terms."

"How hard can it be to kill some sailor?"

"You want to kill him, you go ahead. I do it as part of this package and it's a million dollars U.S. Period. Any other incidental kills are covered by the five percent; plus you get one unrelated noncelebrity kill."

"Fine. Fine. Maybe Anna will buy off the yachtie to protect her brother. Or charm him. Or something."

"I have a feeling about this. It isn't a good feeling. But I will take care of it. Tell Roberto and all your men that they will be contacted by Trotsky for instructions."

"We'll tell them."

"I will need men this time. Many of them. How many do you have over there?"

"Five or six. More on the way."

"Trotsky will coordinate your men. Now they are my men."

"Okay."

Gaudet rose and didn't shake hands or say good-bye, but simply turned and walked out.

On the street he called his right-hand man, Trotsky, on his cell phone.

"You have to get me guns in the States and in Canada. Mac Tens. At least six. Some sniper stuff. Three of those. I'll need three good Frenchmen with passports and no history."

"Expensive."

"When was that a problem? Then I need information and fast. Everything you can get on Anna Wade—the actress. You got a notepad? I'm gonna tell you about a guy who calls himself Sam."

Eleven

The minute Gaudet left, Benoit began kissing Chellis.

"There is just enough time before brunch," she said.

He hesitated, remembering that he and Marie always took a "nap" after brunch.

"Don't worry. She is on her period."

He broke away. "How do you know that?"

"Sisters know these things. I'm surprised you have to ask."

Benoit's hands on his body felt good.

"She must never know. About us."

"Oh, of course not. No one will ever know."

The phone rang. For a moment she slid down the couch and glanced at the screen. He was impatient to resume.

"Data processing."

"Answer it."

She listened for a moment.

"You better tell him yourself."

Chellis clicked on the speaker.

"There's a problem with the BC backup."

"What about the backup?"

"Jason's automated backup program has been reprogrammed. It shows it's backing up when it's not.

We have what looks like a bunch of old formulas. Jason left an encoded message. It says, 'DuShane is hiding on the back roads, in the rivers of my memory, never gentle, but always on my mind.'"

"How could this happen? You're supposed to be checking!"

"We do check—"

"You don't," he shouted. "If you did you would have known the minute it happened."

"Nobody can follow Jason's stuff. We wouldn't know if it was the real—"

"Don't give me that line . . . you just told me it was phony . . . old, you said . . . so you knew. Don't make up stupid excuses for your moronic breach of your duty."

"There is one more thing. A worse thing. He took a backup file of Jacques Boudreaux. A Kuching file."

"When?"

"Recently."

"What was on it?"

"We're not sure."

"You are an idiot. I want a full report."

Chellis slammed down the phone and began to fasten his pants until Benoit stopped him.

"Relax," she said, pushing him back down.

"If Jason gave a CD to Anna it may have had Kuching files on it."

"There is nothing for us to do now but attend to each other."

After brunch with Marie, after he had given her flowers and yet another diamond pin, they were back in the apartment and Marie held his head in her lap and stroked his temples the way he liked.

"Those bankers have worn you out." She smiled a knowing smile and for just a second it pissed him off.

* * *

Gaudet proceeded immediately to Benoit's apartment and removed the beard while he waited, transforming himself into the clean-shaven man who was Dahrr Moujed, his given name at birth.

Gaudet in his natural state was not a bad-looking man, but primarily it was the confidence in the eyes that made the passable appearance. He was just shy of six feet, had small even teeth, relatively thin lips, a very flat pursed expression in natural repose, a small aquiline nose, and the darkest of brown eyes. His hair was very short and very black and pointed up in all sorts of odd directions as if he wanted to be a punk rocker. In reality, the plastics and wigs made long hair or orderly hair a near impossibility.

Benoit's apartment had panache. Simple straightforward designs, with yellows, creamy browns, and a few soft accents. She liked glass and brass, nothing frilly, very clean lines, nearly antiseptic in places, but there was an original Picasso on the wall, one of the lopsided-faced ladies, that DuShane had given her, and works by several other lesser but noteworthy painters, all contemporary, but no abstract work. Benoit said she liked to have a rough idea, at least, of what the artist might have been thinking.

As to the lady portrayed, she might have shared a similar soul to Benoit's. Even Benoit admitted that, what with all the fracturing and displacement in the lines.

If she wanted to know only what an artist was feeling, Benoit was fond of saying, she'd read a poem.

When at last Benoit came home, she wore her disapproval rather plainly.

"I'm sorry," Gaudet said without emotion. "I can't resist baiting your boss. He's so easy, so American."

"He is a French citizen."

"In his head he's an American capitalist, born a farmer and come to the wicked city."

"You were being crazy, talking like that, accusing DuShane Chellis and me of having an affair."

Gaudet grabbed her and pulled her to him.

"Give me just a minute," she said, and went into the bathroom.

From his pocket he removed an exquisite knife with a pearl handle and a carbide blade that would slice silk in midair.

When she came through the door of the bathroom, she wore a short leather skirt and a red sweater that left one shoulder bare. Her legs were tan, bare. She wore patent leather pumps with high heels. She wet her lips with her tongue and looked long at him, saying nothing. Slowly she walked toward him as he played with the blade on his finger. With meticulous ease he cut the sweater off her and freed her breasts, enjoying their shape, like wineskins, slightly pointed and with a sensuous droop. It was a special image and it excited him as few other images could. They had violent sex according to his addiction. Without exception she professed to like it, but he never believed her, nor did he care whether she was lying.

They said nothing until it was over, then watched TV for twenty minutes. When she returned from a trip to the bathroom, she brought a second condom and wore a second set of panties that he could shred.

After he had exhausted himself again, he showered and dressed, returning to find Benoit nude in the bed, with covers to her waist. Gaudet was dressed and ready to leave. Still, it was hard to take his eyes from her.

"I want you with me, and I've never wanted that of a woman," he said.

"That's almost touching coming from you. Now tell me, what do you know about this Sam? I saw something in your face when Roberto talked about him."

"I think I have encountered him before—on a job a year or so ago. At first I dismissed the idea—some coincidences are simply impossible. But I keep thinking about it. The Sam I knew about—I never actually saw him—liked sailboats, lived in LA. He had a big staff and conducted investigations. He worked for wealth. Royalty. Celebrities. Governments. Big money for big problems. If he just happened by, it's an incredible coincidence. And as I told Chellis, it's the coincidences that kill you. I think he was hired to be there. Their rendezvous must have misfired. Perhaps she fell in on the way to meeting him in the yacht."

Benoit lay back, looking as if she was intrigued at the notion.

"You think she hired him before she came?"

"He's exactly the guy a big celebrity would hire."

Once more he went to her and kissed her deeply. If it were not for the departure of his plane, he would have entered her bed a third time and asked her about the science involved—Jacques's science.

"What is love to you?" she asked him suddenly.

"When a man says he loves, he is apologizing for his lust. It means I want to use your body but I'm sorry for it—a form of contrition."

"And what if a woman says it?"

"She realizes that she's being taken by a cold bastard and she begs for security. When a woman says 'I love you' it means: 'Don't leave me for someone more beautiful.'"

"Why do you like me?" she asked.

"Sex with you is the closest I will ever get to religion."

"You flatter me. I think you could forget me in a day."

He smiled despite himself. "It would take more than a day."

He turned to the mirror to check his disguise. When he dressed he had put on a mustache and plastic, but not the beard. Traveling to America or Canada with a beard increased the likelihood that he would be detained, even though he traveled as a citizen of France.

Gaudet didn't like leaving his island these days. The inconvenience and danger of travel kept him home more than it ever had before. Gaudet owned a portion of a small island in French Polynesia where he had constructed a burre on stilts with a thatched roof laid over copper that had turned green from the salt air. Inside it was modern, with a polished stone floor and teak and rock for the walls and Honduran mahogany for the bookcases. A German client, a corporation, had constructed the house in its own name and then quietly sold it to Gaudet's Cayman Island corporation. The transaction was booked as an exchange of services.

He was still thinking of the place while he waited for the cab to the airport. He was not particularly fond of any city, but Paris had many beautiful women. If he didn't consider the presence of attractive women, there were only a few places in the world he liked, and he liked his burre the best. Soon his burre might be graced with visits from Benoit, which would give his island all that he required. It troubled him that she had not agreed to visit him yet. He supposed she imagined that she would be left out of things with her sister remaining in Paris at the Grace offices. Already he had decided that if Benoit would not come to his island, he would for the most part remain in Paris and endure the company of men. But he would never sell the burre because women, like life itself, were transitory.

Gaudet had been born in Oman, the son of a merchant who had moved himself and his non-Muslim family to a suburb north of Paris shortly after his birth. On his third birthday they moved to Paris proper, and when he was twelve they shipped him to a Catholic boarding school in a village about an hour's drive away. After that he saw little of them. Just before his thirteenth birthday they died in a taxi accident, and thereafter Gaudet largely fended for himself. It was made easier by the fact that he had never felt close to either of his parents. But then he never really felt close to anyone. He was able to remain at the boarding school and pay tuition by working during school and during the summer, with additional small contributions from an uncle in Oman.

As a young man he was ambitious and flirted briefly with drug smuggling, then went to work for a man named Jean Lacour who operated a walk-in laundry. It was a rough business, and sometimes turf wars were settled with fists. It was the violence at which he excelled, and soon he hired himself out as a collector to loan sharks as a sideline. He did so well at roughing up deadbeats that he soon left the laundry except for occasional jobs protecting territory with fists and threats.

At the age of seventeen he made his first foray into killing when a man at a neighborhood party picked a fight. He easily won the fight because he discovered in the first few seconds that he had no fear. After he beat the man with a chair and then his fists, the fight ended when some older men broke it up. Devan invited the other fellow to finish the fight down the street, but the man declined. It was then the consensus that Devan was the clear winner. It was no appeasement. When the man was on his way home in the quiet of the night, Devan jumped him with a pipe, crushed his shoulder, and then his head. He left him in the street but because of the earlier fight, was nearly arrested for murder.

It was because of this experience that Gaudet swore off direct methods of killing, which he found wanting when compared to more creative techniques. It worked much better to leave his targets dead and everyone, including the police, wondering how it came to pass.

He was only eighteen when he killed his second man, an elderly fellow named Dubroc who fed the pigeons in the park. The man had put in a laundry a block from his client's business, and his client was willing to pay to make the new arrival disappear. Unfortunately the old man had a large family, including many sons, so picking fights and general harassment was not a solution.

By studying poisons, Gaudet learned about belladonna. The English knew it as nightshade, and although the sweet berry of the plant had resulted in the deaths of many French and English children, it was the root that yielded atropine, a deadly but medicinally useful alkaloid. While it worked well in dilution for dilating the eyes, one-hundredth of a grain of pure atropine ingested would kill a grown man in short order.

Devan was deliberate in everything, and that came to include the preparation of his poisons. What he lacked in experience he made up for in study and contemplation. After watching the old graybeard Dubroc for days, it became obvious that the man liked his pint of whiskey every afternoon, which by evening left him drunk. When Dubroc went home at night, he usually meandered down the sidewalk swaying and jolly, occasionally finding support on lampposts or in doorways. It also became apparent that the man had a sweet tooth, a love of tarts from the local bakery. It took two weeks of careful work for Gaudet to learn to bake such a tart. Even young he had been patient. It was a simple matter to grind the belladonna root fine and to fill a cherry confection with enough to kill a large dog. He doubled that amount.

To avoid any suspicion whatsoever, he baked a tart at the home of a vacationing acquaintance thirty miles distant on a day he knew that the old man would appear at his office above the Dubroc laundry. While the old man was tottering about his chores in the late afternoon, Gaudet slipped into his office and put the tart on the desk atop a piece of bakery tissue. Fascinated, Gaudet remained in the area but heard nothing. A couple of days later Gaudet read the press account. The man was out in front of his laundry unable to speak, reeling about, clutching and unclutching his hands as if kneading unseen bread. When someone grabbed him and called an ambulance, the old fellow was bending at the waist, doubled over, and turning very red at the ears.

Gaudet found the story entirely to his liking.

Since then, during a lifetime of self-development, experimentation, and wet work, Devan had become a master of the accident. He did not shoot, strangle, or stab a victim. Instead he created elaborate tragedies. It was as if he were writing screenplays, and each act of creation left him with a sense of satisfaction he had found nowhere else. Recently, though, he had noticed a yearning to watch his victims die, to kill them directly, and he had decided to make some effort toward that end.

Still, indirect killing held his primary interest, and the range of delivery methods, from gas explosions to neurotoxins, was surprisingly broad. Through Benoit and her work with Jacques in Kuching, Gaudet had even acquired monkey viruses that were almost immediately lethal to humans.

It was a wonder, he thought, that he had found a job that so nurtured his creativity.

Once in the taxi, Gaudet called Trotsky for the final time. "Do we know where they are going?"

"Seaplane to Vancouver. We're guessing private jet out of there to the States."

"Guessing does me no good."

"Anna lives in Manhattan. Just to the west of Central Park. I have the address."

"Have you got people there?"

"Soon. Chellis's group has just found us an apartment across the street. We'll have to lease it for a full year."

"Do it. Surveillance?"

"When we get in the apartment. The normal audio equipment should work fine."

"Does Anna Wade have other houses?"

"At least one in Hollywood Hills and a ranch in Wyoming."

"Americans . . . Get all three places covered but focus on Manhattan if that's her primary home."

"It will take a lot more people."

"Then get a lot more people. We're getting paid for it."

Twelve

October in Borneo ushers in the rainy season following what is almost always a dry September. But this October, now nearly ended, one would never have guessed it was the start of the monsoons, for it had not yet rained. The creeks were a trickle, water was being rationed, the ground was gray and cracking, people were grumbling, plants were dying, and animals were crowding slimy waterholes.

Samir wished for something more effective than Valium. Before his face tropical fish swam in a large tank. They floated and moved in rhythmic muscular ripples, ordered symphonies in motion. He watched the fish only because he had heard that they were found in waiting rooms where their effect was touted as calming.

Perhaps they were helping. He could not be sure. His mind was like a curtained room, round and full with secret fears, massing just out of his sight. He found that if he didn't keep his eyes on the fish, they cast furtively about. At times his body shook as if he were cold, and then out of sheer weariness it would stop. Usually at those moments he slept.

He played a strange mental game, forcing himself to remember what he used to be like, trying to pretend to be the man he once was and to make decisions he once would have made. Frequently he asked Fawd what he might have done before, just days ago, and Fawd tried to conjure the right memory of his boss in full command. Fawd had given him a shot of Thorazine and he was waiting, hoping for some results.

Samir remained determined to break into the laboratory, but it was hard to maintain inertia in the face of his anxiety. Just this morning, while shaving and making a giant O with his mouth, Samir had caught himself wondering if he was still Samir Aziz. DuShane Chellis had done something to him, to his mind. Samir knew that Chellis had gone to a great effort to gas him in the lockout chamber. He also knew Chellis was lying about the entire incident, but he had no idea concerning Chellis's reasons, except that it probably related to the Mossad visit and the new technology Colonel Schenkel had hinted at when he was holding a gun in his face.

He needed to know the truth.

Fawd had spoken on his behalf with Chellis, but the man had only smiled an insolent smile and offered his sympathy for Samir's "anxiety attacks." Before leaving for Paris, he had offered to have Samir seen by a distinguished neurologist in France. It would be a cold day in hell before Samir put his life in the hands of DuShane Chellis. He also recommended a masseuse, but Samir would have none of it.

The man was a strange kind of Frenchman. Chellis's grandparents on his father's side had emigrated to the United States, but had kept their French ways and their French language. Chellis himself was born an American, educated in American schools, and attended the first two years of a university in the United States, but finished in France. His education in France ultimately turned into citizenship. As far as Samir was concerned, the man thought like an American, lived and spoke like a Frenchman.

Thanks to his hookup with Chellis, Samir had become a force in the arms industry—a man with a lot to lose. His company was a major presence at the Paris Air Show, the Abu Dabai International Defense Exhibition, the Singapore Marine Arms Show, and other lesser shows. In the spacious halls of IDEX 2002, Samir could offer just about anything military, from boots to bombs, ready-to-eat meals, fighter jets, and helicopter gunships. He had a very popular air defense antitank system, and was even trading in medium-range missiles capable of delivering nuclear warheads. It was up to the buyer to supply the nuke.

It was Samir's relationship with Chellis and their mutual projects that had propelled his net worth to more than five hundred million Eurodollars and the Frenchman's to more than three billion. Their secret joint venture continued to use medical technology, computer software, and hardware in military applications, but the Grace Technologies name was on nothing. The parts made a circuitous journey to a South American medical supply manufacturer, and from there through many distributors (all paid a small portion for keeping their mouths shut) back to Samir, and then on to China and other interested nations and organizations.

Chellis's association with Devan Gaudet was a new and troubling development for Samir.

Recently, a fellow arms dealer had exchanged a $100-million shipment of surplus Soviet weapons for trunks full of U.S. stocks and bearer bonds. When the bearer bonds disappeared without a trace and the tons of merchandise with them, rumor had it that Gaudet had killed the dealer and several of his men while making it appear the work of Samir Aziz. Most people considered Gaudet a myth; Samir knew better.

It now made sense in retrospect that Chellis might have forged a business relationship with the elusive assassin. Not long ago a French minister who had called for investigations into Grace Technologies died suddenly in an apparent drowning accident. What good fortune for Chellis, Samir had thought at the time.

Samir knew more than most about Gaudet, but it still added up to precious little. He had started out as a thief and a loan shark enforcer, become a hired killer, amassed a fortune, gotten into business, and worked for only a select few. His clients included men with oil money who funded terror. Samir had never seen Gaudet—at least that he knew of—but it was said that the killer favored a beard. Perhaps he would discover something of Gaudet in the lab, but he doubted it. More likely he would discover something about himself—probably something he didn't want to know.

Fortunately Kuching was an easy place to move men and materials. Samir stopped watching the fish and told Fawd that the drug cocktail was good enough—it was time to perform the break-in.

As he waited for his men to take care of the security guards, he hoped he wouldn't fall apart. He tried to calm himself by acknowledging the degree to which he'd planned and prepared for this operation. Long before this trip to Kuching, Samir had had his best men study the Grace lab. He had always known there might come a time when he'd have to look in on his partner's business without Chellis knowing. In general, no laboratory staff members worked between midnight and 6:00 A.M. Only the janitors visited the building, and when they were in, the alarms were off.

Trained security men walked the buildings and

grounds, but there was fatal regularity to their at-
tempts at random patrols and they undertook their
duties in the somnambulistic fashion of the under-
paid. By five minutes after midnight Samir's men
had all four guards trussed and blindfolded and
sleeping soundly from a narcotic. They would wake
in twelve hours on their front porches, smelling of
whiskey and with no memory of anything that had
happened to them. Clinical experience had proven
that the drug erased the memory, and further that
recipients would unconsciously manufacture self-
protective and context-appropriate explanations
for unexpected happenings. These men would convince themselves, upon awakening on their front
porch to the smell of alcohol, that they had finished
their jobs and had a drink. Despite his panicked
state Samir savored the irony that he had originally
gotten this drug from Chellis.

Once his men had carted off the security staff, they
merely waited for the janitors to finish the northern-
most wing. At 3:00 A.M., Samir and his men moved
down the hall methodically. It was just as Samir remembered. Walls bare and off-white, the floor shined,
everything clean, nothing fancy, the faint odor of
caged primates.

They went straight to the neurology wing in the primate building and there they found no files.
Apparently security discipline was being enforced.
Samir had to take another tranquilizer and gather
himself. He sent his men to do the work while he sat
in an office and shook.

His men backtracked to the offices of the scientists
nearest neurology. There they went through locked
file drawers, Samir hoping that human nature would
yield some stray documents. He had told his men that

he wanted files on people, not apes, and that any such files should be immediately photographed. He sent another group to administration, and fell asleep because of the heavy doses of medication.

Fawd reported that the large walk-in safe at administration was hard to miss, but it was locked, had a timing device, and his safecracker could not gain entry. To use powerful enough explosives to open the door of the safe would wake the city and destroy the building. Samir was not about to get thrown in a Malaysian jail—especially with his new anxiety problem.

Disappointed, they retreated to the locked file drawers in the offices of the various research scientists and again awakened Samir. Hundreds of available files yielded only two interesting documents. One pertained to Jason Wade, the other to Jeremiah Fuller. Fuller had evidently been treated for dementia, likely the result of late-onset Alzheimer's. Wade had apparently been treated for a rare brain disease whose course was not well known. Apparently both men had been desperate enough to subject themselves to experimental treatment.

The portions of the files containing treatment details were missing, but the last paragraph of the last page of a technical write-up in the Jason Wade file read:

Production of retro viral vector by multiplying circular vector plasmid using e-coli restriction digestion. Production of coding sequence for receptor amplified from cDNA source by PCR. Coding sequence for blocker by PCR. Promoter amplification from genome DNA by PCR. We introduced 5ml vector times 19 through venus transfusion: one aloquat per each pro-

*moter. Estimated 98% success to infected cells, esti-
mate infection rate 92%. Transdermal application of
suppressor/activator cell agent feasible. Test to see if
JH receptor is in frame.*

Samir ordered one of his men to photograph the
technical language. He would send it to a lab that
might tell him something. He also ordered his lieu-
tenant to find out everything possible about Jason
Wade and Jeremiah Fuller, including information on
family and friends. They went back to the primate lab,
observed the packs on the backs of the two macaques,
and continued looking. In a storage room they found
packs and plastic bottles labeled *JH* with dates. One
was denominated *Potency Exp. 05/05.* Another bore
the label *Transdermal JHRA.*

"What does it mean?" Fawd asked the science expert on the team.

"Whatever it is, they apply it through the skin. I assume from the lab note that SA means suppressor
agent."

"Take all there is. Take the two liters," Fawd said.
"They will know someone broke in, but why should we
care?"

Anna's Manhattan apartment was on the twenty-
eighth floor of her West Side building. She had been
trying to read a book that had been recommended
during cocktail talk at a party. The friend who made
the suggestion was a psychiatrist, a man who had
been happily married for thirty years. Although she
couldn't help bristling at what she thought might
be an implication, however subtle, that she couldn't
stick with one man, she was now reading with more

interest than she cared to admit. Normally she read a book in a few days, but with this one she read slowly, picking her way through the ideas and the feelings. It was titled *Where Did She Go? Where Did He Go?* and purported to study a phenomenon called emotional unavailability. Having resumed her reading of the book upon her arrival from Canada, she had come to realize that she was reading about Sam. She had started to wonder if she might also be reading about herself.

Like a lot of highly motivated and self-directed people, Anna had the mother of all double standards for those with a title like therapist, counselor, psychiatrist, or psychologist. Shrinks of all flavors were fine . . . for the other guy: There was not a shred of shame in consulting them. Anna had found no difficulty in consulting head doctors for the sake of her brother, but since beginning this book she had gone to someone strictly for herself twice in a week.

The phone rang—her publicist. Apparently when the press had called her to ask whether Anna had spent the night with a rugged, American sailor aboard his yacht in British Columbia, the publicist had responded with "no comment." Ordinarily that would be okay, but in this instance it would be taken as an admission. Anna knew Sam would be angry if his name or even his general description ever came up.

"Just call them back, say that you checked with me, and explain that there was no night on a yacht at all. I was with my brother. I did some survival training with an expert. We stopped at the resort for a few minutes, this expert and I, and I signed autographs for some bird-watchers. End of story. Nothing has changed between Lane and me."

She went to the kitchen. When things were tense

she liked to eat, and when she was determined not to eat, she would go to the kitchen and graze with her eyes. Bananas, apples, oranges, tangerines, mangoes, a pineapple, pears, whole-wheat crackers, crusty dark whole-wheat bread. There was the aged balsamic that by itself was good, but when used with olive oil induced massive consumption of bread. New York-style kosher dill pickles. Lazio's gourmet tuna. And then the refrigerator things: special Cajun relish for the tuna; nonfat yogurt that had protein but was full of sugar; the unsweetened yogurt that was a little too tart but okay if mixed with fruit; barbecued tofu sticks from the local deli; lox. And best of all, the jar of natural peanut butter with the oil floating on top.

Anna's most successful and painless diets had been those that she made up herself, and the least successful were those she read about in books. She favored seafood and vegetables and whole wheat and soy products. If it could scream when it died, she preferred not to eat it, and she knew she should never eat in the evening. Of course this was difficult to explain to a man who wanted to buy you dinner at Babbo.

As if summoned by the thought, Lane called. "Hi. How goes it?"

"Oh, fine. I'm hungry and so I'm going to work out. And I miss you."

"I'm missing you too. All the time lately."

From there the conversation spiraled down through a long string of exchanged and rehashed excuses for not seeing each other and Anna's attempt to explain Sam, pretty much without success.

"Look," Anna finally said, "I'd like to tell you more about this investigator guy, but really I shouldn't. The way he works, if I talk I'm breaking my word. Oh, hell. I can tell you. It's a guy who sometimes calls himself

Sam. I know when a person is well connected and Sam is that."

"Well hung or well connected?"

"Don't be crude and especially don't be jealous. I don't know his full name because he doesn't give it out to clients, but he seems very solid. I'm having him checked out."

"Sounds serious."

"It is."

"Listen, you take care of Jason. When you're done you call me. We'll meet. Maybe we can start over."

But she could hear a difference in his voice. There was resignation and sadness, and she knew he didn't really believe what he was saying. What they really needed was a dinner or two to break up properly. It would require a weird dance of words, each party trying desperately not to feel rejected and trying not to make the other feel rejected. A perfect parity parting. That was what Lane was thinking and she knew it. Probably because that was what she was thinking.

Still, she wouldn't close the door. Maybe they could work something out. Then a new thought zinged through her mind. Maybe he had been seeing someone else. These things could be very subtle at first. He had three women in his current movie. Two were single, and it really didn't matter that the third was married. People got ideas, married or single, and LA people were among the worst.

Lane would not cheat, but he might think, and if he was thinking . . .

She tried to shake her bad thoughts. She had absolutely no reason to doubt Lane. More reason to doubt herself. It was so easy to start thinking. It was like food. An iron will was required. Maybe she was thinking about Sam. She hadn't liked the sound of her own voice when she told Lane not to be jealous of Sam.

On the desk was a script. She loved it. If she took it, there was no doubt it would take her further from Lane. Somebody once told her that everybody who makes it to the top is hard in the core. They make sacrifices in their personal life—killer instinct, some called it. God, she hoped it wasn't true.

She called her agent. "Let's make the deal on *August Moon*."

"You're sure."

"Yes, I am."

"Okay, honey. You got it."

Gathering her things, she called to Genevieve, her young assistant, and said she was leaving. Anna normally employed people in their twenties as assistants, people interested in the arts, acting, design, and the like. These tended to be somewhat informal arrangements and she often had four or five in her employ at once, although she usually tried to find things for them to do that would keep them out from under her nose. Sometimes that was difficult. Genevieve would probably never be an actress, but she was the best assistant Anna had ever found.

Anna was having dinner with her ex at his place. She wondered if she should have mentioned it to Lane.

On her way out the door she called Lane again.

"This will only take a minute."

"No. Problem. Shoot."

"Do you have any secrets from me?"

He sighed. "I'm not having sex with anyone else, if that's what you mean."

"It's okay; I've got my secrets too. I'm going to take the part in *August Moon*."

"I see," he said.

"You can assume things or you can keep an open mind."

"Come on, Anna. It takes a lot more time. It's a big commitment."

"That part is true. But we can work around it."

"We didn't use to have secrets."

"I know that."

"So let's get together."

"We will. As soon as I can. Good-bye. I love you," she said after a second. She winced, not because it was a lie, but because the "I love you" had become a thoughtless habit.

While she took a taxi over to Park Avenue she pondered how the evening might go with Josh. It would be important to be warm, but not so warm as to be confusing.

She had married Joshua a few months after Jimmy died. There was a whirlwind engagement, so short it was hardly worthy of the name, a marriage, and fourteen months later a divorce. Just like "his" and "hers" in the linen closet, there was "his" and "hers" when it came to impressions about the breakup.

As is often the case, there was a precipitating event triggering the breakup that had little to do with the substance of their growing disengagement. Joshua had become intoxicated and had gotten sexual with one of her friends. Before that, she was contemplating some attempt to stop the unraveling of her marriage. It had begun occurring to her that maybe there was something inside her that made long-term relationships difficult.

Joshua's indiscretion killed the last of her waning desire to work on the marriage. Initially unaware that he had been caught in his infidelity, Joshua was dismissed from her heart before he figured out she had left, and he still suffered from having been beaten to the punch.

According to Joshua, their breakup was brought about by Anna always wanting control but never wanting intimacy. She wanted appearances and she wanted to be adored and she wanted passion; at home there was to be a festive environment, everybody happy all the time; no problems. She wanted to help the needy unless the needy included her husband. And finally, as a sort of crowning contradiction, she wanted constant emotional stimulation. When every single day could not be filled with breathless passion, she got bored and began withdrawing. And that, according to Josh, gave her the excuse she needed to dump him after a minor indiscretion.

She arrived late at Josh's, but he was his usual forgiving self.

"You made good time."

"That's nice of you to say." She kissed his cheek and came in.

They walked from the front door through the entry and living room in silence, Josh no doubt contemplating his game plan while she considered her own. She wore a simple Calvin Klein pantsuit, and from the corner of her eye she caught Josh looking her up and down.

"You have on your friendly-but-formal face."

She smiled.

"Am I reading you right?"

"Uh-huh."

"The face does not come naturally to you."

Joshua was tall and slender and charming. He had

a large, friendly mouth with perfect teeth, not unlike Anna's. He was nothing like Sam in the physique department, but he was nice-looking, even naked.

More pleasantries followed. He offered her wine, one of her current favorites, a 1996 Turley Zinfandel. Josh loved wine, was very thoughtful about it, and always knew what she was drinking. For dessert he would offer her a Sauterne Chateau d'Yquem 1990 and she would choose a beer.

He lived in a four-thousand-square-foot apartment and was one of the most successful pension fund managers in New York—the youngest and one of the richest partners in his Wall Street firm. He had picked all the right tech stocks, exited before the 2001 collapse, then gotten back in very judiciously. Josh was the quintessential "catch."

They sat on the small sofa by the gas fireplace and near the window where they used to sit, she at her end, he at his. Immediately she curled her feet beneath her, which made her more difficult to approach. Over the wall-to-wall beige carpet lay a beautiful Persian, a wedding gift. The couch they had picked out together after they moved in.

They talked about her current movie, a tale about the desperate girl who is really a jewel, who starts out poor, ends up rich, becomes detached and even cold.

"And of course, as she draws from the hairy-chested man his buried humanity, they fall in love." Anna concluded her summation.

"If you're trying to make this your life story, can I be him?"

"Do you think I'm detached?"

At that Josh grinned.

Thirteen

High-Grade was one of the best auto parts stores in LA. It sold every imaginable accessory and part and also did custom fabrication. The building occupied a full fifty thousand square feet on a single floor. In front of the building a huge parking lot circumscribed nearly half of the structure and ended at a ten-foot-high stone wall. On the wall were signs, every five feet, warning of cut glass atop. Behind the wall and out of sight was a second Cyclone fence with razor wire. At night security patrolled the outer fences. The property was flanked by a large wholesale plumbing outlet and a retail lumberyard.

To the right side of the building was a break in the wall, a large iron gate, and a small guard shack. Trucks with parts came and went through the gate, as did Sam and his staff. Sam owned the building and kept his offices in the back—difficult to find if you weren't one of the chosen few.

In order to gain access a person had to go through the gate in the stone wall, past the guard shack, and through a door on the side of the building constantly monitored by cameras. To get through the outer door one needed a plastic fob to unlock the computer-activated dead bolt. After going through the first door, a room with comfortable chairs, magazines, artwork, and more cameras waited. If Sam's staff liked what they saw of you on the closed-circuit TV, they opened a thick steel door embedded in a concrete wall. If there was some question, you never got in and they called the guard shack for an escort off the property.

The entire building was concrete block, but the portion housing Sam's offices had an additional reinforced concrete wall inside the outer block wall, and lining the office interior under the Sheetrock was a layer of Kevlar. There were windows in Sam's office, but the panes were manufactured from the type of glass used on the president's limousine. The openings looked a little like tunnels because it was a full eighteen inches from the Sheetrock interior to the exterior of the concrete block.

The furnishings and finish of the place felt like a government office—practical, functional, not particularly expensive, and definitely not elegant except for the conference area, which was wood-paneled with built-in bookshelves that housed various collector's items: a ship's telescope from the early nineteenth century; a bread-loaf-sized Inuit polar bear statue carved two hundred years ago from the tusk of a woolly mammoth; a bronze sextant used by Sam's mentor, Professor Alfred Channing, when he was a young officer in the merchant marine; a ceremonial Tilok headdress worn by his grandfather Stalking Bear; and an original Leonardo da Vinci drawing of a partially dissected cadaver that, Sam was always careful to explain, had been made before the pope forbade the artist to dissect bodies.

This was where Sam greeted visitors. There had been a number of visitors in the year before he'd quit to go sailing—government officials from noteworthy gumshoe organizations of several nations.

All such visits were made to enlist Sam's help in obtaining information. These were by no means all of the meetings with these men or these agencies. Many occurred at a beach house owned by Sam, with Paul presiding in his place.

Only the officials Sam knew personally, and trusted, were invited to his office to meet him face-to-face, and when invited they brought no uninvited guests. Everything in life, even true love, comes with a price, and Sam had taken on certain obligations when he accepted certain data downloads from the government.

The government was no more eager to talk about their work with Sam than was Sam himself. Sam helped the government, and usually he helped a great deal, but he never charged a fee that they didn't claim was unconscionable unless it struck him that he should accept favors and information in trade.

Since the advent of U.S. domestic terrorism, the government had been extremely forgiving of Sam's legal excesses, especially when they were producing valuable leads on terrorist activity. The government never seemed to notice that some of their questions could only be answered by means of rather obvious invasions of privacy, such as the time he hacked into a national rental car agency computer and the suspect's personal computer to successfully thwart a bomber who had filled an entire car trunk with C-4 plastic explosive. By the time the FBI had enough evidence for a search warrant, Sam had violated the suspect's legal rights several times over. Hence Sam had to provide the government not only the necessary evidence, but also a legitimate way to discover it.

Anonymous tips may be used in the presence of corroborative evidence to support a search warrant, and Sam was responsible for many such tips—including leaving a suspect chained to a police station guardrail with a sign around his neck. The sign said: I DEFRAUD MY CLIENTS. At the man's feet were financial records in a box that proved the fraud. The state court judge ruled that the sign constituted a legitimate tip and created probable cause to search the box.

The centerpiece of the offices and the heart of all that Sam did was Big Brain. Big Brain's claims to fame were the immensity of its database, the speed with which it could be fed, and its ability to simultaneously operate for its own purposes hundreds of computers over the Internet. The secrets of its success, however, were found in the search tools and computer code that sorted and sifted the data and ultimately decided which of the billions of bits of information were relevant to a particular inquiry.

Even when Sam was off sailing, the data never stopped rolling into Big Brain, and the dozen or so technicians who worked for Grogg never left their stations. At the moment they were crunching and gobbling information about Grace Technologies and thousands of people associated with it and comparing that with information already in the database. Grogg worked to set out parameters in the software that would outline search modes of interest. This activity would increase tenfold with the arrival of his investigators.

Sam worked in a big room filled with cubicles and acoustical dividers occupied by all his in-house investigators. They seldom left the office. The actual gumshoe work was contracted out to licensed and unlicensed private detectives around the nation and the globe.

Sam sat behind his desk, a position he hadn't taken for months, hunched in front of a computer screen and talking off and on to Paul. Paul sat in a special soundproof room, from which he had been listening to Anna Wade's ex-husband, Joshua Nash, speak. Evidently he and Anna were having wine and talking.

Paul was listening to live feed from a huge parabolic mike aimed at Josh's window, along with the transmissions from Anna's cell phone, when she chose to use it, and congratulating himself on the results. Sam and Paul felt guilty about the bug in the apartment's sprinkler system and were trying not to use it. But the parabolic mike was iffy, and faded in critical parts of telephone conversations that were being used as tests, so they had to resort to the internal mike, thereby breaking the law in a more meaningful fashion.

The audio feed also fed Big Brain. Among other things, the computer was making voiceprints for future comparison and pairing the voiceprints with facial-recognition software, handwriting-recognition software, and signature-recognition software, routine procedure for every person identified in Big Brain's memory banks.

"They're getting onto the subject of Lane," Paul alerted Sam.

"She's working around to her brother. I can feel it."

Sam minimized his screen on DuShane Chellis and joined Paul in the booth. He heard a male voice, the voice of Joshua Nash.

"How are things with Lane?" Josh asked.

"You wouldn't ask if you thought they were good." Anna's response was fainter but clear.

"I guess what I'm trying to say is that if you and Lane ever—"

"Josh, it was a symptom. Can't we leave it at that?"

"Isn't there some way you can find to forgive me?"

"For the adultery or for lying to my face about it?"

There was a barely audible sigh. "We didn't actually—"

"Please, let's be real. It's been years. And we aren't going to discuss the gynecologic details of something more than three years old. For God's sake, I've had Lane for almost two years and you've had I don't know how many girlfriends."

A long silence followed. Sam and Paul watched the speaker.

"We gotta turn this off if they start . . . you know," Paul said.

"I know," Sam said. "I know."

Anna wanted to abandon the topic, but Josh kept on.

"Word's out that Lane is cranky. He wants a companion-wife kind of woman. You're a megastar."

Josh followed his remarks with a knowing but sad smile. She knew he desperately wanted sex. Before Lane, but after she and Josh had separated, three years ago almost to the day, she had given him that much, knowing that she shouldn't, knowing it would feed his unbelievable optimism. It had been a moment of insanity that she wouldn't repeat.

Instead she thought about Sam stirring his tofu spaghetti. She thought about the sound of his swimming behind her and recalled her utter certainty that he would follow. Then there was the shouting and name-calling, the competition, and suddenly she wondered why they had been fighting. Something stirred inside her, and whatever it was made her want to fight with Sam some more.

"Josh, I'm sorry, you really are a dear person to me, but I'd rather not talk about that." She watched him, feeling his uncertainty. "Please."

"Okay." He forced the disappointment from his face. "Well, we've got a great dinner ahead of us. And I want a few dances."

"As many as you like, Josh. As many as you like." He carried her wine to the table and acted as though it were a dinner date with a New York cousin. He had his dignity and he wouldn't bring it up again—this time.

She waited until the main course to bring up her brother and Sam. Being patient was killing her. Josh Nash had an armor-piercing mind. Nobody was beyond his reach when it came to information. He lived on information. If anyone could see through Sam's veil, it would be Josh. Just as important, he knew Grace and he knew Chellis. Deep down she still didn't know what they were capable of, and perhaps Josh did.

It took her twenty minutes to tell the story. Josh listened intently and waited until she finished before firing questions at her.

He asked about Sam's speech, his yacht, the books on board, and whether she had seen any personal records. The questions were exhaustive and he took notes. She told him what she knew: Sam had a Ph.D., likely in computer science. His father, now deceased, had been in the military special forces, his mother was Native American and had been to college. With the last disclosure she began feeling lizardlike.

"How are you supposed to get hold of him?"

"I have an e-mail address."

"What is it?"

"Firechief at bluehades dot com."

"You're kidding me."

"That's it."

"Okay, I'll trace that to a server some place."

"I want to know about him but I don't want to get caught looking. Above all else, you can't get caught."

"Are you sweet on this guy?"

"I don't know what we would have in common. I know very little about him."

"What's your gut tell you? What's the first thing that comes to mind when you think about him?"

"Fighting. Wanting to smack him upside the head."

Josh laughed. "This Sam must have done something nasty."

"He saved my life."

She watched the corners of Josh's mouth turn down.

"Come on, Josh, don't worry. I'll tell you when you need to look smitten. We aren't there yet. And you're too big a man to ever allow even a whisper of a whine to pass your lips. Besides, if you're going to be jealous, be jealous of the right guy. Be jealous of Lane."

"You know you are really good. You'd have me holding my head at my own execution and my decapitated face still smiling. I'll try to find out about Sam. Boats are registered. This guy told you things but was very selective. No schools, no Indian tribe. People can't hide. Nobody can. But this guy is sure trying."

"I know. God, I feel like some lower life form doing this."

"Why do you say that?"

"I promised not to talk and now I'm talking."

"You didn't mention that when you went through the list."

"I know. I feel really guilty."

"Listen, it's sensible to know something about this guy before you trust your life to him. Why was he in the vicinity?"

"I know. I know."

He looked at his notes. "The mother thing, if we

knew the tribe or the school, could be the break we need."

"But we don't. And if you ask Peter Malkey, the only mutual friend that I seem to share with Sam, he'll tell him and I'm cooked, so don't make that mistake."

"No hint of a real name?"

"He wouldn't tell me. Unless you want to call Sam of the *Silverwind* a hint."

"Just be careful." He paused. "What else? There's something else, isn't there?"

"Jason gave me a CD-ROM at the lodge. I was going to catch a seaplane that I had called in after he gave it to me. He was so serious about it I wanted to get out of there. It's the reason I was running. Jason is so mixed up by his paranoia sometimes, I can't be sure why he gave it to me. I'm sure it's full of his research. That means it's valuable to Grace. I want to take it to a mathematician that I can totally trust. I want to deliver it myself."

"With all the swimming did it get wet?"

"Not very. It was in a waterproof bag that leaked a little the first time I went in. After the first dunking I rinsed it out in fresh water and I put it in a waterproof Ziploc bag, then back inside the waterproof bag. After that I think it was dry."

"It's plastic. It should be fine. I can get you someone. Probably someone in academia. But you're right about Grace. It's their property. Trade secrets. No wonder they were after you."

"How dangerous are they?"

"I think they are business people. Would they kill somebody? No. They'll try to get their property back. This is really eating on you, isn't it?"

"Yeah."

"It was an honest mistake with Jason. You can't blame yourself. . . ."

"Well, I do. And now to top it off I'm going behind Sam's back."

"You have no ill motive whatsoever. You're trying to protect yourself and Jason."

As she left Josh's she felt guilty, nasty. There had been a little magic cord between her and Sam—something mysterious and indefinable. Now it was gone. At home she sat down at the computer and tried to compose an e-mail to Sam, but she couldn't think what to say.

Fourteen

"What are we gonna do?" Paul asked.

"Hit it head-on and hard."

They waited thirty minutes over some take-out Chinese food that Typhony brought from her brother-in-law's place. He was blond and hadn't a speck of Chinese blood, but he cooked great Chinese.

With one last swallow Sam picked up the phone.

"What have you done?" he said to Anna. His voice was firm but soft.

"Please, Sam, just trust me."

"I trust you fine. You have one chance. Tell me what you've done."

"Don't be a jerk, Sam. You're putting me in a corner."

"I'm gonna hang up now."

"No!" she shouted. "Can't you see I need some autonomy here? Some freedom. You're pulling this ridiculous macho crap on me."

"Listen to me."

He could hear her take a deep breath.

"I'm going to have a sponsor call you."

Before she could ask "A sponsor?" he hung up.

"Well?" Paul said.

"We call Peter Malkey."

* * *

She plopped the receiver into its cradle. She should have known what Sam was capable of. Damn him.

The phone rang.

"Anna. It was great to see you at the party last month."

Instantly she recognized Peter Malkey. The producer was one of the few LA people she trusted.

"Are you calling about Sam?"

"He gave you the 'Sam' card, huh? Then he likes you."

"What if he hadn't liked me?"

"Actually, whether he liked you or not, you might have gotten any one of the other cards. He's got John of the *Silverwind.* Sonny of the *Silverwind.* Or maybe Robert. I don't know them all. Those of us in his little club mostly call him Sam the History Man." Malkey seemed to search for what to say next. "This call is unusual because you already know him. Few people know him before they get this call, and most don't even know him after they get it. Sam works in mysterious ways."

"Well, you tell Sam to get his mysterious ass back on the phone. He hung up on me."

"That attitude won't work with Sam. Not even for Anna Wade."

"All right, what do I do?"

"You told someone to find out about Sam, didn't you?"

"Yes." She sighed.

"Who?"

"Josh."

"Oh, damn."

"What's that mean—oh, damn?"

"Josh still loves you. Everybody knows that. He's stubborn and powerful. Bad combination. Somehow you have to make him stop if you ever want to hear from Sam again. I can vouch for Sam. He's pure gold. Total integrity. Other than stretching the law a little."

"I'm not going to simper. I want to talk to Sam. Tell him to call me."

"A contest of wills. Okay. I told you I can't do that. But he says you have an e-mail address. Write him."

With that Peter hung up.

She typed out an e-mail:

We went through a lot together. You need to help me through this. I need to know you're safe for me.

She sent it. Instantly a reply came back, and a dialogue began.

Trust Peter.
I want to trust you.
Good, that's fine. Trust me.
I need information!!!
Good-bye.
Come back here and fight like a man, you weenie!!!!!

Nothing. Boiling, she called Peter.

"Help me."

"I can't."

"What the hell do I do?"

"Call Josh. Tell him it's imperative that he stop immediately."

She called Josh and argued for twenty minutes. Finally, hearing the desperation in her voice, he agreed to stop, at least temporarily.

She called Peter back and explained.

"Temporarily isn't good enough. Make him stop until you tell him to start."

Josh relented.

Her e-mail in-box dinged.

Good girl.

She typed back:

Don't call me girl.
Remember, Peter said to charm me. So charm.
Crapola on you!
Call Peter for lessons.

The phone rang. It was Peter.

"He wants to meet you in LA as planned, Friday at eight P.M., but you're to meet at the Fish House instead of the Plaza. The Fish House is—"

"I know where it is."

"Okay. There will be a man at your door shortly. His name is Shohei. Don't ask him a bunch of questions. He's Sam's man. He's there to protect you."

She rolled her eyes but said nothing.

"Also he says this about your meeting. Are you listening closely?"

"Yes." She sighed into the mouthpiece.

"You know, you're Anna Wade. You're above whining. Not even a whisper of a whine should cross your lips."

"Peter, how did you know to say that?"

"It's word for word what Sam told me to say."

"Does Sam scare you?"

"In the beginning he scared me every day."

"Does he bug people?"

"Oh, he bugs a lot of people. I'd say he just bugged the hell out of you."

Normally she was in control of everything and

everybody in her life. Even the chaos was ordered. Nothing about what was happening with Sam felt like control.

Growing up, she had not been one of those kids who kept her things organized all the time. Her room was usually a mess. Her mother nagged her when there was a spare moment.

However, at the end of every week she picked up her things, got all the books on the shelf, the clothes in the hamper, the papers in their proper place or thrown away. She started over. Thus, as to her physical space, she presided over a gradual deterioration of orderliness that was always recovered at week's end by a sort of reverse big bang.

Even in adulthood she lived that way when she wasn't traveling. Her assistant was to leave her worktable alone until the end of the week. There could be no inspiration on Thursday if it didn't look like she had been doing something on Wednesday. On Saturday morning, however, she and her assistant cleared her desk so that it was completely free of everything but the telephone and the letter opener. Things would be filed, put away, or shelved as appropriate.

Not only her desk but the entire apartment was to be put back in order at week's end. The magazines that on Friday were on all the little tables, or the manuscripts on the couch, or the week's opened mail at the kitchen desk, were all to be gone by Saturday morning. Normally Anna started before the cleaning lady arrived, feeling as though she had to get the place clean so that it would be presentable to the cleaners. Somehow this struck her assistant, whose back ached along with Anna's, as slightly ironic. Anna couldn't see it as the least bit strange.

People were different. With people she was much

more cautious because unlike things, people could not be put back in place once they moved. She liked the people in her life not to move. Although she found it disquieting, she discovered that she tended to relate to people on the basis of how they fit into her plans. If they didn't have a place in her plans, she tried to be nice, because she wanted everyone to like her, but she didn't want that more than she wanted to get on with her plans. That was especially true by the time she reached eighteen. It made understanding Jimmy difficult because he didn't have any plans.

After her father died, a slow determination began to build in Anna that culminated when she moved out. It wasn't determination to be on her own, or to be a movie actress, or to find the right man. It was a determination to *make* life happen in place of *letting* life happen. That was the only way she could later explain it to herself and the few others who got to know her well.

It seemed as though the day she moved out her mother began paying attention to her. In fact they began talking almost every day. That was the year she wrote the poem. She lied when she told Sam she couldn't recite it.

Day Care

"I'll take you with me," she would whisper each
    morning
and pull strands of hair from the slick of tears
that washed across my face. "Look,
I'll put you in my coat pocket"—
this made me smile, this way she had
of pretending I was still tiny enough
to ride in her pouch—"and you can come with
    me

to all my classes, then at lunch
I'll slip you little bites of my sandwich
and if I get a Coke in the afternoon,
you can have a sip" and I knew she would,
rather than leave me at the day care
with its broken games and pots of dried paint.
Because she knew what it was like to be apart,
like a valve of my heart had closed,
like a lung was slowly deflating.
Everyone else tore across the playground
howling and flinging sand at each other
as if they were born there, as if
they never felt cut off from oxygen,
as if they never held their breath,
turned white and damp, couldn't exhale
until someone came to take them home.
Here I would wait all day,
try to make myself smaller, try to imagine myself
wrapped in the flannel lining of her pocket,
among the lint and bread crumbs
until my pulse slowed to match hers,
until she began to breathe for the both of us,
until I lifted my mouth to her fingers for food,
went back to that place where I was a part of her.
I knew she would take me back, on those morn-
     ings
when she had to leave me in the parking lot,
I knew she would shrink me and keep me with
     her if she could.

Sam knew he had only temporarily cured Anna of
the snooping disease, but told Paul that New York
could dismantle the parabolic mike aimed at Joshua's
window and take it back to Anna's, with the result that

they would have two such mikes aimed at Anna's apartment. They would also need to get the mike out of the sprinkler system.

Next he went to work on the Grady Wade situation. He had run a credit check. Not surprisingly she had a couple of credit cards, but they were billed to a PO box. Sam had a cop friend run a DMV check, and that yielded a driver's license and street address.

Sam took an outdated e-mail address given him by Anna, called for Grogg, and asked him to do what he could with the old address. Perhaps when she changed e-mail addresses she kept the same service provider. When they breached the security for the service provider's database, they found her current e-mail address.

A random password generator quickly concluded that her password was "Tease."

They viewed her in-box and copied the contents. They needed to extract her deleted items and sent items. To accomplish their task they put an electronic watch on her line and waited for her to access the Internet. Fortunately it didn't take long. They sent in a retrieval program based on computer virus technology that went into her desktop to copy and then compress her deleted-items folder, her sent-items folder, and all her personal correspondence under "My Documents." When her computer was at rest, but on, it went to the "connect" function of her modem, and dialed up her Internet provider and sent an e-mail to Big Brain with a "winzip" file containing copies of all of her deleted and sent items as well as the correspondence from "My Documents." The virus then removed the sent-item e-mail that was the only trail back to Big Brain. Thereafter the virus self-destructed, leaving no trace and doing no damage to the computer. They called the entire process and the program a "Grogg Job."

Sam now knew substantially more about her, including her current employer. He called the manager of a cab company with whom he did business, and for a thousand dollars cash asked him to query all his drivers about the Gold Spurs, where she worked. An hour and twenty minutes more and Sam had the private phone of the Gold Spurs management, the names of all three bartenders, the doorman, and the owners, along with names of cabbies who knew Grady or the establishment.

Big Brain broke down the computer e-mails and correspondence documents, isolating all declarative sentences and focusing particularly on any sentence that included a descriptive emotional word or phrase such as glad, mad, pissed off, happy, heartbroken, and the like.

Big Brain then did a loose but revealing personality inventory on Grady, which Sam printed out and placed in an envelope marked "Spring."

In a few minutes they had a cabby on the line who knew the Gold Spurs manager. The manager was new. Very professional. A straight-up guy. One of the cabby's wealthy regular fares went to the place twice weekly and usually paid for the cabby to go in. Since the patron was a high roller, the manager came around. Always count on the cabbies.

Sam was on the freeway, headed to the establishment, in minutes; for another two hundred dollars the cabby greased the skids with the manager and the bartender on duty. (Of course both names went immediately into Big Brain for future use.)

Gold Spurs was a big sprawling place with a lot of limos. Money obviously flowed here; bouncers were thick and Sam saw plenty of tuxedo-clad floor managers. The place featured semiprivate rooms, nonalcoholic beer and soft drinks, chocolate-covered strawberries, and a menu of sorts.

Sam wanted Grady Wade, known as Mirage, in a semiprivate room. Normally the rooms would hold a party of eight and went for three hundred dollars per hour. Plus the girl at thirty dollars a dance for steady lap dances or a hundred and fifty dollars per half hour for friendly chats and lap dances, as the customer required. Before Sam went into the room he needed some background. There was a little bristling from a floor manager at the request for information about Grady, but it could be arranged for two hundred dollars—just local color about her work at the club, no address, no phone number.

Upstairs in the VIP lounge he found Nester, the so-called bartender who poured soft drinks. The guy was handsome, not too smart, and obviously spent the better part of his mornings pumping iron. Sam elected to go straight to the manager.

Two twenty-dollar bills got Nester to flick his head with practiced vanity at the office door.

Sam was greeted by a man with a neatly trimmed beard, a slim build, and a seemingly genuine smile. Not the sort he expected to find.

"I'm Will," Sam said.

"Come in. I'm Guy."

The office was nice, even plush. Guy had putters and golf balls in the corner and a carpet cup and fake green behind his desk.

"What can you tell me about Grady Wade?"

"You don't look like the type to get moonfaced over a young dancer." Guy smiled to take the sting out of the comment. "Or a serial killer."

"That's gratifying," Sam said.

"It would be helpful if I knew your motives."

"I'm a friend of her aunt's. I think maybe Grady needs some help, but I'm not sure, and I want to find out."

"Fair enough."

"Tell me about her. I mean about her, not how she wiggles her ass."

"Men admire her in droves. They follow her around like sick puppies. Her hair is golden, her eyes are the deepest blue. None of the customers can usually catch the sadness. They watch the plastered-on smile.

"She loves to please the crowd, she wants them all to fall in love so that she can walk away and leave them hurting, wanting more. She succeeds.

"She can smile and touch a head or pat a shoulder, and some old guy with his tobacco-stained teeth will lay his head over where that hand touched. He's trying like hell to remember what it was like to be eighteen.

"She likes all the downtrodden. If a rich man cat-calls a dancer, she'll walk up and throw a Coke square in his face. Of course I threaten to fire her; half the men in this strip club are here to watch Grady throw her butt at the door boy. Or they're sitting around waiting until she pats their shoulder, or if the planets are lined up right and the gods are smiling, kisses their cheek and squeezes their ass.

"More than anything else she wants someone to discover that she's something special and yet she's terribly afraid of it."

Sam nodded his understanding.

"She had a baby when she was seventeen. She loved that kid out of her mind. That baby was the light in her soul. Maybe she loved him too much. He died when he was a year old. Name was Jace. Dad's nickname as a kid was Jace. Her dad didn't come to the funeral.

"All the men move across the room to be near her. Her regulars, the guys with the big money that she goes for, have learned to be cool and sit in the shadows. That's how you get to be a Grady regular.

"Her dad has never come to the place but if he showed an interest, he could maybe motivate her to make something of herself. She's smart enough to go to college but won't. She is jealous as hell of her aunt's success and won't admit it. Since you're sort of the Salvation Army, I think she just started coke. Maybe in the last week. Maybe only once, but I think she started."

"When did you fall in love with her?" Sam asked.

The man laughed and shook his head. "Back when I was just a customer, managing another business."

"You couldn't land her. How come?"

"You tell me. Once when she'd had a couple too many Harvey Wall Bangers, I thought I was making headway. We talk but it doesn't seem to be going anywhere."

"Have you slept with her?"

"Of course. Not that it's any of your business."

Sam rose. "You've been more than helpful. Thanks."

Sam held out a fanned handful of cash. Guy shook his head and waved it off.

"Thanks again. I'm going to see if Grady can do something for herself," Sam said.

"Have at it. Once Grady makes up her mind it's history. You'll see. Good luck."

"I'll wait for her to come around," Sam said, shaking his hand. "You think I could buy her shifts for five days, starting tonight?"

"No need. She is a free agent. But you won't get to

her. She wants no part of her aunt and she'll smell you coming a mile away. I could talk to her for you . . ."

"No, thanks. I'll go down in flames by myself." Sam let himself out.

He parted with another twenty-five dollars to find his way to a semiprivate room with the help of a floor manager. Then he parted with the three-hundred-dollar room cost. At least the couch was comfortable. For some reason Guy wanted Sam to believe that he was a straight-up in-love guy. That was interesting. He read a magazine to pass the time.

Grady was standing over him before he realized it. "Expensive place to read a magazine, under that pathetic little light."

The way she said it, she sounded as if she were talking about his genitals.

"You haven't met me and already you don't like me."

"I don't like people throwing their money around asking about me. Especially ones sent by my aunt."

"One hour of your time—a thousand dollars."

"That's a lot of lap dances."

"No dances, just talk. You have to talk for the money."

"What do I have to talk about?"

"Your life."

"Oh, I get it. You're here to save me. That's why Anna sent you."

"That's right. And something tells me you want to be saved." Sam stood and looked into her eyes. "Now do I stay or leave?"

She hesitated. "What's your name?"

"Sam. Make up your mind. I haven't got all evening."

"All right."

"For another thousand you come with me."

"I can't."

"You can. I talked with Guy. He's got no objections."

"Is he part of this?" She looked surprised.

"No. But he seems like maybe he wants you out of here almost as much as you want out. I know you're in this for the money. There's two grand for you to come talk to me. Way more than you typically net in an evening."

"It's just business? Just talk? Nothing more?"

"Just business; go get dressed."

"I'd like to talk to Guy first."

"What's he going to tell you?"

"I don't know. What do you know?"

"I know a lot. Enough to care. Now go get dressed."

While Grady changed her clothes she dialed Guy's office on her cell phone.

Guy's first reaction mirrored her own: This Sam was just another droid sent by her aunt. When Guy couldn't dissuade her from going with Sam he encouraged her, and she thought that a bit odd.

"You promise to stay in touch?" Guy asked.

"What do you mean? I'm just going for the evening."

"Don't count on it. They are going to try to talk you into staying someplace, doing a head-trip on you. You promise to call me?"

"I promise. The minute they stick me with some shrink I'm out of there."

Grady hung up, knowing he would be climbing the walls not knowing where she'd be. When she found out she might just tell him.

Fifteen

Sam waited for Grady outside. When she came out, her jeans and T-shirt made her look like any other young woman on the more beautiful end of the gene pool, perhaps a little harder in her expression and features. They got into Sam's metallic-blue sports car.

"Nice car. Sixty-seven Corvette? Am I right?"

"That's what it is."

"This car has hot shit under the hood?"

"Yup."

"It doesn't look or feel normal. What did you do with it?"

"It's got a bored-out 427 adjustable boost twin turbo L 88 engine with a supercharger that brings it up to 750 to-the-wheel horsepower. We put in a six-speed transmission and re-worked the suspension with hardened axels, Eibach springs, and Bilstein adjustable shocks. We added the roll bar and put in the Brembo brakes. There were other goodies. The air conditioner didn't work after all that. I think that's why my friends call it the Blue Hades."

What he didn't tell her was that the windows were polycarbonate and would stop most bullets and the doors lined with steel and Kevlar.

"Do you really like the feel of the power or is it that you piss a lot of people off?"

"Probably both."

"So, tell me, what do you have against stripping? I saw you looking."

"This isn't about me or what I like or don't like or whether I look or don't look. But you can start earning your pay by telling me exactly what you think I think about stripping for money."

"You think it's a worthless degraded profession. That we don't respect ourselves. That we're druggies and junkies or women who for some reason or other hate men and don't mind taking advantage of a bunch of dumb lonely pricks who spend their money on an eyeful and a pat on the head. Oh, and you probably think it screws us up for future relationships."

"What about the harmless entertainment angle?"

"You think a stripper has to act like a whore. Pretend sex with her body and her eyes. And that when she does that she cheapens sex and cheapens herself. And you're wrong. Sex is good; there's no reason but ignorance to be uptight about it."

"So do you believe any of what you think I think or none of it?"

"You didn't tell me what you thought."

"That's because I'm the paying customer here."

That comment bought him Grady's silence until they reached the airport, where he put the car in a hangar and boarded the Hawker 700 with her for the short flight up the coast.

The beach house was a tasteful place, slightly modern with a high side of the structure that faced the water and a roof that sloped back inland, not luxurious but stylish rustic. There was a lot of leather in the interior design. Sam had owned it for ten years.

"This is Jill, Spring's assistant for our class," Sam

said as they walked through the door and encountered a healthy-looking brunette with curls.

Jill shook Grady's hand and said hello.

"What's she do? Ménage à trois? And who's Spring?"

"The teacher."

"Who are you?"

"I'm your worst nightmare if you get out of line. You now have a chance to make ten grand for the next ten days."

"I'm not staying anywhere for ten days with a shrink."

"Ten grand. You can leave any time you want but you forfeit the ten grand. Yes or no? You have thirty seconds."

"What is your last name, Sam?"

"I'm just Sam, short for Sam."

"When you walked into the club you were Will or something, weren't you?"

"And this place is class and PE. PE is short for physical education. You had PE in high school, didn't you?"

Now Grady looked truly uncertain.

"You have a cell phone. Give it to me."

"No way."

Sam looked at her defiant eyes. "Either give me the phone or I take you back and your best chance to change your life is gone."

He could see the hesitation, but in that instant he knew she wanted to stay. She looked to Jill, who stood by quietly and nodded almost imperceptibly.

Grady handed him the phone. Then she took out a cigarette.

"No way," Sam said and snatched it from her lips.

"Who do you think you are?" Grady shouted as he emptied her purse on the table. Anything that could hold cocaine, including her cocaine holder, went, along with her cigarettes.

"Soon you'll have an investment in your body and you'll feel the same way I do. This morning when you got up and looked in the mirror you were convinced that you weren't much. So you and I nearly agree on something."

"Go to hell. What's that supposed to mean?"

"I'll tell you tomorrow."

"When do I get my phone back?"

"Whenever you want it, you just tell me that you give up."

"Bastard."

"You and your aunt share something anyway."

Sam left so that Grady could begin class; he called Anna. "I've met Grady. She's agreed to start a program. Which is a big deal. But of course it can go bad at any time. We had the little conflict of wills and she decided to stay."

"Well, hello to you too. It was nice of you to call me, what with your busy schedule. Now what are you doing with Grady?"

"I have a counselor, Spring, and a trainer, Jill, and they will work on her body and mind."

"Where is she now?"

"A beach house."

"How long will this last?"

"We shouldn't leave her at the beach house very long. Three or four days and we move her. Chellis and company are in all likelihood keeping tabs on her because if she ever gets on your side, your chances of getting a court order and custody of Jason increase— even in France. They're liable to do something when they discover she's gone."

"You think they'll know?"

"We have to assume they will."

"Where will she go next?"

"The mountains, where nobody can find her."

"Are these the mountains of your tribe?"

"My family?"

"Yeah."

"Your contract will specify that I don't reveal information about myself or my family."

"I want to go with you when you take her."

"Why?"

"She's my niece."

"I don't believe that's the reason."

"It's a good enough reason."

"You're in New York."

"So I'll come early."

Sam disconnected. There'd be time enough to argue later.

Anna organized her day, first in her mind, then on a list. She made lists but never referred to them because she had exceptional recall for any writing whether a movie script or a grocery list. First on the list was to try Jason's satellite phone. She had no idea what to expect.

"Hello, sis," he said.

"Jason." She was elated. "How are you?"

"Just fine. Holding them off. Crackin' the whackers."

"And what are the whackers these days?"

"Modeling a mind."

"Sounds good." She realized she'd had no idea what to say if she got hold of him.

"Did you know that at birth the brain has a hundred billion neuron cells? Each neuron is connected to ten thousand or fifteen thousand other neurons for incoming signals. Your brain, Anna, may just be the most complex thing in the universe. And here I am, thinking I'm the guy to unravel it. Ha! Me, a guy who spends his days fending off Nannites. I can see why they live in the DNA, though. . . . Are you there?"

"I'm listening."

"Right now I'm dealing with electrons, photons, and morons. The morons are the most difficult."

"Chellis's people?"

"I tell them that silicon is crap. Carbon atoms would be much better until we get a handle on a quantum computer. This carbon is molecular-level stuff. Then again, the Nannites may not want us cracking every riddle, depriving the universe of its mysteries. Quirky buggers, them. Quarky, for that matter—"

"Jason?"

"What?"

"I need to ask you something."

"Okay."

"Did you shoot your rocket launcher at a boat the other night?"

"Roberto wasn't really clear on that. He told me it was a Nannite ship, but that was just to humor me. I did it for the tension release. It was a good-looking tub for a derelict. I told Roberto what he wanted to hear about blowing up the Nannites. You know, ho, ho, ho. They patronize me constantly."

"Did you also shoot a cabin?"

"Cabin? Uh-uh."

"The cabin on Sonoma Island."

"Nope. Cabins were never on the menu." Jason paused and she could hear whispers. "Here, Roberto wants to talk."

"Hello? Anna?" Roberto said. "How are you?"

"Just fine. I was enjoying my talk with Jason."

"I'll put him right back on. We are still, you know, concerned about the mix-up. Especially about your friend. If he's going to report Jason, then we should—"

"He's not reporting anybody. Our only concern at this point is Jason and his welfare. I'd like to speak with him again, if you don't mind."

"Ah, well, I see that he's wandered off to his workroom. You know how that goes. Call back about noon. He takes his midday break like clockwork."

She was about to insist he put Jason on when the doorbell rang. Genevieve checked the video screen and inquired about the visitor.

"There's a gentleman here to see you. His name is Shohei. He says he was sent by Sam of the *Silverwind*."

Anna started to tell Roberto to forget about it, but he'd already hung up.

"Ask him how I can be sure Sam really sent him."

There was a pause. "He's talking to someone on a cell phone. Here, you listen." Genevieve turned up the intercom.

"Sam says not to take a cold shower without his help, whatever that means."

"Let him in."

Sooner than she would have expected, a square-shouldered Japanese man perhaps five feet ten inches tall walked into her apartment.

"How did you get up here without the doorman announcing you?"

"He was occupied. I would have . . . let in myself . . . but I did not wish to startle you."

"I'm Anna. Now how do you know Sam?"

"Call me Shohei. I see you do not know rules."

"I thought I wasn't supposed to tell strangers about him. Surely that doesn't apply to you?"

"Ah, yes. Apply to me. Apply to everybody from sea to sea. But you seem, ah, troubled. What you want to know?"

"Everything."

"That would be a lot. I will check make sure things okay. Then I will make rounds. There are men outside."

"Men outside?"

"Yes. They are, I believe, from France."

"How do you know that?"

"Wallet mainly. In amongst American dollars there was French currency. And the clothes. Particularly the shoes."

"How did you look at their wallets?"

"One of them went to sleep."

"Just like that, he took a nap?"

"Temporary lack of blood supply to brain. If you wish to leave apartment we will discuss. We will always have plan and you will always follow the plan."

"What did Sam say to do if I want to do my own thing?"

"I say good-bye. Sam say good-bye."

"You know that man has me over a barrel and I don't like it."

"Why you so angry? Relax. Listen to music. Burn incense. Sam is helping you. Believe me."

"Tell me about this woman Spring who's helping with my niece."

"Spring is very smart lady. A psychologist. And Jill. Jill the challenger."

"Does he work with Spring all the time?"

"Yes. When needed. Spring is Sam's mother. But that is secret."

"Oh. Now that is interesting."

"Yes. And I say too much."

As the day wore on, Shohei moved like a shadow that came and went with the movement of the sun. After a time she almost quit noticing him. Often he stayed outside.

She called Lane and concluded he was pissed because she couldn't come and see him. The discussion didn't end particularly well, which wasn't surprising. Their relationship wasn't ending well.

The rest of the afternoon she memorized lines, muttering scenes over and over, trying to get in a groove with her new character. For two hours she took no calls; at about 4:00 she began returning them. At 4:30 Joshua called. Although he had ended the Sam investigation, he had looked into Dr. Carl Fielding, the applied mathematician Jason had requested by name. Josh had used contacts in the securities industry to get to people close to Fielding, and he'd arranged for Fielding to meet Anna at the Carter Building at 9:30 in the morning. She made an appointment with her hairstylist for 10:45 A.M., as a cover story to feed Shohei.

"It's time for a plan," she said to Shohei.

"You go out?"

"Hair studio. Tomorrow at 10:45 A.M. After my first calls and the mail."

"I see. What is the address?"

"Genevieve has it. It's on Fifth Avenue."

"We're gonna have people following. You like disguise?"

Anna smiled. "I'm an actress. What do you think?"

Anna found herself enjoying Shohei. He was a smart man with a deep sense of humor. Shohei rocked her boat.

She tried on a big floppy hat and sunglasses, the old standby.

"Ah, Anna with a hat," he said.

"How about we just let them follow us?"

"Fine by me. I call Sam."

"Wait a minute. If we were going to call him anyway, why did we just have that conversation? I thought it was you and me. Shohei and Anna."

"We make the plan but then we ask Sam."

"Whatever. I'm gonna be late. Oh, and one more thing. I need to make a little stop at the Carter Building on the way. At nine-thirty A.M."

Shohei's eyes grew wide and he looked into hers. It wasn't a stare but it wasn't a vacant look either. It was tranquillity. It was Sam's look. She turned her eyes from his.

"It is to your credit that you cannot look at me," he said.

"I can look at you," she said, leveling her eyes on his. But in his countenance there was a certainty that she could not match. Somehow he knew she was hiding something. She suspected that he even knew what she was hiding.

"How did you know?" When he didn't answer she thought for a moment. "The same way that Sam knew I was checking him out."

"You drop this little stop on me like big bomb. I'm not supposed to notice this, this . . . this . . . afterthought?"

"I need to drop something very important off at the building. It's personal."

"Your period is personal. We talk about the safety of my ass, lady."

At that she laughed.

"Why don't you cut funny business and tell me what is going on?"

"I just did. I'm going to give someone something at the Carter Building."

"Who someone?"

"It's private."

"I be right back."

Sixteen

Shohei stepped outside the apartment and used his cell phone to call the office.

"Call back. Tell the office to use safe-talk," Sam said. Shohei did it and updated Sam.

"Our rose wants to be watered. Hair, you know. Tomorrow morning at ten forty-five A.M. Oh, and she has little afterthought. She wants to stop for espionage at the Carter Building."

"Carl Fielding. Physics guy. He's good. I'd use him. John Weissman would be better. If we say no, she'll be pissed?"

"You got that right."

Sam seemed to pause to think. "Let her go to the Carter Building. Same with the hair appointment. I'm sure Gwen is still her hairstylist. She's nearby. Try to find out what these shadows are about."

"Hey, Boss, you pretty good. How you know about Gwen?"

The door to the apartment opened. It was Anna. "Is that Sam?"

"Yes."

"I'd like to speak with him when you're finished."

"Sam, you hear that?"

"Put her on."

Anna took the phone and headed back inside.

"Wait," Shohei said, "if you go inside, then you go in bathroom to talk away from any window."

"Why?"

"Parabolic mike. Window is big eardrum."

"Jeez, unbelievable."

Anna's bathroom was large and included a small sitting area.

"How are you doing?" she said as she sat down in her soft-cushioned wicker chair.

"I'm doing well. Are you behaving yourself?"

"Of course. What is our plan for Jason? I spoke with Roberto and he's giving me the creeps. Bad."

"We're gathering information. We're working on making an ally of Grady. I want to go get Jason and take him to another doctor but it takes planning. I need some Canadians with old ties to law enforcement to go in with me. I also need to make progress with Grady. Plus we have to line up a good shrink. It's all coming together and there are a lot of good minds at work."

"I haven't officially hired you."

"We'll work out the contract soon."

"Okay, well, it's hard to wait. I really want to get Jason to a doctor. Our doctor. So how is Grady doing?"

"Fighting. When they argue and tell you to get a life, you know there's hope."

"I see. A scream is better than a yawn."

"Exactly. And how are you doing?"

"Fine. I'm sure Shohei just told you that I need to go out."

"Gwen could come to your house."

"How did you know that? Did Shohei tell you?"

"No. It's my business to know."

"It irritates me that you can find this out so easily."

"Who said it was easy?"

She made a conscious effort to restrain herself. "Do you know anything more about what Grace is up to?"

"I pushed a contact at Interpol and got him to tell me the dark side of Grace Technologies. It is linked in some as yet indiscernible way, they think, with an international arms dealer."

"And what does that tell us?"

"Well, people like that are willing to break the law in big ways, and you really hate to find out that you are dealing with them. They tend to be dangerous."

"So what do we do?"

"We try to be careful and not get shot."

"I need to tell you something," she said. "I need to tell you how I got to where I am today."

"Certainly, if you've waited this long, now would be a good time to tell me."

"I had some resentment toward my father."

"Alleged perfection is always a real bad sign."

"When I was about nine I walked in on my mom and dad making love. Let's just say it was graphic and not exactly conventional sex. As an adult I have no problem with it at all. In fact as an adult I would have laughed. In fact after my dad's death my mom and I worked up the nerve to talk about it and we both laughed. But at nine it was a little bizarre. At the time it happened, my mother freaked, which probably didn't help.

"After that day my dad never had a serious conversation with me except once; it was a rainy day under the tree in the front yard. He put his arm around me and he told me he loved me. That simple gesture and those few words were the only serious communications that I received right up until the day he died.

"All the rest of the time he only joked. Just smiley and friendly but never close, never truly warm. Never hugged me or touched me except to pat me on the head. It was like I knew something and he couldn't wash it out of my mind. So I had leprosy or something.

"This does all relate to my brother but you have to be patient. When I was twenty my brother was married to Sydney. One day she comes over to the apartment. It was Saturday and I was cleaning up my room and trying to clean up the rest of the apartment that I shared with two other girls. It's kind of my ritual.

"About midmoring Sydney was ushered in by a room-mate. Sydney's makeup had been running and she looked bad. We had this conversation. 'Jason is seeing another woman,' she said. She tells me she found jewelry under their bed. After being with her mother on a visit, Sydney came home to discover the jewelry. I pointed out that it didn't prove anything, but at the same time I had this sinking feeling. And I hate to say it, but burned into my brain was the idea that my dad was, you know, oversexed or something. It was crazy, but I thought, oh, yeah, a chip off the old block. Then she tells me she found cocaine in his pants. Grady is only three and he was watching her and I freak out.

"Sydney made up an excuse to leave town, but hid her car and came to my place. Right in the middle of school and work when I had things to do fourteen hours a day, I faked an illness and we took turns watching Grady and following Jason.

"At that time part of Jason's work was in conjunction with a molecular biology lab associated with the university. Often he went to the lab for conferences although his regular office was at the university. On a beautiful Saturday afternoon I was following Jason when he walked to the lab but did not go in. Outside he met a young woman who looked like a student. I figured a graduate student. Although the woman was no knockout, she was slim and not bad-looking.

"Scared to death he'd catch me, but determined, I followed them to a condominium. They walked into the complex and with all the corners, it was hard to follow. Near the swimming pool they disappeared. I was pretty sure they must have gone inside one of the units fronting the pool, but couldn't be positive. It proved nothing, but two days later Sydney reported that Jason had gone to the condo with a woman matching the description and hadn't come out for two hours.

"Thereafter Sydney showed up at my apartment with a bruised face, the result, she said, of a fight with Jason. She had confronted him. There was some counseling, but a divorce followed and I took Sydney's side. I was convinced that Jason was a cocaine-using wife-beating two-timer. There was a divorce and then we had the custody battle. Jason's money paid for both sides. It got very ugly and I was desperate to win. It had almost become my fight; I was pushing Sydney.

"God, I hate to say it but I saw my dad in Jason and I just fought like a junkyard dog. Even Sydney, I think, was feeling driven by me. I remembered every bad thing about Jason that I could, and I used whatever charm I had on that judge and we beat Jason until he gave up. I never personally asked him about the coke or the girl or the beating. In court he said it wasn't true and I just knew he was a lying SOB. Once he tried to call me in the middle of it all, and he tried to stop me on the sidewalk. Both times I told him to go to hell. Now for the really ugly part.

"After Jason went to France he called me. I had just gotten my first really big checks from *User Friendly*.

I had money. And this is the part I really hate myself for. . . ." She choked but composed herself.

Sam was smart enough not to comment. He just waited in silence.

She cleared her throat. "Anyway, he calls and says that he's having some mental issues. And I just told him to quit snorting coke and he'd feel better. Then I hung up. Right after that he got treatment of some sort, from Chellis Labs, and then went off to Canada and I never heard from him again. But his call really bothered me. I think I waited a week and then I went off to see Sydney in California. By this time I was mostly living in Manhattan, although I was spending a lot of time in LA so that I could be with Grady. This was back when Grady liked me.

"Anyway, I talked with Sydney and she was kind of ticked that I was bringing it all back up again. And she started reminding me that we had Grady and that was the important thing. She reminded me that we had fought for Grady. Why did we have to rehash the past? So really my questions about the coke and her story about the beating went unanswered except in the most general way.

"Then things went along fine for a while. At the ripe old age of fifteen Grady got her first boyfriend. She thought it was serious. Sydney and I were determined that Grady was too young, and she was, and we determined that we were going to break it up, and we did. Grady has the strongest will of any child I have ever known. The apple of my eye, my little honey, turned into a tigress. Since she didn't want to hate her mother, she sent it all my way. Every ounce of it.

"Soon thereafter, when Grady was sixteen, Sydney was in a really bad car accident with a drunk who ran an intersection. We thought she might die, but she didn't. I went to see her when she was really bad, and she begged my forgiveness and told me she had lied about Jason. He had been talking about moving to France and it scared her. She knew there would be a divorce and was desperate to get Grady.

"While Sydney was convalescing, Grady begged her mother to place her with her Aunt Lynn. Lynn was what Grady wanted because Lynn worked, wanted the money that went with keeping Grady, and meant well, but had no time. So Grady lived as though she were eighteen when she was sixteen. And I lost her. It broke my heart, but I understood Sydney giving in to Grady.

"With Sydney's revelation I went after my brother and began visiting regularly and here we are today."

"Quite a story," Sam said.

"You're not going to go over how stupid I was, are you?"

"Lectures? Nope. I'm the guy who got his son killed."

For one of the first times in her life, Grady wasn't sure what she should do. A full day and night had passed since she had spoken with Guy. Her trainers had announced a twenty-minute break, during which Grady was to pee, think, and, as Spring put it, find her center of gravity. Spring, like Sam, was a force to be reckoned with.

Grady had only twelve more minutes in her bedroom alone. She closed her eyes and picked up the phone, determined to call Guy.

"Grady?" A knock at the door. It was Spring.

She put the receiver back. "Yeah?"

Spring opened the door, looking partly stern, a little sad, and slightly amused. Jill was with her.

"Why did you have to go and blow the rest of your

time?" Jill asked. "Now it's another one-hour run. Why don't you tell me what you are doing? Don't lie to me."

"I was trying to make a call."

"To whom?"

"It's none of your business."

"Okay. Well, you know the rules. No calls until we have an agreement about calls."

"And when does that happen?"

"When we trust each other," Spring put in.

"That could be a long time."

"That thought had occurred to us," Jill said. "Now start your run."

Devan Gaudet sat in the back of a dark-windowed van down the street from the Carter Building. The leaves were not yet showing autumn color, but the women were cloaking themselves for the season, and watching them was enthralling. They had style, and an aloof self-assurance that he found sensual.

An hour earlier he had seen a man named Shohei lurking around the apartment of Anna Wade. Shohei was a world-class bodyguard who sometimes worked for the man he knew only as Sam, a figure who was more apparition than man, hidden behind a cloud of emissaries, agents, and collaborators. This confirmed his hunch about the "Sam" who had found Anna Wade in the waters of British Columbia.

Had he been sure that Anna was involved with this man, he would have raised his price. When he last crossed paths with Sam he had nearly been caught, which meant that he had nearly failed in his mission. Having to move quickly made this one an especially challenging job.

For once the regular gumshoes rounded up by

Chellis had been useful, setting up first-class electronic surveillance from across the street.

What he was doing now was risky and he knew it, far more complicated than simply killing her. In the new America there were more police, and the slightest hint of terrorism would bring in an army. Laws had changed and the American police had many more surveillance powers and greater numbers and were increasingly wary.

He stepped out of the van wearing gabardine slacks, a white shirt, and a name tag that said BRICKRIDGE TECHNICAL SERVICES. He carried a briefcase, a cell phone, and two pens. Salt-and-pepper gray hair and a neatly trimmed beard along with gold wire-rimmed glasses gave him the look of a college professor. Inside the Carter Building he took the elevator to the fifty-ninth floor.

After a quick survey of the hallways, he proceeded to the roof. The helicopter was no surprise; the people he was dealing with were far too clever to allow themselves to be trapped at the top of a high-rise. According to his sources this was the only office building in Manhattan on which a helicopter could be landed and it required a special permit. Quickly he moved back downstairs and entered the offices of Dyna Science Corp.

He greeted the receptionist who sat behind a large built-in island that looked like a breakfast bar in a modern kitchen. He smiled and showed her his name tag, while she transferred a call.

"Super sent us up here. We're checking for spores. *Stachybachus.* There were some complaints on the fifty-ninth. I'll just be taking some dust samples."

"Spores?"

"Yes. If overly abundant they can cause a significant

health risk. But we can fix it, even if the concentrations are high."

"Well, that's good to know," said the young woman, a blonde with wonderful skin. She also had a name tag. Virtually everyone had a name tag these days.

The phone beeped quietly and she spoke into the headset.

He opened the briefcase and removed a tiny vacuum machine utilized in the collection of dust samples from carpets.

"Maybe I could just take a sample from under here," he said, coming around behind the island. She looked slightly dismayed at having a man crawling around near her legs, but soon got caught up in another call. He pressed a small microphone onto the underside of her desk. It stuck on contact.

He went down the hall to the rest room, where he entered a stall and set up shop. From his briefcase he removed a Beretta semiautomatic with a silencer already affixed. Next he installed an earpiece and commenced the tedious job of listening to the receptionist. It was a full twenty minutes before he heard the serious-sounding male voice of Dr. John Weissman.

He placed the pistol in the briefcase and exited the rest room.

Alder leaves of yellow and mustard brown were strewn in the trail and the wet had matted them like carp scales, making the forest run almost quiet save for the wet thud of tennis shoes and the raspy breaths of tired lungs. Jill and Grady broke out of the park and onto a three-cornered beachfront road where a group of small shops attracted tourists.

"I'm going to use the rest room," Jill said. "You be good."

Grady saluted, and after Jill had disappeared into the ladies' room she trotted to a nearby phone booth, punched in the number of Guy's cell phone, and used her calling card number to make the connection.

"Hey," she said when he answered.

"Where are you?"

"Way up the coast. Near Carmel, I think, maybe Big Sur. There aren't any signs right here."

"Are they holding you against your will?"

"I can leave any time I want. I'm okay. It's rough but I'm okay. I could really use a hit but I guess that's the whole point. Look, any second my keeper will be coming out of the can, and if she sees me I'm toast. So I just called to say I'm fine and I'll call for a real talk as soon as I can."

"Take your time. I know you're working through things but I do love to hear your voice. You need to let me know where you are, just in case."

She set the receiver in the cradle, knowing she could easily be caught. Then she ran toward the rest room door to put distance between herself and the offending paraphernalia. After a few strides Jill came out.

"Were you at the booth?"

Grady hesitated. For reasons she couldn't get hold of she felt very uncertain about her response.

Jill stepped close and put a hand on Grady's neck, then put her head next to Grady's head as if they were huddling.

"Look, I'm starting to like you. Don't let me do that if you're going to disappoint me."

For a moment Jill said nothing more. Grady figured she could be forgiven this one transgression. It was, after all, a nothing telephone call and unworthy of one of their foul punishments.

"You're a druggie," Jill began again, "and I know you probably still think like one—keeping that connection going with the old life. Calling your friends, telling them you miss the stuff. Come on, let's run."

Grady wanted to argue and explain that Guy was no druggie, but instead she put one foot in front of the other back down the trail with a half hour to go, too tired to lie or fight.

Seventeen

Anna sat in the limousine facing backward, as did Shohei. She wore a simple turtleneck sweater, a St. John knit given her by a fatally injured girl whose last wish was to meet Anna Wade. "Who would have ever thought that Shohei would sit on a seat with Anna Wade?" Shohei said.

"I don't think it's really such a big deal, Shohei. Wardy Long sat beside me, held my hand, and tried to propose before he threw up in my lap, and now he works in a correctional center making license plates."

Shohei laughed and nodded. "Okay if I be impressed anyway?"

As they pulled to a stop, Shohei pointed. "Look at that guy over there."

Anna peered through the tinted glass window at a wide-shouldered figure in a panama hat leaning against the concrete. His arms, neck, and chest filled out his leather coat. Sunglasses dangled from the open neck of the coat as if he expected the sun to shine. She looked closer, trying to discern the face under the shadow of the hat, and suddenly realized that it was Sam puffing on a cigar.

Without even thinking about the men who had

been following she opened the door, jumped out, and confronted him.

"You son of a bitch."

"Hello to you too. Shall we go up?" Sam asked.

"Where the hell did you come from?"

"California."

"Sam, don't give me a hard time."

Maddeningly he took her arm and started walking toward the entry. Not knowing what else to do, she walked beside him, Shohei trailing. They walked briskly along the sidewalk to the entry level of the building. They entered a large lobby several stories high and hundreds of feet across.

From nowhere two men appeared in the lobby, escorting them to the elevators.

Instinctively she looked back to the front door, saw several men exiting a dark sedan on the street.

"Are they the ones? In that dark-looking car?"

"Probably, but don't look at them."

"Why are they following me?"

"Maybe they have personal business in the building, like you and me."

"What floor are you going to?" she asked.

"I'm going to fifty-nine."

"And I suppose by some marvelous coincidence you're going to Dyna Science Corp," she said.

"I can't believe it. Is that where you're going too?"

"Sam, I have a private meeting."

"Oh, absolutely. So do I."

"Who are you meeting?"

"Dr. John Weissman."

"Well, I'm meeting somebody else."

"Whose name is?"

"I'm sure you already know."

Sam pushed the button for the fifty-first floor.

"Why are we doing this?" Anna asked.

"Fool the followers. A little—distraction—never hurts."

They stopped at the fifty-first floor and exited.

"Now what?" Anna said.

"The stairs."

They climbed eight flights to the fifty-ninth. By the last stair her thighs and calves were burning. She knew Sam was watching her and she could detect the mirth at the corners of his mouth. As far as she could tell he was completely unfazed by the fast climb.

According to the placard as they exited the stairs, the floor was occupied by Dyna Science Corp. Even the hall outside the offices was elegant with blue red-trimmed carpets, wall tables with blue vases, some paintings of the neoclassical period, and the occasional chair. Everything picked up on the blue and red, whether by echo or contrast.

"I want to attend to my business alone."

"Okay. We'll all wait inside in the lobby."

"I'd prefer you wait here."

"Okay," he said, but continued walking toward the door.

"You said okay."

"Okay, I understand you want me to wait out here."

"So you're refusing to wait out here."

"Why would I wait out here?"

"To respect my privacy. To allow me to attend to my business uninterrupted."

"Okay."

"Screw you," she said, walking in the double doors with Sam and the entourage following.

"To these people I am Robert. Don't tell them otherwise. Get behind me, eyes on your toes. Leave your hat and sunglasses on no matter how dumb it feels,"

Sam said in her ear. Instantly she took off her sunglasses and her hat and turned to look Sam in the eye, radiating her displeasure. Then she gave the receptionist her best infectious smile.

"Good morning. I'm here to see Dr. Carl Fielding."

The receptionist's face lit up. "Anna Wade. How exciting to meet you. They told me Anastasia Wade, not *the* Anna Wade."

"Robert," the receptionist said, still looking at Anna but talking to Sam. "Look at who you've brought us."

"Quite an event, huh?" Sam said.

"It's very nice to meet you, May," Anna said. "You've got a great place here and I'll bet that is your daughter?" Anna looked at a small picture on the woman's desk.

"She's my pride and joy."

"She looks to be at that age where everything is exciting."

"That's so true."

"What grade is she?"

"She's in the second grade."

"Well, give her an extra hug for me, would you?"

"I will. And I know you're here to see the professor."

"Dr. Carl Fielding. I'm wondering where I might find him."

"Well, I was about to say that Dr. Fielding is not here but he suggested you see Dr. John Weissman. Who also has an appointment with Robert."

"This Robert?" Anna asked.

"Well, yes. That's our only Robert."

"This is Sam," Anna said.

"Nickname," Sam said. "We just need one of the small conference rooms for twenty minutes. That's it."

"Okay, let's see. Two-B. And it's open for the next two hours."

"Great. Anna and I will be in the guest office for a couple of minutes if you could get that call going for me."

May nodded.

"We'll be right back." Sam led Anna toward a small office off the lobby. Anna knew how to allow her publicist and agent to handle her and her activities when she so desired. Sometimes it was easier to think about her work and not sweat the details. But right here, right now she wasn't going to be handled. She stopped and turned to May.

"May, did Carl Fielding actually speak with you when he left a message for me?" Anna said.

"Yes. Like I said, he suggested you see Dr. Weissman."

"I see." She turned to Sam. "Somehow this was your doing."

"Only partly," he said. "We can clear this up in this office if you'll just come and listen." This time she allowed herself to be ushered inside. Sam closed the door. "Dr. Weissman is the guy."

"And why are you the one to determine that?"

"Good point. How would you like to decide this?"

"I thought I was doing okay."

Sam stuck his head out the door. "May, is Dr. Fielding on the line yet?"

"Just coming, I'll patch him through."

Sam put a phone in Anna's hand.

"You spoke with my ex-husband, Joshua Nash?" she asked Dr. Fielding, by way of introduction.

"I did indeed. I assume we're talking about Jason Wade's work?"

"Yes. I understood you would meet me."

"Yes. I'm so sorry if I disappointed you by not being there. Dr. Weissman and I have been friends since graduate school. He would be most familiar with

Jason's work. We don't really have a handle on all that Jason is doing, but I could do you no better than John. I would have been there today but I'm teaching this quarter and I'm a little strapped at the moment."

"Well, thank you very much, Dr. Fielding. You've been very helpful."

"If you need anything else . . ."

"We'll let you know."

"So who do you choose?" Sam asked Anna after she had replaced the receiver. "Will John fit the bill? He's Carl's man."

"Carl's or yours?"

"You talked to Carl."

"Why didn't you just tell me all this?"

Sam shrugged. "I knew you'd overlook any unintended slight."

"Let's go talk with Dr. Weissman," she said.

"If that's your choice I can live with it."

John Weissman was a tall balding man with a confident smile and a fringe of once-blond hair. Sam immediately pulled the curtain over the interior glass wall of the conference room, giving them privacy from reception.

"Sam tells me that you would know more about Jason's work than Carl Fielding."

"He's probably right, as far as I can tell," John said. "Based on what little we know of Jason's work, that is. If this is about the modeling Jason's doing with the neurology people—trying to model consciousness— I don't think anybody understands it."

"Well, whatever my brother is working on," Anna said, "he insisted I take this disk. I have no idea what's on it."

"Well, we can take a look and see what's there, at least generally. Now why is it he gave this to you?"

"I'm not sure, but I'm sure it's highly confidential."

"I will say nothing. This will be a personal matter, just between us."

Anna removed the CD from her purse, now in a Bob Dylan jewel box, and handed it to Dr. Weissman.

At that moment Shohei came in unannounced.

When Jill and Spring went to town to shop, Grady was too savvy to use the phone in the beach house. They had taken her cell phone.

As she considered how she might call Guy, she spied two young men walking onto the back patio of the neighboring beach house, obviously contemplating the barbecue and carrying a large piece of red meat.

She would ask for a quick ride to the nearest store, use the phone booth.

"Hi, guys," she said easily with a good solid smile.

"Hi. I'm Clint. This is Seth."

"I wondered if I could impose on you to give me a ride to that store down the road. I want to get some orange juice."

"Yeah."

"Sure," Seth followed up.

"Who is the guy who brought you here?" Clint asked on the way to the store.

"You were watching?"

"We just got here ourselves and saw the Porsche."

"You should see his other car." In some detail she described the Vette.

"Who is this guy?"

"I don't know. He was hired by Anna Wade, my aunt."

"You don't mean *the* Anna Wade? Not the movie star Anna Wade?"

"That would be who I mean."

"You're kidding!"

"Relax, fellas. I don't even speak to her."

When they got to the store she managed to send Clint and Seth to find a patio hummingbird feeder, a marvelous excuse that came to her as they were driving. She went to the phone booth with her enthusiasm mysteriously drained.

"I'm still in the program. I'm doing great. Still can't talk long."

"Where the hell are you?" asked Guy.

"I told you, California coast somewhere." It amazed her that she was lying and she wasn't certain why.

"I want to see you."

"Keep your shirt on and you will. Right now you have to give me a little space to do the program, that's all."

"There's nothing wrong with you that a little snort won't fix." His voice was strong with an edge and quite different.

"I'm not sure that's true."

"Yeah, well, you're probably right. Hey, I miss you. I love you. I'd just feel so much better if I knew where you were."

"I know. I'll call soon."

"They are now two floors below. Temporarily confused, I'm sure. And not too subtle in their searching," Shohei said.

"Go," Sam said.

"What's happening?" Anna said.

"This is the part where you were to have kept on the

hat and the sunglasses and let me do the talking so May wouldn't have a clue that *the* Anna Wade was here."

"Well, I didn't do that. So how about plan B?"

Sam took out a radio. "Grubb in, Scott in," he said.

Sam looked at her, then at John. "If you want to escape what might conceivably be a serious risk of death or injury, you should do exactly as I say."

Seconds later one of her escorts from downstairs, a large black man in a suit looking like a linebacker on steroids, came through the door, followed by a leaner fellow nearly as tall and sporting a platinum-blond crew cut. Even in the loose-fitting suits it must have been an effort for the men's tailors to contain the muscle.

"One in. One out. Anybody strange comes that May doesn't know, stop them—whatever it takes, exclusive of shooting, unless they use heat first. Then kill them. Grubb," he said, addressing the black man, "why don't you stand out front? You make a good red flag.

"Anna and John, come with me."

Anna and John followed Sam out the door and down the hall, away from reception. Sam was watching May, as if to make sure that she didn't see which way they were headed. Glancing back, Anna saw Grubb take a position outside the conference room door with one hand in his suit jacket.

Offices lined the outer wall, each simple and fairly small. To their left were cubicles with four-foot dividers and the usual array of baby and spouse pictures, grade-school artwork, and the typical postings of office humor.

People were moving past them through the hall, looking busy and distracted.

They stopped at an empty office with the placard announcing Norman Rawles and went inside.

Sam closed the door. "I told you I hoped this wouldn't happen, John, and I'm sorry. But it's probably a little safer for you on the roof with us. On the other hand they will expect that you are there. What's best for the safety of this data is for you to use the computer in this office to upload it to your computer at the university."

"I can do that. Hopefully they have a fast pipe here to the Internet."

"It's a couple of T-ones," Sam said.

"I'll do it."

Sam called a woman named Olivia and got a password that would access the computer. "John, you are Norman Rawles until I call and tell you otherwise. Close and lock the door. Leave the blinds open. Start the download, put your feet on the desk, and call the police. Tell them that you have reason to believe a robbery is in progress. If you hear shooting call them again and let them know about the guns. Don't come out for anything. After the download is complete, hide that CD in a drawer or the computer. Don't take it out until you leave. Got it?"

"Got it."

"Look natural and absentminded, like you haven't a care in the world. Come on, Anna."

At the end of the hall a placard announced the offices of one Oscar Feldman, obviously an executive.

Sam and Anna walked in. "Head down, hat on, and stay behind me," he said.

Oscar, a balding man with black bushy brows, barely had time to open his mouth in surprise. Sam beelined for a back door that led to a hallway with rest rooms and janitorial and utility rooms. They came to a plainly marked door with a green sign that said

ROOF—HELIPORT. Through this door they came to another hall, which led to a set of stairs.

"You've been here before."

"Yes."

"I thought it was illegal to land helicopters on rooftops in Manhattan."

"It is. But this building has always had one and if you know the right Feds you can get a permit. Cost me a big favor, though."

As they climbed the stairs, Shohei fell in behind them. On the roof waited a large, white Bell jet ranger helicopter.

Sam paused, turned to Shohei. "It was supposed to be a twin engine."

Shohei shrugged. "I don't know how they screwed it up."

"I never put my clients in a single-engine anything. We're not going."

Shohei appeared surprised but nodded agreement.

"Tell the pilots to leave or stay; their choice. Tell them there is danger."

Shohei ran to the chopper. Anna studied Sam, who frowned and studied the roof.

She let her eyes follow his. Well out of rotor range, the roof accommodated the house over the stairwell, an elevator room, a storage room, and beyond these a lounging area complete with a planter box garden. The patio furniture was bolted down.

The helicopter began to make a loud whining.

"Now what?" she said above the din. "How do we get out of here?"

Sam handed his radio to Shohei. "You might want to tell Scott and Grubb to follow those guys up here."

Just then the chopper lifted off, climbing steeply and away from the building. Perhaps three hundred yards from the building the jet engine skipped horribly, went silent, and the bird dropped with its rotors nearly motionless. A loud crash came from the street level a quarter mile or more distant.

"Come on, come on," Sam said to a stunned Anna. "I need your shoes." She looked bewildered but took them off. Inside the utility building in the far corner, Sam found a green tarp and some sacks of fertilizer and vermiculite for the potted flowers. Turning the shoes upside down to create the appearance of someone kneeling, he jammed the heels under the bags and allowed the very tips of the soles at the toe end to protrude from under the tarp. With the tarp over the bags it was a powerful and convincing illusion.

"Sam, what are you doing?" He was rummaging through some tools; he pulled out a big wrench.

"Stay here," Sam said, walking out the door to the elevator building. Sam used the wrench to break off the door handle with one big whack. The building was a mechanical room for the elevator motor, the cables, and assorted equipment.

Sam returned and grabbed a ladder from against the wall.

"Crawl up on the shelf," he said.

"What are you gonna do?" she asked as she climbed.

"I'm going to invite some gentleman to beat me up. We hope it will be a form of aversion therapy. Shohei will be right here and he will make sure that nobody hurts you."

"I don't get it."

"Self-defense is the only way we can legally break their body parts."

Eighteen

Things were not going well for Gaudet. When he exited the rest room he saw Chellis's little squad standing outside the glass entry door to the Dyna Science offices. He didn't want them coming in and making people nervous. Reversing course, he got on the cell as he went back to the rest room.

"Go up to the roof. Verify that Anna and her group have left in the chopper. If they are still there call me. Don't kill them unless and until I say so." There was a second part to the plan, if they didn't take the chopper. The backup was known only to Gaudet and he savored it. But he detested being thrown into a situation where he had to work with others. He hoped the morons could follow instructions.

Anna's group had left an obvious meat man outside a conference room door. Good trick. Two seconds later a big blond athletic sort, the guy who no doubt could hook and jab in blurs, exited and Gaudet breathed a sigh of relief. Then he realized they also might be headed for the roof. With a throng of body mechanics up top he couldn't be sure what would happen.

Gaudet peeked in on the man who'd met with Sam and Anna Wade. The good doctor looked like the real thing with his feet up on the desk, talking on the telephone. Gaudet walked swiftly but calmly to May at reception.

"I need to get into the offices and I forgot my fob. At the end of the hall they told me I might obtain a general-purpose fob that will access the various office doors."

"For all but the executive offices," she said. "I'll need to check with Olivia or Mr. Feldman, though, before I hand it out. I'm sure you're authorized, but they are so careful about giving these to contract maintenance personnel."

"Of course. Maybe you could just come with me to Olivia's desk? They asked if I'd go get you."

She looked uncertain but rose anyway, then touched a button on her phone.

"Grace, could you handle the calls for a minute? I'm going down to see Olivia."

As they walked down the hall, Gaudet waited until they were twenty feet from the women's rest room and glanced around. No one was in the hall. Taking a significant risk—something he almost never did— he clipped her at the base of the skull and erased her consciousness, grabbing her as she slumped forward. Likely she would remember at least some events just prior to the blow. If it were not for his beard it would be a real problem, but then he never worked as himself. Quickly he pulled her into the tiled and mostly pink, beautifully papered, and wainscoted ladies' room, where he peeled down her hose and her sky-blue panties and set her on a toilet. To make sure she remained unconscious, he squeezed off her carotid arteries for what seemed like a reasonable time.

After locking the stall door he slid underneath, and could barely imagine his good fortune when he got back to the hall undetected. The plastic fobs were in her top drawer right where he expected to find them.

With the fob he entered the office of one Norman Rawles and had the good doctor unconscious in seconds.

After Anna was tucked away in the storage building, Shohei stood by Sam at the entrance.

"You should let me do this," Shohei said to Sam. "These guys too easy for you. Not even good practice. Besides, your arms are not even healed."

"I don't know, Shohei. You're good, but maybe a little light for a whole crowd?"

"You are just jealous."

Sam smiled. "Have it your way."

"Grubb," Shohei said into the radio.

"Yo."

"They show up yet?"

"Just here. But they turned around and walked out right after they came through the door."

"Where did they go?"

"Don't know."

"Pull your guns and get up here. I'm guessing you'll be right behind them."

"Roger that. Say, there was a guy around here with a beard, May said he's looking for spores. Some kind of *Stackybachus*."

"Does she know him?"

"Seemed to."

"Where is this guy?"

"I don't know. He went down the hall somewhere. Seemed like he was taking dust samples from the carpet with a little vacuum machine."

"Get up here."

Shohei removed a 10mm pistol from his shoulder holster and stood back behind the elevator house. Sam retreated inside the supply room. Five men came through the door onto the roof. They spoke French. All but one were six feet plus. The small one seemed to be the leader and talked on a cell phone. They were apparently interested in where the helicopter had crashed.

Oblivious of any danger, perhaps because of their numbers or just foolishness mixed with bravado, they made for the roof edge. Only one held a visible gun—a nasty little Mac 10. The others had their hands under their coats, looking as if someone had told them to dress business casual.

"Hey," Shohei shouted, and leveled his gun just as his own men burst through the access door, each with a semiautomatic pistol aimed at the Frenchmen.

"Drop the Mac," Shohei said. "Hands up." The leader was staring at the broken handle on the utility building door.

"Over here," Shohei motioned.

The foreigners walked over, looking sullen, with soulless eyes and tough-guy stubble. They appeared either drugged or bent on a good round of senseless killing. Sam was almost surprised when they let Shohei put them against the wall to frisk them. He removed two guns and a knife each. When he took the cell phone from the leader, the man snarled some words in French.

"Perhaps you suffer the pain of a bad choice," Shohei said to the leader. "You seem like you don't like me. This is your chance to prove it."

"Which one of us?" the leader said in good if heavily accented English.

"I think you bring all your friends," Shohei said.

"What about those guns?" the leader said, nodding at the two men with Shohei.

"They are to protect them, not me," Shohei said.

"I should throw you off the roof," the man said.

"You are free to try."

From his stance the man appeared to be a street fighter pure and simple. Undisciplined but not to be underestimated.

The man circled Shohei.

The leader muttered something and his men began to circle as well.

Shohei launched himself at the man that seemed most eager, his flying body shaped like a wedge with his left foot leading. Shohei knew to use power on a big target. Sam heard the clavicle bone shatter. As the man went down, Shohei passed over him, raking his face with a trailing foot.

The man floundered on the ground, as if for a moment he had awakened in a bad dream, then put the good arm down and jumped up. Without waiting, Shohei feigned an attack on a second man, but whirled, kicking the knee of a third man, dislocating it with the hard snap of dry wood.

The man held the pain with a tight jaw while his dark determined eyes followed Shohei, then uttered a scream while he quite deliberately snapped the knee back into place. This man had no fear.

The other two men charged with fists cocked. They came with watchful speed like experienced street fighters, but Shohei spun away, dodging their blows and breaking out of the circle. Now he used the wall of the storage room to limit their angles of attack. The leader launched a roundhouse kick, missing Shohei's head by inches. Before he had the striking foot down, Shohei did a judo sweep to the leader's pivot leg, upending him and dumping him with the hollow slap of flesh on concrete.

Shohei kicked another man in the solar plexus, the breath erupting from the man's lungs. He ended the motion by putting his elbow hard into the nose of the leader, who by now was springing to his feet.

Although there were many of them, they were fumbling for the available space, fighting apart rather than together.

Blood streamed from the leader's nose. Apparently the popped-knee man was moving and, judging from the determined line of his thin-lipped mouth, ready to fight again. Even the fighter with the crumpled clavicle was ready.

Too late Shohei realized the man who had been by the door was charging. The attacker used his shoulder to drive Shohei toward the building's edge. The man was a bull in body and mind, pushing him effortlessly backward, even lifting him completely off the ground. Normally a fighter would use the edge of a rooftop to his advantage by playing on the knowledge that his assailant would not want to fall with him and causing the opponent to disengage. Sam could see that Shohei's instincts were telling him otherwise; the man seemed ready to risk pushing him off the building to their mutual deaths. Shohei slammed a palm down onto the man's nose as they moved closer to the edge, but nothing slowed the bull. The second time he was able to rotate his palm striking upward with vicious force. It was a blow that could kill.

There was a near scream, the man stumbled. They were ten feet from the edge. Shohei moved his right arm overhead in a vertical arc, and Sam knew he would land the elbow squarely on the bull's seventh cervical vertebra. It was one of the hardest blows Sam had witnessed in combat. Then in a blurring flurry Shohei struck inward to the bull's throat, crushing the larynx. When the bull hit the ground he didn't move.

The bull's attack had moved Shohei away from the others, spreading them out. Their comrade's death appeared to have no effect on the remaining men. Shohei seemed indecisive. Like Shohei, Sam had fought many men, but these men were clearly blind to their own emotions and without caution. Neither the threat of death nor serious pain seemed to have any impact on their will.

"What do you want with Anna?" Shohei asked the leader, whose nose was literally spouting blood.

"I want only to beat you," the leader said.

Just then the man he had dispatched with a gut strike attacked with his fists. The first blow missed altogether, the second Shohei parried with his left hand, and before the next landed Shohei trapped the fist and delivered an elbow strike to the floating ribs. The wet grunt told Sam a rib had pierced a lung. Involuntarily the man's head snapped down, following the pain, while Shohei twisted the wrist, bending him farther. In close, Shohei brought a knee slamming into his opponent's face, then retracted the knee into a twisting back flip to move away from the charging leader.

Catching Shohei, the leader began punching fast powerful punches. Shohei stepped against the man to take away swinging distance, but took one punch to the jaw and two to the body. Shohei head-butted the man's nose, then smashed upward with locked fists striking under his chin. Since he had nearly bitten his tongue in half, the leader's mouth was filling with blood. Shohei put an elbow into the leader's face on the way to kicking one of the others in the groin.

Instantly Shohei came back for three successive punches to the leader's already broken nose, staggering the man before he stepped back to watch.

Two assailants were unconscious or dead, two badly injured, and the leader teetering woozily.

"Perhaps we agree that you and your men need more practice before we do this?" Shohei said.

The leader shook his head. They were coming at Shohei again.

"You lack the discipline to fight me. You cannot win," Shohei said, trying to enrage the leader.

His enemy with the bad knee was looking for a way to strike with his fists. Shohei saw an opening and kicked to the remaining good knee, knocking him down. He followed with an elbow to the ear. This time the man was rag-doll limp when he hit the deck. Over-protective of the collarbone that was by now twisted bone in flesh, the next man wasn't thinking about his lower body. Shohei went for the knee. The man was quick and blocked the kick. Shohei feinted a fast punching motion at the man, then whirled and struck him down with a kick that snapped his head and turned his eyes vacant.

Whirling the opposite direction, Shohei kicked the leader square in the jaw but not before taking a powerful kick to the ribs.

Amazingly, the leader was still standing. Sam could not recall seeing a man hit repeatedly with that much force without definitive results. Four men were on the deck unconscious; only the leader remained. Normally a leader in this situation would give up, but this man would neither quit nor talk. Instead he studied Shohei, looking for some weakness.

Shohei could hang this man from the roof and get nothing more than *Drop me.*

Sam stepped out from inside the utility building. "Ah, sir, I hate to interrupt but Japan here is wreaking havoc on France. Surely you don't want something more than your nose broken."

"I want to continue," the leader said.

Nineteen

Gaudet worked fast. Weissman had loaded the CD onto the computer and had been uploading it to a remote site. By shutting down the computer he halted the information transfer—whether in time or not, he couldn't be sure. Nor could he know whether a trained scientist might have learned anything significant from the contents of the CD.

Other than killing the man, there was no immediately available cure for the fact that the good doctor would remember that he had been attacked. There were several ways to create an accidental death scenario, all made possible by the supplies in Gaudet's briefcase. None would be foolproof, but each would create confusion and doubt. First he checked the wallet. No medical notice cards.

Opening Weissman's shirt, he was delighted to find a surgical scar. Quickly he checked the lower leg and found two more telltale scars.

He punched a button on his cell. Trotsky answered.

"Screw-up. It's not Carl Fielding, it's John Weissman. But we're in luck. He's got bypass scars."

"I'll make the call. No problem."

"It'll look like a setup if you change the name."

"Use another girl. Simone."

Gaudet scribbled down the new number and hung up.

He went through Weissman's briefcase and found a small, unopened bottle of nitroglycerin tablets. Lucky again. Gaudet had them in his briefcase for such eventualities, but it was much better if the victim actually carried them.

He took an envelope with one Viagra and put it in Weissman's pocket. From his shirt pocket he removed two paper coasters, each with a number written on it. He used the coaster with an A in the corner. He slipped it into Weissman's wallet. Slapping Weissman about the face, he went to work waking him.

"Come on, John. John. I'm a doctor," he said in his accented French. The voice displayed the concerned warmth of a physician. As the professor began to regain consciousness, Gaudet popped a Viagra in his mouth.

"Chew and swallow, John. You've had a little heart problem—this pill will help. Chew and swallow."

John made a halfhearted effort at chewing.

"Swallow, John."

John swallowed. Then he chewed a little more.

"Keep chewing, John."

Next Gaudet took a syringe containing a gel form of concentrated Viagra solution and put it directly into Gaudet's nostrils.

He popped two nitroglycerin tablets under John's tongue. "More pills, John. These will help."

As he worked, the bug under May's desk carried a new sound into his earpiece: heavy boots thumping the floor; grunts and words spoken in Spanish. Two men. They were right on time.

Gaudet had worked hard and carefully to set this up. These men believed they had been hired by a Lebanese businessman. It would not surprise anyone that Aziz might have Latins do his bidding. Samir Aziz would not send Arabs—it could take weeks to get them into the country using Middle Eastern passports. Samir would use people already here or hire Europeans or South Americans. It was such an ecumenical world these days, one never knew from which direction one's enemy was coming.

Gaudet took the CD from the computer. Before leaving he wiped all the gel from inside Weissman's nostrils.

When he closed the door Weissman was nearly dead. It was unfortunate that Anna had given the man the disk. She had killed this man. Gaudet shrugged. Soon he would kill her.

Sam watched the leader once again start to circle, two of his men on the ground, now groaning, struggling, rising to fight on. There was tension that felt like a quivering note on a steel guitar. And then, as if the place were growing too quiet for the stress, the access door to the roof slammed open.

Two quick shots and someone had put bullets through Grubb and Scott, their foreheads opening like exploding pomegranates. Sam stepped back to defend Anna. Two men dressed in black and masked rushed through the access door onto the roof with guns aimed at Shohei. Sam drew down on one of them and dropped the first gunman with a hit to the chest. Flak jacket, Sam thought. The sound of the strike indicated body armor.

The second man fired. A bullet sliced the air and slammed into Shohei's upper torso. There was a contortion of his face, a snapping of his body, and a gush of air from Shohei's lungs, as he crumpled around the wound. Sam shot even before he comprehended, parting the gunman's head in a red spray.

Things happened in a blur, with the remaining gunman firing too fast from the ground, first at the wounded Shohei, then at Sam. Sam jumped back into the equipment room, thinking of Anna.

Now diving and rolling to escape his pursuers, Shohei left a thick blood trail. The leader and the two others went for Shohei with the energy that comes with a second chance, grabbing him and making such a tangle of flesh that Sam saw only struggling bodies. They were a foot from the roof edge. Sam could not risk a shot into the knotted bodies.

Sam saw the remaining gunman jump over and behind a planter box. Without waiting Sam charged the planter and dived, certain the man was popping a clip. Sam hit the middle of the man's body and took out his eyes with finger jabs. Another strike to the head and the man was finished.

Sam turned to Shohei and saw him head-butting and kicking, throwing his own blood everywhere as he struck. The bullet had ripped a lot of flesh. Sam looked at his eyes, certain that the color of life was fading.

The Frenchmen were pushing him to the edge. Not one of them seemed fearful of dying so long as they got Shohei.

Having no choice, Sam threw his knife into the bodies, hoping he wouldn't kill his friend. The dull silver of the razor-sharp blade sank deep in the leader's back. There was a pause as they teetered on the edge; a quiet wind was nature's sigh before receiving her own. They fell.

Sam stepped to the edge.

His breath caught in his throat. Ten feet below, dangling on a harness suspended by two cables, an aluminum window washer's platform shone gray and pitted under the dull November sky. All three men lay on the platform. The two had their hands on Shohei's chest and chin, trying to shove him into space. Sam jumped. From behind him Anna screamed.

The platform shook and swayed with the impact of Sam's landing. One swift kick and a fist strike and Sam had the two men unconscious. In seconds the leader would be gone forever. There was no key to operate the electric motors that would raise the platform. Reaching down, he found a hole in Shohei's shoulder and compressed it with his fist. Then a second hole closer to the chest. Shohei coughed. Death was near. His face was ashen. Sam had to move him to the roof.

Then he saw it. Running down the first twenty feet of the building was a row of steel protrusions held fast in the concrete. The entire logic of a twenty-foot ladder on a fifty-nine-story building escaped him, but the fact of it filled him with hope. His soul was now slightly less bleak than the sky. Putting Shohei in a fireman's carry, he climbed. Anna's worried eyes peered down.

"Shohei, you look a little bruised there," Sam said as he laid his friend on the rooftop.

"Never mind," Shohei whispered.

"It was a great show until somebody brought a gun. You know I'm gonna be really screwed up if you die on me. Damn you."

"You should take Anna to see the cherry blossoms of Hokkaido," Shohei whispered.

"Please don't die on me." Sam heard his own voice crack.

Sam did what he could to stop the bleeding while Anna used his cell phone. He told her who to call. A helicopter ambulance arrived five minutes later to lift out a nearly dead Shohei.

"I'm going with him," Anna said.

"They won't let you."

"They will."

"We can't protect you as well if you do that."

"I don't care. I'm going. Do plan B."

"I have to go get Weissman—we don't have time to argue."

"Good, you can save your breath. Good-bye."

The jet turbines began to whine.

Sam watched her scream at the pilots, gesturing her determination. He couldn't imagine what she would say to get them to bend an unbendable rule, but he wasn't surprised when she climbed in.

The Frenchmen had by now all slunk away, or died, or carried one another off. He didn't care. The only bad guys who'd succeeded in doing any real damage were corpses. There was apparently a second player after the CD who cared not a whit for the French or anyone else.

Anna Wade watched as the medics worked on Shohei.

"Take care of Sam," he choked.

They ran IVs and got blood started.

"Oh, God," one of them muttered, trying to stop the bleeding with a plastic bandage.

They injected medicine, got him an airway, a respirator, blood, oxygen, and stuck electrodes to the part of his chest that wasn't raw meat. Anna saw Shohei watching her from the corner of his eye. His fingers moved like fish fins in calm water and knowing what he wanted, she took his left hand and tried to send her love. But she doubted that he was conscious for more than seconds.

"No," Anna said mostly to herself. "Please don't die."

The monitor that was calling out his heartbeat went flat. The medics grabbed electric paddles. As the life went out of his body they jolted it with current. Again and again they tried.

Shohei never came back.

John Weissman looked to be sleeping at the desk, but Sam feared the worst. He launched a flying kick at the door and broke the lock. In seconds, a small crowd gathered in the hallway.

He found no pulse in Weissman's neck. Lifting him out of the chair, Sam laid him on the floor. Weissman's lips were blue, his pupils dilated; he had a dead man's pallor. Sam began compressing his chest. An officeworker knelt next to him, accepting a small part in the grotesque theater unfolding before them.

"Breathe into his lungs. Two breaths for five beats," Sam said.

Another man came to the door.

"Call an air ambulance," Sam said. "You must go through the government to land on this roof." He gave the man the number. "Tell them what's happening. Tell them it's for Sam."

This time it was eighteen minutes before the med techs were down from the roof with a gurney. They took over, but Sam knew it was hopeless. He didn't want to think about the meaning of it all: Weissman's wife; his kids; the grandkids, the family dinners; holidays. The shared joys were now gone because Sam had decided to stick him in a room instead of taking him to the roof.

The police had arrived and were clearing the area.

Sam threw open the drawers, looking for the CD and knowing it was fruitless. His only hope was that the material had been transmitted to Harvard in time.

He walked to reception, passed a uniformed cop, but May was nowhere to be seen. Obviously the detectives hadn't arrived yet. With his cell phone he dialed John Quarrles, an assistant director of the FBI in Washington, DC. It took him three minutes to explain that he had stepped into a nest of bad people and was going to need somebody big to vouch for him. Some minutes later he had Quarrles's assurance that the New York office of the FBI would tell local law enforcement what it needed to know about Sam's and Anna Wade's involvement in the deaths.

Twenty

Jeremiah Fuller sat in his living room with his eldest daughter, her husband, Marmy, and his two grandchildren. Stacy made a pitcher of iced tea while he checked the steak on the grill and came back inside.

"Okay, Dad," his daughter said, "it's clear that your disease has taken a turn for the better. Can you give us a clue what they did to force the remission?"

"Who cares what they did?"

"Well, do you even know?"

"Actually I don't. It's part of the program. They don't tell you exactly what they are doing. That's why they do it in the far corners of the earth."

"That seems unethical to me."

"But look at the results. I need the pills in my dresser drawer or I get awfully jumpy, but that's the only downside."

"I just can't believe it. Before this you could barely remember that you went to the store for milk. Now you can memorize a dozen digits. More than any of us."

"Ain't it grand?" he said, and excused himself to the bathroom.

Life was good. He was in love with his wife for the third time and all his kids were more or less flying straight and level. Entering the master bathroom, he saw that the window was up an inch. Funny, this time of the year, with the cold weather, Tracy didn't normally leave the windows ajar. He closed it.

He urinated, still a little worried about the slow flow. "If it's not your brain, it's your prostate," he muttered.

In the mirror he checked his teeth, found the piece of meat that had been bothering him, wet his toothbrush, and gave a quick brush. He winced—something seemed to have stung his gums. He looked closely at the brush and saw a tiny wire. As he did so, his chest felt a terrible compression, his vision blurred, he swayed on his feet, and he knew that he was falling and that he would die.

There was an extraordinary brilliance and exhilarating warmth. In the brightness he called out to God.

Four men were dead, one of them a close friend. Instead of sitting depressed and drunk or mourning, Sam took a cab down to Greenwich Village and walked into Babbo, a restaurant known for its out-of-the-ordinary cuisine. Sam was after the Brandiso, a delicious white fish cooked with fins and head, then deboned to order.

The place was a relatively simple, long hall-like affair, white-walled and with upstairs and downstairs dining. It was described as Italian Nouveau cuisine—Italian for those who liked Italian, and Nouveau for those who enjoyed perfectly looped lines of avocado paste on bone-white china impeccably designed with a colorful arrangement of vegetables and greens that even included a flower.

Sam knew that a Babbo care package would help Anna find her equilibrium. He had persuaded Lenia, an assistant chef, to put together all the makings of a Brandiso dinner that Sam would bake at Anna's.

With the loss of these good men, he didn't care if he ever ate again, much less whether it was gourmet fare, but he knew it was expedient that they keep living in every sense. Anna might not understand at first, but soon she would feel the same.

Sam allowed Lenia to include some cream sauce for a side of pasta and a marvelous mushroom salad. He listened carefully as she explained the presentation, although he had no intention of following directions when it came to that. It was ghastly enough to think of flavors and appetites or anything of warmth and comfort in this time of mourning. But the fellowship of those who were fighters was imbued with an unwritten rule that allowed remembrances but no funerals. The mourning would be private; this dinner was to be a celebration of the life lived and a commitment between the survivors to keep on living.

As he waited for Lenia to finish he called Anna.

"You okay?" he asked.

"I think so." Then she was silent.

"Anna?"

"I'm sad. And I'm worried about Jason. We need to do something right away."

"We will."

When Lenia emerged, she paused a moment to look at him. Taking the bag, he kissed Lenia on the cheek, gave her a hug.

"Take care of yourself," she said. "And come and see me when I can cook for you."

It was when he walked onto the street, the cars beating the air into a steady whir, their lights tracing white lines and red bubbles in the night, that he realized he was struggling to answer a question that he only barely understood. As the cabdriver made a blur of the electric light marquees of New York up Seventh Avenue and through the incredible bustle of Times Square and onto Broadway, he gave up the pondering and decided to act.

He called Paul.

"Remember what we heard about six months ago—that Wes King believed someone had gotten to his software codes?"

"Yeah, but we figured we couldn't tie it . . . you know, just a coincidence."

"I was tired. Now I'm not. I want to dig it out."

"But we've got everyone, every resource, dedicated to figuring out DuShane Chellis and Samir Aziz . . . and how to extract Jason."

"While you are doing that, in spare moments, I want any connections between Suzanne's case and this one. Anything."

"Got it."

"How are we doing on Jason?"

"Good. The Canadians are on board."

"Did Harvard get the transmission from Weissman?"

"They got a lot. Some of it is encrypted. Quite a bit actually. They're working on it. You can call Carl at home tonight." He gave Sam the number.

They talked as Sam rode up Broadway to the Upper West Side. By the time he arrived at Anna's block, he was satisfied that all the minds at work in his office were focused on the right issues.

Inside Anna's building a security man, dressed in blue blazer and gray slacks, greeted him as he approached the counter. Another armed security guard wearing a side arm and crisp blue uniform sat in the corner.

"Whom will you be visiting this evening?"

"Anna Wade."

"And you would be Sam with no last name?"

"That would be me."

"I was told you won't be showing us any ID," the man said with a tone of disapproval. "But you might tell us Anna's favorite flower."

"Herb's lilies."

"Go on up."

Engrossed now in how exactly he would conduct the next couple of hours, he floated in his mind while his feet took him without thought to her door. Amidst all the death he began to think about being close . . . making love. He imagined seducing Anna over dinner. Shohei would approve, of that there was no doubt.

The man in the hall in front of her door, a contract private investigator, looked like he could wrestle alligators. The man knocked for Sam, and Anna opened the door.

"You feel afraid," Sam said.

"Kind of shaken up. They were good people and now they are dead because of complications in my life. But still I want to get Jason, to act, before something else happens."

Sam carried his package into the kitchen and put it on the counter. "It's easy to jump off a cliff. It takes more effort and planning to climb one. We gotta climb the cliff and it will take preparation."

"What do we do?"

"We're already doing it. I've got a team assembled to get Jason out of Canada. We're doing surveillance to see how much soldier power they have around him. We're lining up the psychiatrist, a guy in Seattle. There's a whole lot to this and we're going full speed, but if we just roll on in there without preparation we may tip them off, fail, and lose Jason."

"I guess you have a point. It's hard to wait."

"Right now we're going to make ourselves eat, breathe, drink in Shohei's honor."

"You say that so easily."

Sam removed the baguettes along with the mushroom salad. "Knives?"

"In there," she said. She sighed, seeming to resign herself to Sam's plan, and got out some olive and garlic hummus to go with the bread.

"Let me tell you what we've found out."

"Okay," she said as if willing to wait but not convinced.

"Pots and pans?"

"There."

"Let's start with the therapist Grace has Jason seeing. Dr. Galbraith. We found that he went to Harvard, apparently has no publications, at least of note, has practiced for twenty years, is considered an expert in memory loss, has seen a number of celebrities, and has been credited with some remarkable cures. We found several associations with public figures including a couple of press releases where he was named and quoted. Two of the stories concerned people I know and want to talk with because they were said to have made remarkable improvement. One of them was in bad shape."

"Were these clients of yours?"

Sam smiled. And set about getting the fish on a greased baking pan.

"Confidential, right?"

"I'm interested in talking with a guy named Jeremiah Fuller. Apparently Galbraith was Fuller's doctor, and Fuller suddenly got his memory-building capacity back in the midst of a nasty bout with some sort of memory-wasting disease. We'll see."

"I can't relate that to my brother."

"Neither can I. But we'll look into Jeremiah Fuller nonetheless. As for Grace Technologies, Interpol is interested in them. I think that's because of a link to this arms dealer, Samir Aziz. We think Aziz sent the two gunmen on the roof—we think they were after the CD-ROM."

Sam told her what they knew and she listened intently. With the fish baking in the oven, he put some water in a pot and set a colander over the water.

"Why would an arms dealer be associated with DuShane Chellis?"

"Computers are the foundation of all modern weapons systems."

"And Jason's work would be relevant if it makes the computers smaller."

"Or the rockets more accurate. Small and accurate are important in weapons."

It was too soon to cook the pasta or put on the vegetables. The fish would take twenty-five minutes.

"We still haven't talked about my terms."

"Well, obviously I still want to hire you."

"You aren't exactly a team player," he said, watching for her reaction.

"I'll work on it."

"Uh-huh."

"I've had the same agent since nearly the time I started acting."

"My dog loved me and forsook all others."

"Now you're being a smart-ass. Do you know what we're arguing about?"

"Not a clue."

"Well," she said, "how do I hire you? Do we do some secret society thing?"

"You have to have a sponsor—and don't give me a hard time."

"Sounds like AA."

"It isn't. It's practical and it's my system."

"Okay, well, that's Peter, right?"

"Right. And it's a minimum fee of five hundred thousand dollars, but that counts toward my twenty-thousand-per-day fee. That covers my time and basic staff time at five staff man-hours per day. More than that and it's two-hundred-dollars-an-hour staff time. The good news, I suppose, is that my fee drops to five thousand per day after I have put in sixty days."

"What about the days you're not working exclusively on my case?"

"I prorate, but you're my only case at the moment."

"So how much, in the end, does it really cost?"

"It usually runs six or seven hundred thousand a month if we're working steady and I'm not using a lot of independent contractors and staff. My average fee per case for all cases has been one-point-four million. Cheap compared to what you get for a movie."

"I'd like to ask how often you do pro bono, but I'm afraid you're gonna bring up that we don't do free movies."

"Or even give refunds on the bad ones."

"Ooh, you're nasty tonight," she said.

"I do maybe a free job a year or several little ones. Poor people don't usually have particularly complex problems."

"All right. You aren't cheap, but okay."

"Well, that's not all. You have to agree to my contract."

"What's that?"

Sam put on the vegetables and peeked at the fish.

"Let's sit on the couch. You should be comfortable

when you hear this." Sam took the two glasses of wine and Anna carried the bread and cheese. They sat close.

Sam explained the contract at some length, watching Anna's brow get tighter and tighter. Finally she summarized:

"I have to shut up about you forever, unless I get your permission to offer your services to a friend or an acquaintance, and to ensure that I don't make any untoward disclosures I have to post a deposit of one million dollars in stocks or bonds in Switzerland. My heirs get the stocks and bonds and all earned income and appreciation upon my death, and so I lose the use of my money unless you give consent for its removal."

"Hey, if you fall on hard times I can be reasonable."

"You get to know all about me while you attempt to tell me nothing about yourself. Notice I said attempt. If we have a legal dispute, it is decided by arbitration in the Cayman Islands. And if a court says that is not enforceable, we have arbitration in Las Vegas, Nevada, in front of a list of arbitrators all of whom, no doubt, know and love you, and if that's not enforceable, it's arbitration in front of the American Arbitration Association. Who's working for who here?"

Sam shrugged. He knew words would not help.

"And grown people do this?"

"Apparently you're going to do it."

"Okay. When will we actually go get Jason?"

"We leave for California first thing tomorrow while my team makes the final arrangements. For now we relax and have some dinner."

"But when will I see my brother?"

"I can't promise, but perhaps the day after tomorrow. I want to stop and see a psychiatrist on the way."

"The guy you've chosen for Jason, right?"

"Yes. Before you ask who, we're still deciding which one right now."

"You probably think I'm heartless. Your good friend died and I'm talking only about my issues."

"Jason's alive and we can do something. Shohei is dead and we can do nothing for him."

"Have you cried?"

"No."

"Does that concern you?"

"People who don't cry usually aren't concerned that they don't cry."

"Have you had this happen before? When your son died?"

"That was much different. That was a piece of me gone, so it was like mourning myself."

"Anybody else?"

"A woman I loved. I was at the funeral. I stood off to the side away from the crowd mostly. A few people I knew hugged me. I think I examined my feelings more than I felt them, although I certainly felt a great deal. How many people have you had die besides your father and Jimmy?"

"That's pretty much it."

Sam poured a second glass of wine for Anna, re-filled his own glass, and gave her the last piece of bread. He had gobbled six pieces to her one. "When Shohei and I went to memorial parties or funerals I never saw him cry. Out of respect for the dead he would go on living, eat the food, and drink the wine."

"Is that supposed to make this easier for you?"

"Shohei was a professional. He lived with the risks. John Weissman didn't."

"You can't blame yourself for that."

"I can. I do."

Anna put her hand over his.

For a while they talked of Shohei. Anna recited the events of their day together, the way he had smiled, why she had become fond of him so quickly. Then Sam talked of his first meeting with Shohei, their cases together, and tried to recite a few of Shohei's jokes, which were legion, all the while struggling to distill the dry sense of humor and the unbeatable confidence of the man.

"When we were together," Sam explained, "I felt a special energy, like we could do anything. I wish now we had hugged each other at least once."

"You never did?"

"Never. We usually nodded our greeting. That was us. Cool to the end."

They returned to the kitchen and Sam cooked the pasta.

"Dinner is about ready," Sam said. While they waited Sam placed a call to Carl Fielding.

"A big portion of the file is encrypted," Fielding said. "Ask Anna if she would know how to finish a sentence that begins 'Receive for yourself . . .'"

Sam asked her.

". . . the same sun that shines on your brother, the same blue sky that colors his river."

"Any commas?"

"One after brother," Anna answered.

"I'll try it," Carl said and was gone.

"Jason would know that I would know that Nutka painted it on a piece of wood."

"Intriguing—all these codes," Sam said.

"What did the police say? They sure were fast with me."

"I used some pull. They know they don't have the whole story. I told them it was international and that they needed to trust me. They used to trust me for a lot more than this when they wanted my help. I also told them that Weissman's killer could be related to Grace or Samir Aziz. They have no more desire to reveal your involvement in this thing than we do. I had to promise to tell them anything I discover in that regard the minute I discover it."

"What in God's name happened to the helicopter?"

"Well, of course it's not official yet. But a fuel line was put together badly after maintenance. It came apart and starved the engine of fuel."

Sam prepared the pasta and pulled out the fish.

"That can't be a coincidence," she said.

"Right now they're saying it is just that. We may never know."

Out of nowhere Anna said, "Tell me about the psychologist Spring."

"You haven't admitted you know she's my mother."

"Okay." She sighed. "Tell me about your mother."

"I wish she would put what she knows in a book. And I wish people could hold the book and sense the woman when they read her words. She is the best person I know. She is strong and principled and intelligent in her compassion. I feel humbled when she talks."

"Wow. That's quite an endorsement for a mom."

"She is quite a woman. But to learn what she is saying, you have to struggle because her words have to be used if you want to find their meaning. They are like bones, you have to add the meat."

As he put the dinner on the table, Anna nodded, not quite understanding.

"She is a Talth and the daughter of a Spirit Walker."

"What exactly is a Talth and a Spirit Walker?"

"Are we all done snooping around, calling Josh, or anybody else?"

"We are all done with that."

"Talths and Spirit Walkers can be the same or different. Kind of like a priest and a monk can be the same and different."

"Okay."

"A Talth can be male or female and they are a ceremonial and a spiritual leader. In our tribe they are thought to be the keepers of the secrets to harmony of the soul. They know the sacred places and teach the young people. Today not many young people are listening. Spirit Walkers, like my grandfather, are thought to have mystical powers; they are usually loners, but can be married, and they wander a lot. They dream. For them the wilderness is a place of plenty. By the way, I don't necessarily buy into the mystical powers part. I think maybe there are comprehensible reasons why it all works. Then again, you wonder.

"There is a story handed down among my tribe that life on earth was started by Wah-pec-wah-mow, which would mean something like Earthmaker in a literal translation, but we would say God or Great Spirit, and that Wah-pec-wah-mow began humankind through a race of spirit beings that held the secret to inner strength and harmony of soul. Spirit Walkers are thought to be their spiritual descendants. Sort of like a Catholic would say that the pope is the spiritual heir of the apostles."

"I'd like to know more about Spring."

"What do you want to know?"

"Anything. Whatever you'll tell me. Let's start with her legal name."

"Key-atch-ker," he said quickly. "Try to remember that."

"One more time."

"Key-atch-ker. It's actually Yurok, not my tribal language, because she was named by a Yurok Talth, and to honor the woman who named her she left it in Yurok. She took the name later in life—Spring, the time of new beginnings. It's also part of the culture of my tribe."

"What *is* your tribe?"

"We'll get there. We have to get to know each other first. Every year my tribe and some others have a sort of new-beginnings ceremony where they renew themselves and everything in the earth."

"And what do you believe?"

"Well, as to people, I guess I more or less made my living on the premise that people don't change. That's if you want to play the odds."

"Tough outlook, don't you think? I got the impression you were trying to change."

"Yeah, well, I guess I'm trying to beat the odds. What about you?"

"Lately I think the odds are beating me."

Twenty-one

Normally Salice is warm in early November, and this year had been no exception. Samir sat on the balcony on the third floor of the lavish government guest house. It was built around an inner courtyard with garden and fountain. On the first floor a large entry lobby led to a three-way intersection. To the right lay a living area for the women screened by a *mashrabiyya*, to the left a larger living area for the men, and straight ahead an open courtyard.

Designed so that Arab dignitaries might appropriately entertain guests, it had complete daytime facilities so that men and women could be separately entertained. The upper two floors were bedrooms and game rooms and Western-style multimedia rooms. On the third floor there was one less bedroom and a library of sorts.

In keeping with Muslim tradition, the decor featured no artistic depictions of people or animals, lest they become objects of worship. Paintings were landscapes only, with one exception—pictures of the emir of Quatram. Perhaps veneration of the emir was a pardonable sin in Quatram. Despite four of his men behind the door and another eight at various points in and around the building and hallway, and the safe-passage guarantee of the general, Samir sat and watched the tremor in his hand, felt something like a peach pit in his esophagus, and suffered the raw acid of anxiety-driven esophageal-reflux disease eating his duodenum. He imagined red puckered holes growing in the lining of his stomach.

Samir's anxious moments had grown so powerful that they frequently felt like pain. Often he considered putting a bullet in his head. To relieve the tension he took all manner of tranquilizers. By insisting to himself that his mind had been invaded and that his feelings were unreal and unjustified, he remained barely capable of making himself function. Despite the fear, he understood winning and losing, and he knew he was losing. Sheer force of will kept him in the chair where he had promised himself he would sit for twenty minutes.

When it got really bad, Fawd would apply the stuff from the laboratory on Samir's skin. Its effect was almost instantaneous. The doctors couldn't explain it, and were trying to discover some component of the oily substance that was the active ingredient. So far they could discern only that it must contain every herbal remedy known to man and certain trace hormones from an unknown source. It had obviously been carefully mixed by brilliant chemists determined to mask its individual components. Since the supply was limited and he was hoping for a long life, he used the magic potion sparingly.

Tonight he was the guest of General Al Mashriq, one of the emir's many cousins. On the table next to him sat a report on missiles available from some warehouses in the Czech Republic. They were old but serviceable and he knew he could sell them. He had tried to study the technical details, but soon lost interest.

Occasionally he used his laptop computer to access his e-mail account via a server in Lebanon. This time he had an e-mail, sent through encryption software illegal in many countries. Not in Lebanon. Tediously he punched in the necessary letters and numbers until the mail document opened. It read:

> *We have not secured the merchandise. Complications. The butterfly apparently had it and the scorpion went after her. We aren't sure what happened to the merchandise.*
> *There were many defective packages upon our arrival. Concern that consumers may blame us for defects. Other southern gentlemen involved. Prospect of picking up the merchandise is now remote.*
> *Can we shop at the other store?*

Samir wanted to talk to his people, but his paranoia made him reluctant. He didn't know who might be listening and had no scrambler good enough to guarantee security against the best intelligence services. The encrypted e-mail was pretty much foolproof, but even then he wrote only in silly allusions.

For days he had had men monitoring Chellis's Canadian compound. There was no doubt that Anna Wade carried something that had great value to Grace Technologies. Samir's people had followed her to New York, used listening devices, and by tapping her and her ex-husband's phones learned she might have a data CD-ROM that was to be delivered to a world-renowned physicist.

From the opaque message in the e-mail it was clear his men had failed to take the CD. Before they arrived, there had been killing. And some other Latins were involved. His men were concerned about being blamed for the shooting. Now they wanted to go ahead and take Jason Wade, since they didn't hold the CD as a bargaining chip. He knew from a separate message that they had planned to take Jeremiah Fuller, only to find he had died hours before, and they couldn't secure his body or his brain.

Samir sensed the hand of Devan Gaudet at work.

Furiously he typed his answer.

Fawd stepped onto the balcony. "What are they doing?"

"Everything. Nothing. We need to take Jason Wade. What do you need?"

"The general has sent something for your nerves."

"How does he know about my nerves?"

"With all due respect, during your meeting this morning you rose and walked around about one dozen times. Your eyes never stopped moving. Three times you caressed your side arm under your jacket. With all due respect."

"So what does he send?" Samir asked.

"I will show you."

A moment later he returned with an attractive blond Caucasian woman. She showed no dullness in her countenance; no dilated pupils. Intelligent blue eyes looked down at him with some interest.

"What do you do, or should I ask?"

"I am a masseuse. I calm nerves. I will relax you."

"That'll be the day."

"Have someone bring in my things, please," she said.

Just inside the balcony they set up a portable massage table.

"Please take off your clothes and lie on the table."

Samir eyed her. He had enjoyed a few massages in his life. He supposed he could worry as well on the table as in the chair.

The woman appeared ready with her table and towels.

"Everybody out," he said to his men.

Nude, he wrapped a towel around himself and told the woman she could turn around.

"What is your name?"

"Michelle. I go by Mindy."

"Why did my friend the general send you to see a man twisted by his own nerves?"

"Because I'm white. Middle Eastern and Persian men seem to prize white women."

"So what services do you provide?"

"I provide massage and companionship. If you choose to steal it, you can have sex."

"I don't take that from a woman. I am a wreck of a man anyway."

"Let me see what I can do."

As he lay on the table, the only things he could think of were the monkeys in Chellis's laboratory. Chellis was making a monkey of him, using some sort of science fiction to instill a terror that nearly overwhelmed him. Samir imagined what a world leader who felt as he felt might purchase in the way of weaponry.

The massage was good, but the conversation better. Immediately, and almost miraculously, it seemed, he began to relax as he hadn't since the day at the laboratory. It was as if this Michelle had the magic potion from Kuching. She was forthright and not at all slow-witted as he expected. As she massaged him, she told him her story: Her husband, a man from Quatram, had fled the U.S. with their child. She came to Quatram, tried to take the child back to the West, and was caught in Salice and put into slavery by the general.

The general had kept her for his own purposes. It was better than torture, so she worked with it and won his confidence. Samir liked her a great deal; something about her seemed to match something in himself. After the massage they talked and drank wine. Her tenacity with respect to retrieving her son was obvious. She was courageous, at least as clever about men as she was brave, and one other quality amazed him: her seeming inability to complain. Always looking ahead, thinking, plotting, never giving up, even in the face of disastrous circumstances.

At 2:00 A.M. she left, but they could easily have talked all night. It was only after she had left that he cursed himself for his own stupidity. She had to have been sent by Chellis with massage oil that contained the same stuff he had stolen from the lab.

In the morning he went to the ministry offices and met again with the general. They haggled over small arms and rockets. The rockets were a problem. If he sold them to Quatram he would be violating various international laws and treaties. In response to continuing pressure from the general he hedged. Then the meeting ended with backslapping and goodwill. They desperately needed him.

In the limousine Samir found himself longing for another massage and for Michelle's company. He called the general, knowing all the while that she must be a Chellis plant and he would be walking into DuShane's latest scheme.

"I am afraid I don't feel well enough to travel. I'd like another massage from that woman, what's her name?"

"The stubborn one? She's Michelle. She won't answer to her Arabic name."

"It doesn't matter," Samir said. "I just want the woman to give me a massage."

Michelle met him in the guest house within the

hour. "I would like to buy you from the general," Samir said. Her eyes showed hope, then went flat. "Take you to Lebanon, where you would be free. I should like to employ you, but only if you accept. I would try to see that you get to visit your son. And if you work hard enough and smart enough, I will consider helping you get your son back."

"I am required to give you sex?"

"No. Never."

"I am a slave. I cannot leave."

"You aren't listening. You can leave if I buy you."

She seemed to consider; then she spoke quickly. "I accept your offer."

"Good."

Samir called the general from the limo and established a price of $200,000 and the sale of five missiles. It was the missile deal that sealed the bargain. Already rich, the general was not so interested in the money— but he certainly took it.

There was just enough time for Anna to pack a bag before sleep. At 4:00 A.M. she would be going to the airport to meet Sam. When the phone rang, she talked herself into picking it up, knowing it could be her agent.

"Guess what I'm going to get you for *August Moon*."

"Whatever you negotiate. You know—"

"I know you like to pretend the money doesn't matter. Maybe you're not pretending. Anyway, guess why I'm going to get you twenty million."

"Because I have two X chromosomes?"

"Because you're going to get nominated. I'm pretty sure and so is everyone else."

"I wish I had a clever line for that one."

"You deserve it." Despite her deadline at the airport she remained on the line for five minutes, listening to her agent's assessment of who was impressed, who was not, who would be critical, and most of all, who would be jealous and whom she had impressed. These would be the factors that would help determine whether she would win her second Academy Award.

"They want to have a little formal announcement about your taking the part at the studio—and a party. Next week. Thursday or Friday. They're working the details."

"Okay."

"Anna? Will Lane be coming?"

"I . . . I don't think so."

"Will anyone?"

"What have you heard?"

"Nothing. Nothing. Well, maybe not exactly nothing."

"Tell me."

"Well, there was the story about the yachtsman, which you denied, of course. And then I asked Peter if he knew anything . . . and of course he denied it, but his voice said otherwise, or so I thought."

"There is someone. I haven't broken up with Lane, though. This new guy has got the worst case of hide-and-seek I've ever seen. He's seriously the smartest man I have ever met."

"Have you fallen for him?"

"Officially I don't know he exists."

"How does he feel about you?"

"He doesn't know yet. I haven't told him."

"Normally that would be something he would tell you."

"I'm working on it. I'll get him to take me to the studio party. I'll just have to work fast."

"I guess you will."

Anna took a deep breath and dialed again. "Lane?"

"Yeah?"

"This is really unfortunate but I need you to be just dead-on honest with me."

"Okay."

"Sometime here we are planning to have dinner. And I think we will both be jockeying for one of those really sweet, we're-great-pals breakups. That's what I think. You tell me right now straight out if I'm wrong."

"Who is he?"

"His name isn't important and . . . well . . . it's the fellow who is helping me with my brother . . . Mr. Secrets."

"Her name is Julie."

"Have you slept with her?"

"No. Of course not. I've barely talked to her. Well, maybe I've talked to her. And she went home before we actually slept."

"You're a gentleman. Go have your way with her. Under any other circumstances I would do this better. You deserve better. You are a good man and some woman will be very lucky. We are now officially good friends."

"Okay. You tell your publicist first. Mine will confirm. It was mutual, we remain best friends, blah-blah-blah. And there were no third parties involved. I do want to know, though. Did you sleep with him?"

"No way. Never even considered it. Until now."

Twenty-two

When she heard the whine of the hydraulics and the thump of the landing gear doors, Anna began the talk with Sam in earnest.

"What's happening at Harvard?"

"Your code phrase opened the file folder, but there are many other folders that are also encoded and they have to be decoded with a random-numbers generator. We're using Big Brain and sucking up the power of several computers. They did get a bunch of science, but of course everyone is most curious about what is hidden. Human nature. So we wait."

"I am excited about *August Moon*, but it's difficult to feel excited about anything without feeling guilty."

"It's like laughing at a funeral."

"Anyway, they're having a little party at the studio."

"That's great. Give you a chance to show the world it's business as usual for you."

"Right. Except for it to look normal, I need an escort."

"What about Lane?"

"We're officially just friends now."

"So?"

"Well, if . . . you break up and then attend something like this, it fuels rumors and starts talking. You just don't do it without some time passing, and even then . . ."

"Well, I'm sorry to hear about Lane."

"Thanks. There is a solution, though. . . ." She put her hand on his and gently squeezed.

"Oh, Anna, I'm . . . I'm flattered, and honored, but . . . rumors and publicity. I can't . . ."

"Yeah. I thought you probably couldn't, but it would, you know . . . mean so much."

"I can't."

"Maybe?"

"I think we may be repeating ourselves."

"I'm sure you are right. I'm sure you are. But just in case there is a way, maybe you could sleep on it. Not, you know, make the final decision."

"All right. We'll let it rest for now."

"Thank you."

"You're welcome."

A few moments of silence followed.

"Maybe you'd consider just arriving with me, maybe come in the same limo, then wander around."

"I would love to. It's just the occupational hazard thing."

"Riding in the same limo. Just being at the same party, maybe now and then talking or walking together. Look, I'm sure you are right. I'm a schmuck for pushing the issue. Or at least I'm feeling like one."

"I will ride in the car with you. Then we will go our own ways at the party. Okay?"

"That's cool. And really thoughtful. And I think a step forward."

He was quiet for a moment. "You're ignoring the fact that I've built my career on anonymity."

"Which conveniently removes many of the women that might interest you."

"So when you go to the store are you one of those people that picks through all the fruit, testing each one?"

"It's just dating."

"That's me, I'm just dating too."

"But you will . . ."

"Take you to the party."

The Seattle cabbie had a walrus mustache and spoke Russian. After talking to a Russian-speaking dispatcher, the man seemed to understand where they were going.

Sam listened intently on his cell phone to Paul rattle off the tail end of the report on Dr. Galbraith. Anna was trying to put her head close to Sam's so she could hear the story as Paul told it. Sam blew in her ear, causing her to pull away, and grinned.

"So you checked the title records and found a few million in commercial real estate?" Anna asked when Sam had hung up.

"That's right. House is expensive, no mortgage, no car loans, no credit card debt. We had somebody go through his garbage and find his stockbroker. He had three. We called all of them, claiming to be a friend and wanting to adopt the same strategy as the good doctor. We emphasized how much the doctor thought of them. One of them was candid enough to say that Galbraith made most of his money on stock options in Grace Technologies and the brokerage house had nothing to do with the choice. In fact they wouldn't have picked the stock."

"No kidding."

"I think we've established that he's well off through some association with Grace Technologies."

"So he's in their pocket."

"Seems so."

"And you're absolutely sure that your fellow, what's his name . . ."

"Yanavitch, George Yanavitch."

". . . has no connection with Grace."

"I am. Plus he's a leading authority on schizophrenia and its physiological correlates."

"And you think that helps because? . . ."

"If somebody were going to do something to screw up your mind, they probably disrupt the electrical chemical activity in your brain. That is a physiological process."

"Okay," she said. "When do we leave for Jason's?"

"Paul will have my friends outfitted and ready to go in a couple of hours. We have the intelligence we need."

The cab sped past Virginia Mason Clinic and up to a large brick residential-looking structure that was actually a suite of medical offices.

They paid the cabbie and got out. There were four psychiatrists listed on the bronze plaque by the door. In the offices they were confronted with an empty receptionist's chair, antiques, and a carpet that Anna carefully inspected. Checking the nap from the underside, she pronounced it genuine handwoven Persian.

"This isn't the place they do the scans and physiology stuff."

"It looks nearly like the office of an art broker."

"Yeah, well, no law against taste."

At that moment the receptionist returned and showed them into the office of Dr. Yanavitch, a pleasant bearded man, round in the face and with hair gone silver-gray.

"My goodness," he said when Anna took off the hat and the glasses.

"Pleased to meet you," Anna said.

"As between the two of us, I'm sure I'm the one who's pleased. Sit down."

They sat in stylish wooden chairs next to a large overstuffed chair that Sam surmised was the proverbial couch.

"I'm afraid we've had a little hitch."

"Hitch?" Sam said, immediately alert.

"I know you said that no one was to know about your inquiries. But we goofed. Routinely we get referrals. Our physiological work leads many therapists to want to eliminate functional disorders before they begin treatment. They want to work with as healthy a brain as they can get. Sometimes our studies lead us to recommend drugs that alter the brain chemistry and make therapy more effective. At any rate, my staff knew that Jason had been seeing Dr. Galbraith and unfortunately assumed it must be a referral despite my admonition. So they contacted Galbraith's office and requested records. That's the bad news. The good news is his office sent the records and I opened them before they called, in a panic, and asked for them back. I also, as you requested, have had several discussions with Dr. Carl Fielding about the contents of the disk. And in addition, as you requested, we have talked with others at Harvard and MIT."

Sam tried not to look sick about the disclosure to Galbraith. "What did you learn?"

"Galbraith's office said they'd need the consent of the patient's guardian for me to release their information to Anna Wade or anyone else. And they asked for it back."

"But you didn't mention the disk."

"That never came up."

"Uh-huh," Sam said. "We have a lot of resistance from those responsible for Jason. Anna is his sister. Maybe without going into specifics you could tell us what might account for Jason's behavioral problems."

"Well, let's just assume he's paranoid as you describe, nervous, afraid, makes up imaginary enemies, and so on. But otherwise he's brilliant. To tell you the truth, I've never seen asymmetric right prefrontal brain activity combined this way with diffuse amygdala activity and some limbic system activity in patterns that I see with Jason. Let's just say hypothetically that if he had pathology in his prefrontal cortex, amygdala, and limbic system, you would expect abnormalities related to fear, perhaps the memory of fearful events, or even the inability to be afraid, or at least the inability to respond appropriately. Prefrontal activity similar to this, although not quite the same, is associated with anxious temperament. The amygdala is critical in processing unconditioned fear responses such as what you might expect if you show a zoo-raised monkey a deadly cobra." Yanavitch slowed, seeing that his guests were not following him. "Let me tell you a little about the brain if I might, because it will be relevant in talking over Jason's work."

Sam nodded, and the concentration lines on Anna's forehead made it apparent that she was girding herself for a mental battle.

"The brain consists of a hundred billion neurons. They transmit and receive electrical impulses using chemically operated circuits. For our little discussion about how the brain makes a mind, a neuron looks something like this." Yanavitch stood and placed a large drawing on a white drawing board. On the drawing there was something that looked roughly like a rubber squeeze bulb sprouting brushy fine hairs around its surface and, at what would be the small end of the squeeze bulb, a branched stalk. The fine bushlike things protruding at several points were labeled *dendrites*. Then the single branching stalk with its several forks was labeled *axon*. At the end of each axon was a tip called a terminal button. At the base of the axon was the axon hillock.

"We have incoming mail on all these bushy-looking dendrites and outgoing mail on this axon through the terminal buttons. On the dendrites there are proteins that act as receptors for the chemical signal that crosses from the terminal buttons of the neuron before. These transmissions cause the generation of electrical waves that traverse the neuron body. The straight line here with branching toward the end is the axon, and is outgoing, carrying an electrical pulse toward the next neurons. So the transmitting neuron communicates by sending electrical output through its axon and generating a chemical signal across the synapse to the receptors on the dendrites of the receiving neuron, thus perpetuating the electrical signal.

"Just to avoid confusion, we will be talking only about those neurons associated with conscious thought and emotion, the cerebral cortex and the limbic system."

"I am reaching back to undergraduate biology and it's a little fuzzy," Sam said. "And you are moving into deep waters."

"I have read a little," Anna said.

The doctor nodded and cleared his throat. "I should add that the neuron is not an 'on and off' switch, in case you are thinking of something like a binary computer.

"It's more like a rheostat. It can receive waves of

various amplitudes through its dendrites. The neuron sums the input signals at the axon hillock. Nerves aggregate as inhibitors and activators. For example, some aggregations may increase hunger and some may decrease hunger. Exercise stimulates cells that inhibit hunger. There are cell aggregations that activate fear and those that inhibit it. Any model of the brain must take into account a myriad offsetting nerve groups. Individual nerves fire an impulse out their axon if there is sufficient incoming signal strength. Inputs are summed at the axon hillock. Once triggered at the axon hillock, the axon normally fires with uniform strength through its various terminal buttons.

"As an aside, the human body isn't big on growing new neurons, maybe some, but unfortunately not enough to keep up with neuron mortality. Furthermore, synapses that aren't used dissipate. But the good news is that neurons make new connections with learning. That's why you should keep thinking and stretching your mind into old age. Read, play a musical instrument, work puzzles, keep the mind zapping itself and those interconnections growing. Anyway, I digress.

"Now if you were as smart as your brother, Ms. Wade, you might be able to mathematically model the various potential relationships between a population of neurons. There are billions of neuron brain cells with total interconnections numbering in the trillions in one human brain. On your brother's computer CD, Carl Fielding found equations along those lines. Utterly impressive work, even given the fraction of the data that seemed to have been successfully transferred."

"I can't imagine math can describe the creation of human consciousness," Anna said.

"Yeah, well, a lot of us have a hard time imagining

that consciousness exists and is replicated every time an infant is born and matures. So the mathematicians may never have a perfect model," Yanavitch replied. "And I haven't mentioned the other complicating factors. For instance, at any moment a neuron may be receiving more than one pulse at a time, summing up impulses and in addition recognizing the firing activity of neighboring neurons.

"Just to review: A neuron receives electrical waves of varying amplitude through the dendrite and sums them. If the axon is triggered by the input, it fires a uniform signal through all of its various branches.

"This allows for an incredible amount of signal variation and integration among multiple neurons. Which is wonderful for the elegant brain but tough on the mathematician.

"To further complicate matters, one neuron can detect incidental parallel stimulation of other neurons. That is to say, a neuron can make a biochemical note of the triggering of other related neurons. Certain molecules, such as glutamate from a neighboring axon, will stimulate a chemical response in a dendrite more easily if the neuron to which the dendrite feeds is likewise stimulated from another source. The cell becomes more readily stimulated if parallel messages are being received by other neurons. Conversely some neurons are inhibitors; they dampen or counteract a particular response. For example, in a holistic sense a hunger response can be dampened by exercise."

Sam and Anna nodded dumbly.

"Dr. Fielding believes that Jason has derived one of the most complex equations they have ever seen in order to model brain function. And Dr. Fielding's colleagues in neurology are in misery because they didn't receive all of it."

"We knew he's a genius," said Anna. "We're trying to figure out what's wrong with him."

"There is something else. We can tell that Jason was postulating an increased potential. Maybe an induced response, for example, with a drug— Only the drug he was apparently thinking of doesn't exist."

"What was he thinking of?"

"Nannites."

"Give me a break," Anna said.

"I know, but it was on the disk," Yanavitch said. "Judging from his notes, Jason really believes in some factor that he ascribes to Nannites."

"You don't believe in Nannites?"

"No. But the first day somebody suggested that light was disappearing in black holes, I probably wouldn't have believed in that either. Look, I can't take it seriously, but I can't make any final conclusions until we get the rest of his data. Especially the code."

"What is that?" Sam asked.

"After we used Anna's code, there were other codes to access files within the first file. They're using your computer to break it."

"I'm aware," Sam said.

"Dr. Fielding learned that it's against U.S. law to use such a lengthy encryption." The doctor paused and was dialing the telephone. After a few queries he hung up.

"Dr. Fielding is at a lecture. They'll have him call me the instant he returns."

"So you'll see my brother if we can get him?"

"Oh, absolutely. Go anywhere, do anything."

"You may have to," Sam said.

"Is my brother fixable?" Anna asked. "Of course I know before I ask that you can't answer."

"You're looking for some hope and I don't blame

you. I can't say. But I know the question to ask: Why the fear message? He's clearly getting fear messages or neuronal activity in the fear areas of the brain. The brain's intellectual tendency creates an explanation for the fear. Which in his case is the Nannites."

"If someone is mostly normal but just a little emotionally unavailable, how do you fix that?" she asked.

Sam wrinkled his brow.

Yanavitch thought for a moment. Looked at Sam, then back at her. "Well, before you go into Gestalt therapy you might try this popular book . . . what is it? I think it's called *Where Did He Go? Where Did She Go?*"

Twenty-three

"You look like you've run out of room."

Roberto found Jason staring at an equation he'd written on a white board. The formula covered the board from edge to edge and nearly from top to bottom. "Yes, well, I'm going to take a digital photo and put this up on a screen. Then I'll start with a fresh board."

"We think we should move you."

"Why is that?"

Roberto tried to look sincere. "Trick the Nannites."

"You don't believe in them."

"It should be clear to you that we believe in you and your work. So if you believe in Nannites, that's good enough for us."

"How would you propose to trick them?"

"Make them think you died."

"In the beginning what was to be the universe was packed into space almost infinitely small. Then something happened. Maybe God said good morning. The big bang, some have called it. A tenth of a millionth of a trillionth of a trillionth of a trillionth of a second later the universe had started cooling off and was about a hundred million, trillion degrees and we had gravity.

"I won't bore you with what happened next. Suffice it to say it took another three hundred thousand years and an average temperature of three thousand degrees for atoms to form. That was the Nannite moment and the world of the Nannites began in our world. They must have gotten here from someplace else, but now they could start to develop their carrier in our universe. We are the most highly evolved carrier.

"Given that Nannites were here before we even became mammals and that they had all that time to evolve, beating us by over five billion years—given that we don't even know how much longer than our universe they have been around—what makes you think we can fool them?" His eyes were wild. "I think you're dull, Roberto. You just don't get it."

Roberto didn't know how to respond.

"How did they get to you?" Jason asked.

"They didn't get to me. I'm trying to help you."

"I want to work. Leave me alone. And stop acting like an idiot."

"Look, why don't you go outside, get some fresh air? We'll go for a walk and talk about it."

Jason put down his marker and walked out the door with Roberto, nodding at the refrigerator-sized Frank Stefano.

"I wish Chellis would feed you to a meat grinder, whip up some Roberto tartar with ground olives and mushrooms, a good dose of garlic, fresh horseradish, and a little pimento on top."

"Let's enjoy the walk," Roberto said. "It's beautiful here, but we can find an even better place for you to work."

"There is one certainty that arises out of all of this."

"What's that?"

"Human consciousness for all of its glory is a miracle that has not yet sufficiently advanced to free us from sick mutants such as yourself."

"Tell me," Roberto said. "Do the Nannites have a sense of history?"

"Good question. Keep moving in that direction and we may have some hope for you after all." Jason looked at him. "I don't think it's the Nannites you want to fool, Roberto. I think it's Anna."

"Don't be silly. She'll come to visit at the new compound."

As they walked along the trail in single file, with Jason ahead and Frank bringing up the rear, Roberto felt watched, even though foliage was so dense it would be difficult for someone to follow them undetected.

The trees around them were smallish, maybe sixty feet tall, mostly Douglas fir, a few silver firs, and the occasional big-leaf maple. The conifers had branches all the way to the soil that tangled and competed with the ground-loving species. A son of Italian farmers, Roberto had learned a few names of the things that sprang from the earth in this place of green and mist. Unlike the south of Italy, things grew so tight that the machete line became a wall in places, as if someone were contemplating hedgerows.

"Wait." Roberto stopped to listen.

"What?" Frank said.

"I don't know, I thought maybe I heard something."

"It won't be Nannites," Jason said.

Roberto thought it was sarcasm, but he never knew for certain with Jason.

The path had gotten muddy, their boots slushing noisily. He listened in the new silence. A black-capped chickadee was doing its dee-dee-dee and a kingfisher flitted on uneven wing beats with its rattle call, before it landed on a snag, sitting proud and blue like midget woodland royalty.

There was a slight whirling autumn breeze in the islands, and in the distance honkers called in V formation, always seeming to reach for somewhere that never came.

"Okay." Roberto shrugged. They began walking again.

As they approached a familiar bend, Roberto was sure he heard radio static for just an instant. This time he drew his unloaded gun and wished it were full of bullets.

Ten feet in front of him a painted face rose from out of the wall of green, then another. Roberto whirled, looking. As he did so the forest became a mosaic of plants and faces. They were surrounded by at least a dozen men wearing combat fatigues and carrying what looked like futuristic military rifles. Roberto's chest constricted; he could be dead in seconds. Suddenly his head was plunged in darkness, his arms were pinned to his sides, the gun yanked from his hand, and all he could see were his feet. Then a zipping sound up his neck and he could see nothing. Before he could think, he was helpless and struggling. They laid him on the ground and began tying him. Frank was swearing and thrashing in the bushes.

"If you couldn't fool these Neanderthals, you sure couldn't fool Nannites," Jason muttered. The way he spoke, it sounded as though he was watching rather than fighting. Roberto wondered if somehow Jason was in on whatever was happening, but that seemed impossible.

In seconds the attackers were gone and Roberto lay with his arms tied and some sort of tape holding his wrists and ankles. He couldn't move. His head was zipped in a nylon bag, almost suffocating and foam-filled. He heard the dee-dee-dee of the chickadee again. He no longer heard Frank; the assailants may well have killed him.

He thought of the dark; then he felt the dark, the staleness of his own breath, the soft foam clinging when he stuck out his tongue. With his first rib-expanding gasp he felt velvet closing around his mouth. He tried another breath and then again, faster. He could suck but he couldn't fill. Soon he sounded like a marathoner gone mad; eeee, haw, eeee, haw, the breaths came and their frequency mounted with his fear. Soon his body was shaking, nearly convulsing. Eeee, haw, eeee, haw. Breathing sounds and the want of air took over his mind. He was crying and choking and still the breaths came harder and harder, faster and faster.

His mind was a lizard trapped in a tiny cave. Then arose something worse, the fear of not being able to end it, to kill himself.

Roberto screamed and remembered the souvenir turtles in Mexico. The workers laid them on their backs in the sun. The necks came out. Then the legs. Stretching and reaching, the turtles slowly became frantic. Finally their limbs started to dangle, and then at last they simply waved, as if saying good-bye on their way to a slow death.

Sam wanted to make calls from the airport. He still liked pay phones more than cell phones because he claimed that talking on a cell phone was about as private as screaming from your back porch. Anna thought the phone companies had fixed that problem, but didn't bother arguing with Sam. While waiting, she had some thinking time, and to divert herself from nagging worry about Jason began imagining how intriguing it would be to undertake a little investigation.

As she thought about the phone call she might make, she exited the jet on the tarmac and walked away from the plane so as not to be heard by the pilots.

"Hey, you," she said to Peter in her usual way.

"Anna, great to hear your voice. I hope everything is going grand with Sam."

"Just grand. That's not what I called about."

"Oh?"

"I have a screenplay that might be good for you."

"Really!"

"Uh-huh, it's great." Then she went on for five minutes.

"Man, this sounds exciting."

"Ah, Peter, there is one thing you could do for me."

"Uh-oh."

"What do you mean uh-oh?"

"It's about Sam, isn't it?"

"I do need a favor that has to do with Sam, and clearly I brought it up right in the midst of discussing a mutually advantageous proposal—which I might add you deserve anyway—and I want to do it with you no matter how this conversation turns out. You have my word on that."

"I'm not going to do anything that Sam wouldn't like."

"You know I wouldn't ask that."

"All right, what is it?"

"You're his friend."

"Yeah. So?"

"Does he have a girlfriend?"

"No. I don't think so."

"See? How easy was that?"

"Uh-huh."

"Now just one more little question. How sure are you?"

"Very sure."

"Who was the last?"

"Oh, no."

"All right, all right. Just tell me if she was a celebrity. If it was secret."

"You know I can't do that."

"Now think about this. Do I want to know this to hurt Sam or to get some much-needed insight?"

"Anna, you're killing me."

"I can just feel that it was a celebrity, but Sam has told himself that he has to have secrecy to the point where he may actually believe it."

There was a long pause. Peter let out a breath. "Well, you've got it half figured out. I don't know why you're asking."

"Thank you. You're a sweetheart. But exactly how did it end? Did she give up or did Sam?"

"Maybe nobody had the opportunity to give up."

"Nobody had . . . Wait. Did she die?"

"I didn't say that."

"You're a darling, Peter. Thank you. I have my answer. Suzanne King was beautiful. The right age. There was all that publicity about the stalkers. She died in a plane crash about a year ago."

There was silence. She let him go.

Next she called her agent and her script reader in quick succession. For every screenplay idea they latched on to, they looked at hundreds. Nothing in the latest crop looked that great. She had a three-movie-deal commitment, so that had to be worked into the equation. Then she called Genevieve and asked that they tell Prada, Christian LaCroix, Missoni, and Vivienne which dresses she would keep. She reiterated that the dresses were to be purchased and not received with compliments. They had sent about six each, and she'd been sitting on them for three weeks and only planned to keep a few.

She hung up and called her publicist.

"Lane and I are breaking up. It's the usual, we'll always be friends. We both got all we could out of the relationship and came away better people. Mutual. No third parties. We still talk all the time. And one other thing. This is very sensitive. I don't want too much volume on this, just a little. But I definitely want something."

"Yes?" Now Sally sounded interested.

"Create a little buzz, a little mystery about who might escort me to the party at the studio."

The publicist could do it all in her sleep.

Twenty-four

The Beaver seaplane landed on the small inlet that they called Lodge Bay and made it past the breakwater arriving at the dock on momentum alone. It was a slick, fast landing with the radial chugging and spluttering typical of these old twelve-cylinder workhorses. When Sam stepped off the pontoon onto the dock he noticed the clear water, the white sea anemones, maroon starfish, and the small minnows visible below.

It was a blustery day with mottled, battleship-gray clouds with folded, dark creases. Sam, Anna, and three armed-to-the teeth Canadians—two ex-Mounties and one ex-military and all licensed private investigators—walked up the dock and took in the wilderness: bald eagles teetering on the wind, the rush of blowing trees, and the grandeur of towering granite. Any more men and it would have looked like an invasion.

Of the three men that Sam brought along, T.J., one of the ex-Mountie officers, was the natural leader. He was a brown and silver-haired, mustached forty-five-year-old who looked sharp and acted tough. Sam knew he was both, but also knew that he had fallen on hard times. A painful divorce and kids in college had left him broke. Sam worried about such things affecting a man's performance under fire, but in this case he seemed committed and it was obvious that he was totally impressed by Anna.

Duke, black-haired, squat, and broad, an amateur fighter with stone hands, seemingly more oak than man, walked second to last and carried his weapon as though he expected to use it.

"It doesn't feel right," Anna whispered to Sam. He nodded but didn't reply, concentrating on detecting what might be hidden.

Bringing up the rear was Jeff, a tall and quiet man who lived like a coiled spring.

Sam kept his finger on the trigger of his assault rifle, an M7, and the others did the same. Only Anna was unarmed. At the head of the dock a broad plank walkway traversed the rock and boggy heather beyond. A small stream murmured but did not put them at ease. The slap of their feet on the wood diminished as they hushed their footsteps.

After walking inland a good three-quarters of a mile, they came to the side door of the lodgelike main house. Sam moved along the windows, ignoring the door for the moment. Someone was on the floor and judging from the alabaster-white skin of her legs, it was the housekeeper fitted with a gray bag over her torso and trussed up so that she couldn't move. Beside her was a man in well-worn blue jeans—maybe the handyman— then next to him another groundsman and beyond him another woman—a cook or housekeeper.

"Someone's been busy," Sam said. In a couple of minutes they had broken the door and were inside untying people.

"Where is Jason?" Anna said.

"They didn't come back from their walk. The men must have taken them," the first housekeeper answered.

"How many were there?"

"We saw several," the man spoke up. "Maybe six but there were no doubt more."

"Weapons?"

"All kinda strange guns."

"Where is Nutka?" Sam could see the worry in Anna's eyes.

"Still with her family. Coming back this afternoon in time for the massage."

"Let's go." Anna turned to run down the path Jason would have taken.

Sam grabbed her arm and spun her around. "Plan. Remember the plan."

"The plan is we go look for him."

"Whoever did this is dangerous," Sam said.

"That's why we're in a hurry."

"Just a minute." Sam turned to the staff members. "I'd stay here if I were you."

Sam started walking. "This trail here?" he asked Anna, pointing to a route just above the beach.

"If they were going to the point, that's where they'd go," Anna said.

Running down the path would be dangerous, but moving slowly off the path in the brush would be extremely time-consuming; he opted for speed over safety. They went quickly, guns drawn.

Sam slowed at every corner and peered around the nearest available tree, listening intently for any sound. Now they were strung out with at least thirty feet between them, winding along the base of the mountainside through the thick foliage and dense new-growth trees, over the small footbridges, through the mint-green clover, all the way feeling completely vulnerable to ambush. When they had covered about half the distance to the point, Sam thought he heard something. They were in an unusually dense thicket. He raised a hand for the others to stop and crept forward by himself. There was a muffled scream and he guessed what he would find.

Sam looked back at Anna and held up his hand, knowing her tendency to charge headlong. As quietly as possible he stepped off the trail to the right and began a slow circle. The others remained in place. Forcing himself to be patient, Sam listened and looked with every step. Whoever was doing the muffled yelling could be victim or bait or both.

After he had circled ahead of the sound he moved slowly toward it. He found the two bodies trussed on the ground—helpless. One of them was screaming, out of control and hyperventilating badly. Still, it could be a trap, so he retreated into the forest and came full circle.

"There are two men on the trail," he told Anna. "From their builds neither is your brother.

"They sound in agony."

"It's their fear."

"Then let's go."

"I'm sure it's Roberto."

"So?"

"We could learn something."

She studied him, and then he could see that his idea was dawning on her. "That's inhumane. I am ashamed of you that you would even say such a thing."

"Okay. But remember it's your brother's life. Now I want you to bear with me."

Sam nodded at T.J., who got in front of Anna.

"Please, just stay here for a minute."

Anna shot around T.J. and Sam grabbed her.

"I swear to God I will handcuff you to a tree."

With that, some of the fire went out of her eyes.

"Okay, but I'm going with you."

"On this, with your brother's life, there is no plan B."

He waited while the moans down the trail continued.

"No plan B," Anna said.

Just around the bend they came upon the two figures.

Sam knelt down near Roberto's thrashing head.

"Roberto," he whispered. The head slowed. "Roberto."

"Help me," he shrieked, hoarse and breathless.

"I will. You can get up and be free, but first you have to tell me some things."

"Please, please, please!" He was hysterical and barely rational. Sam reached down and ran the zipper halfway up, providing a little airway.

"Relax. I'm not letting you out until you relax."

The man whimpered and cried, nearly incoherent, but his breathing slowed.

"Okay, Roberto, now all you have to do is tell me the truth. And I will let you up."

"What do you mean?"

Suddenly it was as if the old Roberto had come back. Sam sensed resistance.

"I thought you had learned. I guess not." Sam reached out and closed the zipper. Roberto's body jumped as if Sam had hit him with 120 volts. Suddenly he was screaming and shaking. T.J. winced and looked at Sam, obviously worried, pointing to his heart. Anna bent, her lips low to Sam's ear.

"Please, Sam, I can't take this."

Sam loosened the zipper; maybe he was pushing it. If it didn't work this time, he would let the man up.

"Roberto, I think we may just leave. Up here somebody may find you. Or when we move you off the trail they may not."

"What do you want?" He became incoherent. He was crying and had defecated in his pants.

"Tell me where Jason is."

Roberto talked.

Sam pulled the zipper down; he supposed Roberto could see light. When they had established that he knew nothing of Jason's whereabouts, that Jason had been taken, Sam knew they should move quickly.

"Who shot the rocket at my boat?"

"Jason."

"Were you with him?"

Silence. Sam reached for the zipper.

"I was."

"What did Grace Technologies do to Jason's brain?"

"He had a rare disease and they experimented. I don't understand it. Something about changing his brain cells. Chellis and his scientists understand it. Chellis knows how to make Jason paranoid so he stays close to home. The massages help his symptoms— it's the oil, but I don't know how."

After a few more questions it became obvious that Roberto didn't understand the mechanisms involved. They would need to go elsewhere.

Ten people or more had kidnapped Jason. Probably across the island. Sam released Roberto and listened while he cursed.

"Panic is your worst enemy, Roberto. If you don't tell Chellis, I won't. Seems to me you ought to be on our side."

"Fuck you," Roberto screamed, no doubt imagining the fury of Chellis and the death of his own career. Now that he was up and looking at them, he surely realized that they would have freed him with or without the confession. Humiliation fused with anger made him hateful, and Sam could see it in his eyes.

"Relax. Any one of us could have had your reaction. Once the mind starts flying free you never know where it's going to come down. You just flew a little further than most."

"You are despicable," Anna said to Roberto. T.J. stepped out of the brush and handed Sam a filterless cigarette butt with a small gold insignia stamped on one end.

"Middle Eastern," Sam said.

"We should chase them in the helicopter," Roberto said.

"Very handy, a helicopter. A beanie on a coffin. They'll blow it out of the sky about the way you blew my boat out of the water."

"Jason did that," Roberto corrected him.

"While you watched," Anna said.

"Well, I'm sending the chopper anyway."

Sam just nodded; he would try to take advantage of the idiocy.

"We'll need boots, water, warm clothing, preferably wool or moisture-wicking, a lighter, water, knife, and some fully automatic weapons if you have them."

"We have the weapons."

"And a rocket launcher?"

"We have one of those as well."

"Good." Sam moved off toward the lodge at a jog. "Let's roll."

As soon as they started they heard a seaplane circling low and dropping. Sam ran, suspecting that the plane was to pick up the intruders at Lodge Bay. If they had not done so already, at any minute the intruders would discover that their plans were being interrupted. Even as he thought it he heard the approaching plane apply power and fly low over the island. It sounded to Sam like a large twin-engine seaplane. No doubt the intruders had gone back toward the lodge, then turned and gone overland toward the other side of the island.

It took only five minutes to get everything on Sam's list. They grabbed some food bars for good measure and some of Nutka's salmon jerky.

"I suppose you want to go with us," Sam said to Anna.

"I can act the part of a commando. My performance will be convincing."

Sam allowed his eyes to tell her she was a dope.

"Give her a gun," Sam said. She snatched an M-16 from T.J. It was made of camouflage-colored plastic and steel.

"Can you use it?"

Anna popped out the clip, pulled back the bolt, and checked the chamber. With a business like *ka-chink* she replaced the clip.

Sam nodded his approval.

Sam, Anna, the men, and Roberto left the lodge before Sam said what was on his mind.

"I want to have the pilot take us to the far side of the island in the Beaver. Roberto, you can come when your helicopter arrives.

"The Beaver will be there before the overland troops. It will come in fast and low and land. Still, it may get shot up. These kinds of people are going to have a lot of firepower."

"Okay, I'm going," Anna said.

"It will hold five. But you really shouldn't go."

"Why the hell not?" Anna said.

"Death. Horrible disfigurement. Those good enough reasons?"

"I'll risk it."

"What if it increases the risk for the rest of us?" Sam let his serious eyes make his point.

"You can't make me stay, Sam."

Sam hesitated, gauging her, then took her aside. "Look, I'll spend my time worrying about you and I won't be as effective. Neither will the others. T.J. will be busy trying to save you."

"Sam, don't do this to me. I can shoot."

"I'm not taking you. You're obsessed with your brother—you don't think straight."

"How are you gonna stop me?"

"We're wasting critical time." She locked eyes with him and he knew he had a problem. Her hand went into her purse and she came out with a satellite phone. She unfolded the antenna.

"I gotta go," he said. "Keep the gun. You may need it. Go in the house with the others."

Anna said nothing, but she knifed him with her look.

Sam turned and trotted to the dock with T.J., who had been a few paces back and was listening.

"What's she gonna do?" T.J. said.

"I don't know," Sam said while he watched her.

"I hate to say it but she looks like a woman who has you by the gonads."

Even with the distance between them Sam knew she was looking right at him, and he could feel each punch of the dialer as if it were drilling his chest.

"Damn that woman," Sam said. She was coming back toward them and talking on the phone.

"We should leave now," T.J. said.

Sam walked up to Anna. "What are you doing now?"

"Just a minute, Harold," she said before covering the mouthpiece. "I'm on the phone with the *New York Times*. Harold Butler. I'm going to give him an interview. If you get in that plane without me you're going to read about yourself in the *New York Times*. You're going to read how you left me standing on the dock at the residence of a bunch of criminals. Not only that, you're going to read your life's history. I can afford to forfeit the bond. And you can sue me if you want to."

"But if I take you . . ."

She indicated the off button on the phone.

Sam was looking at a woman who was crazy with determination.

"This is what I get for saving your life?"

"No. This is what you get for trying to run it. Nowhere in our contract does it say you can make life and death choices for me. I am your equal. Get that through your head."

"If you come you fight my way."

"Since I don't know any other way to fight, I suppose yours is as good as any."

"You are something else."

"I'll grow on you. Let's go," she said. "Harold, I'll call you back later." They both ran back to the plane.

T.J. looked worried.

As Sam was walking to the plane a bad feeling almost paralyzed him. He tried to shake it off. He considered that the intruders were far ahead, trained and heavily armed, and probably impossible to catch. His small group wasn't ready for this.

"Come here," Sam said, pulling T.J. away from Anna.

"What about me?" Anna said.

"Just stand there," Sam growled, about as mean as he ever sounded.

"I don't think we should take Anna and I'm afraid this could end in disaster," Sam said.

"You stay. The boys and I will go. If you sit here she'll stay and there isn't a hell of a lot she can do about it."

"I don't want you dead, T.J."

"It's the job. I wanna go, but I sure as hell don't wanna take Anna Wade."

"If you fly right over to the far side you could be flying into automatic weapons fire. If that happens you'll be dead."

"We won't go straight. We'll come in at the end of the island and go overland."

"It's your choice."

"What are you saying?" Anna walked over to where they were standing.

"You and I are staying here to run the radio," Sam said.

"No way."

"Anna, I'm staying here and so are you. T.J. and the boys are going."

The pilot was slow in reaching for the door. He cleared his throat and spoke. "What are all these guns, and this?" he said, speaking in a tight voice, his eyes hard with fear.

"Little problem," Sam said. "These gentlemen need to go to the other side of the island, up at the other end, and look for someone."

"With those?" the man said, still eying the armament.

"Lotta bears over there," Sam said.

"Bullshit," the pilot said.

"Twenty-five thousand dollars if you take them."

"Am I gonna get shot at?"

"Probably."

"Fifty thousand cash plus you buy the plane if it's damaged. And I want it in writing now."

Sam took out a pen and scrawled the deal.

"And the movie star here signs it."

"Listen, asshole, we gotta go," Jeff said.

"Take it easy," Sam said. "The man's being reasonable. And now that we're paying him fifty grand he's officially agreed to fly through live fire."

The pilot swallowed and looked at Sam as if he might rethink his position. The three men jumped into the plane. Sam shut the door, practically choking with frustration.

He and Anna stood in silence while the plane taxied and took off.

They watched as the seaplane flew down the island, made a turn, and disappeared in the distance. In ten minutes they got a radio call.

"Sam, they are long gone. No seaplane, no boats, no nothing. We watched as the Otter took off in the distance. There was a chopper nearby that could have come into the old orchard back here. We're coming back." Then there was a few seconds' silence and T.J. came on again.

"We've been hit. We've been hit. Somebody stayed behind. We're going to try to land." Then more stridently. "Duke and Jeff have both been hit bad. Automatic weapons fire."

Sam called seaplanes and a medical helicopter. The pilot got the Beaver on the water.

Twenty minutes later T.J. came on the radio.

"Damn it, Sam. Duke and Jeff are dead. Both gone."

Twenty-five

Sam and Anna sat in a Hawker 700 jet that had leveled off at 32,000 feet.

"We have to go after them. The longer they are gone, the harder they will be to find."

"You know, you're trying my ego. Supposedly I'm an expert at this. We have fifty people or more working their butts off nearly twenty-four hours a day looking for escape routes from Canada. We are monitoring phones, we're nudging the Canadian government, we're getting informal help from the FBI and Scotland Yard without yelling too loud because of the circumstances and because governments can screw things up. They left in a private plane, and we'll find it."

"I know. I just can't stand it."

"We lost two more men because we couldn't wait."

"I know. I know. We've gone over this."

"Until we know where they went, you need to get your mind off it and give the appearance of Anna Wade going about her business as usual."

"Yeah, well, you can just haul your cute butt down to my studio party."

"I said I would ride in the limo."

"But we aren't going if it will in any way affect the hunt for Jason."

"Absolutely."

Anna began eyeing the small couch in the back of the jet's cabin.

"Lie down if you like," Sam said.

"Will you come back so we can talk before I fall asleep?"

"Sure," Sam said. He took a mint-green blanket and white pillow from a forward baggage compartment, ushered her to the back of the plane, and sat in an upright seat across from the couch. Anna, already in her stocking feet, lay down.

"Why don't you sit here?" she said.

Sam got the idea, moved over, and put the pillow in his lap.

"Tell me about the letters in the picture book," she said.

"Maybe I should be the one on the couch."

"Come on, Sam."

"The thing with the sat phone and the *New York Times*. I didn't like it."

"It was just a bluff. You were being a butt head. Let's not digress." She put her hand on his arm and patted it.

"No." He said it with a tentative tone to soften what was not soft.

"I know. I was wrong. Wrong. Wrong. I won't do it again but I'm sure I'll be tempted."

"One of the letters was to my son. It was in English so you know what it said. Mom found it in his things.

"The other was in the language of my tribe. It was from my grandfather to me."

"And what did it say?"

"It was very similar to the letter I wrote to my son except for the last line. My grandfather didn't mention the sunset or the beer."

"And?"

"It said 'Do not neglect the gift that I have seen.' Loose translation."

"What is that gift?"

"I have dreams. Sometimes hunches. They are just normal things. Most people have them."

"Your Grandfather was a Spirit Walker?"

"Yes."

"And he had these dreams and hunches?"

"Uh-huh."

"Methinks you doth protest too much. In the cabin when you jumped up and said we had to get out. Was that one of those dreams?"

"Yeah."

"When was the last time you had one?"

"Before getting in the seaplane at the lodge; on the roof of the Dyna Science building before getting in the helicopter. But you know that was logical. It had only one engine. I usually use one with two turbines."

"When before that?"

"When I was sailing past the mouth of Devil's Gate. I turned in."

"It's how you saw me."

"Well, it made it easier."

"Come on. Would you have seen me if you'd kept going?"

"Probably not. I had the same bad feeling about putting you in the seaplane."

"So what is this?"

"It's nothing."

"What did your grandfather mean?"

"My Grandfather Stalking Bear decided that I inherited the Spirit Walker thing."

"Fascinating."

"It's intuition pure and simple."

"Did all Indians around these parts believe the same?"

"Well, there were some distinct differences. Only my tribe believed in Spirit Walkers, but all the tribes had the spiritual leaders known as Talth."

"So tell me your tribe."

"You can keep your trap shut?"

"Of course."

"You threatened me with the *New York Times*."

"I said I was wrong. I concede."

"I'm a Tilok."

"What's your name? Your real name."

"Oh, no." He shook his head. "Let's go back to Indians. Even in things as basic as language there were differences. The Yuroks spoke a language related to the Woodland Algonquian tribes of the northeastern United States, while the Karuk spoke Hokan, the oldest language in northwestern California, and the Hupa spoke the Athapaskan, which was a language common in the Pacific Northwest and the Southwest. Pretty amazing to have such diversity in one small area of northern California."

"What do the Tiloks speak?"

"A dialect of the Algonquian tribes, but Mom says it's pretty different. Before English, none of these tribes could talk to each other without a multilingual translator. Their economies, social structure, and spiritual beliefs were similar but there were differences. My mother can tell you what was common and what was not. Tiloks were travelers, not so much lowland Indians except seasonally. In spring and summer Tiloks went to the high country. They were hunters, trackers, and traders."

"Why does she say that your soul lacks harmony?"

"I told you that you need to leave me with a few secrets."

"Okay, just a little more. Tell me about your dad."

"He was the penultimate tough guy. Life was about holding out the proper facade no matter what. Laugh at adversity, joke when others cry, never have a really serious conversation, and never under any circumstances be vulnerable."

"Must have made a heck of a one-man platoon."

"He was a parajumper. The bad-ass rescue patrol. The president or a cabinet member goes down, needs rescuing, or a pilot behind enemy lines, or a hiker on Mount Denali . . . the toughest rescues around are given to the parajumpers. That's what you wanted to know."

"I'm not spying on you, Sam. Relax." She squeezed his arm. "I do, though, fully intend to find out everything there is to know about you."

"Curious creature, aren't you?"

"I am," she said, and quickly drifted off to sleep.

He didn't really doubt her. It seemed that he was seriously losing his grip with this woman.

He used the plane's satellite phone to call the office. Typhony answered.

"How's it going?" Sam asked.

"Really good but I can't talk now, so I'm giving you Paul."

That's weird, Sam thought.

"Yo," Paul said.

"Are we making progress?"

"You bet. I called Hal Godwynn. Apologized for the middle-of-the-night wake-up. Said you'd be talking to him, that you really needed his help. He's cranking up as we speak. He knows it's big and says there'll be a lot of mouths to feed. Fifty thousand dollars to try, with a fifty-thousand success fee and fifty thousand more as a home-run bonus. Success is that he finds a plane leaving Canada with Jason on it and tells us where it landed. Another fifty-thousand home run if we actually find him and we get him back."

"Okay." Sam heard something in Paul's voice.

"We're thinking Jason was smart enough to circumvent file-folder security but never cracked the code to open the document. So he gave us a folder that he locked with a document inside that was encrypted by Grace Technologies. We're working on breaking it. Grogg is going to run about two hundred big computers in series for about an hour and see what he can do."

"We need to break it open. Jason had to have a reason for thinking it would be interesting."

"So when you gonna be here?"

"Soon. Tell me what's wrong, Paul."

"Oh, it's nothing critical; it can wait until you get here. Some people want to talk with you."

"Which people?"

"Trust me on this one, Sam. It's one of those things you should get into when you get here and it will definitely keep."

"It's why Typhony wanted off the line."

"Uh-huh."

"Okay. I'll be right there. I can hardly wait."

Someone had screwed up. Sam knew that. And the miscreant wanted to tell his or her story.

"What's wrong?" Anna asked.

"You faker."

"Tell me what's wrong."

"If you could hear, you know they wouldn't tell me."

"What do you think?"

"Don't know."

"Who's Hal?"

"A retired FAA administrator. He has a knack for tracing aircraft flying in controlled airspace."

"I hope he figures it out."

"I do too."

"Sam, I want to go to the office with you."

"That's out of the question."

"If you let me come, I'll . . . well . . . I'll pay closer attention to what you say."

"Oh, that's a real concession."

"You're looking for my brother. That's where everything is happening. You've got what . . . bunches of people in there all working phones and computers and God knows how many people out in the field feeding you information."

"You can't come."

"What if I promise to follow orders? How about that?"

"For the entire job you promise to do what I say?"

"Nearly."

"What kind of lie is 'nearly'?" Sam laughed. "At least be convincing. You get the anemic lie award."

They drove through the streets of LA, she watching his face in the flickering of the night-lights, Sam talking easier now. She sensed he had decided to take a chance. He pulled through the gate, past the guard shack, and into what was obviously a very private parking area. She saw a lot of cars for what she considered the late hour.

"Looks like your crew is hard at it," she said.

"That's one I don't understand, though." He indicated a sporty-looking Porsche. "Four hundred and twenty horsepower, 413 foot-pounds of torque, zero to sixty in ten-point-oh seconds, and all-wheel-drive. It belongs to Jill, and she's supposed to be in the mountains with Grady." Then he leaned forward and peered down to the end of the row. "What the hell?" he said. "That's my mother's car down there."

Sam had a look on his face that she hadn't seen—a cross between anger and worry.

Inside they were met by Typhony and Paul. Jill stood just behind the pair. Everybody in the office was looking out of their cubicles, most standing.

Sam saw his mother in the doorway to the lounge. Beside her was Grady with a yellow pad. There was a hush about the place, none of the soft clicking from the keyboards. Everybody was watching as though he were a cop breaking down the door of a bookie salon. For a second nobody spoke or even moved.

"What's happening with Grady?"

"I brought her here and put her to work," Jill said.

"Paul?"

Paul looked at Jill.

"Paul said no way. Said we would have to follow procedure and that she wouldn't work here for months, if then. I argued and he said take it up with you. But I brought her in anyway, when he wasn't looking."

"You broke a company policy?"

"I'll be happy to fire her ass," Paul said.

"She was just trying to help . . ." Grady called out.

"Go back to your desk, Grady," Jill said. "This is my business."

"I'm speechless but I'm sure it won't last," Sam said. He craved a cigarette.

"I want to explain," Jill said.

"In there." Sam nodded at the conference room.

He felt like the King of Siam when the Englishwoman challenged him about Tup Tim. Security had to mean something.

"I'd like to speak with you privately," Spring said.

It gave him the excuse that he wanted not to react immediately.

"Okay," Sam said.

They went into the conference room first and closed the door. "Jill only told me after we arrived and were inside that you would not approve. Shortly before you arrived here she explained the significance of what she had done—that it was a major breach of your security rules."

"It certainly was that. And she ignored Paul."

"And so you need to fire her."

"That's right."

"And yet you know she would bust her butt for you in a tight spot."

"I know that."

"So you don't want to fire her. So maybe there is a better way."

"I'm listening."

"Let her come up with a means of making recompense that satisfies everyone she put at risk. If it satisfies you and everyone else, then she can stay."

"But she's not a child, and this is a job. We don't do detention."

"Sam, I've watched these people. It's a little community."

"It's a community with rules and principles that we all follow. Myself included."

"I'm not going to waste your time. But everybody here was threatened by the breach and they have worked out something, subject to your approval."

"Well, I wouldn't hold out a lot of hope. This isn't a halfway house. But I'll listen."

"You know I'm right."

"Just please don't make a treaty with Anna Wade and declare war on my psyche."

They opened the door.

"Can I talk to you now?" Jill came in.

"Talk," Sam said.

"You can't run your kind of business and have people doing their own thing. I know there is never a good reason to breach security."

"But?"

"No but. You should fire me."

"Then why did you do it?"

"At the time I thought you'd understand, because of the danger to Grady. Then when I mulled it over, and after Paul started literally shaking me, I realized maybe you wouldn't. Originally, I thought, maybe you'd get mad but somehow . . . overlook it."

"But why did you think I'd understand?"

"Because our research shows that Samir Aziz is probably dangerous and that Chellis is perhaps deadly, but so clever that we can't prove it. Chellis will kill Grady because she's the key to getting Jason free of Grace's control. Aziz will abduct her for the same reason. There isn't a safer place than here. Finally, I have a feeling about this girl. We can trust her. She should work here. That's why I did it."

"There is a safer place than here. Even if you were right, that doesn't justify—"

"You're not listening. I told you it doesn't. That's why you have to fire me."

"Unless we come to some . . ."

"Understanding."

"Like what? I have a strung-out stripper kid in the bowels of my office."

"Sam, don't call her that."

"You're right. She really has nothing to do with the rank piece-of-crap trick you pulled on all of us."

Sam took out a single Marlboro, his last.

"You don't smoke. Do you?"

"Hell, no. I quit long ago."

"Besides, that's against company policy."

He tossed it in the wastebasket. For as long as he could remember he had never seen her look this worried.

"We all talked about it. Your mother asked me a lot of questions. And we came up with something."

"Okay," Sam said. "What is it?"

"Of all my material possessions nothing means more to me than my car. We'll all take a blowtorch and cut it into two-inch squares and we'll put the squares in a giant box by the door to rust."

"And everyone agreed to this?"

"No, that's not all. For Paul that wasn't enough."

"Okay, what else?"

"I made a deal with Paul to drive some piece-of-crap car for a year. He will pick it out and it will come complete with rust spots. That is, if you agree to all this."

"This is bizarre. It's kindergarten. Tell me honestly: Would you do the same thing if you had to do it over?"

"No. I would ask you and if I couldn't convince you, I would leave it alone."

Sam thought for a moment. Two years ago she would have been out of the building by now. Getting soft in this business was scary.

He made sure to take his time and look her square in the eye. She took that to be his answer.

She turned and opened the door and walked through the office, aiming for the exit. They could all see the sorrow on her face and Sam saw the anger in their eyes.

"Jill," he shouted as she waited for the heavy door to open. "If everybody agrees, then it's okay by me."

"I can stay?"

"Yeah. I just wanted you and everyone else to see exactly what it's going to be like if anybody does it again. Anybody."

Sam shut the door, wondering if he had done the right thing.

There was a knock. He opened the door and found Grady bursting at the seams to speak.

"Can I talk now?"

Sam nodded.

"I think I can do the job. I know you can trust me," Grady said, looking at Sam. "You don't even have to pay me."

"You don't know what you're asking. We will be on your ass for two years. You'll have to be in school and getting grades."

"Fine."

"If you drink even once you're fired. There is no compromise on this job."

"Fine."

"You would have to counsel with Spring by telephone twice a week for the first three months when she's available. And you will have to go to a substance abuse group chosen by Spring."

"Fine."

"You would have to live with Jill and exercise five days a week with her. I would tell her to torture you."

"Fine."

"You would have to take a polygraph should Jill ever

ask for one. But most probably, if I think you are dishonest in any respect, you're fired. I wouldn't trust you for a long time."

"Okay."

"You do as Jill says at all times without question."

"I know."

"You never tell anyone about the company or your work without my permission. Break that rule and you're fired."

"Uh-huh."

"What is uh-huh?"

"Yes. I agree."

"You'll see a lawyer and sign a contract. With the help of Spring and Jill you are going to create guidelines that will give a lot more structure to your life." He hesitated. "It has to be a structure the rest of us can believe in."

"I know."

"You still want to work for my company?"

"Yes."

"Pay starts at ten dollars an hour. Nice even number."

"You won't be sorry."

"Time will tell." He looked up to see Jill standing behind Spring.

"And, Jill, you are committed to this?"

"Absolutely," Jill said.

"You know Jill is doing this for you?"

Grady nodded and held out her hand to shake Sam's.

"I'll shake your hand in a month. Right now performance talks. We both made a decision today. I'm counting on you to make it a right decision."

When Sam left the conference room he noticed that Anna was talking to Spring.

Great.

Twenty-six

An hour later, Sam introduced Anna to Grogg and Big Brain. She learned that Sam had roughly fifty people worldwide gathering information around the clock, in addition to the fourteen staffers in Sam's office. Detectives were checking credit cards, phone traffic, looking for disgruntled former associates, people with ties to law enforcement, and into all manner of databases. Each iota of information was funneled into Big Brain, which stored images, driver license numbers, car VINs, Social Security numbers, telephone numbers, cell phone information. If it could be rendered digital, Big Brain stored it.

In the beginning, before the computer began to draw correlations and aggregate people who knew each other, it all seemed somewhat useless. Gradually, however, patterns emerged. Even more significantly, for years Sam had kept records that could not lawfully have been retained by many law enforcement agencies even after the war on terrorism. A few people in law enforcement did not like the limitations and had private webs kept at home on large PCs, and Sam had downloaded several of these. Much more significantly in off-the-record trades with the U.S. and other governments, he had downloaded various government databases. It was a dumping ground that hungry government spooks could come back to—a place they could find things that had to be wiped from government computers.

Terrorism had helped create the flexibility that Sam needed, but it had started long before the 9/11 attacks. Since bad guys tend to run in packs and deal with (or screw) each other, Sam already had information on both DuShane Chellis and Samir Aziz, along with hundreds of thousands of others. It was now becoming apparent that Samir and Chellis seemed to know some of the same unsavory people. Scotland Yard suspected that DuShane Chellis used a hired killer who had been employed by other criminal types.

"I'm so impressed," Anna said when the short tour was over.

"Everything here is backed up on the East Coast every day so if something happened, not a great deal would be lost. If both Paul and I die, a board of my employees along with five other guys, law enforcement and former law enforcement, get it all. Ultimately it would be used by the government for antiterrorism and organized international crime. Of course they may have to delete a lot of it. Legality for government data is a big issue."

"I'll bet the government would love it right now."

"Actually they get pretty much what they need. But in bits and pieces. They don't have the software to handle much at a time, and they aren't even close. The database without the software to search it is not nearly as productive as it could be. My data warehouse programs are proprietary. The problem with sharing everything with the government is that my clients are not always odor free. But there isn't really a bad person among them, inasmuch as it's for me to discern such things."

"Can't they subpoena stuff?"

"Paul is a licensed attorney and our general counsel. I also am a licensed attorney. I went to correspondence school and passed the bar a long time ago, when I was young and could sit on my ass for hours. You also sign a contract with Paul and me acting independently as your attorneys. There is a clause that, at least purportedly, makes information that you give us subject to the attorney-client privilege. Much of the rest of the data is covered by the attorney work-product privilege. I have the best lawyers in the country protecting my stuff and the government, of course, has learned that the hard way. Not because I beat them in court but because we never get there. They know they would have to fight and go to court to get the stuff. That takes time and they have to ask what happens if they lose. And if they win they have to ask whether it will be there and whether they will be able to retrieve it and more importantly whether the public would stand for the government having this stuff.

"Not to mention, if Grogg goes quiet on them, or wants to screw them, they have a real problem. I have far too much that they want for them to fight with me. For them, cooperation and trading is the preferred alternative. And sometimes I have to get signed waivers from my clients to give them certain material."

"This is impressive," Anna said. "So how do you detect associations between people?"

"If we are doing an investigation and we see people in a car or at a meeting together. If other people are mentioned in a person's garbage, maybe just a Christmas card, or a simple note, it all goes in. Every person that comes in contact with someone we might be even remotely interested in goes in the database—everything we can get on them. That's one of the things the technicians do all day long. We try to search every public record on every person significant to any investigation. Maybe they show up on real estate title reports as buyer and seller or maybe partners in property or in a corporation. When we are gathering information nothing is too trivial to go in our database—even things that seem completely unrelated at the time. We love phone bills. And the computer remembers forever that Jack Jones had a postcard from Nick Smith in his garbage can. It's a link, and we will never lose that link."

"I'll worry about the moral and ethical quagmire after we rescue my brother."

"Uh-huh. My clients tend to look at it that way."

Next Sam showed her the bunk rooms. For the women there were twenty bunks, dressing rooms, four tiled baths, and color. The room was cocoa with white trim, art and photos on the walls, dressers with wooden name placards, a wooden bookcase with some books and more photos.

"Now for the men."

Although the color was the same and the baths were similarly tiled but with boy blue, there was no art or photographs; metal lockers stood in place of solid hardwood dressers, benches instead of chairs. It was much smaller, and the eight bunks were crammed together.

"Maybe you should ask the girls to fix up the boys' place," Anna said.

"Yeah. Maybe."

"Inside you're saying 'Go to hell.'"

"It's a place to sleep. When you're awake enough to enjoy the scenery, you're supposed to be out working or on your way home."

"I knew it."

"And what were you talking to my mother about?"

"I'm way too sleepy and I'm going to go try one of the pretty bunks in the girls' room."

"This smells like revenge."

"You can handle it."

They walked down the hall to the larger dorm. Anna stepped inside and turned around.

Sam gave her a peck on the cheek.

"Not truly an inspirational kiss. But nice nevertheless."

Sam turned to leave, anxious to get back to work. And somehow he didn't like what had just happened to him. Turning, he walked back to her. As if she were expecting it, his lips met hers and their tongues explored their passion, which he found considerable.

"I shouldn't be doing that," he said. "But the only thing that seemed worse was not doing it."

"Sam?"

"Yeah?" He stopped as he turned to leave.

"Now that I've seen where you work, I want to see where you live."

Early in the morning Anna rose and found Sam sleepy-eyed and hunching over a cup of coffee in front of a computer screen. There was a certain oddity in this sculpted gym rat staring wide-eyed at dull narratives and mind-numbing details about lists of people that probably had nothing to do with anything that mattered. Sam was a jock in geek land, she thought. The entire main portion of the office was a myriad of computer screens, server lines, and phone lines, information coming in from France, Lebanon, and other faraway places, all supposedly relating in some manner either to her brother or to the men who seemingly had controlled him.

"Come to my place for brunch," she said, watching him as he pointed and clicked.

"Okay," he said. "I'm going to get a few winks in the boys' room."

"I'll take a cab. And I'll see you at eleven," she said.

She had decided to remain in her Los Angeles home for the duration of the hunt for Jason. Like many other houses in Hollywood Hills, it was large and white and stucco with a red-tiled roof, something of a standard formula for the area. Individuality in the architecture of such mansions lay in shapes, corners, windows, what was round and what was square.

This house had two stories and about four thousand feet per story, with a third-floor lookout turret in which she occasionally read. The view from the tower was of brown hills and other white adobe red-tile-roofed homes. The turret had a bar that she seldom used because she drank only wine and the occasional Tom Collins. The house had a screening room, a library, a family room, a gathering room, and a living room. Most of the time she lived her life in the family room-kitchen area.

After arriving home she slept again. At 10:30 she awoke and looked at the luminescent red numbers on the clock atop the TV cabinet. Startled, she sat upright trying to think about homemade granola and what she would wear and what Sam would think.

She walked to the kitchen and crawled up on a stool overlooking the granite kitchen bar. She noticed that the pattern in the granite sort of shimmied, and hoped it wasn't some weird neurological problem.

On the counter was an article about Steven Spielberg and the history of his moviemaking career including his youthful efforts at filmmaking. The man's passion for the craft appeared relentless. Next to the article was *Atonement*, a novel that began with Briony's passion for her play. Because she was just a child, Briony's passion was unmetered by doubt. Anna could connect both with Spielberg and Briony.

Anna's mother, being a Catholic, taught her that the chief end of man was to glorify God and enjoy Him forever. For Anna that seemed a distant way to define her life and not quite close enough to the pavement. Life for Anna was founded on a first truth. It was at once a revelation and a premise. The chief end of man was to make responsible use of his freedom.

In Anna's mind people had the best chance of squeezing the most out of their choices if they focused their attention on just a very few simple things. Sometimes only one or two.

Such focused attention on a single detail of life was what Anna called passion and it was the bedrock of her being. Great lives could be formed around many kinds of passion: a passion for God, or the expression of man's woes and triumphs as in art or theater. It could be growing roses in the backyard or being a good steward of some treasure.

If she had a steely spine, as some said, it was only her passion for a single simple thing. She wanted to use her lips, her body, and her mind to tell great stories. There were, of course, obstacles, and steel spines were good for overcoming them.

Now it was occurring to her that one passion might not be enough. Perhaps a second could be fit into the stuff of her life and she might use her freedom to cultivate this second passion as well, but as yet it had not been made simple. That was a prerequisite. She knew that a part of finding her second passion was in turning around Jason's life and the damage she had done. She was deeply suspicious that this second passion might also be related to getting to know the right man.

As she pondered Sam's visit, her old impatience to help her brother returned. The phone rang.

"I'm on my way." It was Sam on his cell phone.

"Great. You like granola?"

"Yep."

"Have you learned anything?"

"Hal hasn't finished looking. I did learn something interesting, though. Tell you when I get there. Not on a cell phone."

"Well, hurry up, Sam."

Despite her anxiety over Jason, she felt a strong sense of anticipation that Sam was coming. She found herself looking in the mirror pondering her hair, and the complete lack of any makeup. She could wear a thick robe or a thin one, silken or soft and shapeless. She daubed Joy perfume and felt completely ridiculous, then began with her hair. After a few minutes she figured it was decent. Going to the "old and comfortable" section of the closet, she grabbed a Lands End terry-cloth robe.

In her closet there were two full-length mirrors. She looked at herself and thought about Sam, his cool good looks, his easy confidence.

"Damn," she muttered, walking back to the bathroom, brushing her hair more vigorously and applying a little rouge before the doorbell rang. When she started getting a crush on a man it didn't matter about Oscars, or the adoration of millions, it mattered only about the one.

She trotted back to the closet, put the terry-cloth robe on a hook, and grabbed a Donna Karan robe instead. Blue with gold trim. Stylish but not steamy.

"You nut," she said aloud as she glanced in the mirror one last time.

When she arrived at the entry she found Sam wearing a leather coat, a gray sport shirt, and black pants.

"Hi," he said, and kissed her cheek.

There was only a brief, slightly disappointing hug. Something was on his mind. With other normally inscrutable men, a few actually, she could feel their mood when they walked past. It occurred to her that most such men had either been her lovers or were related to her.

Suddenly she had a hunch about what—other than her brother's disappearance, dead friends, and a wounded pilot—might be bothering Sam.

"You're worried about the kiss. That's so touching."

"Touching?"

"You're afraid of hurting me."

There was just a ripple across Sam's cool.

"And you came all the way out here to talk about it."

Sam looked at her, saying nothing, knowing that there were many weak words and few that were strong. He could talk about his need for privacy and that would be nearly indistinguishable from whining. Reasoning would be obvious and trivial, for there would be no logic on this subject that hadn't already occurred to her.

So he watched her. As he did he noticed the brown amber of her eyes, and the way she half smiled but without the usual confidence. Normally there was a great evocative force to her personality, but she was not using it. Instead she seemed like an accomplished but vulnerable woman. Once again her hair was studied chaos with even more curly ringlets. There was a softness about her that made him want to crush her in his arms and whisper things. He could imagine that she would giggle softly in his ear and tease him with her fingers.

Apparently on impulse she stepped forward and kissed him, tentatively at first, then a little harder. Sam responded, then stopped.

"So?"

"I suppose we should . . . I know I kissed you yesterday and it was good. And this was better. But I'm thinking that until we get this figured out . . ."

She kissed him again, her tongue like a butterfly, her lips firm. He let his arms stay around her for a long moment, then released her.

"That was just one for the road until you get it worked out," she said.

"You're an amazing woman."

"And?"

"We've got to put your brother first. This . . . kind of thing will slow us down."

"I see."

"What do you see?"

"That must be the right thing—keeping our relationship professional. It's just that . . ." She stopped and took a deep breath. "Well, of course I understand." She gnawed on her lip. "I still expect you to accompany me to the studio party." But she smiled when she said it so that he knew it was a tease and not a weight around his neck.

"I have been thinking about it. Maybe I could take you. Maybe you could say I was like the friendly security man or something. But it's still a bad idea."

"Shall I take that as a complete capitulation?" she joked.

"And might we add the little detail that you will

never consider talking about me? I mean other than the security-man story at the party."

She batted her eyes to tease him. "You are as safe with me as I am with you." She kissed him on the cheek and ran her hand over his bicep. "So what were you going to tell me? Your tone suggested something important. You talk while I start on the granola."

Using a mixture of oats and almond and walnut fragments, she ladled on some canola oil and some honey, spread it on a pan, and popped it into the hot oven to bake.

"You've been asking about my former love interest," Sam said.

"I'm busted. Peter is a statesman and a snitch. But this can't be what you were going to tell me."

Sam paused and thought about how to approach it. There was a tension in her body.

"To understand about our latest discovery you need to understand about my former love interest. And the death of my son."

She had heard the tone of his voice change—her eyes showed it. She sat down. He joined her.

"It was an assignment. Suzanne King—you know enough about her, I assume?" She nodded. "Suzanne had a stalker. He was coming onto her property and taking pictures. Even intimate pictures. My son and I set a trap at her house to catch him. . . ."

Twenty-seven

A droplet of sweat hit the yellow pad, slightly fuzzing the blue line on which it landed. Sunlight through ten-foot windows was broiling Sam alive, and the flak jacket under his shirt exacerbated the effect.

He pressed his eye to the camcorder that scanned the gardens, large veranda, and pool. The kidney-shaped Olympic-size swimming pool lay translucent blue—the South Seas hue created by tiny square ceramic tiles laid across its bottom.

Suzanne, who rarely consented to wear less than one-piece bathing attire in her movies, swam in a thong bikini, doing a slow crawl with perfect form, just as her father, now deceased, had taught her. The August sun beat on her tawny arms and glistened her splashes. Sam found her as beautiful as any woman ever created by God or gazed upon by man.

Sam's son, Bud, moved along the terraced hillside among the rhododendrons, azaleas, dogwood, myrica, sunflowers, japonica, and lilacs, looking for the same thing that now eluded Sam.

Every inch of Sam remained totally alert. Three feet away was the door to the veranda, cracked open. He had been very clear with Suzanne that there was an element of danger. Personally he didn't like using this seminude swim as bait. For some time he had felt that Suzanne's stalker was mentally deteriorating. It was evident in the notes sent by this strange left-handed peekaboo artist. The laws of testosterone, buttressed by the shoe size of the print in the garden, dictated that it was a man fond of composing his notes with letters clipped from magazines.

The intimate and candid pictures the stalker had taken of Suzanne, and thereafter shared with her and others on the Internet, were at once compelling in their beauty and composition and at the same time chilling. It was inconceivable that someone could get so close so frequently and remain undetected. There was no technology to be found, no miniature cameras or telescopic lenses, on the premises. Sam had been careful to search.

Judging from the angle of the sun apparent in the photographs, the stalker made his daylight forays around 2:00 in the afternoon. One picture had been shot through the louvers ventilating the dressing room in the poolhouse complex—a striking nude. Sam had received a disturbed look from Suzanne when he jokingly complimented her. Sam was always serious, but seldom acted that way except at moments of peak vulnerability for his clients; when they wept he tended to ease up on the dry humor.

In searching for the stalker they had considered gardeners, housekeepers—anyone with regular access. They had all checked out negative.

At one end of the pool were small boulders and palms, at the other end marble statues of recent vintage amongst solid granite tables with blue and yellow parasols. To the far side of the pool, similar tables were placed under a massive pergola eighty feet long by fifteen wide and thick with vine-sprung leaves.

Hills the color of wheat were set off by an occasional

dark-barked green-leafed oak—except in places like this estate, where gardeners used irrigation and soil amendments to defy the earth and climate. This ten-million-dollar home had been constructed on a natural bench carefully groomed with brick-fronted terraces in the Hollywood Hills.

Sam used his camera to scan the four-thousand-square-foot poolhouse annex, then swept up the hillside until he saw the boulders and palms on the far left. Monotonously he repeated the sweep, stopping every minute or so to look with his naked eye. It wasn't enough to see the intruder; Sam had to capture his presence on film. That way the local police, who were at this point thoroughly buffaloed, could be convinced that they were looking for something more than one of Suzanne's publicity stunts. Sam believed her. But even he was finding it taxing.

Normally he would farm out this sort of chase-'em-down job to someone like Shohei, or with a little more training from Shohei, perhaps his son, Bud. Usually his contracts were far more sophisticated than catching a clever stalker. But this fellow had so successfully eluded authorities and private detectives that Suzanne had finally persuaded Sam to solve her problem, paying his rather extraordinary fees.

More than anything else this stalker was patient, willing to wait weeks to get a single good photo. Last time, the final straw, he had photographed Suzanne painting her toenails in the bedroom. Carefully reviewing all the photos and the dates when they were apparently taken, Sam concluded that the man had a penchant for sneaking around the day before a full-moon night. Everything about this case was utterly bizarre. Sam knew they were dealing with a badly twisted mind, and it worried him.

He studied the buildings, the grounds, the pool, squinted, and did it again. Nothing.

The stalker seemed to have an uncanny way of knowing when to arrive. Suzanne, wanting to end it, thought the swim in the scanty suit, the day before a full moon, would make marvelous bait if the stalker had any means of observing it.

Sam had placed banks of infrared motion detectors and video cameras. Suzanne kept a dog, Grendel, making it seemingly impossible for a stranger to enter the grounds without triggering either a red blinking light on Sam's control panel or a yapping dog alert.

But there was something Sam hadn't figured out and he knew it. This guy had an edge that nobody understood.

Sam picked up the radio. "Bud, come back." While he waited he made another sweep with the video.

Sam had hoped Bud would be drawn to a slightly more intellectual calling, but it was not to be. Bud liked the most literal side of fighting bad guys and there was no dissuading him. Close all their lives, Bud and Sam were inseparable. They both loved the daredevil stuff in their spare time and more often than not did it together.

Because he'd had longer to work at it, Sam was by most measures stronger than Bud, but at forty he was no longer faster. "Come back, Bud," he spoke again into the microphone, slightly concerned. Nothing. Bud was normally back to him in three seconds. Maybe bad radio. Just then, Grendel the Doberman began an ugly bark in the dense garden behind the poolhouse.

"Bud, you out there? I need a comeback."

A light turned red on Sam's panel. Abruptly the dog went silent. Someone was in the garden. And the light indicated that someone was in the house. But that was impossible.

Suzanne swam, oblivious.

"Bud, you there?"

Damn.

Sam moved toward the door; time to get Suzanne out of the pool. Still nothing more from the dog. Before walking out the veranda door, he glanced back—no more lights were blinking on the control panel, so it was unlikely that whatever triggered the sensor was still in the house.

He slipped out the veranda door, holding the mike to the PA system.

"Suzanne," he said.

She stopped swimming.

As if by magic, a man appeared, sitting on the roof of the poolhouse. He held a camera mounted on a crossbow. Sam swung the camcorder onto the poolhouse roof and punched the police call button on the alarm pad. That done, he sprinted onto the veranda and down the six feet of steps.

"I wouldn't do that, if I were you," an amplified voice said.

Sam froze. The intruder was talking through the stereo system piped around the pool. If the gunman's finger moved a fraction, Suzanne's perfect body would be sliced with a four-bladed hunting bolt.

"Get out of the water, Suzanne," the man said.

The intruder wore a mask, but at least two video cameras with separate feeds were capturing his image. They were also recording the voice unless he had somehow managed to disable the microphones.

Suzanne stopped at the edge of the pool, broadside to the intruder.

"Out now," the man barked.

Suzanne didn't move.

"Ten seconds and you're a dead goddess. I suggest you move."

Suzanne looked at Sam. He nodded. He needed time. Where was Bud?

"Take off the suit," the man said. No doubt he was clicking pictures as he spoke. Suzanne didn't move. "I said take it off."

She looked at Sam. He nodded again, his eyes trying to pick out Bud. Suzanne's shaking hands reached behind her to untie her top. As she moved her hands and turned to the side, Bud came flying over the peak of the poolhouse roof and sent his body like a missile at the back of the intruder. The man's neck snapped with such a pop that Sam heard it from several yards away. The man rolled down the roof, hit the concrete, and moved in ugly spasms. Suzanne screamed and ran, trying for the short way around the pool to the house, thereby actually moving toward the poolhouse and the quivering body.

Sam drew his .357 magnum and walked forward, his eyes never leaving the man on the ground. Suzanne began yelling crazy, hysterical screams all over again; a second man stood in the poolhouse door, just ten feet from her, with a pistol leveled at her chest.

"Nobody move," the man said, "except you." He spoke to Suzanne. "Come over here to Papa." Like the first man, he had a dark plastic mask hiding his face.

Suzanne just shook.

Grabbing her around the neck, the man dragged Suzanne back toward the poolhouse where Bud still stood on the roof, at least twenty feet away.

"Put down your guns and come down here or I blow her brains out."

Sam's mind was whirling. What stalker would risk

this? And how could there be two men? Something was dead wrong. Whatever the case, if the guy was a sexual psychopath, Suzanne was likely dead if he got her alone—anywhere. If he was only pretending to be a sex nut, anything was possible.

Sam started walking, trying to will Bud to ignore the gunman and retreat over the roof to strike again.

Instead, Bud dropped from the poolhouse roof to the patio.

That was wrong, son.

"Stop there," the stalker said to Bud.

Thirty feet from Sam the intruder had a chokehold on Suzanne and his gun to her head. He began walking Suzanne the last few feet to the poolhouse. Sam couldn't let that happen. Bud was closer but could do nothing. For a second the intruder released Suzanne to open the poolhouse door. Suzanne started to bolt, but he grabbed her and pulled her back. Bud vaulted a patio table toward the pair, and the gunman fired, hitting Bud square in the chest. A second shot fired from the hip caught Bud in the head.

Before Sam's eyes his son thrashed and shook. Somehow the gunman's first shot at Sam missed.

Sam leaped to the side behind a garden boulder. Bullets spat against the stone.

The sounds of Bud's shaky breath all but paralyzed him. A sorrow so deep that it took power from his legs displaced his rage; he couldn't turn the emotional corner. Sam stared at the ground, knowing that the maniac was dragging Suzanne to some insane torture. He forced himself to move, to peek around the boulder at his convulsing son.

The door to the poolhouse was now closed. Sam sprinted recklessly to his boy. There was a thumb-sized bloody hole above his right eye. He propped Bud's head in his hand and devoured the bloody face with his eyes. For Sam there was no face like this in all the world and never would be again. For the briefest moment there was a flicker of recognition in Bud's eyes; then he was gone.

With nothing more than grief and duty in his heart, Sam marched to the poolhouse door. The large workout area was empty and undisturbed. Out the back door Sam saw nothing. All he could think was that his initial suspicion had been correct: These guys knew something he didn't. They must have had a way into the compound. If they didn't glide on a parasail, maybe there was an underground passage. Suzanne had not mentioned tunnels when asked directly about them, but this property had been in use for years. Just yesterday he had learned that somewhere in the immediate area of the estate, there had been a silver mine.

The poolhouse had a large mechanical room. Once it had stored coal for a 1930s-style furnace. He would start there.

Sam ran down the hall past the showers and into the large game room. To the right he remembered one door. He found two. The first opened into a large storage closet. Nothing inside. The second led to the mechanical room, whose ancient concrete floor, uneven and tilted in some areas, held a cast-iron cover Sam didn't recall seeing.

Careless.

He pointed the .357 at the cover and lifted it clear. Nothing but a four-foot-deep hole. Jumping down, he looked around at a big earthen pit blackened with coal remnants.

The chamber was bounded on four corners with old concrete stub walls. Disgusted, he climbed out, thinking he'd better search the whole building fast.

As he made for the door a swatch of black fiber caught his eye. Clothing. It had been trapped under a concrete chunk that was part of the fractured floor. The cement block wouldn't budge when he used his fingers. He went to the room's workbench, pulled down a pry bar, and tried again.

It came up. Beneath the wooden frame on which the jagged piece of concrete had rested was a black hole, a tunnel. Returning to the workbench, Sam found a light, shined it down inside.

Jesus.

He estimated a ten-foot drop; a ladder hung in place. These guys had done a lot of work.

First Sam hung into the shaft upside down with light and pistol. It had the smell of dead air, fetid with the cycle of living and dying. On the floor of the shaft lay fresh loose earth from their recent excavation under the poolhouse. Although the shaft went in two directions, all the footprints came and went away from the direction of the swimming pool and toward the nearest property boundary. His eye followed the footprints to a bend in the shaft some forty feet from the hole.

He turned and climbed down the ladder in the conventional manner. Obviously he was descending into one of the old silver mine tunnels. There wasn't time to be cautious. Once on the floor of the tunnel, he ran with the tracks.

Sam had almost reached the bend when he heard the sounds of a struggle. He turned off his light and slowed.

"Don't make me ruin your face."

Suzanne's assailant was standing at the base of another ladder. She was on her knees naked in front of him.

"Go to hell."

Sam rounded the corner and walked silently toward the gunman.

"I'm not going to kill the best piece of ass in North America. Not yet."

Sam aimed at the gunman's head, but it was indistinct and would be hard to hit in the semidarkness. He dropped his aim to the center of the man's shoulder.

He whistled loudly.

Startled, the man whirled reflexively. It was the only excuse Sam needed. Lead poured out of Sam's pistol, hitting the man's torso as if little patches of the gunmen's hide were exploding. Sam felt only a sting in his arm before the return fire caught him square in the chest and sent him flying. *Tough son of a bitch,* Sam recalled thinking before he passed out. . . .

Twenty-eight

"When I woke up in the hospital the world was a different place," Sam told Anna. "Losing my son was everything, and it felt as though nothing of me remained. I just wasn't there anymore without him. I gave my staff a large severance except the people feeding and maintaining Big Brain. Suzanne insisted that I go with her to France where she was making a movie. It wasn't then that we talked about it—about us. She came to the hospital, told me, and said she'd be back. I managed to tell Typhony, my on-again off-again girlfriend at the time.

"They wheeled me to Bud's funeral with two nurses and two IVs. When I got back to the hospital Suzanne had returned with a whole squad.

"She rented this place in the French countryside, the Loire River Valley, the heart and soul of France, she called it. I was completely depressed. She brought doctors and fed me happy pills.

"Suzanne came and went and physically I got better. I noticed the nurses got cuter.

"I couldn't go out with Suzanne without news coverage, but we saw each other each night when she came back from location, and gradually we got to know each other.

"Things started tending toward the physical and we

both got nervous. I wanted my quiet anonymous life, still thinking I might somehow go back to work, I guess. She didn't want a boyfriend who couldn't take her to an opening. I thought maybe I loved her at the time, but I had always told myself never to get involved with a celebrity. I don't know if it was that or the depression and the guilt that initially kept us apart.

"We took a breather, so to speak, and for a few days I went for long walks around the green lawns, through the rose gardens, into the vineyards, past the fish ponds, and along the Loire River. There didn't seem to be a solution.

"She called me and said we had to find a way to be together and she was coming to talk about it. They had been in Spain to shoot some scenes. I never talked with her again."

"The jet crash," Anna whispered.

"Yeah."

"First Bud, then Suzanne." Anna shook her head. "Did you love her?"

"I don't know. I still don't know what we could have done. I went back to work."

"The way you explain it, you see yourself as a victim of your profession, which demands you not take up with a celebrity. Tidy little package. Circumstances may change, but your whole life will always be a set of clever tricks you use to make sure that intimacy never happens. Passion, yes. But not the rest."

"I take up with a celebrity and the media will soon know when a person's in trouble. Right now they don't notice that I've shown up because I don't exist. That's important."

The phone rang.

"Answer it," Anna said.

"I have two big pieces of news," Paul said. "Hal

called. A G-Four landed at Campbell River and took off for Fiji. They even learned that the people getting on the plane in Canada came in on two Beavers from the Alert Bay area."

"Fiji. I'll be damned. Which island?"

"The airport at Nadi. After Nadi the G-Four went to Lebanon, but a number of passengers got off in Fiji and took a limo to another part of the airport. If they boarded another plane, Hal says it's only a matter of time until he knows whose plane and where it goes. Apparently it's hard to keep secrets in Nadi. But if they stayed a few days and then flew out, it could be harder than hell to find them."

"Lebanon tells me it's Samir Aziz," Sam said. "Trouble in paradise—partners at each other's throats."

"Right. We're exploring that. But Big Brain has a new entry in the diagram." Paul went on at some length to explain the strange correlations in the data.

"And you must have something on Wes King," Sam said.

"He died of a heart attack a couple months after the break-in. You were in France."

"Well, we missed it and now all we can do is play catch-up."

"What?" Anna took his arm as he hung up. "You look sick."

Sam was still sifting the facts in his mind. "It'll take a few minutes to explain. You ready?"

Anna checked the oven. "This stuff burns easily because of the honey." She pulled out the granola, served it, and got them glasses of orange juice.

"Okay," Sam said, and sat at the table. "Suzanne King had a kind heart. Suzanne allowed her ex-husband, Wes King, to hang around her house. Of all these divorced celebrities who allegedly remain 'good friends,' this was that rare couple that actually did remain on good terms."

"It's not a bad idea to maintain the friendship."

"Uh-huh. Well, there wasn't any spin with them. And Wes stayed at the house mostly when he visited town on business. The study remained his and I guess, according to the maid, the deal was that he could keep using it until Suzanne found a serious boyfriend. Wes had a wall safe—which of course we didn't know at the time of the stalker case—where he kept the source code to a valuable software program his company had developed. It was called Auditor, and it had made him a fortune. All you need to know is that it was a very sophisticated accounting program that integrated other manufacturing and production functions and was unique at the time. But to set it up and to make it run with other programs you needed the source code. It's very long and complex and virtually can't be figured out."

Sam started nibbling the granola as it cooled and nodded his approval to Anna.

"Somebody wanted it for use in places like China, where its sale was forbidden by federal law. Supposedly because of its potential military applications. The whole thing with the stalking and photos of Suzanne was a diversion to distract attention from the real motive for invading the property. The people who were after the software's source code found themselves a couple of real live perverts with a record of stalking and assault."

"But why go to all that trouble?" Anna asked. "If you've got the tunnel into the estate, why not sneak in when nobody is home?"

"Because they couldn't do it with only one entry into the house. You blow up the safe and everybody can guess what you're doing. The software theft only works if people don't suspect that it has happened. That's the big difference between this and a theft of cash or jewelry. Suzanne believed that stalkers were invading her house—she was distracted. I doubt she even knew the contents of the safe. None of us, not me, not the police, and evidently not Wes, were thinking about theft or planning for it. We were all thinking about people on a weird power trip posting nude photos on the Web. That's how we interpreted all the break-ins, the entire experience."

"Okay, so what information connected King's software and my brother's case?"

"Big Brain. I told you the feeding of Big Brain never really stops. The tech staff was feeding Big Brain even when I was off sailing. What we had thought of as a solved crime—namely Suzanne King's stalkers—suddenly became an unsolved crime when the news about the safe and the source code became public. The techies fed in the information as the police released it. And the FBI guys that know me and know Big Brain paved the way to feed data for their own purposes. That created a hot spot or high-priority area in the database on anything related to the King case. If there is any genius in Big Brain's software it is taking these seemingly unrelated facts and finding connections. Sometimes it just seems like trivial information but you'd be amazed at what comes of it.

"In the car used by the stalkers there was a shaving kit, and in that kit was a paper cocktail coaster that had a phone number on it. The number belonged to an executive for Systemtechnik, a German company. We never made anything of that because the stalker was a cousin of the executive's wife. That explained why he had the number. But before we figured that out we tapped into a computer contact list for Systemtechnik and downloaded the entire contents. And of course we never throw anything away. Big Brain has nearly infinite memory space. One address in those thousands of company contacts was a Cayman Islands address that will become important. Big Brain drew a correlation and the executive with the stalker's phone number was the same executive who entered the Cayman address in his company's computer.

"More recently Big Brain highlighted the name of an exporter of gift cheeses in France because it appeared on an invoice retrieved from the garbage of a Grace Technologies employee named Benoit Moreau. The cheese package bore a shipping address—a post office box in the Cayman Islands, the *same* post office box in the Cayman Islands that had popped up in the Systemtechnik records. That meant a connection to the Suzanne King case.

"To thicken the plot some, a French software company called Belle du Jour had received construction drawings from that same Systemtechnik executive. Belle du Jour also received money and sent billings to Grace, so Big Brain noticed that Belle du Jour had dealings with both Systemtechnik and Grace, and in the case of Grace the ROCs—"

"Wait, what's a ROC?"

"ROC, record of communication. . . . The ROCs were to one Benoit Moreau."

Anna looked confused, but she motioned for Sam to continue.

"Next comes the exotic twist. A little while back, for a completely different project, we managed to download one of the databases from a very large overnight delivery company. We're talking major data volume here, but handling it is something that Big Brain does

better than any computer in the known universe. Big
Brain found a package sent by Benoit Moreau—a
shipment from a sex gadget company. Now Moreau is
close to Chellis in the corporate structure, so she creates red flags any time Big Brain notices her. She sent
the sex toy to Belle du Jour, but the contact phone
didn't match any of the numbers we had for Belle du
Jour. The number turned out to match a satellite
phone, and it also appeared on the phone logs of a
cell phone used by one of the stalkers. It was also dialed by the Systemtechnik executive and a phone at
Grace headquarters in Paris."

"So that tells us a criminal, the Systemtechnik fellow, and this Benoit gal all called the same sat phone
number." Anna's eyes widened, as if she could see the
possible significance.

"Uh-huh. They did. Next step is to find the address
associated with that sat phone number; turns out it's
registered to a company, the Freight Stop, in the Cay-
mans. You could search for that company for years
and find nothing on it . . . but . . . Big Brain had noted
that someone at Belle du Jour had sent a document
to the Freight Stop. And at one time the billing address for Belle du Jour was a Cayman Island address
that had all mail forwarded to a certain Polynesian
island address.

"Because of this, Big Brain assigned priority to the
Polynesian address.

"That led Big Brain to do some handwriting-
recognition analysis. Remember the cheese? In Benoit
Moreau's garbage was a card that she had sent to the
Cayman address, which forwarded it to the Polynesian
address. A joke was scribbled on the card by the recipi-
ent, who sent it back to Moreau—return address:
Polynesia. The joke was in French and it said: 'Keep the

G spot warm.' And it was signed *G*. Now do you recall the guy checking for spores in the Carter Building?"

"Yeah?"

"He signed in with the receptionist as G. Gousteaux. Big Brain matched the G on the sign-in form with the G on Benoit's card. And when he was printing his name on the sign-in sheet it matched the print of the joke on the gift card. That makes the man at the Polynesian address the man of Belle du Jour, who is associated with the Freight Stop, which does business with Grace Technolgies and Systemtechnik. This fellow is almost surely the lover of Benoit Moreau and is definitely the spore man who killed Weissman and who in all likelihood masterminded the assault on the Carter Building."

Anna whistled, shaking her head.

"What really tortures me is that he also probably controlled the two perverts who harassed Suzanne, one of whom killed my son. The good news is that we've put this all together. The bad news is that this guy is very clever and very deadly and now opposes us. One more thing. When we gave all this to Interpol, they thought it might be a man who sometimes calls himself Devan Gaudet."

"That's incredible."

"About like the granola," Sam said, taking the last bite.

"So now that makes this personal for you."

"I'm afraid it does."

Twenty-nine

Devan Gaudet strode lazily down the sidewalk, an air of calm certainty masking what he was about to undertake. On a leash he led a fine-looking bulldog as harmless as May daisies. It amused him that the good guys were so predictable. At times like this he was practically ready to believe in God, for only the miraculous could account for his good fortune.

Naturally Grady *had* to tell Guy that she was going to go to school. (It was entirely predictable that the Sam man would try to ruin a perfectly good stripper by giving her a job and sending her to college.) With her background she would start either in a small state university or a junior college. Using about a dozen skip tracers he and Trotsky identified the school in three days.

That would have been impossible to accomplish in the short time frame if she hadn't also reassured Guy that she wasn't moving far. She had called from a phone booth on the street right after registering at school and according to her story walking some distance through the neighborhood before stopping to use a pay phone. Although she didn't say how far she walked, they assumed no more than thirty minutes. On the tape of the call there was the sound of a harbor whistler buoy in the background. There was one junior college in the greater LA area that would be within earshot of a whistler buoy. Benoit had sent the voice recording as an e-mail attachment so that Gaudet and his men had it almost immediately.

Using an old ruse, a seasoned private eye had gotten Grady's mailing address out of the school. Of course it was a PO box. Since the post office needed a physical address or phone number, a complex bit of bribery completed the work. Immediately he put three of his best men on the house. At least that was Trotsky's assessment of this trio. When they saw Grady leave in a rusty-looking car driven by another young woman they called him. The bodyguard types around the house had vanished, so he concluded that she would be gone for a while. No suitcase had been in her hand, so she wasn't on a trip. Now he was only gambling on her swift return.

There was something unusual about this job—something in his state of mind. For some time he had allowed himself to fantasize about watching this particular young woman die. He knew that she must be beautiful if she was anything like her reputation. The vision growing in his mind was becoming a compulsion, and although he knew it, he found himself drawn to the point that his will was riding on a tide of strange emotions. Nothing about the situation seemed to be blunting his analytical skills; he was not unaware of the risk involved in a face-to-face, hands-on killing. As he thought about it he concluded that his will was very much intact, that there was no element of irrationality. It was simply that the reward inherent in what he was planning merited the risk. It was nothing more than the pursuit of pleasure, the way some men risk their lives for a shot at the summit of Everest.

The house had an alarm equipped with motion

detectors. The best way in was under the house through a duct that had been opened with heavy shears, but before going into the house he had some chores. He crossed the street at the end of the block, careful not to jaywalk. Wandering a little, letting the dog piss and sniff as he went, looking here and there, he made sure to give the appearance of a man out for a stroll.

When he arrived at the front gate he tied the dog and it sat. Then he walked through the gate and into the shadows, where he pulled on plastic surgeon gloves, put rubber slip-ons over his shoes, and pulled a key from under his raincoat. Next, staying in the shadows, he went to the side of the house, unlocked a padlock that fastened a three-foot-high door allowing access under the house. Chellis's men had exchanged locks after they had cut off the original with bolt cutters. It took seconds to find the splice between the heavy lengths of duct tape; he disconnected them at the elbow. Another two minutes to find the depression in the ground that had been covered with cardboard, burlap, and dirt. It was carefully constructed so as to be invisible to the naked eye. He left it open so that he could crawl in quickly, but hoped he wouldn't need it. Next, he moved up under the grate and slowly pushed it aside. The motion detector did not trigger the alarm.

He pulled a plastic bag from the large pocket of the overcoat. Without hesitating, he stood up with his torso above the floor and triggered the alarm. He went straight to the cupboards, found a bowl, and filled it with the contents of his bag and placed it on a table with a note. The alarm was raucous. Moving fast, he found the trapdoor to the attic in the bedroom closet. There were foot pegs up the wall for access. He tilted the overhead trapdoor on its hinges and put his head up into the attic, illuminating the musty space with a flashlight. It was a sizable storage area and had a plywood floor supporting a large number of boxes. The woman was a pack rat. When he left, he did not replace the trapdoor, but instead left it open for easy access. He then jumped back under the house, replaced the heater grate, and fit the duct back in place, applying tape. The alarm had been sounding for three minutes. Crawling out from under the house, he walked to the front, took the dog, and immediately encountered the neighbor, clearly the neighborhood busybody, just as his men had predicted. An older man with a pipe and a paper under his arm looked eager to talk.

"I am from France, as you can tell by the accent, and I saw this place and thought sure it was my friend's, and now I see that I am turned around and in the wrong neighborhood. I feel so bad. Somehow when I knocked loudly on the window I must have set off the noise sensor."

"Only a girl and her friend live here."

"Yes. Well, I wish the police would come so I could explain."

"I don't know what it is like in France, but here it can take twenty minutes for the police to arrive. I'll tell them. Last time it was a spider crawling over the which-'em-a-call-it. I turn the alarm off and reset it when she isn't here, but I have to wait for the police to check everything out."

"You're sure? I'm very sorry for the racket." As if he hadn't a care in the world, Gaudet walked down the block, turned to the left, and disappeared from the neighbor's sight. Turning the dog loose to wander off down the street, he doubled back behind the house, jumped a neighbor's fence into the backyard of Jill's house, and went immediately to the grate. After about seven minutes from its initial sounding, the audible alarm automatically turned off and became a steady beeping inside the house. It was another ten minutes before the neighbor who had the code was in the house with the police. Footfalls made it obvious that they were walking through the house, checking superficially.

"Hey," one of them whispered. There was silence for a time.

"Hell, there's nothing up there. They just left the trapdoor open."

"You gotta check, though."

Then they were back at the front door and he could hear the neighbor resetting the alarm. He would have sixty seconds.

"You know it's fifty dollars for false alarms," the officer said.

"Guess I should have collected from the guy with the dog," the neighbor said as they closed the door.

Rushing up through the grate, he replaced it, and was up in the attic before the alarm once again became effective.

Gaudet sat in the attic and waited, amused that it had gone so easily. Had they been more watchful, it would have been necessary to wait in the hole in the ground under the house. This way it was so much more comfortable. Taking out his light and a small book, he began reading the published journal of a bondage slave.

There were a couple of lamps radiating a soft glow, one in between a small sitting area and the breakfast nook, and the other in the living room. Then there

were night-lights in the wall outlets along with various
things that emitted pleasant scents; and these electrical deodorizers were in addition to hand-tied bags of
aromatic herbs; and there were special sounds like the
heat pump fans, the rather loud refrigerator freezer,
the hot-water pump, and sometimes the Jacuzzi tub.
To Grady, Jill's house felt as if it nurtured life, even
had a life, as opposed to just containing people, and
in that respect it reminded her of a large jetliner flying over oceans in the dead of night.

The place seemed more feminine than one would
expect, given an owner who favored rock climbing and
fast cars. All the furnishings in Grady's room were done
in an amber-colored oak except the Early American
amoire, which appeared to be pine. Two paintings featured flower gardens created by making myriad dots in
oil. She didn't know the correct name for that type of
painting, but had made a mental note to find out.

Grady had arrived home late, having seen the den-
tist, the doctor, and run a number of household
errands with her bodyguards. Lately she found herself
looking over her shoulder. As Grady understood it,
they had her father and there was nothing more for
them to get but her.

After she changed into her sweats, she pulled on a
robe and found Jack outside the back door, sitting on
the porch.

"Hey," she said. "Wanna talk?"

"It's the middle of the night." He turned and smiled.
"Sure I'll talk, but we need you sleeping. You're still
freaked about the alarm, aren't you?"

"Well, it's my third night and it happened today."

"We walked through this place. Looked in all the
closets. We went over with the alarm company that
it was the motion detector in the kitchen. But it's

impossible to get to the kitchen without triggering other motion sensors. We can't find a point of entry. Probably the guy with the dog knocked on the window and some time near that moment a bug crawled across the detector or a mouse ran across the floor and it went off. The guy thought he did it. That's all."

"I know."

"We called Jill and she said it was probably nothing because the alarm has a hair trigger."

"You really think it was nothing?"

"Would you be here if we thought there was any danger? Really, the odds that some French company is going to get together a killing squad in a week is a little far-fetched. But that's not to say we shouldn't be careful. So if you think of anything, you tell me. We'll all be right here. Soon I'll be in the living room. If need be I'll sit in the bedroom and watch you sleep."

"No. No. I'll go back to bed or read or something. Do you want some soup? Jill left a big bowl on the table."

"No. No, thanks. You have it. Maybe it will help you sleep." Talking to herself about how safe she was, she went back and got in bed.

All this fuss over her father was a further irritation. She had never allowed herself to be impressed that he was a famous physicist. Although she had not previously wasted more than a few minutes thinking about him, she now was becoming curious. More accurately, she was beginning to worry. Maybe he was the best guy ever. Perhaps, in some strange way, he had cared for her but never let it be known. Now she might never know.

Hot and still adrenaline-alert, she tossed off the blankets and glanced at the phone. It was 11:30 P.M.

and Guy would be leaving the club. She wanted to talk with him one more time, and that would be the end of it for a few days. Jill wasn't home and the security people seemed to be staying outside. She picked up the phone and made a collect call.

"It's so good to hear from you."

"Yeah. I'm sorry I haven't called very much. I'm starting to realize that you probably cared about me."

"I *do* care about you. How's school?"

"Well, I'm just auditing a class. It's the middle of the term so I don't really start for grades until next semester. But I also have a job. A new job. I'm done with stripping, done with drugs, done with clubs. I'm moving on."

"That's so great. I am too. New job starting next week. I'm managing a bar. A bar where people leave their clothes on. So what's your job?"

"I can't talk about it. It's research."

"Sounds fascinating. Whatever you can tell me I would love to hear."

She hesitated. She knew she could trust him. "I'm researching things—interesting things. Like today I was learning things about Fiji. Taveuni Island."

"Fiji?"

"Yeah."

"What about Fiji?"

"You know, I shouldn't get into it. Not even with someone I trust. There are rules here."

"I understand. Will you be going to Fiji?"

"No. But others will."

After more small talk she hung up, feeling intrigued, more so than she could remember. He was a nice man. She grabbed her robe and headed for the refrigerator. There were men about the place, so she had been told to wear something.

As she walked down the hall past the living room and into the kitchen, she saw the bowl of soup again on the table and the note from Jill.

She tossed the note and sat down with the soup after she had crushed some saltines and sprinkled them on top. A quick blast from the microwave and inside of four minutes she had the soup down.

It was savory, surprisingly so, heavy with spices and the flavor of barbecue sauce.

She decided to call Jill at the office.

"You can't sleep?" Jill said.

"My body seems to be on full alert."

"Still thinking about the alarm?"

"Uh-huh. You know, I have hated my father for as long as I can remember and I don't even know him," Grady said.

"At least you feel something and you have a name for what you feel. What is your first memory of your father?"

"Seeing him at work on his chalkboard. It's about the only memory."

"There's some yogurt in the fridge and some marion-berry jam."

"Sure, why not? Might as well get fat now that I don't get naked for a living."

"Don't ever let El Numero Uno hear that. We'll be running to New York."

It was a roomy kitchen with a breakfast table in an alcove. For some reason Jill loved Early American decor, and the place looked like the inside of an up-scale farmhouse.

"Grady?"

"Yeah?"

"Don't you think you should wait until you meet your father before you finally decide about him?"

"He's an asshole. He had to be. Think about it."

"You're not sure."

"How do you know?"

"Because you're still fighting yourself about it."

"Yeah, well, the Dad part of me is losing. I promise."

"I would like to meet your father."

"Good luck. He's a paranoid creep."

"Uh-huh," Jill said.

"I have a guy I like," Grady began. "I was worried about treating him like shit. I promised to call him. Anyway, I broke the rules and called him a few times to let him know I was okay."

"What do you mean? When?"

"Four times. Twice at the beach house, once when I registered at the junior college, and once tonight. But tonight I said good-bye for a few days until we get the rules about phone calls worked out."

"We've got to tell Sam. Don't you understand this is not about deportment? It's about security. This changes everything about the alarm, about everything. And Sam is going to kick my ass. I'm responsible for you. Don't you get it?"

"Look, it was nothing. I told him nothing. I just said I was all right."

"You should have told us. Tell me word for word everything you said."

"The first call was when we were at the cabin when I couldn't call. Then at the phone booth."

"I knew it. The day you came running."

"Well, that too. But I did it again with a guy named Clint from next door. He and his friend drove me."

"Clint is a distant cousin of Sam's. He was a plant. The call at the phone booth was bugged."

"Wow. Should have figured it. I'm sorry."

"Yeah. Now what about the last two times?"

Grady recounted it, afraid of what Sam would say. More afraid than she would have thought possible.

"So all you did was tell him that you are in college, you have a job, and you're okay?"

"I told him I did research because I wanted to impress him."

"You said nothing about where you were, who you worked for, or what you did except research?"

"That's right. Way back when, I said the beach house was near Carmel."

"I'm telling Sam right now. He just got here. The Chellis people could find you with what you told them. Especially about college. We would nail your ass with that info. If your boyfriend is on their payroll, they will probably find you."

"He's not selling me out. That's ridiculous."

"Still, you screwed this up big time. You and I are going to have to move out of the house. You'll need a new name. New school. Do you realize that?"

"Why?"

"I'm too upset to explain right now, Grady. Let me talk to Sam and I'll call you back."

"Do you have to?"

"You know, it's a real problem that you have to ask." Jill hung up.

"Hello, kid."

Grady jumped as if scalded. A strange bearded man stood in the corner. He held a silenced pistol.

"Who are you?"

"Afraid I can't say. On the other hand, since you're going to die, maybe it doesn't matter."

"I feel funny," Grady said, suddenly dizzy.

"I hope you enjoyed the soup."

"What was it?"

"What you're feeling is an alkaloid extracted from

Chondodendron tomentosum, Strychnos toxifera, and a few other ingredients. Then there was something to cause it to quickly enter your bloodstream through the stomach lining. That's the brilliant part."

Grady stood and grabbed the table for support. A terrible weakness was overtaking her.

"My leg is shaking."

"Yes, I can tell you liked my recipe. You may have heard of the active ingredients referred to as curare. That's a native term for a group of organic molecules that come from certain plant species, and are mixed by the natives of South America with poison from bugs and spiders. I rely on the primary plant alkaloid mixed with various pharmaceuticals. Without purification and treatment the stuff is too bitter to disguise even with barbecue sauce and herbs. I'm actually very proud of the recipe."

Grady's face sank near the tabletop; her whole body was shaking now.

"I will pick you up."

He threw her over his shoulder.

"Bastard," Grady gasped.

"Soon you'll long for my kisses—it's the only way you'll be able to breathe."

Grady tried to scream and failed. She watched, fully alert, as he carried her into the bedroom. She could feel everything down to the hair on his arms and the warmth of the bedclothes under her back. But she couldn't move, not even to roll over.

The room was dark, lit only by a night-light in the wall socket. She saw a match strike and watched him light a candle. Her abductor stepped away, and she heard the sound of the shower in her bathroom. He returned to her side.

"The beauty of this drug is that you remain fully

conscious. I don't have to listen to you scream because you can't."

He turned her head so that she could see him. Then it occurred to her that he wanted to see the terror in her eyes.

"Soon you will not be able to respirate."

He pulled his chair very close, pressed his lips to hers, and she could feel the monster's breath expand her lungs.

"Breath from heaven." He actually smiled. "Or is it from hell?"

Again he pressed his lips to hers and filled her lungs. Her vision was as if down a tunnel but he was there, his face in the flickering candlelight. He pulled off his beard. Again he pressed his lips to hers and breathed for her.

"I want you to see me as I am. I want you to see the man who is breathing the breath of life into you and the man who will snuff it out."

Even as her body became dead, her mind became more alive. It was all she had.

"I can't let the relaxant kill you because you may not be able to see me at the last. And that is not good enough. So I'm going to put you in the bathtub and give you a cardiac glycoside that is derived from *Acokanthera apocynaceae*. The principal chemical is ouabain—two-thousandths of a gram will be completely lethal. The second I give it to you I will drop in your electric razor. If the authorities are brilliant they will probably conclude that you were poisoned by the operatives of DuShane Chellis. If they are only marginally competent, they will decide that you were electrocuted." His eyes grew distant. "You won't see me again."

With her mind sharp and undiluted by any hysteria,

she felt his foul mouth on hers, then his tongue, and his breath hot and sweet pouring into her. And he was right. She craved the next breath. She did not want to die at twenty.

Thirty

"We're going to need all the firepower we can get," Sam said.

"Aye. As long as it shoots rubber bullets, right?" Aussie was his guy in Fiji.

"I know it sounds strange, but it will actually give us an advantage."

"I've got to live here after you leave, you know."

"I understand. I want to move on this thing. What if we come in three days?"

"No way. Huge mistake. It's going to take me more time than that unless you want to throw rocks. I can see them settling in, but I've got to get the boat in place. Half the heat I have is still coming. It'll be a bloody miracle if it's in place in a week and a half."

"Then do it in a week. It's important. Anna Wade is bouncing off the floor."

"Do you think she'd bounce off my floor?"

"Very funny."

"We'll try, but *do not* arrive before we can move. The longer you're in this backwater, the more attention you draw."

"Okay. A week. Precise arrival time by e-mail."

"You got it."

"Keep your phone on."

Jill was tapping him on the shoulder. "I'm worried.

Grady has a boyfriend of sorts. She's been talking to him."

"And?"

"It isn't good. She said she was going to school."

"Oh, no."

"You know the alarm went off this afternoon and we never really found out why."

"Come on." Sam grabbed his cell phone and punched Jill's home number as he ran to the heavy steel door, shoving it open as fast as it would move. They sprinted through the waiting room into the parking lot and jumped into Blue Hades. "No answer."

"Jack," Jill said on her cell. "You've gotta move. Something's wrong inside." A pause. "Break her door down, shower or no shower."

"Good move," Sam said.

"Jack said she's been in her bedroom for a while. The shower's been running."

Sam figured he could dodge traffic at eighty miles an hour; they were in front of the house in eight minutes. There was an ambulance siren sounding in the distance. Sam hit the door with a flying kick, knocking it off its hinges. They burst through into the living room and ran to the bedroom. Grady was on the bed, white and dry like chalk. Jack was hunched over her, breathing into her lungs. An ambulance pulled up, and Sam took over the breathing while Jill checked her pulse.

"She has a heartbeat. Feels strong and normal. Maybe a little slow."

Sam breathed in her lungs and stared at eyes that were strange with something he'd never seen. She was utterly still; no part of her moved.

"A drug."

Jack ran out the door, and came back with four guys and one woman, all in blue suits. Immediately they were on her with a stethoscope. Sam kept pushing air into her lungs.

"She said there was soup on the table," Jack said. "Jill, did you leave soup?"

"No soup. None."

"A drug," Sam said. "Must be."

"BVM," the lead man said. "We'll take it," he said, putting an airway down her throat with a squeeze bag fitted atop. "She looks like somebody gave her sux," the woman said. "Let's go with Versed as soon as we get the IV in her."

"Pump every last ounce out of her stomach and ask questions later," Jill said.

They had her on a gurney and out the door in seconds. The bedroom window had been broken out and the torn curtains moved in the gentle breeze; the sheer white shreds and the blackness behind were a grim prop for someone's death feast.

Sam pulled Jack aside. "What happened?"

"I went to the door and knocked. There was this huge crash. I went in and somebody had gone through the window. She looked dead but her heart was beating. So I did the CPR with the mouth-to-mouth thing. It seemed to help, but she didn't breathe on her own. I called an ambulance in between breaths, which was tough, and I knew you'd be along any minute."

"Any idea who went out the window?"

"Not a clue."

"Didn't the other guys see?"

"No way. They heard something and came around, but they didn't know what they were looking for and it was dark."

"You would think they'd have seen something."
"Yeah. You would."

Samir summoned Michelle into his workroom, pondering the complications in his life.

"Leona will come back next month. I have never had an office as such but I will get an office in Beirut and a spacious apartment nearby. It will be yours if that pleases you."

"It does. I know I cannot be here when your wife is here."

"If I were Muslim I might have more than one wife, but I am supposedly Christian Maronite. On the subject of having one wife, Leona is very religious." Samir chuckled.

"You are looking so well, but you know we're running out of oil."

"I know. And life is hell without it. There is a difference between what we took from the lab and what you get in the mail. If only we knew what it was."

"There is something I must tell you."

"Yes?"

"Please believe me that I am growing attached to you."

"Yes?" Samir suddenly had a bad feeling.

"I was not in Quatram when I came to the Middle East. I couldn't get in. I was seeing lawyers in France about my boy and working as a masseuse when I was summoned to the offices of Grace Technologies. I gave a massage to DuShane Chellis. It was a good job and I came regularly."

"So did he, I should think. Go on."

"You do not have to be crass."

Samir chuckled before she continued.

"I think it was a very odd relationship he had with his assistant Benoit. She is the sister of his wife. Very odd. Anyway, I told them about my son and that I was seeing lawyers. To tell you the short version, they got me into Quatram through the general and they promised I could get my son out of the country if I could entice you to hire me."

"You are working for Chellis?"

"I am telling you what I am not supposed to tell you, so I guess I am working for you. But my son's life is at stake."

Samir nodded, keeping his face neutral. "Go on."

"They said it would be easy to win your favor if I did exactly as they said. For massage I was to use the blue-tinged oil that I now use on you."

"So they are poisoning me or playing with my mind."

"Yes. But it isn't what you think. I have the oil on me, and on my fingers, and it does nothing to me."

"So what are you saying?"

"Just that the oil by itself doesn't seem to do anything."

"What did they tell you?"

"Nothing, except that I was to use a different oil today."

"And did you?"

"No."

"Why?"

"Because I couldn't deceive you."

"You like me?"

"I know in some respects that you are cruel, but you were kind to me. You are powerful, very powerful, and maybe I need someone like that."

"I could split you like a chicken for conspiring with Chellis."

"I know that."

"Why did you think I wouldn't kill you?"

"Am I wrong?"

"No." Samir chuckled. "You are not wrong, but what does a man like me know of love or loyalty? I buy women."

"Even your wife?"

"Especially my wife. Her price is diamonds. I knew you came by way of Chellis somehow because I knew the oil in the laboratory was a stronger version of what you used. No massage could make me feel that good."

"Why didn't you kill me?"

"To be honest, you intrigued both my head and my loins. Few women do that. You were desperate. Equally important, I simply cannot live without the effects of the oil you brought. And I like how you use it. Now where is this oil you were supposed to use today?"

"I have it in my bag."

"Get it."

In moments she returned to the workroom with a white canvas bag. "Here it is." She held a small bottle.

"Put a dab on my back. Let us see what it does."

"What if it is deadly?"

"They do not want to kill me now. They need me for the business. They want only to control me. It is not poison. I suspect that where the other oil lessens the jitters and diminishes the torture, this one does the opposite and would make me mad with fear. So just a dab. Then get the other oil."

"It comes in portions, remember. If I use a portion of the regular oil now, that will be a few drops I don't have for another day."

"I stole some from the Chellis lab but I use so much for those damn doctors who still can't figure it out. The reason I am normal some days is that I get not only what you have but also I get extra from the other supply."

"I am so sorry," she said.

"Unless they can figure out what is in it, we are going to run out. Well, we will risk it. Just use a dab of the other and get ready with the usual stuff."

Dipping her finger in the untried oil, she reached under his shirt, smeared it over his back, and held him close. They waited for a few minutes, talking quietly.

"That works fast," he said. "It is as if someone loosed the hounds of hell in my head. Quick, give me the other."

She smeared a little more of the regular oil and after a time it calmed him.

"So we have solved another small part of the riddle." He patted her head and growled, "I will kill the bastard."

Benoit rang Gaudet as he drove through Los Angeles.

"I would have said that the stuff from your snitch," he said, "this Guy fellow, was nothing. But I've traced a private flight from BC to Fiji. I'd been examining many international flights on that day, but this one is suddenly more interesting. Tell Chellis to try a bluff with Samir. Act like we know where he has Jason. I have my people going to Taveuni tonight. If he's there they will find him by tomorrow night, unless they've made very careful arrangements. By the way, our little angel has gone off to heaven."

"Are you serious?"

"When do I joke about stuff like that?"

It was a relief to have Grady Wade out of the picture. Benoit found Chellis down the hall from his office, leaning in the treasurer's doorway. He waved good-bye to the treasurer. "Did you tell Michelle to use the other oil today?"

"Yes. He'll be paranoid as hell when you call." As they walked she told him about her conversation with Guy and her most recent conversation with Gaudet.

"Perhaps you'd like to go get some things done," Chellis said. "I'm liable to be a while with Samir."

"I'm fascinated to see how you handle him." She put her hand under his arm and leaned close.

"And if I kick you out you'll be hard to find."

"I'm never hard to find. I just go to the labs sometimes in the course of doing my job. I do have a job."

"You can stay."

They sat on the couch, where he picked up the phone and she threw her leg over his, making sure that he could feel the warmth of her body on the meaty part of his thigh.

Samir's assistant answered.

"Samir and I need to talk," Chellis said.

"He is very sick. But he will try you in twenty minutes."

"Maybe if we're going to find him in Fiji anyway, we shouldn't bother with a deal," said Benoit.

"Finding Jason and bringing him out without them killing him are two different things," Chellis replied.

"I suppose you're right. We just need his work. It doesn't matter who guards him for the next little while."

Benoit knew that Samir would make his way to another phone line at a relative's used only for occasional important calls. It had a scrambler and would not be tapped. She would receive the call through a router from another number outside the building taken in the name of a dead person. It would ring into the office from a relay to a special private line. It had all been swept for interception in the last twenty-four hours. Even if a government tapped the satellite link, the scrambler would disguise voices beyond electronic decoding so that voice-recognition sweeps aimed at either man would not sort the call from the millions of other calls going on between millions of other people. No doubt the government could develop software to detect scramblers, if it hadn't already done so. But there were so many scramblers that it left a large number of transmissions to be decoded, and no one knew exactly the level of government success in unscrambling these signals.

"I have a feeling the Fiji thing is a good lead," Chellis said while they waited. "It's out of the way. Politically I recall it's controlled by chiefs in fiefdoms. There is no intelligence agency, and like all third-world countries they love foreign money. There's no dictator to undertake kidnaps and other crap."

"Maybe. It wouldn't have been my choice, but maybe." The call rang through.

"Samir, old friend," Chellis began. "I understand you're nervous. I don't really blame you for taking my scientist. But we both desperately need him to continue his work and he can't do that without Grace Technologies."

"What has that to do with me?"

"Listen, I know you have him in Fiji. In an hour I'll know exactly where he is. Let's not fight. I'm willing to give you the security you want, but we need a joint team down there protecting Jason. A very powerful man is after him. He is aligned with Anna Wade, the American actress and Jason's sister. They have the American police and the Canadian Mounties on this.

We need to work together, not fight each other to the death. Because unless we work together, that is what it will be."

"What exactly are you proposing?"

"You and I hire Devan Gaudet—you've heard of him—to trap the American hired by the actress. You and I watch Jason together. My men and your men. I will send a small contingent to Fiji. Four men. Together we will hire more. You will have four of your men. Gaudet will be in charge of the trap."

"And how do you know the American will come?"

"If he is as good as Gaudet says he is, he will come. They won't wait for years of red tape in an undeveloped country."

"I will have ten of my men. You will have four, or no deal. And I always keep control of Jason while you are working with him."

"You know Gaudet from France and the South Seas?"

"He is not a man. He is not even an animal."

"Yes. Well, he's working for me. You agree he will be there to take care of the American. So can we make a deal? You've ten men but Gaudet runs the war with the American and works for me. You keep your ten men with Jason; I have only four?"

"It is a deal. But don't cross me."

"Hey, I want my research to continue. That is all."

"Can you fix me? My head. You have scientists."

"I will see what I can do. But if you don't trust me with Jason, how are you going to trust me with your head?"

They knew they had him. Even when Samir said he would call back, they were pretty sure of his answer.

Chellis hung up the phone and rolled Benoit over

on the couch. Their sex was fast and for her as mechanical as the drawbridges on the Seine.

"God, that relaxes me," Chellis said.

"Why don't you go home early? I will call your
masseuse."

"Good," he said.

Thirty-one

Benoit called Jacques at the Kuching laboratory.

"So what's happening?"

"I'm in the lab cleaning up spilled crap. Somebody got agarose and ethidium bromide all over the workbench and on the floor and didn't clean it up."

"You have people to do that."

"Not in the wee hours. I still like to play in the lab. I'm cutting some plasmid."

"So?"

"So if you really want to know, we are getting a better handle on the interaction between the amygdala and the thalamus. When a visual danger signal is processed, it goes to your thalamus. At that point the signal diverges and goes both through the cerebral cortex and directly to the amygdala. We have some information about the cascades and the feedback between the cortex and the amygdala that . . . well, let's just say I think the fight on the roof would have gone better. We are getting some promoters for soldier profile that will knock your socks off. We already have the receptor coding sequence down pat."

"Good, good. I need to know more. Gaudet wants to understand the science."

"You don't understand the science. Just tell him that."

"Yeah, well, in the strict sense that's right, but I know what you've told me. I know what I've seen. And he knows I'm not stupid. So I am going to have to give the basics."

"We did that. He's the one who first suggested putting the vector in Chellis."

"He wants a little detail. He knows I know some of it."

"Something about telling Gaudet even the general outline of the program bothers me."

"I will be vague."

"You won't breathe a word about the soldier profile."

"He knows we did something to those guys on the roof. He didn't understand it but he heard enough to know."

"Could have been a drug."

"Look. I'm mostly going to explain all the legit stuff. Curing anxiety disorder, curing psychopaths. I told him how that research led to Jason and Samir."

"You didn't tell him the difference between Kuching and the other labs."

"Just the most rudimentary basics of Nervous Flyer. No Soldier profiles. None of the new stuff. I said you do monkeys in Kuching and we do rats in France."

"You didn't even hint—"

"Will you relax? I didn't. I won't. I made it sound very preliminary."

"Okay. I miss you. I want to see you."

"Patience, my love."

"And I want a crack at our beloved CEO. When I walk into the room I want him shaking in the corner like a poisoned rat, tongue out, eyes dried like little raisins, squinting, trying to remember a world that is no more and trying to escape a mind overrun with goblins."

"Jacques, what did he ever do to you?" She laughed. "Don't answer that. You will get your chance to fill his head with goblins. Soon. But don't you think turning Chellis into Mother Teresa would be more of an accomplishment?"

"Too bad we can't kill him."

"Well, we can't. The trust provides that Marie and I have control only as long as he lives. After that the lawyers and banks take over and we'll be out on the street."

"When do I get to see you again? You always screw and run."

"Don't be shallow. You know I love you. We just have to be patient."

"It would be a lot easier to be patient if I could hold you in my arms, share wine, sit on the veranda every night."

"Let's not get into this on the phone."

"No one is listening, for God's sake. That scrambler thing . . ."

"Okay, Jacques . . . You know, I heard that the gal in your records department has taken up with your new neurologist." She got him off onto office gossip, which he liked, particularly if it related to women and their lovers. It took about fifteen minutes to establish the connection with the man that she sought.

When she saw the phone light with another in-coming call, she got off the line, wishing that Marie could help her with Jacques the way she helped with Chellis. It was Michelle, and she had a disagreeable tone in her voice.

"You know our talking like this is dangerous," Michelle began.

"Did you get a chance to use the oil?" Benoit asked.

"Why?"

"It's part of the deal, you don't have to know why."

"But if I knew why or what—"

"Did you do it?"

"Yes, and now he's climbing the walls, he shakes, he won't talk to me. It's like he thinks he's going to die or something."

"Okay, you can give him the regular stuff later today. I will leave you a message when it's time for the second rubdown. If you want to see your son, do it my way. Only eight more months and we'll buy him. That's the deal."

Chellis came in and out, wanting news of Jason, and when there was no news he went to the gym to work out. She was grateful he didn't want sex. She was busy. Finally Gaudet called her back.

"I found him."

"Good," she said. "Here's the plan. . . ."

Anna told herself that it would be irrational for Sam to back out of the party. But here it was, 6:57 P.M., and she could imagine him at the office grinning.

She called him on his cell. "Where are you?"

"Don't worry. I'm not tricking you from a tavern. I'll be there in two minutes."

At exactly 7:00 P.M. her doorbell rang and he appeared in her foyer. This was not Sam in the straw hat.

"Breathtaking." She realized she was smiling too broadly. "Absolutely breathtaking."

"You aren't bad yourself," Sam said. "But to the extent that I'm noteworthy, that is bad."

"Don't be silly. You're my escort. You're expected to be spectacular."

"That's what I'm afraid of."

"Don't worry, the press coverage will be minimal. A couple of publicity shots. Nothing more.

"Let's go. Before your worry puts a chill on the evening." She gave him her arm and they walked past the Blue Hades to the waiting limo. She kept talking all the way there, partly out of guilt and partly to avoid more questions about the press.

When they arrived at the studio, it appeared that her press agent had said just a little too much. The journalists were stacked up like the shoe boxes in her closet.

As she slid over to the limo door, Sam asked, "Anna, did you set me up?"

Outside, she took Sam's arm. To his credit he stood tall and took her through the crowd like John Wayne on a spring morning.

A wall of cameras sparked the night and blackened the sky, and they stepped through them like seraphs passing through diamonds. It was exactly the way she wanted it—upon reflection. Sam could just cope.

"Ho, ho, you nailed me," he said.

"You like making me happy?" After they passed inside the studio, she turned to him. "Nobody knows who you are. And I intend to keep them in suspense."

Sam nodded to her. "I'll join you in a minute."

Slightly disconcerted at his departure, she moved forward, shaking hands and greeting people.

Anna had sprung a not-so-subtle trap. It amused Sam and troubled him at the same time, and that seemed to be the way with this woman, both on-screen and off. As he walked away from the throng of reporters, a short, aggressive fellow with a determined grip on his green steno pad stopped him.

"Anna is just stunning this evening," the man said.

"Yes. Well, it's not my job to notice. I'm just security. But her date is arriving by separate limo. Should be here any second."

"No kidding. This is straight?"

"Oh, yeah." Sam took an earpiece out of his inside coat pocket and popped it in his ear, leaving a tiny cord coiled back around his lapel. "Hey, I've got to run and check out the crowd."

But the reporter was already busy telling the guy next to him that Anna's beau would be arriving any second. Sam heard them guessing celebrity names. After nodding at a few cute girls, he grabbed a glass of sparkling water, gulped it down, and retired to the men's room, where he took a couple of big drags on a Winston, then, not trusting himself, threw the pack in the garbage.

After a pass through some spectacular food, where he had some exceptional lox but skipped the bagel, he removed the earpiece and found Anna.

"Stick around," she whispered, nearly gritting her teeth.

He nodded. "Do you have a confession you'd like to make?"

She hesitated, no doubt wondering if he was still bugging her calls. "I just mentioned it to the publicist. That's all. I told her not to make a big deal."

"Yes, I can see the press is oblivious."

"You look so good in that." She put a hand on his lapel. There was no question that she was letting everyone know what she and her hand thought about the tall guy in the tux. There were no press nearby.

"Be right back," Sam said as a well-known producer approached.

Sam wandered deliberately through the crowd with his earpiece until Mr. Green Steno approached.

"So where is the boyfriend?"

Sam moved close, giving his best confidential cock of the head. "I can trust you not to reveal the source—right?"

"Absolutely."

Sam put a doleful look in his eye. "The beau didn't show."

He'd planted a medium-sized, second-page headline in the morning news, the way he had it figured.

It turned out to be a big headline, but like a worthy adversary Anna played the good sport and refused to let him see her consternation. Sam wondered if he had made the right move.

He sat in the seat next to her; the eight men accompanying them had spread around the coach-class cabin of the 747.

"Coach is just fine," Anna said.

"How long since you've even been on a commercial flight?" Sam asked.

"I would do it."

Sam laughed.

"You know I'm fine with it. You're just trying to needle me, and it's working. Now will you finally tell me who we're meeting in Fiji?"

"Aussie. Real name is John Hammer. A retired CIA agent. He emigrated to the U.S. from Australia as a young man, became a citizen, and joined the government service. Pacific Rim specialist. When he retired, he integrated into Fijian society pretty successfully, for a white man."

"I gather he's good."

"The best."

"I want to check on Grady."

"I already did. She'll be safe with Spring. They're staying with my cousin Kier. Nobody but nobody will find her, and if they do they'll wish they hadn't."

"Well, I hope she's okay. You know, mentally. How awful to be paralyzed and fully conscious." She shuddered.

"I think that was the point. This guy gets his kicks watching people die by inches."

"Will he go after Jason directly?"

"It's you and me they want dead. I'm guessing that's job one. And that's not going to happen."

"I appreciate everything you're doing."

"You're welcome."

They fell into silence. Sam was mildly surprised that Anna hadn't asked him about the details of the plan. It seemed proof that the trust between them was near complete, despite their game-playing.

Aussie was managing the details, starting with the equipment, which had come to Fiji from Australia and New Zealand via Federal Express. They'd have plenty of weapons but only rubber bullets. Sam hoped it would be enough. This was to be a ploy, not a mass killing.

Each of the eight men had worked for Sam on more than one occasion. On the ground T.J. would give most of the orders, leaving Sam free to think and to modify the strategy for the mission as needed. Two men had come from Japan. Both did security work for the emperor's family on special occasions, as well as providing protection for Western celebrities traveling in Japan.

Both had been friends of Shohei and wanted to make things even. One of the men, Yodo, had been a student of Shohei's. Three were English, outright mercenaries who had been in live combat on several occasions. The two Aussies had served in their government's secret service. Sanford, an ex-linebacker from Florida State University who couldn't stand the tedium of private detective work, had jumped at the chance to join one of Sam's more exotic assignments. Also he had a promise of dinner with Sam and Anna. Already Anna had autographed her picture, and been corrected when she started writing it to Sandy, a name his friends used. Turned out that Sanford always wanted to be called by his full name.

"I think that's good," Anna had reassured him. "If you don't feel like a Sandy, then insist on Sanford." That advice and her grin obviously had made him feel like a new man.

Yodo sat behind Sam in the next row back. When Anna would rise he would always nod his head, and when she went to the rest room he was an ever-present shadow.

"He seems like all he does is watch. Does he ever read?"

"Yodo is fierce and loyal. He never relents and that's why he's protecting you."

"Oh." She nodded. "Aren't you fierce and loyal?"

"Do you want me standing outside the rest room when you pee?"

"Good point."

If these men had anything in common, it was an unflappable disposition that allowed them to be rational and calculating when other more ordinary men would be distracted or shaken by serious fear. Each of these men had climbed Denali with Sam, and thus had contemplated their own death seriously on at least one occasion.

Sam had asked them not to talk about the details of the assault in front of Anna. Until she learned or demanded otherwise, the plan was for her to wait out of harm's way while they snatched Jason Wade.

It took half an hour for Sam, Anna, and Yodo to get to the Fiji Air departure gate in Nadi that would take them to Taveuni. T.J. and the others would take later flights. Anna wore a hat, sunglasses, and a blond wig, at Sam's suggestion.

The Fiji Air ticket counter attendant greeted them. "Bula."

"Bula," Sam replied. It was the universal greeting; everybody said bula to everybody all the time.

The agent took their tickets and produced boarding passes. "The departure gate is just down there."

At the gate a man was saying their names loudly. "Sam Brown and Anna Brown, please." He couldn't pronounce Yodo's last name, so Yodo nodded and the man nodded back.

It was an agent standing on the far side of the screening machines, motioning them through. Sam carried their luggage straight through the metal detector, while Anna paused. No one seemed to be performing any screening.

"Come, come, come," the man called to Anna. She walked through the metal detector with her handbag, looking like a horse eying a suspicious bridge.

"Even after New York?" Anna said.

"About like it was last time I was here," Sam said. "It's only this way in the interisland flights. Going back to the States or practically anywhere outside Fiji, it's the full pop."

"I wonder what Fiji Air will be like," she said.

"Like a horsedrawn airplane," Sam said. "Manufactured near my birth and painted like a sixties flower-power Volkswagen bus."

Sam's description, based on prior experience, proved remarkably accurate. They climbed in and watched the pilot stow their luggage on the backseat. The plane accommodated about fifteen passengers. There were four including Yodo.

"Tourism has never recovered here. Aussies come. New Zealanders come. But since the war on terrorism any country that's had a coup in the last five years gets little tourism from the U.S."

As they sat, the pilot climbed into the plane. "Bula," he said. "Fasten your seat belts and read the information card."

"That was succinct," Anna said.

"Are you ready for this, Mrs. Brown?"

"Remember, I'm one of those wives who didn't take her husband's last name."

"Yeah, I got that. You were born Brown. It was just a coincidence that you married a Brown."

"So I'm Anna Brown-Brown."

"Well, if you wanna be. If you're just Anna Brown I could have taken your last name, I guess."

"So where are we meeting 'Aussie'?"

"Upon arrival. You'll like him. He's good, too. He knows the chiefs."

Anna's look said she didn't understand.

"Fiji is controlled by a group of chiefs. Each island has its own, and together they form what we would call a committee. Although the country has a president, he'd best not cross the chiefs or he'll find himself deposed. Aussie has made it a point to know most of the chiefs, especially the more powerful ones."

"I hope this works."

"I won't lie to you. It could be tough. We've rushed this a bit."

"I know you've done the best you can."

"These things take a lot of planning." Neither said anything for a moment.

"You'll be at the airport when this goes down." Sam saw a new strain in her face as soon as he said it.

To his surprise, though, she didn't argue, but watched the terrain as they flew away from Nadi. To their right was the high plateau country, to the south the Nandrau, and more northerly the Rairaimatuku. Falling away from the mountainous plateaus grew jungle; scattered villages and dirt roads led to the sea and the lush river valleys.

They passed over the Vatu-i-ra Channel barrier reefs and myriad coral heads showing almost white in the azure sea. When they arrived, the landing was steep and fast. Anna squeezed Sam's arm until they stopped on the tiny runway. Beside it stood a terminal that looked like a 1950s-vintage American gas station. Behind the terminal a two-lane road ran parallel to the runway, and to the far side a loosely strung wire cable the diameter of a silver dollar ran through the palm trees.

"You see the line there in the trees?" Sam asked.

"That's the power line?" Anna asked.

"No. There is no power line. Everybody with electricity has a generator. That's the phone line."

"Just hanging from the palm trees?"

"Pretty quaint, isn't it?"

"There's a man," Anna said.

"Crapola," Sam said.

"What do you mean?"

"There are several men. You picked the right one out of the crowd. You noticed his good looks. His confidence."

"That's Aussie?"

"None other."

Aussie smiled at them with teeth like a white-board fence. Yodo nodded and Aussie nodded back.

Sam shrugged at Aussie, feeling Anna's shoulder against his, the warmth of it, the way she was familiar to him, like a woman on a date.

And he liked it.

Thirty-two

From the airport on Taveuni Island the road continued a mile or so in both directions before it turned to dirt. It was the one well-traveled road on the island, and European and American luxury homes as well as several small resorts lined the paved section.

Anna, T.J., and Sam were staying at the Coconut Palms, Sam and Anna posing as husband and wife. The grounds featured short-clipped grass flower beds, and burres spread amongst palms, breadfruit, kava, imported banyon, and tropical ornamentals. It was three o'clock in the afternoon. A pleasant scent hung in the warm humid air. The people seemed to nap on their feet, and even the bugs appeared tranquilized.

"There's only one bed," Anna said when they walked into the air-conditioned room. "Are we both going to sleep in it?"

"There's a roll-away," Sam said.

"Even if there weren't and I were a vestal virgin, I would sleep like a baby." She was checking out the closet.

"Because?"

"You haven't figured any way to touch me with anything but your brain."

Sam took her arm and turned her around. She came close to him, letting him smell her hair.

"Sam the frustrated man," she said. "You needn't worry. You have both your clearly delineated principles and your roll-away bed."

She gave him a little mocking smile, but stopped short of closing the last two inches between them.

Flower scent came through the louvered windows and became part of the seduction.

"God, I want you," he said.

"Tell me, which version of me is it that you want to sleep with?" She turned as if distracted by her suitcase and the shirts she was pulling from it.

Sam pulled out the roll-away and lay on it with an audible sigh, the moment lost, for now. Before he realized he had fallen asleep, he woke to Anna Wade in a blue sulu, the native wraparound skirt. Atop she wore a smart white blouse of raw silk. She was handing him another blue sulu.

"Put this on. Men wear these around here."

Sam considered it, but found still too much of his dad left in him to seriously consider a garment that was in fact a skirt.

"You go topless and I'll wear that."

"Okay." She began unbuttoning the blouse. "You've been wanting a look for days."

"Wait. You don't have to prove—"

"You wanna see my chest? Let's just get it over with."

"I was kidding, okay? I won't mention it anymore."

"Promise? Now put this on. I bought it for you when you were sleeping."

"Crapola."

"Don't crapola me. Put it on."

Aussie met them for dinner. He apparently felt it incumbent to give them the pan-Australian grin and wolf whistle. Anna smiled at Sam in his skirt.

"What?"

"You're pouting. You're actually pouting."

"I don't usually cross-dress."

They ate dinner on an outdoor veranda, and the food was exquisite. Anna and Sam asked Aussie about his life, learned that he lived on Vanua Levu, just down from Suva Suva, in a house on a little acreage overlooking the ocean and Bakabaka Island. He was planning to use the money he made from this job to build a large, covered porch.

Finally Aussie pushed away his plate. "Look, I know you both need to talk some business, so how about I retire to the burre?"

Sam nodded, slightly relieved. In view of the impending drama, a threesome wouldn't allow him to relate to Anna and her prejob jitters.

"If you'll excuse me a moment." Aussie smiled at Anna and pulled Sam aside.

"You know we could really use her in this. As one element of a distraction she'd be terrific. She's an actor, mate. Dress her up in some skimpy doodad? Get my meaning?"

"I don't know," Sam said.

"You're sweet on her, I know."

"The woman sizzles. I'm not the only man to notice."

"Well, why don't we ask her if she wants to help? It is her brother."

Sam paused. Without good reason he did not let anyone, any time, change a plan just prior to execution. On the other hand it would keep Anna with them, save some resources, and reduce the amount of chance in the equation.

"All right. Part of the diversion before the show starts?"

"Exactly, mate."

"I can guess what you have in mind," Sam said.

They returned to the table.

"I know you're gonna hate this but we have a job for you," Sam said.

"You do?" She appeared almost girlish in her enthusiasm. "What?" Now slightly more cautious.

"You could help with the scam if you want to. Aussie here has it worked out."

Aussie nodded, at a rare loss for words.

"You know I'll do it," Anna said.

"Right," Aussie said. "Now the locals have told me all about the resort. The island chief is big time on our payroll. He doesn't know what we are going to do. He doesn't want to know. But of course I had to swear that we wouldn't hurt anybody." Aussie looked at Anna. "Everything in Fiji is ultimately up to the chiefs."

She nodded her understanding.

"Fortunately the chiefs like American dollars, so we white folk are pretty well received. The locals think a famous writer with a huge satellite dish just moved into this resort with a staff and armed guards. The rumor is that he wrote about certain terrorists and had to go into hiding. Locals do the cooking and maintain the grounds; word is they like the bloke but think he's crazy."

"That would be Jason," Anna said.

"We'll have to execute this flawlessly. There are two Dobermans on the grounds and at least five guards."

"What do you mean at least?" Sam interjected.

"Recently there's been more activity. The chief wasn't sure, just seemed like more people, he said. But the guards aren't visibly armed. I'm assuming they've got guns aplenty but they're keeping them hidden so as not to disturb the locals. That's a big advantage for us. Locals think they're French."

"So maybe Chellis for some reason had one contingent of his organization snatch Jason from another. Doesn't quite make sense." Sam pulled a map from a slim leather briefcase and went over the plan in detail. They had a scale drawing of the resort. After he was finished he had Anna repeat the plan.

"Now when I'm here at the gate, supposedly fallen drunk on my ass, you are holding me up and wanting to use a phone to call our resort," Aussie said. "Sam lets you in."

"Do I make noise before you let me in?" Anna asked.

"No," Sam said.

"Okay, then I come just a few feet inside and carry on with Aussie here," Anna said.

"That's right, and when you hear the first pop, or see people running, or any kind of commotion starts, you and Aussie put on night vision, run down the road, and around to the beach just like we discussed. You better not be in that yard longer than two minutes, max."

"And you're sure they won't just shoot us."

"You in a bikini top? Not a chance."

"We could start making out. You could maybe flash them a little," Aussie chimed in.

She eyed Sam. "Did you put him up to this?"

Sam chuckled. "Two people gonna screw on the lawn. It would be distracting. And after all, this is a distraction."

"You're smoking something besides tobacco."

Sam took her arm. "I think we're ready to go. No flashing."

Aussie smiled at Anna. "Peace?" he said with a cheeky grin.

She winked at him and left with Sam for their room. Sam knew something about the suggestion had bothered her. Or perhaps something about the way he handled it. And he thought that odd, because she was certainly not a prude.

"Look, I'm sorry I didn't immediately come to your rescue."

"You think I can't take care of myself?"

Sam smiled and shook his head.

"Well, being chivalrous with one's friends isn't all that out of vogue."

"Aussie was joking."

"No, he wasn't."

"I got it. You want me to be possessive."

"That's not so strange, is it?"

"You're interested in me because you can't have me."

Silence.

"You don't know what you feel or what to call it," he said.

They brushed their teeth side by side.

"I haaaa newer hearrr"—she spat—"anything so ridiculous. I want what stirs my soul. And you, Sam or Robert or whatever, stir my soul."

"Uh-huh."

"Say something."

"Look, you're right. I know what you meant about possessive."

"Now you're patronizing me."

"I'm trying to agree with you so we can get a little sleep."

He adjourned to the bedroom to go over his notes. She put on light linen pajamas and emerged from the bathroom. Sam turned out the lights and they retired to their respective beds.

Sam lay in the dark, thinking, wondering if she had gone immediately to sleep.

"You could get in bed with me if you didn't make a big deal about it."

"Is that realistic?"

"That's up to you."

Sam thought for a while. "It's always scary before a job. Especially if you've never done it before." He rose and went over to her bed. He climbed in behind her and hugged her back.

She put her hand over his.

"Thanks," she said.

Minutes later Sam heard the deep breaths begin. He crept back to the roll-away and managed to fall asleep.

They came down the beach at 1:30 A.M., running the fiberglass-bottomed inflatable at eight knots. It was nineteen feet, eleven inches long, and was powered by a pair of 250-horsepower Mercury outboards. In order to accommodate the horsepower, the transom had been beefed up and ballast added to the center of the boat. It had been a rich man's plaything and at full throttle moved along at fifty-five to sixty miles an hour. Sam, T.J., and all eight men were on board.

They cruised slowly just outside a shallow coral reef, using a depth sounder and GPS to remain at least three hundred feet from the beach. Without night-vision goggles the massive broad-leafed trees lining the shore were shadowy billows in the dark. They were called vutu. Like supplicants to the sun, they grew out over the water, then bowed up as they reached for the sky.

They were in Somosomo Strait, the place of the sharks. According to Aussie, each chief of Taveuni had to swim out into the strait in full ceremonial regalia, and if the sharks spared him it was a signal from the gods that he should be installed as chief. Apparently there were plenty of sharks in the strait, but as Aussie told it, he had speared fish there without incident, making him think the chiefs' odds were pretty good.

The air hung heavy with moisture and was deathly still. Tropical heat lay across their shoulders like wool; the only sound was their boat churning a sudsy wake. As they drew near the landing site, Sam had them slow to a few knots until the sea stopped tracing their passage.

At four hundred yards from the compound they turned in to make a landing. As they approached the shore, all of the men shifted to the back of the boat, raising the bow high. The beach was a mix of rock, dead coral pieces, and silt, but they managed to put the V of the boat's prow on a spot of the sand. Jumping ashore, they broke into two groups; the first group, with T.J. in the lead, moved off quickly down the beach and spread out.

The group led by Sam secured the boat. The boat's pilot, the only one remaining aboard, backed the boat into deeper water with a pole and dropped an anchor off the stern.

The men wore camouflage from head to toe and camo paint on their skin, plus a helmet with night-vision goggles. Each carried an M4 carbine with attached grenade launcher and a Beretta M9 pistol. The M4s were fitted with massive sound suppressors; the grenades were only stun grenades, and all the rounds were rubber. Everyone had microphones and earpieces wired into their helmets, adjusted so that they worked well with whispers.

Sam's group moved onto a trail just above the beach that followed the contours of the steep hillside. The compound sat on a high bluff perhaps 150 feet above the water on a natural bench. There were eight burres plus a two-story house and the main lodge facility. A well-maintained asphalted path ran up from the beach on the right side of the compound, snaked up the hill in switchbacks, and exited beside a large pool.

Directly to the front of the compound was a sheer, soil-covered, near-vertical embankment that could not safely be climbed in the night without ropes. To the left side of the compound, where a wealthy American had a large home, ran a less-maintained dirt trail partially overgrown with palms, breadfruit, taro plants, and creeping vines with huge leaves that lay like a carpet.

T.J.'s group came up on the left, Sam's on the right. Halfway up the hill Sam whispered to T.J.

"In place at station one. Sanford's up."

"Roger that," T.J. said.

T.J.'s group would now be pausing halfway up the hill, waiting for Sam's forward man to locate and dispatch two Dobermans with two dart guns. The dogs were vicious, not big barkers, well trained, and would attack unknown intruders in the night. Or at least Aussie had assumed they would. Certainly they charged the fence well enough.

Sam crept up the hill after Sanford, hoping the dogs would attack without a lot of racket. At the head of the trail a locked gate stood in the six-foot fence.

Sanford used heavy sheers to clip most of the links in a two-foot-square section of the fence. He bent back a corner, creating a hole large enough to comfortably aim the dart gun. After three minutes they'd still seen no sign of the dogs.

Sanford rattled the fence. Still nothing. Sam exhaled impatiently. The first little problem. The gardens were lush enough inside the compound that his men could hide, especially by night, but not if they were going to be jumped by Dobermans.

A single long wispy cloud had draped itself across the sliver of a moon, making fewer shadows. There were no lights illuminating the gardens save two lights a hundred feet distant and mostly obscured on the main veranda dining area. Sanford rattled the fence again. Still nothing. Sam knew the others would be nervous about this development. It was imperative that the compound be alerted only when the team was ready and only by the distraction that Sam had planned.

It was impossible to know where Jason would be staying. According to Aussie, they moved him from one burre to another as a precaution. Most of the time he was kept in what had been the Honeymoon Burre near the cliff edge.

The plan was to create a distraction that would draw the guards out of the burres. Given Jason's propensity for working without regard to his environment, especially into the wee hours, he would likely be housed in whichever burre did not immediately have its front door flung open. In order to watch every burre, the men would need to be widely dispersed. They would then have to move quickly and coordinate without a hitch. Otherwise someone might die.

It had been nearly five minutes of quiet fence rattling and no dogs. They took out the chunk of fence.

Sam sneaked up the hill and motioned Sanford forward.

"No joy yet. T.J., move to the perimeter," Sam whispered.

Then they were through the fence and Sam's blood

started pumping. With his goggles he would see infrared beams, but not necessarily trip wires or motion sensors or night-vision-equipped cameras. Aussie believed there were none, and that would have to be good enough.

They stayed along the edge of the lawn, following the garden beds. The fear was that someone would throw a switch, blind them with light, and shoot them before they could react.

Sam's heart pounded a few beats faster. He reminded himself that success came to the player who got more deliberate and more determined with each bit of added stress.

Fifty feet inside they stopped, and just in time. Two black shadows streaked across the lawn, no fence to slow them. Sanford took careful aim. Sam doubted he could hit both animals. There was a pop and the lead dog tumbled and began whirling and nipping at its chest. The dart itself was heavy enough to pack a wallop. The second dog came on and just before he leaped for Sam, a second pop came from the pistol.

When Sam saw the animal's jaws open, he dropped and kicked the dog in the throat. There was a yelp and the dog went over him, but came back like a demon. Sam charged the dog with total concentration, leading with a combat knife. As he plunged the knife in to the hilt, frothy lung blood burst from the wound all over Sam's arm. As the animal went down, Sam strangled the remaining life.

"Shit," Sanford muttered when it was over. "I missed."

"Yeah." Sam hated killing dogs but would not let himself think of it again until this was over.

"We have joy," Sam whispered into the microphone. For a few minutes they lay absolutely still, waiting to see if there would be any response. They couldn't afford an ambush. Sam already knew the dogs had a habit of charging the fences, so it wouldn't necessarily bring the sentries.

Everything remained quiet. They moved forward another hundred feet until they were near the main building.

There were two guards sitting on the dining veranda at the lodge, drinking something he hoped was alcoholic.

Sam and T.J. sneaked to the right of the veranda and headed toward the far right side of the lodge and the planted gardens. Once in good cover, they came back toward the sentries to a narrow pathway between a burre and the edge of the veranda. One man was large, almost fat, the other slender, not more than 160 pounds. Only one weapon in sight—leaning up against a nearby table. Their security procedure evidenced an ease and lack of concern that Sam found hopeful.

They were in some kind of conversation, speaking French, fairly animated. Sam spoke some French, but it was hard to hear them and they were talking rapidly.

One of them seemed to pick his nose incessantly. The other scratched and picked at a bald spot on his head. Sam and T.J. quickly devised a plan.

Sam removed his boots and socks. T.J. went into a planting bed next to the building and made sounds of rustling, gradually escalating in intensity. Finally one of the guards rose and walked to the end of the veranda—fortunately without the firearm.

"Okay," Sam whispered.

The guard continued walking down the three steps off the veranda.

"Shoo am yaamil hal kalb hallaa?" he called. Clearly Arabic. An unwelcome surprise.

"C'est seulement quelque genre de fidjien gaufre— probablement."

French from the other man. Sam guessed they were speculating that the dog was chasing some kind of Fijian gopher. The fatter guard rose to watch the first.

Sam rose and sprinted alongside the lodge around to the front, and then looked back through the double-wide entry doors and beyond through a bar and sitting area and saw the large guard some hundred feet distant, still on the veranda and seemingly absorbed in his partner's explorations. Sam drew the silenced pistol and trotted on tiptoe straight at the guard with his gun leveled at the man. As the first sentry reached the edge of the thick foliage, he leaned forward and peered through the bamboo. More rustling. The man began making a guttural sort of "shooing" sound, and then quite suddenly disappeared in the foliage.

T.J. was taking him down. Sam took two more long steps and delivered a powerful blow to the base of the other man's skull.

"Okay," T.J. said.

"Okay," Sam responded, dragging the heavy man to the garden to join the first. Taking no chances, they administered hypodermics to the carotids of both men that would have them unconscious for enough time to finish their business. Sam and T.J. retreated to the initial staging point just beyond the fence.

"Team one," Sam said. His team crept forward one at a time. As each came, Sam tapped his shoulder and sent him to his predetermined ambush point. Coming from the sea and heading inland past the lodge, four of the eight burres lay in a row along a large entry garden that was a good part lawn. At the inland edge of the entry garden was the driveway, and beyond that the public roadway. Also to the landward side of the lodge and on the left of the entry garden stood one burre and a two-story house.

Aussie had been pretty sure that management lived in the house and each of the five guards had a burre. Sam put two men to the side of the Honeymoon Burre. Six men in the garden covered the doorways of the five burres and the main house, their weapons ready. Sam did a roll call. Each man had a number corresponding to the number of a burre doorway on the map they'd studied.

Sam thought it was time for a stroke of luck. He and T.J. crept up on the Honeymoon Burre, hoping to find Jason working inside. All the windows were in the front for the ocean view as was the veranda that might have a sentry, but there was thick foliage to the side that prevented easy viewing. Aussie was not absolutely certain about the size of the staff. If they made a mistake and an alarm were sounded, every guard exiting a burre around the main garden, or for that matter the main house, would take a rubber bullet to the chest from a silenced rifle. Normally it wouldn't kill, but it would temporarily debilitate.

They crept through the foliage. Sam had not replaced his shoes. T.J. refused combat boots and wore light sneakers. Sam was a couple of steps ahead of T.J. and to the right of him. Through a break in the foliage Sam saw the porch. Nobody. No light. He moved forward while T.J. remained still. The cabin was completely dark. Opening the door could easily set off an alarm.

Sam retreated.

Now they would have to do it the hard way.

* * *

Aussie and Anna climbed into the jeep at 1:00 A.M. Unable to think apart from nervous worry, she had paced incessantly and driven Aussie mad until he finally distracted her by insisting that they go over the plan one more time.

"I scream that you're acting like a whore. 'Why didn't you just have sex with him right on the table?'"

"And I say, 'Your ass is sagging and your dick is a marshmallow.'"

"That's not what you say."

"I know. I'm an actress, remember? I do this for a living. So stop trying to distract me and let me sit here and worry."

Aussie let it lie.

Thirty-three

T.J. went around the lodge and Sam put on his boots. They met in the front garden and waited. Five minutes to go.

As he sat in the complete quiet, watching the bats dart overhead, plainly visible through his night-vision goggles, it struck him. This had all been too easy. Something was wrong.

He heard a car drive up. Loud voices, some in French and one seeming to speak Arabic. Five in all, and one of them appeared to be Jason from the pictures he had studied.

"Clap three times," one said in French.

"What happens when you mix kava and booze?" another asked.

Kava was a local delicacy that had a mild narcotic type of effect. Although it tasted like old dishwater, it had a bit of buzz if consumed in large enough quantities. Clap three times was a reference to the kava ceremony. He remembered that much. This could be good. Then again, it wasn't the plan.

The group walked up the middle of the grass toward the lodge and the bar. Sam decided to move.

"Jason—red shirt with the glasses," Sam whispered. "On three. One . . ." Then he stopped. "Wait." He looked again at the Jason character. He wasn't sure.

He had been right the first time. Something was wrong.

Aussie pulled the old jeep off to the side of the road at a wide spot created by a driveway entrance that parted the heavy foliage. When he turned off the lights the road was plunged into black. Along the road were more massive vutu trees that held the darkness and made the air heavy with scent. Sweat poured from Anna and the adrenaline in her made the heat a dull ache. She knew she could get killed for real on this gig. For just a second she wondered if she should have stayed a little farther from the action.

"It's just up ahead," he said. "The lady who owns this driveway runs a campground and has groups of kids from Australia, New Zealand, Europe, and the U.S.A."

"Jason's just around that bend?"

"You got it. Are you ready to look like a drunken tourist?"

"All ready." She slipped off her shirt so that she wore only tight jeans and a bikini top. Aussie grabbed his hat. A big Stetson.

"I thought you didn't wear hats around here."

"Right. It offends the chief. But I'm supposed to be a dumb tourist."

Aussie took the mag light from between the bucket seats.

"All go, jungle man," Sam's voice crackled in their earpieces.

They walked up the road toward the bend where they would step off into the thick foliage. "Ten minutes," he said as they walked.

A vehicle came around the corner. It sounded like

a truck. They kept walking, moving over very close to a large ditch that ran down the road edge. The truck slowed as it approached. It frightened Anna, but she didn't know why. She told herself that there was nothing so unusual about a truck in the middle of the night. As it drew close she could see that it had a roofed-over cargo area in the back. On the sides were canvas curtains.

The truck pulled up, making an unmuffled rumble. It was white under a film of mud. A bright and blinding light pierced the night from the driver's-side door. She saw men jumping from the back.

"Run," Aussie said. He plunged into the bushes and she followed the white of his T-shirt. They galloped over and past bushes clawing at their clothes, her tennis shoes sliding. Lights flashed through the foliage and pockets of darkness leaped out at her. Then a man was right behind her, grabbing for her. He tackled her and she fell hard.

Aussie appeared above her, fighting; then came others. A big man held her to the ground. She couldn't move.

Two of them attacked Aussie, knocking him down. A third man started clubbing him with a rifle butt.

"Stop," someone said.

A blond, mustached man with a scar under his chin appeared. He had a coldness about him that felt like snakes on a carcass.

"Hold him," the man said. Now she saw that there were four of them plus the leader. Aussie was unconscious and bleeding badly from the nose. One of them held Aussie's head by the hair. The leader pulled up Aussie's eyelid and shone a light in the pupil.

"Cuff them both."

Roughly they put handcuffs on her and on Aussie.

"Go back to the truck."

The men looked at each other, confused.

When they were gone, he turned to Anna.

"Shut up and stay there or I'll beat your face in."
The accent was heavy French. He stared at her as if to
let his words sink in. "You get to watch. This is the easy
way to die. You don't want the hard way. Those animals would love to torture and rape you."

Then he pulled out a syringe and stuck it up
Aussie's nose. In seconds his body shook and
spasmed.

"No," Anna screamed.

A fog enveloped her face and she was choking,
dying, hot mush filling her lungs, taking her air.

"I thought I said shut up."

"Wait," Sam whispered. "Hold fire."

As the group strolled forward the leader stopped.
"There's nobody here," he called out.

Sam wasn't sure whom he was talking to.

"I'm going to bed. Hey, Chief. You can come out
now. This is stupid. We've done this for three nights
and there's nobody here."

"Make sure you're under cover," Sam whispered
into the mike, and moved farther back in the bushes.
Obviously it was a trap, and the leader was now breaking discipline.

"Aussie?" Sam said.

He heard a grunted response.

"Get Anna back."

"It's too late."

It was another voice.

"Switch to Robin," Sam said. Reaching down to his
radio, Sam keyed in a code.

"Listen up. There's no time. If lights come on, shoot them out. Take off your night vision."

Just as Sam said it the place lit up like a stadium. His men responded with rapid fire and within seconds, no lights.

"Night vision back on," Sam said. "Take 'em out."

There were muted pops from all around, and in two seconds the men that had been fleeing across the lawn lay flopping on the ground like so many boated fish.

Return fire came from the trees. A muzzle blast lit the night. Sam's men shot back without an order. Stun grenades began going off in the trees, people falling to the ground. It was a war. Sam knew better than to listen on the old radio channel. He didn't want to hear the ultimatum. He knew the guys in the trees were only part of the enemy force, maybe not even the main force. There would be many others on the trail back to the boat.

"Holt, Gomez, Ruby, stay here, mop up. Everybody else, follow me," Sam said, running.

Somebody had completely outthought them, and he had nearly gotten them all killed. Now Anna was probably as good as dead.

They ran down the road, around the bend, and saw the truck.

"If it moves, shoot it," Sam said. Men jumped from the truck and took a volley of silenced shots. Anna and Aussie weren't in the truck. Sam noticed the break in the foliage. No Anna. Down the road there would be a car. Sam suspected they had been taken by the occupants of the truck while on foot.

Spying another break in the foliage he tapped T.J. and jumped into the brush, running, then stopping. He heard struggles and a woman's groans.

"Let's die trying," he whispered to T.J.

They charged at the bushes, firing rubber bullets everywhere, not worrying if they hit Anna.

Gaudet worked fast, wanting to know what Anna knew before killing her. The big man's heart was fluttering but hadn't quite quit; Gaudet knew better than to leave him prematurely. He sprayed more potassium chloride and felt for a pulse again.

With Anna it had to be done much more carefully, had to look like a real accident, and that was becoming impossible fast. The Chellis and Aziz men at the beach had radioed no sightings of men retreating to the boat. Anna's friends had all been killed or wounded. It would take Aziz's men a while to figure out that she was missing, and by then he would have her in the helicopter.

The pepper spray had turned her into a choking mess. To shut her up completely he'd need to kill her, and he wasn't ready to do that. "Screw it," he muttered to himself, tired of waiting for the man to die. He picked Anna up and threw her over his shoulder. It was at that moment he suspected that he might have made a major miscalculation.

"If it moves, shoot it," he heard.

He began to run, but it was hard without a light and a light would bring them. There were shots, lots of them. Some very muted. A few unmuted.

After he went about twenty feet or so bullets began pouring past him. They didn't know he had her, he reasoned, or they wouldn't be shooting. Then something slammed into his thigh, nearly breaking his leg. Another bullet hit him square in the back. As the pain electrified his body he realized the bullets were rubber and knew he had made a mistake. He dropped her to her knees and considered killing her. He listened, trying to locate them. She rose and stumbled into the brush. Only an instant of time flashed before discipline took over. More bullets poured past him. Never kill except exactly according to plan. The rule had kept him alive and free of the law.

"Later," he said into the darkness. Then he ran as best he could with his bad leg.

Sam hadn't gone twenty feet when he heard more movement. He charged headlong. The other men did likewise.

There were more groans. Quickly all the men crisscrossed through the thicket.

"Here," one of them called. Sam burst into a little hollow and found Anna leaning on a tree near to collapsing. "Aussie," she choked. Back a ways Aussie was lying completely still. Sam felt his carotid. He was dead. There didn't appear to be a mark on him other than a broken nose. Then his instincts told him there would be a needle mark somewhere. Maybe the same needle mark that had been missed on Wes King.

Pepper spray. Gingerly Sam examined Anna, who was now on the ground. Like a parent checking a baby fallen from its crib, he felt her face and body. She was gasping horribly, panic in her eyes.

"You'll be fine, I promise. Keep the others at the compound, nobody goes back toward the boat," he said to T.J. He turned to Sanford, who had been watching Anna. "Carry her to the truck," he said. The big man hefted her carefully. Sam looked at Yodo. "Let's hope they left the key. Leave all the bad guys trussed on the ground. Give them a dose."

If it was a setup, Jason could be anywhere. At that moment he heard a helicopter and figured they had lost the group's leader, the man who'd killed Aussie.

"Chopper One," he radioed.

"Yo."

"Lift off and watch for a chopper down by the point. Probably low and fast. Follow it now."

"Roger that," the pilot said. The airport was less than a mile away. If they got airborne fast they might catch whatever just took off. Sam considered that they probably were keeping Jason away from the fighting and near his satellite dish in the compound.

"Back to the resort," Sam said. They climbed into the truck and drove through the gate. Cuffed men lay everywhere. Most were out with an injection; those they hadn't gotten to yet were in a lot of pain, judging from their cries.

"Search every building, especially the house," Sam said.

The men went to work. T.J. remained in the central garden and began interrogating a couple of the conscious guards. Frenchmen and Arabs. By sheer luck, and maybe a tad of instinct, Sam had one man who could interpret some Arabic. French was not a problem. Sam went into the house. Nothing about the place looked like it might have been occupied by Jason. His men were systematically searching every closet and cupboard.

Sam walked out, through the lodge, and into the Honeymoon Burre. It looked like Jason's place: a lot of books everywhere, a giant white board covered with equations, two computers, a world globe, and a model of a carbon atom.

So where was he?

Sam opened a few closets and then stepped out

when two men came through to really search the burre. They would look for any place to hide, trapdoors, built-in cupboards that might house an entry or a secret space.

Sam walked out to the two burres that were supposedly not in use. On the way he noticed a window at the end of the main building. Walking up on the veranda and into the sitting area, he went to the only door, opened it, and walked in. An office with another door. Behind the second door, which he had to break for want of a key, was a long closet with shelves and a leather couch that looked completely out of place. On the couch lay a sleeping Jason, obviously drugged.

There were pills in a box and a blue liquid in a squeeze bottle. He remembered Anna's story about Jason and the oil. He took both the oil and the medication.

In sleep Jason Wade looked content. Sam shook him. He groaned, but that was it. Sam checked his eyes. The pupils were dilated, the eyes rolled back. They had used strong stuff.

Sam clicked on his transmitter. "T.J., you have Bravo?"

"I do."

"Let's get the hell out of here. I've got the goods. Meet you on the road. All hands meet me at the gate. Chopper, you there?"

"We're here. We've got the bogey chopper headed to Venua Levu."

"Damn," Sam muttered. "Break off. Come and get us out of here."

"Roger that."

They jumped in the truck and arrived at the Taveuni Airport, where they learned that Anna had recovered sufficiently to curse the man who had killed

Aussie. They put T.J., Jason, and three of the men on the chopper. Sam motioned to Anna to get in so he could send it off.

"I'm going when you go," she said in a voice so hoarse she could barely make herself understood.

He picked her up and put her in the helicopter. "No plan B," he said, ready to handcuff her to the seat.

She raised an eyebrow, but he couldn't read the dark eyes or the emotion that she held submerged. For some reason what he did at this moment seemed to him very important. Whether he would stay and T.J. would leave or whether he would take T.J.'s seat beside her. All of her concentration was on him; she looked nowhere but into his eyes.

T.J. looked from one to the other.

"T.J., would you mind waiting for the second chopper?"

"Not at all."

As he went past him, Sam turned.

"Do my cheeks look hollow?" Sam whispered.

T.J. looked puzzled for just a second, then began to laugh. "At least it's a fine ass you're kissing."

Thirty-four

They flew at Mach .9 in the Gulfstream planning a nonstop to Victoria, BC, where they were to meet Grady. Anna made it a point to sit beside Jason on a couch as they began the trip. By the time they took off, the pepper spray had largely worn off, although she found herself a little red-eyed and blinking.

Sam had given Anna the blue oil and she rubbed it into Jason's back. He became unusually relaxed. Anna hoped they could make the oil last until they got to Nutka, who had a small supply. After that it would be a serious issue.

She put her arm around Jason and hugged him mercilessly while Sam watched and chuckled. Anna finally got a chance to lay out her apology to Jason. Sam noticed that she didn't leave out any details and took more than her share of responsibility. Jason listened but said little until she was finished.

"Sis, you know when I make a bad equation, I spend my time trying to get it right. That's what you've done. You've got it right so the way I see it, the old equation is outdated, lost in the dustbin of history."

Anna had gotten her lip gloss on, and was now planting butterfly circles all over Jason's right cheek.

"Most of the men in this country would just love what you're getting, Jason."

"She's my sister." Jason smiled. "She's pretty but she's my sister."

Anna felt ebullient.

"I suppose the morons want me back," Jason said.

"I would like to fight for you, Jason. Maybe get rid of a guardian of your person altogether or get me appointed. How would you feel about that?"

"No more Mr. Roberto? That would be grand. I think he's gone over to the Nannites."

"We're going to meet Grady. She's going with us," Anna said.

Jason thought for a minute.

"I'm worried," he said. "I'm afraid she won't think well of me because I haven't seen her."

"I'm nervous too, partner. I haven't been her favorite. I saw her at Sam's office but we haven't really talked yet. She's in love with Sam."

"I know you will do great with Grady," Sam said. "Anna will too, but you know they both are a lot alike, which makes it interesting."

"Well, if we're so much alike, how come she never argues with you?" Anna said.

"Oh, she did." Sam smirked a little. "Now are you going to ask how come you continue to argue with me?"

"No, I don't think I'll ask that."

After a time Jason went to sleep and Anna looked at Sam. "What?" he said when she continued looking.

"I'm sleepy."

There was another couch. Without a word Sam found a pillow and put it in his lap. Anna lay down, put her head on the pillow and her hand in his. Soon Sam leaned back in the corner of the couch and fell asleep.

* * *

Although Jill had accompanied Grady to Victoria, the plan was for Jill to return to Sam's office in LA. They were staying at the Empress Hotel under alias names because they were uncertain about when the Gulfstream would arrive. Sam had them remain at the hotel preferring to meet them there with the crowds, and the activity.

As they unloaded into several cabs at the Victoria Airport, Jason appeared nervous. Anna knew that it was too soon for the oil to wear off.

"Relax. She's your daughter. The second you tell her that you love her and that you've been sick, she'll start to respond. I promise."

After they were in the cabs Sam leaned over to Anna. "You look as nervous as Jason."

"Grady and I never really talked. You know she's dead set on pleasing you so she just smiled grimly at me."

"Relax," Sam said. "You just lived through Devan Gaudet. How bad can this be?"

They called the Empress and told them to be on the boardwalk along the waterfront across the street from the hotel. They drove along the harbor and found Grady and Jill easily.

Anna decided to move decisively and end the drama. Without waiting she jumped out of the van and hugged a startled Grady.

"I've made some huge mistakes with your father. And as to you, I've been a know-it-all overbearing aunt. I'm sorry and I want to start over."

Grady barely hesitated. "You're fine. I've been jealous because you had a perfect family, a fabulous career, and my family has been screwed up and my life a mess. I hated you for it. Ah, you also like to fix things."

"Yeah. I'm a real control freak. Maybe you and I can make it. You can fix me for a while. Your dad and I have made a start. I want to make a start with you."

Grady stood looking in her eyes for the longest time.

"I'll try," she said. "Let's go."

Jason was in one of the cabs with the bodyguards, sitting beside Yodo, who now understood that he was to guard Jason at all costs. Grady got into another cab with Anna and Sam. Jill took her leave and grabbed a taxi for the airport.

"We have one more passenger," Sam said.

Anna looked at him, curious. "This group needs a shrink."

They drove a short distance to the Museum of Natural History, where they found Spring waiting out front. She loved museums, especially those filled with Native American exhibits.

They took vans to Sydney and awaited the ferry to Galliano Island.

"Would you like to meet your father?" Anna asked.

"At a ferry?" Then quite predictably for Anna, Grady looked at Sam.

"It's forty minutes until the ferry. How about if Grady and I take a walk over there by the water? Anna can get Jason from the car behind. I can tell you that you will also get Yodo."

"I don't want to be a wuss but I'm nervous," Grady said.

"Come on," Sam said. Grady bounded out of the car and went with Sam. Anna went for Jason, who seemed to have taken to Yodo, who now followed him around like a towering shadow.

The wind was blowing and there was a chill. White-caps dotted the water, gulls circled, and bundled-up fishermen watched their rods and played in their plastic buckets, no doubt trying to figure how to make their bait look intriguing to a codfish.

"She's waited a long time to talk with you, Jason," Anna began. "So she'll be a little nervous and a little excited all at the same time."

"Since I'm normally nervous, this feels pretty usual." He gave her his twinkling smile. When they walked up to the rail along the beach, Sam and Grady were facing the bay. Jason came up and stood beside Grady, who turned when he arrived. They stood apart for a second. Grady threw her arms around him.

Anna watched Grady's face and knew it would work out.

Sam and Anna walked back to the car, not looking back.

"So far that was easy," Anna said.

"All the ingredients were there. You just had to shake and stir."

When they arrived at Galiano, they were picked up in a car borrowed by the crew of the *Inevitable* and taken across the island to Montague Harbor. It took three trips in the car to move all the people and luggage.

Normally bustling in the summer, Montague Harbor was completely abandoned now with not a single yacht at anchor. The small store and resort on the bay was closed up and the place was entrusted to a caretaker until spring.

Across the channel the small town of Ganges on Saltspring Island was likewise buttoned up for the winter, the moorings and docks largely pulled in for the southerly storms. As on Galliano, only the year-round island residents were about and street traffic was light, coffee shops were opening late and closing early. The ice cream parlor sat forlorn in its solitude.

The caretaker at Montague Harbor, a young man with ponytailed hair, lived in Ganges and most nights commuted by boat across the channel. He had a pregnant bride at home. He stood on the dock watching until T.J. engaged him in conversation, leading him off from the group. Sam came over after a minute, looked at the young man, and smiled.

"Everybody is curious about *Inevitable*. What would you like to know?"

"Where are you going?"

"Up north. All the way to the tip of Vancouver Island, up the Inside Passage. We're just the crew and maintenance people, but we brought a bunch of friends along for the ride. In the winter the owner gives us a free trip. This time it's kind of a bachelor party."

The young man had plenty of questions about the boat, its range, horsepower, and cruising speed.

Perfect.

Anna stood to the side just to be safe. With her stocking cap, glasses, and platinum-blond hair, there wasn't much chance that she would be recognized.

"What is it doing here?" Anna asked, glancing toward the giant yacht at anchor in the harbor.

"The owner is a friend; he's letting us use it until we can make other arrangements. I figure in a couple weeks we will have found something more permanent for Jason. Something with a bomb shelter. So to answer your question, the boat is here waiting for us."

When they pulled away from the dock, they could barely see the yacht in the gray drizzle and mist that hung like wet flannel, dampening sound and creating an eerie indistinctness that made one yearn for the warmth and definition of an open-hearth fire.

"Nice boat," Anna said when she stepped off the

large gangplank. "Where's our room?" She looked weary. "We've been traveling for twenty-four hours."

"It was a tortured route, but then nobody knows we're here."

"The last time I was on a boat it met with a sad ending. Isn't this a sitting duck?"

"In this weather it's nearly invisible. Of course we could try a Vancouver police station with our story and see how it goes."

"I just thought maybe a house with a large grounds."

"This moves constantly and in this weather is nearly impossible to find, unless you knew exactly where to look."

"I'm not entirely convinced, but you've managed to keep us alive so far."

By the time Sam showed her the owner's stateroom and living space just behind the bridge, the weather had closed in so thoroughly that no land was visible even though they were less than a half mile from shore. The crew had weighed anchor and they were inching slowly forward out the narrow mouth of the harbor.

Sam took her to the bridge that by itself was worth a million dollars in electronics. They turned south, edged across the channel, and stopped midway, still completely fog-bound.

"What's happening?" Anna asked.

"We're getting off," Sam said.

"But we just got on."

"Surprising, isn't it?"

"That's why you told me to leave the bags on the deck."

In minutes Sam, Anna, Grady, Spring, T.J., Yodo, Sanford, and an anxiety-ridden Jason got into a Zodiac inflatable speedboat and quietly motored off into the fog.

"I'm not believing this," Anna said above the whispering motor.

"No one else will either. And that's the point." Sam said. "If anybody figured out that we went to Galliano, they will eventually find the dock boy. And what's he going to tell them?"

"We went north. To Alaska. A bachelor party."

"And when they learn about the yacht they'll figure we can tick off over three hundred nautical miles every twenty-four hours—easily. Leaves a search area that's utterly massive. We could have gone out the straits of Jaun de Fuca and down the coast to California, we could have gone to the west side of Vancouver Island, or Puget Sound and Seattle. Or as I said, we could head all the way to Alaska."

"Where will the *Inevitable* go?"

"First to Vancouver, where three women and two men will leave the boat and board a private jet for Europe. They will land in London, leave the plane, and disappear. The yacht will sail on."

"And go where?"

"Wherever they want as long as they keep moving. Those guys get a free winter cruise. But they will act exactly as if we were on board and they were protecting us. When they go into a harbor the men will watch the boat from the shore."

"So all the guards went that way?"

"Uh-huh. All those guards did. We have others."

"And was I the last person to find out what's going on?"

"Oh, no. The crew and all those men were planning for us to be on the yacht. They had no idea we were getting off."

"When did you tell them?"

"I told only T.J."

"God, you are paranoid. What is this costing?"

"I've learned through hard, sad experience that a ruse works better if everyone involved actually believes it. People act according to their expectations. I pulled in some chits to rent the place we're going for less than two hundred thousand dollars. A bargain for a woman worth two hundred fifty million."

They traveled through the fog and mist to a long, slender harbor at the very end of the bay. There a passenger van waited, cloaked in the night, its engine running and lights off.

Anna knew only that they were winding up the side of a mountain, the headlights flashing on the green of trees, grasses, and ferns, a few aluminum mailboxes on white wood posts, grass a foot tall clumped at the bases. There were no streetlights and, after a time, no houselights, only the black illuminated to gray, and then it became so thick that they crawled up the road clinging to the center strip. Billions of tiny droplets grabbed headlight beams and spread them to a halo of rainbows—the result of driving in a cloud.

Finally, after going higher on an island than Anna would have thought possible, they came to a wide drive with beautiful iron gates. The driver pushed a button and the gates trundled on steel wheels.

Devan Gaudet's mind was like a free-flowing river finding its way down a familiar canyon. Within ten minutes of leaving Taveuni, using a cell phone shipped out of the U.K., he was talking to his travel agent in Geneva. Fifty minutes after his arrival at Nadi Airport, he was on a jet to Sydney, Australia. Given years of discipline, he was able to sleep the entire flight. Upon his arrival in Sydney he went to work. First he would get control.

In a safe house in Sydney established the week prior, Benoit had seen to it that the GE phone costing about $50 was replaced by a scrambler phone built by Grace technicians at a cost of about $150,000.

"I'm afraid that moron, your boyfriend, will screw up our lives," Gaudet began when he got her on the line. He liked to bring up that she had sex with Chellis, hoping that if he rubbed it in, her hatred for the man would continue to grow. "We need to move up the timetable. Doing nothing is not an option. We've got to move fast and hard or we're going to lose this. Chellis will get too aggressive or talkative, so it's time to proceed as I have laid out. You'd better call your friend Jacques."

"Okay," she said, exhaling a bit too long.

"Did you send a man to Grady's apartment?"

"Of course."

"And?"

"She had a cat."

"So?"

"She boards it when she's gone. A place called the Critter Sitter. She also has a computer. We've got the password and total access. Our guys have also broken into the Critter Sitter's computer and written a program to divert any incoming mail from Grady. We will get it instead, and she'll think she's talking to the Sitter. We're hoping she'll use her e-mail account from the road to check on her cat."

"Long shot," Gaudet said. "Sam wouldn't let anyone use a local computer to send anything. She would have to break the rules, and I wouldn't count on that. It nearly killed her the last time. I've got another way. They need Nutka and the oil. She had a supply. I'm working with Samir. Some strangers came for Nutka in the night and I'm sure it was the Sam group. But we were faster, we have a radio transmitter in her bag, and more important, Samir has men in a cabin with her family. If she doesn't tell us where they take her, Samir makes AK-47 stew. And I have other means."

"Samir would do that?"

There was a quiet that made Gaudet smile and the quiet spoke more than words. Even with their lovemaking, she didn't trust him.

"I didn't know you talked with Samir," she continued.

"Did I forget to mention that?"

"You're an aloof bastard."

"Don't you suppose that's how it is with most people who kill others for a living? The real standout here would be the personal assistant who screws everybody for a living."

"You're talking your way out of my bed." The ice over the line pleased him. He liked sex with the rebellious ones.

"A woman of great poise can take a small joke."

"Soon you'll be no fun."

"I will make it up to you." It galled him to say it, but he wanted this woman. Apparently there were lines that he could not cross. Maybe in the end killing her would provide his only complete satisfaction.

"You mentioned other means of finding them."

"Nothing is certain. It is, shall we say, a real coup d'état? Something that is working out very well. You can trust me. We needn't go into it."

* * *

Samir Aziz paced in the waiting room of the laboratory, ignoring the magazines, *Le Monde,* and the receptionist. It seemed small and chintzy for such a prestigious lab. It irritated him that these people, on whom he had pinned his hopes, had cheap furniture and cheap paintings.

Michelle sat on a chair and clasped his hand as needed. He was extremely anxious to know what was in the oil, why it worked, and whether it could be duplicated. He was not sure that he could stand to live without it in the shadow of an anxiety so powerful that it sapped all satisfaction from his life.

At last the door to the working portion of the lab opened and Monsieur Dupré entered and offered a firm handshake.

"I'm afraid we still can't tell you much. There are organics. Complex molecules that are very hard to figure without a clue. There is nothing that would affect your state of mind by itself, so it must be working in combination with something else, and right now neither the lab nor your neurologist can imagine what that might be. Maybe they have genetically altered your brain, but we have no details. We don't know how they would do that. The note is not enough. It could be anything. In that oil there is every herbal remedy known to man. There are trace molecules. It's a stew. Eventually we'll get it if we don't run out of material."

"So you will keep looking."

"Oh, yes. But it would be helpful if you could talk with the manufacturer of the oil."

"Yes," Samir said.

"What are we going to do?" Michelle asked on the way out the door.

"My men have taken your son. That is a first step."

Obviously shocked, she threw her arms around him in the parking lot. It was the desired reaction.

"When, where is he?"

"On his way to Lebanon. It was a bitch getting him into the country without a passport. But in three hours when we arrive back in my country he will be at your apartment in Beirut. I wanted to surprise you."

"How did you do it?"

"By promising them I would deliver some software that Chellis won't. The software will be no more difficult to obtain than the oil recipe. I had to get your son because Chellis and company are apt to suppose that you have turned on them."

"You are not the man I thought you were," she said. "Not at all."

"No, I am that man. But you could say that I am adapting to your kindnesses. Or maybe that where you are concerned I envy all other men their power, and so I have moved to diminish it in order to enhance my own."

"It is necessary for you to portray yourself so harshly?"

Samir's cell phone rang.

"Yes?" he said, expecting one of his men.

"This is your new friend."

"What new friend?"

"You know what new friend. The friend that will have the recipe to the oil and all you need of it for the rest of your life. And not the crap you've been getting, but good stuff that will get you back to normal. I know exactly what's going on, and soon I will control Grace Technologies and all that it possesses."

Samir hung up stunned, knowing that Gaudet would not be lying. Gaudet's power was growing. Immediately he dialed the number of Chellis's offices.

When advised Chellis was out, he put one of his men on to getting hold of him.

Gaudet was a predator, and Samir had a growing feeling that he might be on the menu.

Thirty-five

Benoit was trying to train the hair on the back of her head into a more perfect wave while she rehearsed exactly what she intended. Marie had gone to Marseille with a friend, probably trying to forget what was happening. Given her knack for reality distortion, she would probably treat the events of this day as one of life's unforeseen tragedies.

It wasn't a bad day given the sunny wintertime weather and the elegant simplicity of their plan and the certainty of its execution, but it wasn't a good day because the most difficult and personal part was yet to come.

Jacques had delivered the aerosol in a container with a crude label indicating that it was roach killer. Fitting, that.

Benoit dressed as if she were going to the company's annual gala. Elegant and form-flattering, her gown was black, and slit up the front from floor to thigh. Although she wore a garter belt and old-fashioned stockings, she wore no undergarments. At about ten minutes to ten, as she dabbed perfume, the telephone rang.

"Yes," she said, expecting Gaudet and trying to keep the fear out of her voice.

"How is it going?"

"Fine."

"Don't deviate from the plan."

"I'm not going to give him sex."

"Unless you have to." When he said, that it was as if her stomach were on an elevator. Not because she minded at all having sex with Chellis, but because for a few insane moments she had convinced herself that Gaudet cared. If he didn't, she was in danger and she knew it.

"I won't have to."

"Good. Is the room completely ready?"

"Of course."

"And you're sure they can restore it to just as it was in a matter of hours?"

"Ten hours. Yes. I'm sure. The metal plates will remain in the walls and floor but nothing will be visible."

"This is going to be smooth, perfect, actually."

"How is your other thing going? Are you tracking Jason?"

"It is superb because I am in charge."

"But you are not saying."

"I am not. Trust me. I am Gaudet."

To win Gaudet's trust she had explained generally about Jacques's research into the Nervous Flyer profile. It seemed to have worked with the exception of whatever secret angle he had going with respect to tracing Jason. Maybe it was nothing—just a ploy to make him appear invincible.

When Benoit heard the knock she took one last look at herself. As she walked past the Picasso she wondered why she felt no guilt whatsoever—it was, after all, an extraordinary treasure that DuShane had given her, and it was only one among many. Before opening the door she paused for a moment, knowing

that nothing would be the same after today. As she unbolted the door for him she acknowledged to herself
that it was something of a pity that they couldn't just
kill DuShane and be humane about the whole situation. There were, however, extenuating circumstances
that they could not escape.

"Handsome man," she said softly as he walked
through the door.

From his eyes she could tell that he was excited in
the way of a child utterly distracted by a rare treat. He
wore a traditional deep blue blazer with a black turtleneck, and had been liberal but tasteful in his use of a
men's cologne.

"Wonderful style and very stimulating," he said as
he came through the door, admiring the dress or
more probably her form beneath.

They went to the couch, where she poured him a
glass of port.

"I can't get this mess off my mind." He took a sip. "I
try to conceive of R and D without Jason and I can't
do it."

"Gaudet will fix it. He is hard after them and will
have Jason soon. They came to get Nutka as we knew
they would."

"It wasn't smart of them. And you know our lawyers
are going to tell the court that the Americans are trying to steal our scientist pure and simple. He was
kidnapped while on a retreat to Fiji. When Anna and
Sam disappear and we have Jason, the French court
will thumb its nose at any Americans who try to continue. Of course this does depend on Gaudet doing
his job."

"He will do his job."

"We'll see. We think Samir has taken Michelle's
boy."

"Yes, I know." She kissed him deeply and invited a hand up her leg. "Come, I will make you forget all of this."

She took him into what had been her spare bedroom. Unlike the rest of the house, it had recently been done mostly in gray and deep red. Heavy draperies hung over every window. The door was massive and out of place for interior use. There was a brass bed with a long scarf affixed to each corner.

"I am going to tie you up so that we can play."

He looked awkward. They had never done exactly that, but she began kissing him and popping buttons on his shirt, making sport of the garment's destruction.

"What will I wear home?"

"I have a new one in the closet."

When he was nude, she got him started on her body and moved him to the bed.

Although he looked a little uncertain, he let her tie his hands and she did so firmly. It was going more smoothly than she had hoped as in her mind there had been a real question about whether she would need to wait for the drugs mixed into the port. Now that it was all ending, she suddenly didn't want him to touch her any more than absolutely necessary. Once he was tied, she pulled the cuffs from their hiding place under the mattress. Before he knew what was happening the first was locked and closed.

"What are you doing? The scarves are fine. Why the cuffs?"

"It's a game, DuShane. You'll like it."

"Benoit? What are you doing?" She closed the second cuff and went to his feet. At the head of the bed the cuffs were on a chain that was bolted into the wall where metal plates could easily withstand a one-thousand-pound pull and any amount of jerking that a man could generate using nothing but his flesh. At the foot of the bed the cuffs were affixed to the floor. Gaudet had insisted that everything had to be foolproof times four.

As soon as he was secure she told him the facts.

"If you scream no one is going to hear you but as a precaution I have this." She held up a large can with a label: BEAR GUN. "This is pepper spray of a strength great enough to knock down a grizzly—you know, the big guys in North America. It will choke you down. If that doesn't work I have a tazer that will knock the dinner from your bowels, and if you foul my bed I will make you suffer."

"What are you doing?"

From a drawer she retrieved a large mask and tried it on.

"The Nannites are coming, DuShane."

She took it off and set it aside.

A look of troubled recognition crossed his face followed by outright horror as the facts began to marshal themselves and he became like a mouse facing the talons of an owl.

"Help me," he shrieked.

She pressed the button on the stereo remote, filling the room with sound, a much better alternative than the pepper spray, which might linger in her apartment. She took a syringe loaded with succino coline and came to the side of the bed. "I'm going to hit you with a tazer. If you shut up and lie quiet I will only do it once." She hit his chest and he jumped. Quickly she put the drug in a vein in the back of his hand.

Next she went to the closet and removed a foam-filled box that was hinged at the top and opened at the bottom. It was quite heavy, weighing a good fifteen pounds. As she carried it to the bed he shook himself lucid and became nearly hysterical.

"Whatever I did I can make it right," he shouted. "Whatever I did. Listen, we can talk. This is insanity." She noticed that he had the look of a beast in his eyes. The whites appeared larger and the eyeballs appeared to rotate inside his head, casting side to side, as if by looking enough he might spy his deliverance. As she sat on the bed to encapsulate his head, he began pulling on his restraints and bouncing up and down, screaming incoherently. At least she didn't notice any words. It was becoming a primal state.

She had a feeling that twice with the tazer might not be good. He had to live a long life. When she tried to put the back half of the head box under his head, he threw it side to side, making it difficult. Finally she could see that the effort was bruising her arms and he was screaming incessantly so that even the music might not be sufficient to disguise the noise.

This part of the ritual had been prescribed by Gaudet, more, she thought, as a form of torture than anything else. The drugs might take another five or ten minutes or they might not be strong enough for a man wild with panic. Primarily, the succino coline would erase his memory of events in this room. Gaudet had given her another more potent hypodermic but for some reason didn't want her to use it unless she felt compelled.

"DuShane," she said calmly.

He stopped his struggling and his screaming. It was a powerful feeling.

"You don't want me to put you to sleep with a syringe. You'll be unconscious. I would think you would hate that."

"Let me up."

She went back to the closet and took out a black box. In front of Chellis she opened it and took out the second hypodermic.

"One stick and you are floating among the stars without even a memory of what has happened to you. Do you want us to steal some history? And if I have to use it, you never know what I might do."

The illusion that he might yet hang on to a little power amused her and was like a narcotic for him. Apparently DuShane reasoned that if he was awake he still had some control. "One chance, DuShane. Let me put the box on you and I'll leave the trapdoor open in the front. I'm not going to bruise my arms playing with this contraption."

"Damn you." He began screaming again. "Help, somebody help me."

Her own miscalculation made her angry. Being very careful with her aim, she took the bear spray and shot it at his screaming throat. Then she stepped way back, her eyes stinging, and opened the bedroom door, retreating into the living room while she watched. The reaction of his body was dramatic. He turned white, then red, and looked as if he were trying to swallow the room.

She wondered why she hadn't thought to use the gas mask. Holding her breath, she ran to the closet and put it on. Now she could watch the spectacle in comfort. He gasped terribly.

Although she knew he was trying to talk, it was a while before she could read his contorted lips enough to make out his words.

"Take me to the hospital."

It was becoming tedious.

After a few minutes he appeared paralyzed; all he did was breathe, and he didn't do that very well. This time she easily slipped the box under the back of his head and closed it. There was a trapdoor in front that she opened.

"There now. That's much better."

After a half hour of reading *Cosmopolitan* aloud to him, the English version, he was pretty much back to normal—that is, he was starting another screaming fit.

"Shut up or I'll close your door."

He quieted, but he looked so angry she thought he might burst veins in his eyes.

"Just tell me why."

"It's simple. I want what you have. If I kill you, then your living trust provides that the trustees for the brat takeover, Marie and I would get a pittance, and we lose the company. Those jackal lawyers of yours would have us escorted off the premises."

"Marie would get millions."

"Twenty, dear. Only twenty. What is that compared to the billions you control? On the other hand, if you are incapacitated, then Marie and I are in charge. Surely you remember how and why you set it up that way. You said, I think: 'I don't want those bastard lawyers taking over unless I'm dead and stinking.' Isn't that what you said? So don't crap your pants and die, honey." She closed the door of his head-box and he began his muffled screaming. After a second she opened it. "Look, you get to live. If you are good, we will give you oil and some days, at least Christmas and Easter, you won't be far off normal. Sort of like Jason. Well, a little more paranoid than Jason, but still alive." She closed his door again.

As a test she left the room, and noted that his words were unintelligible and the sound not particularly audible even with the bedroom door open. It was time to deliver Jacques's vector in the manner prescribed. This was definitely an important experiment. It would be the first aerosol use and it was imperative that they know exactly the amount DuShane inhaled and that he inhale the amount prescribed by Jacques. After dosing him she would begin his education.

The phone rang.

She knew it would be Gaudet, and it was one of those rare occasions when he would be gleeful as a schoolboy over their progress.

Thirty-six

The place reminded Anna of Jason's lodge, the way it was laid out and even the aesthetic aspects of the design. There were five bedrooms in addition to the master suite, as well as two guest houses with three bedrooms each. To further supplement the living space, a large banquet tent had been placed on the lawn near the pool. Normally it was used for summertime parties, but now it was being used as a barracks. Sam, Anna, Spring, Jason, Grady, and T.J. each took a room in the main house.

With a grin, T.J. had won the toss for accommodations in the primary residence. That left six men to the tent and six into the two guest houses. There was a lot more coin tossing. Anna unpacked her stuff in the master suite knowing that Sam would be busy for a while with the men. Whether it was necessary or not, she knew that Sam would feel compelled to have a meeting to set things in order.

Although laid as unobtrusively as possible, sandbags now lined the interior walls of the house, rising to window level in the living room. In the event of a full-scale assault the living room would provide the final shelter other than the safe room. More "safe" than "room," it consisted of a large concrete-reinforced, habitation-adapted, steel safe that sat inside what had once been a utility room. If it got down to the safe room, Sam was counting on the Mounties to arrive before it was breached.

After unpacking, Anna took from her closet a silken robe that she had acquired from Japan. She had never worn it, having resolved to keep it for a special occasion. It wasn't a special occasion, but it felt right for the moment. Under the robe she decided to wear a silk nightgown that looked vaguely like a cocktail dress. For a second she pondered something more translucent, but dismissed the idea. A quick check of Sam's room revealed that he was still roaming around with the boys. She should have known that he would need to mark his territory before retiring. She hoped to talk for a while before leaving him to sleep.

She was nearly done with the biography of the Warner brothers, and decided to finish the last chapter.

There was a soft knock.

It was Spring.

"Hi, I would have thought you would be asleep," Anna said.

"No. I have been wanting to follow up on our prior conversations. You finished the book that your friend gave you."

"Yes."

"I wondered if you figured out where she went."

"I have always resisted any notion that we are somehow the product of our upbringing. I like to feel like the captain of my own destiny. I don't like introspection as much as I like goals and making choices to get where I want to go."

"So you're captain of your ship. And who is captain of Sam's?"

Anna laughed at that. "Oh, I have a sneaking suspicion that he feels the same way I do. But then you will say: If Sam is in the grip of his past, then who is to say that I'm not? Is that it?"

"I thought all this contemplation might have provided a bit of insight."

"Into what?"

"Into your situation with Sam. Maybe I'm just a meddling mother interested in Sam. If so, I'm sorry."

"It's a confusing situation."

They talked for an hour and ended with Anna's poem, which she had not recited since junior college. Spring had her repeat it.

"And you are close with your mother now?" she asked.

"I think so."

"When you wrote this poem you seemed to be flirting with a feeling that you don't really express."

"I never liked day care. The place smelled bad and they ignored me."

"And what did your mother say?"

"About what?"

"Day care."

"We've never discussed it."

"What if you one day showed her the poem?"

"It's no big deal. After all these years it would be mean. Don't you think?"

"There is a Tilok story that I would like to tell you and I would like to tell it to you while you wait for Sam."

"I'm not admitting to waiting for Sam in a silk robe and a nightgown." Anna smiled.

* * *

Grady was thinking about Clint and the strange exhilaration of getting to know her father. And his strange nature. Clint was out in the guest house, Anna's room was to the right of her, and to the left was her father's, and nothing had ever felt quite so bizarre. She hated to admit it, but she wasn't sure how to actually build a relationship with her father and she was equally confounded by a man like Clint. There probably wasn't a large chance that Clint didn't know about the strip club and that, in a way, made it easier, because if they became friends she would need to tell him before they became lovers.

On the other hand, she wondered if any invitation to friendship that she might venture would be tainted by a thousand other invitations, a thousand other clever lines echoing like old words in a prison hall.

In this beautiful house she wished for her Panzy, the ultimate feline source of comfort. She'd seen that each of the rooms was equipped with a computer and access to the Internet. She could check her AOL account for any messages from the Critter Sitter. The rules set down by Sam for e-mails and the Internet, however, were clear. She was not to access her computer at the apartment because it might be traced. Also she knew she had to view her e-mail through the previewing function and could not per se open it. Under no circumstances could she send an e-mail anywhere, nor could she enter a chat room of any kind. Curious, she turned on the machine and used the password taped to the inside of the Microsoft Guide.

She punched an AOL icon, dialed in, and used her screen name and password. Aside from the junk mail, she had two messages: one from Guy and one from the Critter Sitter, with an urgent subject line. The heat of adrenaline-fueled worry coursed through her body as she thought about Panzy. Maybe sick. Maybe dying. She could not call anyone anywhere except Jill and her other friends at Sam's office without special clearance, and then the answer would probably be negative. Although certain it wouldn't hurt, she decided not to even preview the e-mail without asking Sam. It would only take a minute to find him. As she rose, she saw her father standing in the doorway, looking a little uneasy.

"Jason," she said, still not used to calling him Dad. "You don't look well."

"The Nannites. I'm sorry. I don't want you to see me like this, but I just wanted to look at you for a moment. To see that there is some good in the world."

"Anna will give you some oil."

"Yes. I'll find her."

"Anna says Nutka will be here soon and she can give you a regular massage."

"They keep saying that." He raised his hand. "What are you doing?"

"I miss my cat."

"Panzy, right?"

"Yeah. I am worried about her. I was going to find Sam to ask him something."

"About cats?"

"Not exactly. I need to get into some e-mail. I'll be right back, okay?"

"Sure. The Nannites aren't going anywhere. Neither am I. The little bastards."

Jason desperately needed Nutka. But Anna could give him oil and that would cure the Nannite nerves. He also needed the board that they were now putting together so he could work equations, and he needed his computer. Grady was his only consolation. He had never wanted to get near her for fear the Nannites would commence their plague. But now she was here and it wasn't his doing and he wanted to know her.

He walked over to the computer and squinted at the screen. AOL. An in-box of sorts. Someplace called the Critter Sitter had sent an urgent e-mail regarding Panzy. No wonder Grady had been distraught. Clicking the mouse, he opened it.

> *Need immediate treatment authorization for Panzy. We have detected a large sarcoma tumor in her abdomen. Surgery may save Panzy if performed immediately. Please respond by e-mail so that we have a record of your authorization.*

If it were his pet, Pasha, he knew what he would do. He wrote:

> *Take all necessary steps to save Panzy. You have my full authorization for any and all treatments.*

He sent it and felt better immediately. Then he got an idea. Perhaps he could call Grace Technologies and access his own e-mail. It would be fun to send Chellis a message. He clicked out of AOL and thought how he might access the satellite. Then he considered all of the weird goings-on and how Sam and Anna had traveled and seemed to be hiding. Better to wait and discuss it with Anna.

"Grady, listen carefully. No way do you access your e-mail. You are going into AOL over an eight hundred line?" Sam asked.

"Yeah."

"Did you open anything or send anything?"

"No, I would never do that without asking."

"If it is a trap, if they've figured out about your cat, the second you open that e-mail they'll know you've called the account and that could be the beginning of the end for us. Responding with your own e-mail would without question give away our location unless we did a whole lot of programming that hasn't been done here."

"They can find that out?"

"A corporation like Grace would make up some bull-shit story and they would be able to easily discover the local carrier that put that eight hundred call through. AOL has to keep track of all eight hundred calls for billing purposes. The local carrier will know the physical address of the phone that placed the call. Or in this case the modem. We use these techniques all the time."

"God, Big Brother."

"I'll send someone to check on your cat. Don't worry about it."

"There is no way I can read that e-mail?"

"Too risky even to do that. Let's not take chances."

Grady returned to her room and found her computer displaying the desktop icons and her AOL screen gone from the monitor. Certainly her father knew about computers, so he probably went off on the Internet or something. It was just as well. She wouldn't have to look at that e-mail again. She shut down the computer and looked at the clock. She would read the book that Anna had given her. Oddly she seemed to find herself the subject of every chapter. It was called *Where Did He Go? Where Did She Go?*

Thirty-seven

Anna found Sam bent over a desk strewn with maps of the house and grounds.

His room was large to accommodate three walls full of oil paintings, a king-size bed with a massive oak headboard, and a big-screen television mounted in a mahogany entertainment center. Although the room had several lights, Sam worked by a single desk lamp, and so the cream and faux gold walls were softened and enriched by the man-made twilight.

"Secluded homes often don't make good safe houses. Bad guys can hide in the woods."

She nodded, looking at the maps.

"But this place is perfect. We are in the middle of a two-acre lawn manicured with flower beds and low-lying shrubbery. There is a fence all the way round, three dogs, and good electronic security. It's the summer retreat for a contractor who builds nuclear plants and he likes his peace and doesn't want to be disturbed by environmental activists."

"You really had me going with the yacht story."

Sam smiled and turned around in his seat. "You and my mother have been talking incessantly."

"She told me a story."

"Yeah?"

"An Indian girl grew apart from her husband and

found a single man to take as a lover. Many nights she sneaked across the stream. To make it easy she planted large stones and learned to dance across and keep her moccasins dry even in the dark. Then her lover took a wife and left her alone. Every day she looked at the stones and was reminded of him. One night she danced across the stones and found her husband waiting. After that meeting, so the legend goes, they prospered and had many children and every night her husband waited for her at the other side of the river. Over time the story of the stones got around the village and dancing across them in the dark became a game amongst the young women, and soon they placed more stones and made more elaborate crossings.

"Have you heard this story?" she asked Sam.

"Yes," he said. "But keep going. Sometimes my mother's stories have a fork in the road—which fork depends on the traveler."

"Then you know that as time passed, crossing the river on the stones became a wedding ritual for brides, who would find their husbands waiting on the other side to take them off to a secret place.

"Then one day a Talth went to the people and said this ritual was not right because the stones were a memorial to treachery and should not be part of a wedding celebration. Wanting to keep the tradition, the people went to the chief and inquired about the message of the Talth.

"The chief said that time for love must be stolen from the cares of life or it will fade. So the ritual was good because it taught an important lesson."

Sam smiled as if he understood the point. "And what did you get out of the story?"

"There is something about escaping cares and com-

mitments and just stealing time for love that perpet-
uates it. For a lot of people, it's sort of in the blueprint
for marriage that duties are more important than
love."

"But?"

"Love seems dangerous. If you don't want to feel it
you can escape it, but you then become emotionally
unavailable."

"She really is getting to you."

"Are you feeeee . . . ling something, Sam?" she
asked teasingly. "You won't get this overnight. How
did your mother tell the story to you?"

"It was the same story with a different emphasis. It
was all about the path in your mind that not trusting
makes. You know, it leaves a trail like the stones. She was
telling me that my dad left a trail in my mind. Of course
the moral had to be that it's up to me to give the stones
a new meaning. In the story the woman's husband and
the whole tribe gave the stones a new meaning. With
the new trust came new feelings. It's a versatile story."

"Funny. I wrote this poem. It seems like she would
have told me the meaning she told you. The part about
reinterpreting something that happened in the past.

"Anyway did the story soften you up, Sam?"

"Give me a break. What man with any balls is going
to be softened by a story?"

The phone rang. It was T.J.

"We got an e-mail. They're ready to talk at Harvard."

"Okay. We'll come to the scrambler and place the
call."

Sam turned on the speakerphone and everyone
but Sam, Anna, Grady, and T.J. cleared the office area
that had been set up in the house's spacious library.

"I think we have it licked," Fielding began. "We elected George to explain it."

"I don't know how much you want me to try to cover on the phone."

"The whole thing," Anna said. "I want to know what's wrong with Jason."

"Well, as you know there were two codes just to get into the main files. Paul cracked the second, but then individual files were encrypted and we had to go back to Big Brain four times. Jason had hacked into various parts of the Grace computer and downloaded backup files from the lab in Kuching. We are the first to read them, and it took a whole team of us including some folks from the University of Washington and a private foundation lab. But we got their game or at least part of it. And it is fascinating."

"How does it affect my brother?"

"Okay, maybe I should start with the rather glum conclusion and then explain it."

"Yes."

"They altered his DNA. The DNA of his neurons. His brain. It's probably permanent unless the lab that did it has a fix. But there does seem to be a treatment and we know the active ingredient. It is a temporary antidote that will relieve the effects of the DNA alteration for about twenty-four hours. If he takes it every twenty-four hours, he may not feel the effects of what has been done to his brain."

"So he's paranoid because of this?"

"I'm afraid so."

"This seems incredible."

"Well, there is a lot to it. I can explain if you like. I will tell you that we can send you some hormone that will make him feel better."

"Yes. Yes."

"All right. Where to start . . . let's see . . . they needed to alter just certain of his brain cells. They started with neurons in the limbic system, the prefrontal cortex, and the amygdala. They alter them genetically. Once changed, they have radical effects on people's state of mind. To change them genetically they alter the DNA. To do that they deliver new DNA that affects certain predetermined neuron cell types."

Anna seemed to pale.

"Okay. We're all ears," Sam said.

"Okay, to begin with, if we're trying to influence anxiety we go to the cells that influence that mental state. Anxiety is largely controlled by certain brain cells in the limbic system, amygdala, and prefrontal cortex."

"Okay."

"There are two kinds of cells there. Some enhance a response, such as anxiety, and others reduce it. Activator cells or inhibitor cells, we call them. Grace calls the inhibitor cells suppressor cells, so we'll go with their lingo. If you increase the sensitivity of anxiety-suppressor cells, you will actually be suffering less anxiety, whereas the opposite is true if you increase the sensitivity of an activator cell. To increase sensitivity to a neuron they add what we call a receptor. It's actually a molecule on the dendrite."

Sam let George know that they'd become familiar with the workings of dendrites and synapses, courtesy of Dr. Yanavitch.

"If I understand this," Sam said, "my next question is how they forced the DNA changes in Jason's brain."

"To deliver the DNA coding sequence they use a structure that is in some respects like a virus and it is called a vector. To make it they break apart a virus and strip away its protein coating. Then they insert two pieces of DNA. One causes the formation of the extra receptor molecule on the dendrites and that is called the coding sequence. The other is called the promoter strand and it identifies the cells that are to be changed by the coding sequence. It's like the passkey to changing only the neurons that make a difference in the anxiety response.

"Specifically, Grace breaks down a monkey herpes virus. They splice in the coding DNA and the promotor DNA, reinstall a new protein coat around this new ring of DNA, and bam, they have a delivery vehicle that infects a foreign cell and installs new coding sequences. All body cells of different function are defined by the proteins that they make. What defines those special proteins that make a cell unique are the promoters that are active in the cell to produce their unique proteins. For cells that have specialized functions like a cell in the amygdala of your brain, involved in an anxiety response, there must be unique proteins produced by that cell and cells of the same function. Each cell type will have its own promoter.

"If the vector enters a neuron that doesn't recognize the promoter, then there is no change in that cell. They introduce the vector (which for these purposes is like a virus that won't replicate) and it invades all or most brain cells indiscriminately. The protein changes forced by the changed DNA will only apply to the desired cells of the brain. So if any given neuron happens to be a brain cell concerned with anxiety, the vector basically says, 'Honey, I'm home,' and the cell recognizes that voice.

"Now this is something of a simplification because Grace has identified over a dozen unique cell types involved in the anxiety response; therefore they used a dozen different forms of the vector, each with a different promoter but all having the same coding sequence. Remember that the coding sequence is just the formula for producing the extra receptors."

Sam looked at Anna, who was nodding her head as if in shock.

"Here is how the research progressed. Grace started with rats and mice but moved to monkeys in their Kuching, Malaysia, lab. First thing they discovered was that it's easier to take a calm monkey and make it permanently nervous than vice versa. So that is how they started. In effect, to learn about making nervous monkeys calm, they initially studied the reverse process. To make a monkey nervous all the time you put extra responders in those activator brain cells concerned with the fear response. You just turn up the sensitivity of the activator cells."

"And this is what they did to Jason?"

"Well, we're not there yet but this is the research track they were taking. They were making calm animals nervous as a prelude to curing anxiety disorders. Now remember that a vector is just DNA with a protein coat, and—"

"We understand," Sam cut in. "What about the opposite process?"

"I was just getting to that. To make Jason calm they don't touch the activator cells or turn down their sensitivity; they use a hormone to stimulate an inhibitor or as they call it a suppressor cell."

"A hormone?"

"Yes, and get this, it turns out they use insect hormones, called juvenile hormones. They aren't produced in mammals."

Sam looked to Anna, shaking his head, wondering what was next.

"The activator cell receptors and the suppressor

cell receptors are sensitive only to juvenile insect hormones. Each to a different hormone. They got part of the DNA sequences for the receptor molecules from insects and mass-produced the hormones in the lab."

"This is sick," Anna said.

"Yeah. So they can install receptors that make the calm person nervous by making activator cells more sensitive. To counteract the effect you introduce the hormone that sensitizes the suppressor cells to make the subject calm again. To make him very calm you just superboost the suppressor cells."

"Or you could do the same thing in reverse," Sam said.

"Right. We could stimulate the activator cells and do nothing to the suppressor cells and create hyperparanoia. But the hormones have no effect on someone with normal DNA."

"The applications for this are almost unlimited," said Sam.

"Right. They have a profile known as the Soldier profile. On demand they hyperstimulate fear-suppressor cells as well as activator cells associated with extreme aggression. They also stimulate suppressor cells related to remorse. In sum they can create fearless, aggressive killers with absolutely no remorse."

"Why haven't we heard about this for gene therapy for healing applications?"

"They cured the so-called bubble children with DNA fixes to the immune system using retro viral vectors to place genes in the bone marrow and altered the DNA that way. The problem with vectors is the human immune system. It tends to attack foreign bodies and a vector is a foreign body. With the bubble children there was no immune system and hence nothing to fight the vector as a foreign body. We know that Grace somehow solved the problem with the immune response because Jason was not a bubble boy and had a fully intact immune system. Jason didn't steal that file."

The French fighters from the rooftop flashed in Sam's mind.

"They take an ordinary individual, alter his DNA, and apply hormones to make him an ultrasoldier," Sam recapped. "When they want him normal again they wait the twenty-four hours or so until the hormone dissipates or they create the opposite reaction with other hormones. And I heard you say this: To accomplish a permanent alteration of a subject's DNA, all it takes is for the subject to inhale a real good dose of the vector. But how about discipline, intelligence, strategy, and so on? For soldiers?"

"Don't know."

"I faced a group of fighters that had no fear. Now I have a theory about them."

"I doubt they had the full pop that we've been reading about or you wouldn't be here. You've heard about the 110-pound woman who lifted a car off her kid? That's what you'd be dealing with. There is one more thing I want to tell you, especially Anna.

"All of earth's life, plant life, mammals, invertebrates, single-celled organisms, is ultimately made from a DNA blueprint. All life is controlled by its DNA. DNA, you may know, is just nucleic acid molecules strung together in pairs. There are only four nucleic acid molecules. Just four. And the order of them in strings is what controls life. We humans have three billion nucleic acid base pairs in our string of chemical beads. It's the order of the base pairs that makes us human.

"Jason believes that Nannites live in the DNA and that all of life on earth is for the purpose of hosting DNA. That's the Nannite strategy. Somebody monkeyed with his DNA and since he believes the Nannites have their abode in DNA, he ascribes his troubles to them."

"I like my mother's Christianity better," Anna said.

"Well, I'd like to think I'm not a Nannite sanctuary. I hope Jason is wrong. Otherwise we're nothing more than good hosts for DNA."

"So that's what you know that you can readily explain to the likes of us," Sam said.

"That's it."

"You have discovered plenty, and we appreciate it. Somehow we'll try to sleep."

Thirty-eight

Sam felt close to her, perhaps closer than he had ever felt with a woman. And it happened so fast he didn't know what to make of it. When they came down the hall from the conference call, she followed him into his bedroom. There was a love seat and some overstuffed chairs around a coffee table.

She sat on the love seat and patted the spot next to her.

He sat. "How are we doing?"

"I'm okay," she said. "All that matters to me now is that we have Jason, and we understand the antidote."

"We're also leaving here soon," said Sam. "But say nothing."

"And I imagine you don't want to tell me where?"

"It's far from here. Knowing where is only a burden. What if you were captured and I got away with Jason and Grady?"

"I see what you mean." She took his hand. "I don't want to die never having made love to you."

She untied the belt of her robe, and as the knot loosened, he began helping with the buttons. Her scent and the intimacy of her eyes and the fingers on her clothes aroused him.

Then he watched her as she stood and dropped the

robe, and with his eyes he told her what he was starting to feel.

Her nightgown was a beautiful blue and left her form partially revealed. Across her chest it lay open to display a gentle cleavage at her breasts. And the swell of them and the dark of the nipples barely visible beneath the gown made a tightness in his groin. Slowly she lifted the nightgown until she slipped it over her head. She wore slim blue panties with white lacy trim. Her breasts were a dark red at the aureoles and petite. Firm. Something about the way they turned out and pointed enthralled him. There was faint coloring at her neck, where the sun had caught her and freckled her, that contrasted with the paleness around her breasts.

Sam stood and picked her up, slight and easy in his arms. As he walked to the bed he could feel himself start to harden and the flush spread over his own chest. When he put her on the bed she lay back to watch him undress. He did not hurry with his shirt and T-shirt, and she seemed to warm at the look of him. She came up to her knees to do his jeans and put her hand over the mound at his fly, watching his eyes as she gently rolled over him with her fingers. Then she slipped down his jeans. When he put his hands on her shoulders to come over her, she resisted with a whisper, "I want to play," and peeled off his underpants. Using her hands and lips, she did things so exquisite that he wondered at the delicious agony.

Then he lifted her up and stripped off her panties, fascinated at the reddish tinge in her pubic hair and the perfect form of her thighs.

He buried his face in her; she was rich with scent, her sweet perfume mingled with the musk of her body. Gently he teased her with his tongue until he felt her swell. Then he kissed at her breasts, bringing the nipples full and engorged.

"Oh, dear God, Sam," she whispered at the cooperation between his tongue and fingers.

They lay down and he moved inside her. She held him close, her arms tight on his ribs, and she fit herself to him and he let her find her rhythm until he could hear the tune in her soul and feel the beat of it. He pressed himself to her and kissed her, and in those moments he could feel a renewal of his hope and knew that for him the world could, after all, be reborn and his heart pulled from its slumber.

There was a brief respite in their movements while she let her body hold him and he felt her insides squeezing down on him. There was a feeling in her body through his fingertips that told him she was gathering herself. His eyes locked on hers and explored the life in them, and tried to discern the emanations and the unusual brightness that spoke to him of eagerness and hope.

He kissed her deeply—she tasted like the sweet spice of her cinnamon mints. The movement of her tongue stirred him and the feeling of her against him brought his hands low to cup her buttocks. He knew to lift her as she wrapped her legs around him.

She wanted him, but loved the slowness of his lovemaking and the patience that obliterated time. After her exuberance had nearly overtaken her, she rolled him over and sat astride him, feeling the sweet torture down to her thighs where his hand now became the genie of her imagination.

The want of him was almost painful, but she didn't

utter a sound; she was sure that he was hearing more from her than she knew to speak.

"I love you, I love you," she finally whispered, feeling her breaths go nearly desperate, the sweat running down her sides and making the bedsheets wet.

Perspiration poured from her body, and he pulled her close to taste it with his tongue. At her throat as he mouthed her shivers, he could feel her clutch telling him things that she would not say. Once again he let her find her way until she gave herself to a waltz that he slowly began to hear. When he had found the rhythm of it, he learned her new dance and took her waist in both his hands. It was narrow and taut, the muscle of it firm, the movements of it growing strong. There was a clench in her thighs that told him she was nearly spent. He used their sweat to slide her like a car gone wild on a rain-slicked street.

When they had exhausted each other, she sat astride him with her head bowed and she looked and saw that she was naked, and she giggled and fell on him, leaving him to wonder if it would ever be that good again.

She lay with her face inches from him, her eyes not leaving his. The amber brown hues of them were at once soothing and exhilarating.

She leaned and put her lips to his ear. "Who are you?"

"I was born Samuel Browning. My name now is Kalok Wintripp. My father was of English descent. He was an Air Force parajumper. I grew up in Alaska. I received my Ph.D. from MIT when I was twenty-four and I took it as Kalok Wintripp. Grandfather picked my Indian name. It is the Tilok word for Eagle."

* * *

"I have an idea," Michelle said to Samir over breakfast. He was less shaky than usual, as she had used extra oil that morning.

"Hmm?"

"I think we should give you a huge dose of the oil so that you can think like you used to think. A window of sanity, so to speak. All or nothing—figure out what to do to end this torture."

Samir rang a bell and a servant appeared.

"Get me Fawd," Samir said.

The man appeared in two minutes.

"Tell him," Samir said.

She explained her idea and elaborated, this time emphasizing that the old Samir would have found a way out of the current predicament.

"I agree," Fawd said.

"Okay," Samir said. "Get it and let's start."

Michelle could see a difference within fifteen minutes, and marveled at how simply some unknown chemical or drug transformed the man. Ironically, it was his vulnerability that in part had drawn her to him, and now it faded fast.

This time when Samir walked into the five-star hotel in downtown Kuching, he felt like the billion dollars he was worth. He and Fawd had spared no expense when it came to men, and Fawd had been smart enough to keep a large contingent parked around various cheap hotels in Kuching and some in tents camping in the jungle. This time they would not bother to approach the compound so cautiously.

Benoit spoke quietly to Chellis, who sat behind an ornate desk longer than he was tall. His head was bowed over his hands and a thumb rubbed each eye.

They were in an eight-bedroom country house that was nearly a mansion, with surrounding grounds that measured in all over forty hectares. It was a gentleman's farm an hour's drive from Paris and located on a hillside near Chevreuse in a pastoral setting chosen by Benoit more for its security than its notable tranquillity. It was prime real estate, with privacy and a view at the end of a long, tree-lined drive. Clearly it would be hard for Chellis to leave undetected.

"Do you have to leave?" he said to her as she gathered her gloves.

"I do. I have to run the business. But I'll be back. You'll be safe here, I promise. You've picked the guards yourself."

"But the Nannites."

"Yes. We went over that. With the iron grids they can't get in here. You're safe anywhere inside this house."

"You're sure."

"Yes."

"I feel as if I've gotten the vector somehow."

"That's silly, DuShane. You've been so edgy since we left my house."

"But didn't you say the Nannites were coming?"

"I did. And wasn't I right? As tragic as it is, didn't they come?"

"Yes."

"So you see. We've fixed this place up especially."

"When are you coming back?"

"I'll stop by this evening."

"You promise?"

"Yes. And Greta will give you a massage."

"Oh, good."

She turned the television to the financial channel to distract him and left quickly, hoping he wouldn't start to weep again. She had no idea how Jacques had supercharged the Nervous Flyer profile, but it certainly had worked, as had the large dose of drugs she'd hit him with right after the port wine. As Jacques had promised, DuShane had no clear memory of that day.

"He's really bad today, just cracked like that," she said to the supervisor of security just outside the door. "You mustn't let him outside. If he wants to leave remind him about the Nannites. It's a part of his fantasy, and the doctor says it's okay to use it to keep him from hurting himself or others."

"I know, mademoiselle. You have explained it very thoroughly."

"I'm sorry. I'm repeating myself. It's just that we want to keep him safe."

It took an hour in light traffic to return to downtown. Soon she and Marie would move him back to the Paris apartment. She walked into her new office, originally Chellis's, which she was fast making over, and looked expectantly through her messages. She was growing concerned that she had not heard from Gaudet. He was the one remaining person who worried her. Sometimes she imagined that he might read her thoughts, and if he did he would slit her throat—if he was feeling charitable. He would do worse if he was not.

The phone rang. She grabbed it. "Hello?"

"This is Jacques."

"I haven't heard from Gaudet."

There was a strange sound. Then a new voice. "Neither has Jacques."

She recognized the voice. It sounded like a reborn Samir Aziz.

"Mr. Aziz?" she asked, her mind whirling to understand what could have gone wrong.

"So you recognize me. And I you. Jacques here tells

me that DuShane Chellis is indisposed. Permanently. Right, Jacques? Tell her where you are."

"I am in the primate wing." Jacques's voice sounded distant.

"Oh, come on, Jacques. You're in a monkey cage. Tell her you are in the monkey cage. And tell her who is with you."

"I am in with Centaur."

"And what is Centaur wearing?"

"He's wearing his backpack."

"Benoit, do you think an adult male macaque in a full fighting rage could kill a man?"

"Unarmed?"

"Good point. Fawd, let's give him a club. What about if we give the man a club?"

"Centaur will kill him."

"What will you give me not to push Centaur's buttons?"

"Have you given Jacques the vector?"

"No. But I have it right here. But you're getting ahead of me. I wanted to see Centaur do his thing."

"Don't do it. We can talk. We can make a deal."

"I'm listening."

"You can have all the antidote you want."

"I already have it. I told Jacques I would make him a nervous rabbit like he made Chellis and he promised me all the hormone I need forever."

"So what is there to talk about? We both need Jacques and his research."

"What about half of the private half of Grace, which would be twenty percent."

"What about five percent of Grace Technologies?"

"Come on. I have half of the brainpower of the corporation right here in a monkey cage. The other half is up for grabs—depends on who gets Jason. If

you take out Grady without them tracing it to you,
then maybe a French court will let you hang on to
Jason. Then again maybe not, and all you'll have is
Jacques. And since I have Jacques, it seems to me that
five percent is ridiculous."

"There is a lot more to Grace than weapons and Soldier profiles. Don't be greedy or you'll get nothing."

"We should meet and talk, my dear."

"Okay. In the meantime leave Jacques's brain
alone."

"Actually, I think I'll relate to him better if he's
paranoid."

"Then for God's sake give him Jason's vector profile, not what he created for Chellis."

"Which did you give me?"

"Essentially you have Jason's profile. We want a
whole brain here or we won't have anything to bargain over."

"Benoit, don't let him do it," Jacques shouted.

"Did you have the speakerphone on?"

"I thought it was only fair that he hear you giving
his sanity away. Call me when you have a reasonable
proposal." And with that, Samir hung up.

Thirty-nine

"We have a problem," Benoit said when she reached Gaudet.

"Well, I have a few myself. Why are you calling me?"

"Samir Aziz has Jacques at gunpoint in the laboratory and he's gotten all the hormone he needs to be fearless for the next decade."

"We'll deal with it tomorrow. Any more good news?"

"The lawyers are in court. They're anticipating Anna's people, and they are filing papers saying that we want an order halting any interference with Jason's guardianship. Roberto is of course asserting that he is the lawful guardian. What we really need is Jason in our custody back in France. That way we can get someone here appointed even if it isn't Roberto. Someone with ties to Grace."

"I know you need Jason back in France, but it will be hard to explain a war over here in Canada, and he is heavily guarded. I'm trying to do it quietly."

"The lawyers say we need him on French soil now. Do whatever it takes. We'll explain that some mercenary got out of control if we have to. That's better than not having him at all."

"That's a messy way to handle things. And I'm the one who stands to lose when the authorities decide to hunt this 'mercenary.'"

"We'll blame DuShane's men. Or Aziz. But we can't continue on without Jason. So get him or we're finished."

"What do you mean finished? How can one man—"

"His work is worth billions and it's not complete."

"This can't be done 'now.'"

"If you don't do it we're beaten."

"You know what we're risking if I use maximum force."

"I know."

She hung up furious, wondering if Gaudet would get her condemned to a French jail for the rest of her life. She picked up the phone. She had exaggerated Jason's importance, but not by much.

"Claude. Claude Balford. Head of security. We need to talk about his mental stability."

"Huh?"

"I think he's become unstable. He's off in Canada. I'm worried he'll do something crazy. We will need evidence of his instability. Do you understand me?"

Sam was sitting on a ridge across the valley from an ancient cave known to the Tiloks as Man Jumps. The cave was in the side of a formidable gray cliff spotted with the green of stubborn trees that had crammed their toes in the rock and made a home of a seeming vertical wasteland. Sun glistened on the mountain's face and poured down her blue-gray flanks. There was green in the wet algae near seeps as if nature had thrown Irish sparkles. Around him on the ridge it was quiet. Strewn at his feet were wild-flowers whiter than an eagle's crown spread over grasses lush from spring rain. As he watched the cave a woman, Anna, appeared. She called to him in her trouble and was frantic about the sheer drop and the death awaiting her if she fell. He tried to call to her, to beckon to her, but she did not see his hand or hear his call. He rose, frustrated at the vast gulf that lay between them.

Two men appeared behind her, grabbing her. They fought, and he saw her arms flying as the man tried to draw her away, back into the cave.

The alarm filled Sam's ears. He grabbed for Anna, who was coiled around him, then jumped at the sounds of automatic rifle fire and nearly threw her from the bed. The shooting was on the perimeter. The digital clock read 4:00 A.M. He had been sleeping in his flak jacket and had made Anna, Grady, and Jason wear them fully clothed to bed.

"Come on," he said, his head still full of the dream.

"All right. To the safe room?"

"Yes."

They took Grady and Jason and went toward the living area, then down a narrow hall. The safe room had been built like a bank vault, but with human habitation in mind. It contained air bottles and masks, enough for twelve hours of isolation. Ventilation could be totally sealed. The insulation inside was more than a foot thick. To get somebody out would take a blast that would kill them.

The safe room stood freely except for its back wall, which fit snugly against the back wall of the utility room and its base that was sunk in concrete. Sam had been told that even the utility room walls had been reinforced with multiple layers of plywood to shield the box from external explosions.

"Put them in. I can shoot," Anna said. Sam just nodded, unwilling to waste critical seconds arguing. They put Jason and Grady through the six-inch steel door and according to instructions it was then locked from the inside.

Before they got to the living room, T.J. had all the lights out inside the house.

They found a man on watch with a radio, and T.J. alternately barking orders into a microphone and nervously chewing on a plastic coffee stir-stick. They had turned the living room into a command center by moving back sofas, storing furnishings, and placing an old dining table from a local furniture store in the center of the room. It struck a discordant note, like discount fiberboard furniture in the lobby of a Four Seasons hotel.

An umbrella rack by the front door held four M4s and on the hat rack above several pairs of night-vision goggles and a half-dozen gas masks. The two-acre grounds were normally lit by hundreds of walkway and shrubbery lights that actually created the feeling of perpetual twilight. Now the outdoor lighting was being knocked out with bullets. They took up night-vision goggles and placed them on their foreheads, ready to use. Each of them, including Anna, held an M4. Sam handed Anna a gas mask.

The weapons fire was deafening. Muzzle blasts flashed everywhere. Men screamed. Men swore. The radio crackled constantly.

"Did you get the Mounties on the phone?" Sam said.

"I'll do it now," T.J said.

Heavy fire poured through the house. All over the groundsmen were shooting, each man with his own personal war.

"They're everywhere," a harried voice shouted.

"Roger that." There was a roar of shots running together.

After a second of fiddling, T.J. shouted: "Lines down. I'll use the cell."

After a minute he spoke again. "Nothing."

"Let me try." Sam pulled out a cell.

"Hello, hello," the police dispatcher said.

"We have a firefight up the hill from Ganges," Sam said.

"Mister, I got a whole war up there."

"That's right. Send officers, tell them to be careful."

"There are three Mounties on the island, a boat at Galliano. Won't be much. Won't be fast."

"We're losing good guys up here."

"I know, I know. We'll do what we can. I'll have them call you."

The cell lost the signal before he could give her the number. The place wouldn't be hard to find.

"These assholes won't quit," somebody shouted.

"Just blow them to pieces," another man replied.

There were three explosions. The first blew out the windows. The second knocked the texture from the walls and buckled the ceiling and Sheetrock. Dust was everywhere. With the third explosion the entire structure shook and strained like a groaning old man. Two fighters came through the windows, and their bodies were ripped with bullets from outside and in. One of them lost at least half his head, but for seconds the breath of him still wheezed bloody froth out the trachea.

"We have a shrinking perimeter. Our men are withdrawing to their clusters around the house and grounds." Sam saw Anna shooting next to him. Something in him reacted and he pulled her low to the ground.

"Be careful."

As if to punctuate his words, rifle bullets began popping through the room and blowing holes in the wall. They remained hunkered behind the sandbags except when Sam rose, looking for shadows in the half-light. Outside it might have been Gettysburg, the way the smoke drifted in the night breeze. Men were down and screaming, calling out their anger as blood ran from ragged wounds and the cold of death crept through their bodies.

Bullets continued pouring through the windows, shattering remaining shards of glass. Sam could feel the jolt of the sandbags as they took rounds through the wall. Tear gas sailed through the window, streaming a picturesque arc of noxious balls of light before it hit the floor. They threw on the masks.

Then a .50-caliber machine gun began answering from just outside the house, and soon a similar gun responded, shaking the walls, blowing apart the studs. Wood flew from the ceiling as it knocked chunks out of the timbers. Then more huge explosions.

"They're back into the rockets," Sam said. "What have they got?" he shouted into the radio.

"No armor. All stuff you can carry. Rockets, fifty-caliber stuff. These bastards are crazy. You blow parts off 'em and they keep coming."

Just then the wall behind them exploded and a cloud of white went everywhere.

"I got him, I got him."

Sam knew that some soldier meant the guy with the launcher. Then a second rocket hit the house above their heads. "Must be more than one," he muttered inanely. The concussion was bad and they were swathed in cotton-white dust clouds. Without the masks they'd have been choked nearly dead.

As the dust cleared, one of Sam's men jumped through the window. His arm came off in midflight, leaving only red muck and the white of a blood-spurting artery.

Anna screamed from down the wall. In the confusion she must have moved away from him.

"Everybody out," T.J. cried.

Sam knew he was right. The house was a target and the enemy had rockets. Either they were not that worried about Jason or they knew about the safe room.

Sam crawled after Anna just as another explosion ripped through the room. Able to see nothing, he crawled ahead, grabbing for her, but somehow she must have moved away from the wall. He could see nothing.

"Anna," he called.

"Out, out," T.J. said. "I sent her out."

Sam scrambled, hoping Anna had indeed run out into the night. Grady and Jason would be safe in the concrete and steel.

He leaped through the window and crawled clear of the house for maybe thirty yards, shouting, looking for Anna. Finally he lay in the winter grass. Shots were being fired on every quarter. There were pockets of light and fleeting shadows, the rush of adrenaline, the craze of killing. One of Sam's men sat on the grass holding a torn arm and wrapping a belt around it, trying to stop the blood. One of the enemy crawled with only his arms, his back obviously broken by a bullet, but undaunted.

Soldier profile.

Sam aimed at his head, but couldn't or wouldn't shoot. He wasn't sure which. The man had no rifle but wore a pistol on his belt. Sam crawled over and yanked it away as the man struggled for it. There was a grenade belt that Sam also stripped. The man continued on. It appeared he was still attacking the house.

"You're going soft," T.J. said.

"Without a doubt." Sam's men were in little clusters, making no line that could be charged. Approaching the house could be a deadly sport and going inside worse—just as it had been for Sam. Now the enemy would have to slow down or be shot to pieces.

"Have you seen Anna?"

"No. I thought she was ahead of us. She could be anywhere around here," T.J. said.

He looked at the cavernous black of the blown-out windows. Then his dream came back to him. Anna calling from a cave. He knew what was happening.

"You manage things from out here," he said to T.J., and ran for the house.

"Like hell," he heard T.J. say.

Forty

Nothing in Anna's life had prepared her for the intensity of the killing frenzy going on around her. War movies were not war. The man's arm had landed beside her and she'd stared dumbfounded at the wedding ring. A naked dangling artery spewed the man's life onto the wool carpet. Before an explosion blew him away, she had put her hand on the flesh trying to squeeze off the great fountain that spurted obscenely over everything. T.J. came and helped, shooing her away.

"Go with Sam," he said, pointing into the cloud of white. When she couldn't find Sam in the immediate rubble where T.J. had pointed, she struggled to move farther until she felt him tugging on her arm. Instinctively she moved with it.

"Sam, I'm so glad . . ."

Bullets pounded through the house and she was crawling fast.

He tugged her to go faster. Past the safe room she crawled, following a very determined Sam. Then the air cleared slightly and she looked ahead, finding Sam wearing black. But Sam had not worn black. Sam had worn camouflage.

"Hey!" she said. The man was faster than a cat, and

in an instant a heavy French accent pierced the pounding of the bullets.

"Come with me." There was the dull metal business end of a razor-sharp carbide blade at her throat. "I'll kill you if you give me the slightest reason."

He yanked her by the hair. She screamed and went with him when she felt the knife hot and stinging slice the skin of her neck.

He had her.

Sam knew it without knowing it. The man from Polynesia, the man whose initial was G, who had killed John Weissman, who was responsible for the death of his son. This man had Anna.

Sam crawled through the destroyed living room, knowing now why the rockets and the massive assault. It was cover for a desperate man who needed a bargaining chip. What would he do with it? How would he play it?

Sam made it quickly through the house past the safe room to the other side. It was alternately dark and light with muzzle blasts and explosions punctuating the night. The air was heavy with a smell like hot wires. Smoke curled in columns and hung in clouds. It was a primitive struggle with ghastly killing devices rending flesh and destroying a home. Half the men had to be dead, and the fighting was starting to ebb. Perhaps they had learned that there was no getting at Jason.

He picked up his radio. "Any word on Anna?"

"Nothing," T.J. said. On the back side of the house Sam tried night vision between flashes. Looking off into the blackness all the way to the tree line, he scanned and scanned again. He saw men crawling and crouching, but no one really moving except the occasional man pulling back. His radio clicked.

"Monsieur Sam."

"This is Sam."

"If you will look at the trees by the pump house."

Sam looked at the pump house and then saw a man step from behind holding someone in camouflage.

"You have Anna."

"Yes. Still wet with your come."

He knew it was a psychological jab, and still it worked.

"What do you want?"

"I want the two in the concrete box in exchange."

"You're Belle du Jour. You're Freight Stop. You're wanted for the murder of Wes King and the theft of his software. You are the lover of Benoit Moreau, the servant of DuShane Chellis."

"Of course you know that men like me disappear every day."

"But you're not sure, are you? Men like you get caught by men like me."

"Not before I am through with your woman."

"If you want to bargain you're going to have to go for something I can give you."

"Like what?"

"Like me."

"What do I want with you?"

"You won't get Jason. You can have Anna Wade, but to you she is just a toy and she can only die once. Kill me and you improve your own chances of survival considerably. I think you know that."

"I didn't come for you."

"No, you didn't. You came for Jason, but it didn't work because he's locked in a box with twelve hours of air and the Mounties are on the way. It's all about timing, and it's getting late. Of course, even to have a chance of getting in that box you need me dead, don't you?"

"You come, she goes."

"Anna, come here," Sam called out.

Anna started walking with Gaudet's gun pointed at her.

Sam walked toward her and the man in black. The shooting had quieted. T.J. had come up close behind him and was following. For some reason Gaudet did not protest. Other men were creeping to the edge of the field. Now there were many guns on Sam and many guns on Devan Gaudet.

"This is crazy," T.J. said.

"Sam, don't go," Anna said, now almost even with him.

"If I don't go, he and about ten other guys are gonna put bullets in your head."

"I don't care. Don't go. Tell the men to shoot."

"We'll all be dead. We're in the open." Sam walked past her and kept walking toward the man he meant to kill. T.J. fell away, going back with Anna.

As Sam approached he saw a mustached man wearing night-vision goggles. The man took off his mask and a bright light came on. It was aimed at him so that Gaudet was in a shadow.

"You are Devan Gaudet."

"Some days."

"You killed my son."

"Now I understand what a triumph that was. I know you have in mind killing me, but before you try you should turn around."

Sam looked back. What he saw sickened him. T.J. was holding a gun to Anna's head. The other men were keeping their places.

"This is bullshit," one of Sam's men called out. "Whose side are you on, T.J.?"

"The money side. Everybody who wants an easy hundred grand, step up here."

None of Sam's men moved except to point their guns at T.J.

"What's the way in?" T.J. called.

"There is no way in. You can kill Anna and me all day long and there is no way in. That thing has twelve hours of air and it isn't opening a moment sooner, no matter what I do or say. I told them to stay the full twelve hours. Even the cops won't get them out. You blow it up and you'll kill them with the concussion."

"All right. Then we'll put a rocket into that thing and kill them."

"Have at it."

"T.J. is a little small-minded," Gaudet sneered. "I have a pneumatic drill and several diamond-tipped bits. They will go through anything."

"Slowly," Sam said, suddenly feeling a chill.

"As you said, if I've got you, I've got time. Granted there will be a few dead Mounties, but that's no problem."

Sam was ten feet from Gaudet and slightly to the side. Gaudet had a pistol aimed at his head, as did three other men. Too many men. Too many angles. It was impossible.

Grandfather.

Sam could think of nothing.

Without the sun the great horned owl lays waste the eagle's nest.

"Maybe now you'd like to drop the gun before we begin killing your sweet Anna."

Sam sensed that there would be no later chance and therefore any risk was acceptable.

Sam kicked both feet for the sky and as he fell shot a blast at the light.

Black. Men fired shots across the field and there was instant war. Sam rolled even as he was knocked three feet over the ground by a bullet.

Searing-hot pain shot through his ribs but he kept rolling. The bullet had hit the steel of the chest plate in his flak jacket. There was the excruciating pain of cracked ribs but nothing else. Beside Sam a man fell, shot. Sam took his weapon and hunkered behind him. Five bullets, at least, hit the body. Pulling his goggles down, Sam saw Gaudet step behind a tree, still blind without his night vision. With his chest aching like a grapefruit-sized tooth cavity, Sam ran for the tree, figuring to end Gaudet.

As he ran he caught a glimpse of T.J., dragging Anna back into the house.

"This is the Canadian Mounted Police," came booming over a loudspeaker.

A rocket streaked across the field and a car exploded in liquid fire.

So much for the police, Sam thought.

Standing against the large tree, an oak several feet in diameter, he tried to imagine what Gaudet might do. A noise came from above; he looked straight up, fired a single shot. A body fell. Not Gaudet.

Whirling around the tree, he saw nothing. Gaudet was gone, his men pulling back to a sandbag bunker. Maybe Gaudet was with them. Firing erupted and Sam pulled back as well.

Someone had prepared. Of course . . . as soon as T.J. had arrived he told them where to come. Along the way he no doubt had given them information. Even the travel was made easy.

"Sam, we are going to kill your Anna." It was Gaudet's French accent over a loudspeaker.

"Listen up," Sam said into the quiet of his radio. "Converge on the house. Anybody gets any kind of a shot at T.J. just take it. They'll kill any hostages anyway."

Sam ran straight to the house, taking only slight cover when he could. Incredibly he had drawn no fire by the time he made it to what had been a side porch.

He wondered about T.J. actually killing Anna. Maybe, maybe not. But Gaudet would certainly kill her if he could get into the house.

Once inside, Sam moved quickly to the hall around the corner from the safe room. Paintings worth thousands caked with dust hung on the wall or rested on the floor. One depicted red-coated gentry and hounds and the bloody plight of the fox they sought.

"Grady, I'm gonna take Anna's hand off one finger at a time until you come out." T.J. was talking into the intercom box.

"Save your breath," Sam said. "I disconnected it. They're not coming out."

"I'll kill Anna. So help me God."

"No payday for that, I'd imagine. Better get your drill."

Sam could hear T.J. retreating down the hall to the utility room that housed the safe room. Anna was struggling against him. Sam retreated around a corner and waited. From behind him he saw a shadow. Maybe Gaudet.

"I have her now, Sam." It was Gaudet's voice. But not from where he had seen the shadow. Sam's skin chilled and tightened. How did Gaudet get into the house and to the safe room that fast? Maybe it was a bluff.

"How shall I kill her, Sam? You know me. I will find a way to enjoy it."

"You're a tough guy, I know."

A motor started—the sound of a heavy drill.

"We'll be in within an hour," Gaudet called to Sam. "Perhaps a half hour. Come on in. Watch Anna as she gets the treatment."

"Can anybody see the generator?" Sam whispered into his radio.

"They're all dead, Sam," Gaudet said.

Sam tried to ignore him, waiting for a response. "Anybody, come back."

"A lot of wounded. We're pinned down. So are they."

"It doesn't sound good, does it?" Gaudet's voice came through the radio.

"Let's bargain." It was T.J.

"No deal." Gaudet. It was obvious he had no regard for T.J.

"They must have used lightweight concrete. Probably shorted the cement. It is going faster than I hoped," Gaudet said.

Sam could hear the drill grinding. Above him the ceiling had been blown out and holes ripped through the walls. He tried to think, searching for a way to get Anna.

"Soon we'll be at the steel. Maybe they used cheap steel too."

The sound of a large helicopter shook the night air. It was far off but coming closer. An explosion reverberated through the atmosphere.

"The Canadian government just discovered we have missile launchers on top of the mountain."

"Victoria's not far. Neither is Vancouver. They'll have more."

"Yes. And we will shoot them down at five thousand

meters. Then, Sam—they'll be cautious. We will have ample time, I assure you. One thing I've been wanting to do is give Anna a good shot of the Nervous Flyer formula. I think I'll take her with me. She can screw me for the oil antidote. Where we're taking her they'll appreciate that."

Sam tried to clear his mind of anger and frustration. Anna was weeping.

Suddenly Anna screamed an incredible shriek. Sweat poured down Sam. His body shook, his mind threatened to betray him. Still he didn't move. With Gaudet using Anna as a shield, he couldn't even sacrifice himself to kill them. Grandfather had given his life. Gaudet would not give him that chance. Grandfather was fond of saying that a man's ideas were more deadly than his arrows. More than bullets, Sam needed something completely unexpected.

A new plan brought him energy. Running out the back of the house with near-reckless abandon, he made his way through a rapid stream of bullets to the tree line. Three rounds grazed him as he dived into the forest. The shooting came from men skirmishing from various haphazard bunkers or corners of the house. He found Yodo, wounded in both arms but alive and functional.

"We have to take the bunker in the trees."

Yodo nodded.

"I need one rocket."

Gaudet would have been talking to thin air as Sam ran, and any second it would start to worry him.

"You've left us, Sam. I may have to kill her after all."

"I'm here," Sam said into the radio.

"What are you doing?"

"Getting ready to catch you when you escape. I've already lost Anna."

Sam didn't listen to the response; he ran with Yodo, making a big arc. Nobody would be expecting an attack on this bunker from the ground. It was too far from the house. They went into the trees and passed through gaping holes in the chain-link fence. They used night vision, but made no effort to be quiet and still drew no fire. Sam wondered if Gaudet's men were deserting, or more likely dead or wounded.

Twenty yards from the sandbags they stopped.

"We go in shooting," Sam said.

"For Shohei," Yodo said, and with one hand on his automatic he charged the bunker, Sam immediately behind.

As they neared the sandbags they heard a radioed voice in the bunker—Sam thought it Gaudet's. After a clipped response the man rose to shoot, his outline green and ghostly through Sam's goggles. Sam and Yodo both fired, and the man's body jerked as the rounds worked their way up his torso.

Sam vaulted the sandbags and hoisted a rocket launcher, nodded at Yodo, and left as quickly as they'd entered.

"What are you doing, Sam? I'd whittle on Anna's face but I have a lot of men that want her."

"Me too," Sam said.

Gaudet laughed.

"Getting back to the house might not be easy," Sam said to Yodo.

"I go first," Yodo said.

Yodo ran and Sam followed. They both shot at muzzle blasts on the way in. Yodo went down, hit after about twenty yards. Sam dropped and crawled to him, the rocket launcher slung on his back. Yodo was trying to use his belt to tie off his leg, but it was a struggle with his already injured arms and hands.

"You go," Yodo said. "I cover."

Yodo shot and reloaded as Sam crawled frantically for the side porch.

He climbed through the ruined doorway and ran down the hall without incident.

Anna was crying.

"Here I am," he said on the radio.

"Good. The drill is going through the steel quickly. Would you like to know how we're going to get them out?"

Sam looked up at the holes in the ceiling. "I imagine you'll tell me."

Huge pockmarks in the walls would make climbing easy. Keeping the rocket launcher tied over his back, he began climbing. He hauled himself up through the hole and into the second story.

"We have a special form of mustard gas we will drip in through the hole a bit at a time. It sticks to the skin and peels it like you might peel an orange. They'll be out in no time. What do you think, Sam?"

"Hell of a plan."

A bathroom stood above the safe room. The floor consisted of bare marble and carpet over marble.

"The beauty is that even while it doesn't kill them, nobody could stand to remain inside. Look, we are almost through the steel. This was a real cheap installation. The owner should seek a refund."

"I'll make a note of that."

"Tell me, do you prefer Anna's breasts or her thighs? I want to know what to leave you."

"Frankly I was always partial to her smile."

Sam knew that in the end he would have to guess. Right now he wanted so much to believe in magic. Outside he heard a flurry of shots and the occasional rocket concussion.

"Sam, I am warning you, you need to be careful about charging in here. With the gas canisters out, you could have us all with no skin. Anna has beautiful skin—I don't think she'd like that."

Sam suspected that the gas wasn't in the safe room yet. Maybe it didn't exist at all. Something about the tone of Gaudet's voice told him. Now he heard Gaudet talking on his radio, but couldn't discern the words.

Sam closed his eyes and leaned against a wall near the tub. He had to know the unknowable. He concentrated on the safe and the utility room below him, remembering every detail. The top of the safe extended up between the floors; its rear wall lay directly against the utility room's. But there had to be two or three meters of space between the safe's sides and the utility room's side walls.

Given that those walls were reinforced, a blast at the back of the room would funnel both shock waves and debris around the sides of the safe and toward the hallway door, following the path of least resistance.

Gaudet would have his men arranged to provide the greatest cover from a conventional attack. Anna would be in the utility room's doorway, facing the hall and farthest from the safe—a human shield against any hallway assault. Between her and the safe would stand T.J., Gaudet, and the others, with T.J. and Gaudet nearest Anna. This meant that Anna would be partially shielded from the blast by her captors' bodies—perhaps enough to save her life, perhaps not.

A direct hit to the top of the safe could kill Grady and Jason inside, so Sam would fire the rocket to strike a glancing blow at the top of the box. He could scarcely believe he was considering doing this. But what else *could* he do?

His feet moved silently across the floor. Keeping the

first-floor layout in his mind, he stepped into the bathtub and aimed the rocket at an angle to the floor
toward the rear wall, the point of entry where the carpet met marble. It was a huge risk for Anna, but Sam
did not expect to be around to see the result.

"Are you still there?" asked Gaudet over the radio.

"Guess."

Sam pulled the trigger, launching the rocket.

Forty-one

Sam awoke in the bathtub. He had no idea how much time had passed. Probably only a minute or two. His arm felt broken and was clearly bloody. Likewise his shoulder was torn up, but probably not broken. Hardly any floor remained in the bathroom; the wall next to the bathtub was mostly gone and the tub itself rested next to a giant hole where the rocket had blown away a series of floor joists.

Below him he saw Clint bending over a bloodied Anna, who lay facedown on the floor, the blast having come from behind her. Clint was telling her not to move—that the medics would come. T.J. looked to have been broken in the back since he V'd the wrong direction. His body had sheltered Anna's from the blast, as had the three other men lying motionless on the floor. None at first glance appeared to be Gaudet.

Gaudet had left a calling card. Sanford was hanging, tied to the hot water heater. His face had been mutilated and rags stuffed in his mouth. Gaudet had cut a small hole in Sanford's belly and pulled out his entrails. That would explain Anna's hysterical screaming. Gaudet had kept Anna unblemished but still had genuine sound effects.

The safe room appeared intact but for a giant black spot across the top of the box. As Sam intended, the back wall of the utility room was blown out having received the brunt of the shock wave. The concussion forward toward the hallway had killed those in the utility room nearest the back wall and farthest from the hallway entrance. The occupants of the utility room had been between Anna and the blast wave.

"Is she going to live?" Sam said, his voice so weak that it surprised him.

"I think so. She has a nasty cut on the head."

Sam struggled out of the tub, nearly screaming at the pain in his arm.

There was enough left of the stairs that he could walk to the first floor.

Clint used a couple of belts to stop the bleeding in Sam's arm.

"You okay?" Sam asked Anna.

"Head hurts, bottom hurts."

"What happened to Gaudet?"

"He left the room just before you blew it up. The radio silence seemed to scare him off."

"Where'd he go?"

"Turned right toward what used to be the living room."

"Out the windows," Clint said.

Medics were coming and two of them approached Sam; one a young wide-eyed fellow with a sincere intensity worthy of a brain surgeon. His partner with a cowboy belt was more laid-back.

"Please get right down here on the stretcher, sir." It was Mr. Intensity.

"Just a minute," he said.

"Do what they say," Anna said from the floor as two more medics prepared to slide her onto a stretcher.

"I'll stay here," Clint said. "I'm not leaving until Grady and Jason come out of there."

Ignoring the medics, Sam looked at the bullet wound to Clint's arm and the one to the leg. They appeared to go just through the meat and were being patched with big gel-covered plastic bandages.

"Those are gonna hurt like hell, and an Excedrin won't cut it," Sam said. "Grady will be all right without you."

"I'm staying."

"Look, Clint, she's not coming out for another ten hours. The Mounties will be here. I'll send more people. She'll be fine."

Clint looked doubtful.

"I cut the intercom," Sam said. "She won't be coming out early. Unless they run low on air they're staying put for the duration. I think Grady has learned to follow instructions."

"You think that's true in her love life?"

"You're on your own there. She's as stubborn as her aunt. Now let's get you in an ambulance. Hell, if they sew fast you may make it back before they come out."

Sam then turned and walked beside Anna as his medics carried their stretcher empty, still imploring him to lie down.

They rode in an old ambulance, Sam sitting on the bench with the attendants working on Anna. A couple of the new rescue vehicles had been blown to tiny pieces by rockets, the result of being parked too near the Mounties. In addition to the one remaining new ambulance, they were using station wagons, vans, and cars to meet the ambulances coming from Victoria and Vancouver. Helicopters from Victoria and Vancouver were taking out the worst cases.

"I wish you were a better shot," Anna said as the sedation kicked in. "That was a rocket?"

"We're taking over her airway when she's completely

out," the attendant said. "Just to be sure she doesn't get sick and aspirate."

Anna had already nodded off.

"It isn't bad, is it?" Sam asked.

"She's the luckiest woman in the world. Another thirty-secondths of an inch and the shrapnel or whatever might have pierced the skull and there would be a lot more issues—like bone fragments in the brain. As it is, I think she'll just have a hell of a headache and a scar under her hair. You won't see it unless you look close."

"She's gonna be pissed. Her hair's pretty burned."

"They'll cut it anyway to sew the cut. But there's always a wig."

"You don't have a smoke, do you?"

"No. You can't smoke in here. Do you smoke?"

"No. No. I quit a long time ago."

Sam waited at the Executive Air Hangar for Anna at the Orange County Airport. It was a better-than-average lobby with tile floors and great furniture, mostly leather. It had a good selection of magazines, but Sam carried plenty of his own. Next to Sam's chair grew a ficus so perfect that it looked like plastic. Harry sniffed it vigorously; Sam figured some other dog must have peed on it. Harry was just starting to get back to weight, but he'd lost none of his spunk. Island life had not been kind to him. If the people at the oyster farm hadn't found Harry, he'd have died. They told Nutka about Harry, and it'd been she who figured it all out.

Aside from enjoying his dog again, Sam thought he might pull out a copy of *Computer Weekly* and see what was going on with the latest processors.

"Sit down, Harry," he said. "You know she's usually

exactly on time, and we're a whole ten minutes early."
Sam flipped open the magazine. Harry lay at his feet.

Now that he was back in business, he was thinking over the upgrade to Big Brain that Grogg had been suggesting. Always something better.

It was a balmy warm day for the end of December. Today his cast didn't itch much. There were six jets on the ramp. A Falcon 50, a couple of G-IVs, some Hawkers, and a Citation X. No doubt Anna had been on the phone to her agent, her mother, her publicist, and the studio all the while having the last-minute pedicure she'd insisted on. Apparently she was planning on spending a lot of time with no shoes on.

He decided to call Paul. "Any word on Gaudet?"

"Still the same. No trace. Canadians are mad as hell. And stumped."

"Well, he didn't leave happy."

"Granted, he isn't happy."

"How's Grady?"

"Haven't seen much of her. She's spending a lot of her time with her dad. The rest of it with Clint. Doesn't seem quite as intent on work as before, but I trust that'll change after the novelty wears off."

"If we're going to pay her a real wage, it will."

"Give her a little more time; then we'll work her butt off. In fact, assign her to me."

Paul had a good laugh at that.

"Did they come out this morning with the final charges against Benoit Moreau?" Sam asked, thinking that he wished he had taken the time to read his e-mail. Anna had wanted to meet him for an early breakfast to celebrate their trip. She started hinting about seriously dating, but he was staying very clear of that idea. Although since they seemed to be seeing each other, he wasn't sure what it would mean to be seriously dating.

"You didn't read your e-mail? What were you so busy with this morning?" Paul interrupted his momentary reverie.

"What do you think?"

"When you get around to it you'll find an e-mail from Typhony. Officially they haven't charged Benoit. But she'll be up for murder and everything on down."

"It's kind of ironic the way Gaudet left her holding the bag like you wouldn't believe. She was, after all, the grand manipulator."

"Same for Chellis and their lead scientist, when they're fit to stand trial. This morning in your e-mail you'll find another missive from Typhony. I guess Samir, or whoever it was, really messed with old Jacques Boudreaux. So far they can't fix him with the bug juice, apparently because he was given Raging Soldier, a version of the vector that they were going to sell to terrorist organizations and third-world dictators. Imagine those out-of-control reactions you've seen on video of looters or violent crowds. Raging Soldier is that times ten. No discipline. No thought; just violent hysteria. Right now they're keeping Jacques toned down with every tranquilizer known to man."

Sam hadn't responded, so Paul checked to make sure he was there. "You won't believe this, but Jacques Boudreaux killed Centaur, a big male macaque that had shared the cage. Killed the damn monkey with a club. Jacques was bit to hell but he got the monkey. I guess Samir pitted Jacques against the monkey. Raging Soldier profile against Soldier profile."

Sam obliged Paul with a long, low whistle.

"I hate to think what they would have done with this technology."

"It's pretty easy," Sam said. "If you want to destabilize a government you begin by infecting as much of the leadership as you can with Nervous Flyer profile. All it takes is a couple of good inhales and they'll be scared of their own shadow. If you're the government, you give a bunch of enlisted men Soldier profile; if you're the opposition and you have some people you don't like and you figure they're expendable, you give them Raging Soldier and make suicide bombers by the hundred. Then you get your rebels to inhale Soldier profile, feed them the hormones, and stage a coup. Hell of a deal."

"Yep."

"Do you think Samir Aziz is the one who got Jacques Boudreaux as payback? You were gonna check on what the Malaysians are saying."

"I guess the Malaysian authorities are looking for a guy named Claude Balford. Head of Chellis's security team. Their theory is that Gaudet actually ordered Balford to turn Jacques Boudreaux into a nutcase killer. Not to mention locking him in a cage with a crazy monkey. According to their theory Balford would have assumed the order came from Benoit, who would have gotten it from Chellis. Balford denies it, and I, for one, believe him. It was Aziz."

Sam grunted his agreement. "Where is Aziz?"

"Off in the desert of Quatram with a lifetime supply of blue oil and a mistress by the name of Michelle. He doesn't take calls."

"Are you finding me Gaudet?"

"We're looking. He's a shadow among shadows."

"I'm going to find him. First I'm going to Hawaii. On a lighter subject, do one thing more for me. Have somebody pick up the book *Where Did He Go? Where Did She Go?*"

"You're not gonna read one of those dumb chick books?"

"Don't be ridiculous. It's a gift for one of Anna's chick friends. I have to buy something, and that's what I was told to buy. I don't know why Anna picked it. She doesn't normally read that pablum."

At that moment Anna drove up in her Volvo. Sam signed off and walked out on the ramp to meet her.

She was already giving him a look.

"I'm telling you, the wig looks completely natural."

"I still wish you had been a better shot."

They started helping the pilots load the baggage while they waited for the mechanics to fix some fuse in the Falcon 50. Sam worked one-handed keeping his cast clear of the fray.

"I like the damn Hawker Seven-hundred."

"Well, it won't fly to Hawaii. And I offered to go commercial."

"I could see you wanting to kiss in first class."

"Only if the *Enquirer* was there. Otherwise I'd go for the water closet."

"Who needs Hawaii? We're from LA, for God's sake."

"Manhattan."

"Yeah, well, that's you."

She grinned and kissed him on the cheek, and then insisted on a lip-smacker right in front of the pilots.

"You haven't set me up on this trip, have you? Are there going to be reporters?"

"Are you slipping? You should be monitoring my calls."

"I knew it. You've probably ruined my cover."

"Sam, relax. A little trip to Hawaii is the least you can do after shooting me."

"You'll use anything. Guilt, whatever it takes."

"You of all people, Sam. All's fair in love and war. You should know that." She patted his cheek and stroked his back.

He could feel his engines warming despite himself.

"Well, at least we understand the ground rules."

"Damn straight. You're taking me to the Oscars."

"No way. I said Hawaii."

Now it was his turn to smile.

"You'll see," she said.

*For a sneak preview of
David Dun's next novel, THE LAST CLIMB—
coming from Pinnacle Books in 2004—
just turn the page. . .*

The first thing Sam noticed was the owls. They were northern spotted owls and they roosted in an old dead tree. They suddenly began hooting, coming down to lower branches, then moving away. They had been fed live mice by so many biologists that their response to a creeping person was to come close and look for a mouse on a stick. Since they had already established that Sam wouldn't be feeding them, all the hooting and hopping down near the forest floor might, among other things, indicate that someone was out and about.

The wind moved through the trees, ruffling the stiff yellowed leaves like a million flapping tongues. Sam clicked and Paul clicked back. Clouds were blowing through, alternately veiling and unveiling the three-quarter moon. There was not much light out of the forest and on the forest floor it was black. Grandfather had taught Sam to look from the corner of his eyes and to see with his other senses. A friend of Grandfather's kept a blind horse, a horse that didn't even have eyeballs. When approached with an apple, the old horse could easily find the hand that held it. When people approached the horse it acted quite similar to a horse with vision. Grandfather's comment was that people had no means of telling the horse he couldn't see. Although Sam was sure there were perfectly logical explanations for the horse's behavior, it none-the-less impressed him when Grandfather told him not to allow anyone to suggest he couldn't see on even the darkest night.

After a time, he clicked the radio and got nothing from Paul in return. Next he did a radio check and got nothing. Pulling himself out of the sleeping bag into the cool air brought him fully alert.

"Well, Harry, we do have a problem." Sam straightened Harry's blanket, getting half of it under him and half on top. "Shush and stay, Harry." Harry scrunched down. Sam took three steps back, put on his field pack, and picked up his night-vision goggles and his M4 combat rifle. "Stay," he said, also using a hand signal. He knew the dog would not move.

Immediately Sam walked off into the forest. If Gaudet was active, he would expect Sam to check on Paul, so Sam determined that he would make a giant circle in an unexpected direction. Initially he would travel away from Paul toward the owls, being careful to remain silent. Much of the time he felt his way through a world of subtle shadows and pitch-black spots. Branches were everywhere and in places logs crisscrossed into windfalls, but he managed to pick his way around them. He stayed low to the ground but remained on his feet because he could be quieter and move faster. There was a lowland area that was wet and contained flowing water in the rainy season. Traversing it without sloshing was difficult so he moved up to the steep-sided canyons until he reached a place where he could easily cross in silence.

Once he was on the other side he moved back down the canyon, taking only a few steps at a time. He had been moving for nearly an hour when he stopped to study a small opening near the place that he imagined the owls had gone. Unbelievably, he saw the glow of a cigarette high off the ground, apparently up in a tree, near the old road that served as a main trail. No doubt it was a rear guard who was so far from the action that he figured he could smoke. On the other hand it could be some mixed-up hiker who had wandered off-course and just loved climbing trees in the middle of the night.

Not likely.